A PREFACE TO MAN

Praise for *A Preface to Man*

'In its historical sweep, original craft and mastery of narrative, Subhash Chandran's *A Preface to Man* takes its place in the front row of modern Indian fiction, heralding, along with the works of several young contemporaries, the rebirth of the great Indian novel in the twenty-first century. The Indian novel is flourishing where it should—in the heart of India, the rich, black, upturned soil of the Indian languages.'

— Paul Zacharia

'A book of such brilliance needs to be translated into every language. Deeply moving.'

— Anees Salim

A PREFACE TO MAN

SUBHASH CHANDRAN

Translated from the Malayalam by
Fathima E.V.

HARPERPERENNIAL

HARPERPERENNIAL

First published in English in 2016 by Harper Perennial
An imprint of HarperCollins *Publishers*

Building 10, Tower A, 4th Floor, DLF Cyber City, Phase II,
Gurugram Haryana – 122002, India
www.harpercollins.co.in

This edition published in India in 2019 by Harper Perennial

2 4 6 8 10 9 7 5 3 1

P-ISBN: 978-93-5302-494-9
E-ISBN: 978-93-5302-663-9

Typeset in 11/14 Adobe Devanagari
by Jojy Philip, New Delhi

Printed and bound at
MicroPrints India, New Delhi

For those who were born in the last century
and are living in this century

'If a human child, who is born fearless, independent, and above all, creative, ends up craven and bonded in sixty or seventy years, spending his creativity solely for procreation, and finally dies as a grown-up child in the guise of an old man, and if this is called human life, my beloved girl, I have nothing to be proud of in being born as a man.'

—from a letter Jithendran sent to Ann Marie

Contents

Prologue

'Man is the only creature that perishes before attaining full growth!'

It was in his fifty-fourth year, while listening to music with his wife in their eighth-floor flat in the massive building that had recently sprung up on the ground where he had played cricket as a child, that the pain that began as a tickle in his lower abdomen rushed to his heart. Bewildered at not being able to enjoy the beautiful violin rendition between the *anupallavi* and *charanam*, he remarked thus and, rather involuntarily, died.

Except for a recent swelling in the prostate gland, he had had few illnesses to speak of. Since he had reached a stage of incontinence where he was emptying his bladder too often, he had just started inserting baby diapers into his underwear. Whenever his wife suggested adult diapers, he stopped her.

'Not those,' he had said, laughing. 'If we buy those, the shopkeeper will know that one of us is peeing in our clothes. Even more shameful would be him coming to know that we are getting old.'

Therefore, pretending it was for their grandchildren, who were coming to celebrate Onam and his birthday with them, she bought baby diapers and multi-coloured plastic flowers. He began to leak away into them secretly, regardless of day or night. In his childhood, such disposable nappies were not available in the local market. Though the word 'readymade' had already entered common commercial parlance, it had seldom been used in connection with menstrual or nappy cloths. By the time diapers began to appear in local shops during the last decades of the twentieth century, he had turned a young man.

When his children were toddlers, old cloths were deemed good enough to stem the flow of all effluents from urine to blood, thanks to his wife's reluctance to give up her habit of thrift, ingrained in her while living through lean times. This meant his children were not fated to use store-bought diapers. As was the case with many things in his lineage, the fortune of using readymade diapers for the first time befell him, even though at a rather late stage. Standing without embarrassment in his baby diaper in front of his wife, as if to gauge the acuity of his yet fecund powers of self-deprecation, he declared, 'See, the urinembodiment of manliness!'

In the extended history of mankind, he was of the generation that had used many things for the first time. In the years of his adolescence and youth, children were effortlessly handling gadgets that their parents could not have imagined even as late as the last decades of the twentieth century. Televisions with remote control; mobile phones; computers with their endless possibilities; mammoth apartment buildings that ensured one had neighbours not only on four sides but also above and below; mechanized domestic appliances from brooms to coconut graters; prophylactics that titillated—those were the miracle years when all these were like newborn animals springing to their feet as soon as they were delivered. His was also the last generation of children who found happiness in simple toys made by inserting the spines of coconut leaves into the spongy centres of small, unripe coconuts thrown down liberally by coconut palms.

Now, a bittersweet smile in remembrance of those things played on his lips as he lay on the sofa, dead. Noticing the frozen smile, she shook him by his shoulders and asked, with more alarm than sadness in her throat, 'Gone?'

To prevent others from seeing how those unusually melancholic, large eyes that had remained wide open for fifty-four years were beginning to wilt like dying flowers, she pressed them shut with trembling fingers. Then, switching off the music player gifted by their eldest daughter on his birthday two weeks ago, and which had started playing only moments ago, she got up and phoned next door. 'Yes,' she told her disbelieving neighbour, in a voice that hid the tears, 'please inform everyone. Here he is, sitting serenely on the sofa!'

In those moments, she hoped that she was caught in a bad dream. He was still sitting on the sofa in the living room, resting on huge yellow pillows, with his pale blue lungi folded above the knee, a cashew nut trapped in his curled right palm. Next to him, on the floor, was a glass with only a sip of rum left, still mixed with one of his last breaths. She quickly removed the glass and the bowl of cashew to the kitchen, so that the visitors would not take him to be a drunkard. His shirtless body leaned to the left when she pulled out one of the pillows. Unable to bear the weight of the hapless head, the neck stretched like the stalk of a flower. With the help of the two women and an old man, who were the first to reach, she laid him out on the sofa and pulled down the lungi that had come undone, to cover his thighs and knees.

Then she noticed that his skin was a mass of goose pimples and his nipples were erect from the enticing touch of death.

That was on a wet evening in the month of September, two thousand and twenty-six. The prime minister, who was almost his age, had had two terms in power and was now in hospital in critical condition, after an attempt on his life was made while he was campaigning for another stint. Bored by all ninety-eight channels airing only this news, he had switched off the TV and decided to listen to some music. After its thermocol packing was removed, the new music system came into his life like a newborn separated from the placenta and freshly bathed, their lives intersecting for only a few moments. With his eyes shut, and as if picking lots, he had taken out a disc from the crammed cardboard box with its astonishing array of music from his youth. Film songs of the twentieth century that people had more or less forgotten. It was when he was reading the titles of the songs from the fading covers of the long-neglected discs that he began to experience the mild pain that had initially felt pleasurable, like a tickle in his lower abdomen. With his right hand pulling into place the tiny diaper that had begun to slip from its position inside his underwear he had walked into the kitchen. When he could not decide which bottle of alcohol to choose from the upper shelf, he decided to pick that too through lots. There were two or three varieties, though he was only an occasional drinker. Taking care not to topple the bottles over, he had closed his eyes, extended his hand, and picked one at random. In that bottle, left unopened for years, was an excellent rum, darker than black tea. When the top of the bottle was snapped open as in a post-mortem, the joy of his youth bubbled up along with the smell of sugarcane and caramelized sugar, and reliving it, he had come out to the living room carrying the glass, water, and cashew nuts. He had called out to his wife, who was on her way to the balcony at the back with her spectacles and newspaper as usual. He made her sit next to him and started the music, after blowing the dust off the disc. Watching the September rain weaving threads in the eighth-floor sky, as the singer stretched his 'O…' through three levels on lower octaves before uttering the invocation to the enticing 'kaattu chembakam', and feeling the tickle in his stomach getting heavier and rolling up, he had exclaimed to his wife: 'Our A.M. Raja!'

Because it was a second Saturday, as soon as the news got out, the neighbours crowded around the body in the seventeen-by-twelve-foot hall. Though there were five doctors living in that apartment building, not one was able to reach on time to confirm the death, because of their busy schedules. Finally, a dentist, who had recently moved onto the thirteenth floor, was summoned. Having been brought up as the darling of indulgent parents, he had not quite acquired the necessary edification in matters in which grown men are well versed—such as alcohol and death. When he bent over the body and lifted up the eyelid with his thumb to check the pupils, he was assailed by fumes of rum from the open mouth; he also spotted the crooked tooth in the lower row. Smelling the mouth of a corpse for the first time, and trying to hide his confusion at not recognizing the smell of rum, with unwarranted foreboding, he declared in English: 'Before it starts reeking further, let's begin the funeral rites!'

Some people moved the chairs and the large cane teapoy aside. The dining table was carefully placed with its glass top facing the wall, and its pointed legs were swaddled with worn towels and a soiled mundu. It was the first death among the twenty-eight families living in the new building. Neighbours took charge of the preparations as if training for future deaths that were liable to occur in their houses as well. By then, the undertakers too had arrived.

Though their charges were rather high, they were acclaimed for beautifying corpses and making them appear better looking than during their lifetime. After the dead man was shaved and stripped naked for his bath, they laughed, spotting the diaper with the image of a coy duck on it, forgetting that it was on the genitals of a corpse. Still, even the neighbours did not realize the diaper had been bought specifically for him, and took it as something of an accident that he had had on him one of the baby clothes left behind by his grandchildren.

She resented being stuck in the midst of women in the inner room, which prevented her from watching the proceedings, while others lifted and placed on the floor his tall, slim body, now bathed and sheathed in white, a body that she alone had held in power for twenty-six years since their wedding. As she deftly flung his brown underwear under the bed, yanking it from the bedpost on which it had been deposited lazily the previous night, she could not help habitually muttering, under her breath, the usual admonishments: 'Damn! What would people think if they were to see?'

The truth was that, for some time, she could not assimilate the fact that she had been newly elevated to the role of a widow. Initially, she smiled warmly at each person who had walked in after paying respects to the body laid out in the front room. Many a time, she almost asked them to be seated and nearly offered them tea with the practised ease of hospitality. Only when the bitter odour of something that had been rendered vacuous wafted into the bedroom, along with the aroma of the incense sticks that had wafted listlessly in the cramped flat, did it finally dawn on her that she was a bereaved housewife.

However, the man who had died with a child's diaper on him was floating like a leaf on an ocean of comprehension far greater than hers.

A quarter of a century ago in another place, at the fag-end of a honeymoon, and yearning for an offspring at the age of twenty-eight, he had had his first unprotected intercourse in a bed in a rented house still stained with filthy water from the sewers and shit overflowing the septic tank. Having finally decided to submit himself completely to an average life with no claims to anything extraordinary, his life was split into two equal parts: the first half was that of a soul that had burnt away, having failed to find a medium for realizing something he firmly believed would light up the lives of his fellow human beings, despite once believing he had the power to do so, based on a number of assumptions accumulated since childhood about the greatness of man. The second half was comparatively simpler: the unduly serious continuance of a job that least bewailed the wastage of a lifetime; a wedding that began in debt and a marriage that continued in debt; one or two changes of residence accompanied by small lorries stuffed with household things; property partitions accomplished by hating one's siblings, being hated by them in turn and making God laugh; two or three liaisons with other women, attempted purely for the ineffable joy of indulging in forbidden transgressions, and with no carnal pleasure derived; some loud mirth here and there; tiny, inconsequential hurts that friends and relatives had handed out like gifts; accusations and offences that could hardly be blamed on circumstances; quantities of medicines swallowed for illnesses that would have healed on their own; the two or three occasions in life when he had had to endure the tedium of acting responsibly, dictated by auspicious times.

Yes. A pitiful body that would have crawled through so many commonplace situations that even a novice of a fortune-teller could have read similar occurrences on anyone's palm—and could have predicted that he would, one day, die unsung.

Until their two children and their families—who must have cursed him for making them return after a gap of only fifteen days—arrived early next morning, the body lay preserved in a refrigerated display box. The service lift for transporting heavy objects had been under repair for the past week. Hence, when the freezer came late that evening, it had to be hauled up the stairs to the eighth floor and brought down the same way the following day. The funeral being on Sunday, a few more of his relatives had arrived. The corpse had to be taken down in the small passenger lift to the ground floor, inviting frowns from the other inhabitants.

During the attempt to take him down from the eighth floor, and because the lift was too small to keep the white-swathed body horizontal, once again with the help of others, it had to be propped up vertically, and for one last time it stood upright on the ground. The exertion of the pranan to hold upright a seventy-four kilo body was registered with a shudder by people who weighed more.

Nevertheless, the fifty-four-year-old body that burnt down pliantly that Sunday in the suburban Electric Crematorium for Nairs, was only the second half of his life. The first half had conclusively ended in a moment in his twenty-eighth year, when he had failed, after admitting that it is impossible for man to attain his full potential and that the only thing possible would be a helpless splitting into the next generation. Yet, in those first twenty-eight years, he felt the leaden and invisible burden of at least five generations that had preceded him and who stood with their feet planted on his soul.

Rain kept pattering down. That man, who had been born centuries before his birth, had actually died much before his own death.

His name was Jithendran. He was a Malayali.

Part One

Dharma

All that is known variously as the one and the other,
When considered, is but the primal self-form of the world.
All that is done for the delight of the self
Ought to bring happiness to others as well.

—Sree Narayana Guru *(Aatmopadeshashatakam)*

ONE

The Address

It was on her first day of widowhood, after the funeral, alone in the flat bereft of kith and kin, that she rediscovered a whole trove of words that she alone had believed to be priceless, though her husband had, a quarter of a century ago, discarded them with pained contempt. They were a collection of letters and the summarized outline of a novel he had yearned to write in his youth. She had once salvaged it from a pile of books sodden from the gutter water gushing into their house, and had put it away with care after drying. There were the forty, many-hued letters he had written to her in the final ten months—between March 1999 to January 2000—of the interminable six years that had felt as long drawn out as the lifespan of the ageless Manu, starting from the day she was chosen to be his wife and extending to their wedding day. Most of those letters were replete with words that reeked of love—not much different from the kind any lover would write to his woman. While reading them in those days used to make her heart and fingers tremble, now, in her fiftieth year, she could return to them unaffected, as if they were written by an unknown man for an unknown woman. But reading them now, she was distressed as never before, confronted by this chronicle of the persistent anxieties about the dignity of individuals who had tormented him even at that young age, and who kept cropping up every now and then in his letters. She read and reread those sentences that were unlikely to be written again by any young man to any beloved or any friend. With a wildly palpitating heart, she read those parts of the novel that he had abandoned unwritten in his twenty-eighth year.

She felt that the angst that had tormented him while writing still seemed to lurk in them, despite the passage of a quarter of a century. Her fingers burnt when she ran them over the letters. They began to swell and grow inside her like the seeds of lofty trees conserved for the future. She had had no right to access them for a quarter century. He had shown incredible aplomb in being at peace with himself, without talking or thinking about them. Whenever she had reminded him of those summarized notes that could have blossomed into a novel, he laughed them off, as if they were someone else's life. It was one of those rare instances when he had laughed his open-mouthed, hearty laugh. But now she had all the time, the rest of her life in the helpless loneliness of her widowhood, to reflect again and again and to transform those word-seeds, dear to no one else, into gigantic trees and dense forests.

That a man's expressions of truth had the strength to survive beyond his death was a realization that was dawning on her: those words that no pyre could consume demanded to be taken and venerated as the preface to an entire human life.

'And these were the names of those mighty hills:
Chokkaampetti, Paachi, Kaali, Sundar, Naaga, Ko, and Valli.'

Grampa had taught Jithen the couplet that strung together the names of the hills that had given birth to and nurtured the Periyar river. The seven splendid hills stood blanketed in green in the Western Ghats: four women and three men. They were sweating with the kind of exertion Jithen would understand only when he was older. Those sweat channels had merged to form the river.

'Boy, can you tell which of them are men, and which are women?' Grampa challenged, to pass the time as he squatted on his haunches under the coffee shrubs, straining to empty his bowels. Resting the bell metal *kindi* on the ground, Jithen began to count with his fingers, 'Chokkaampetti, Sundar, and Ko are men; Paachi, Valli, Kaali, and … What was the other one? Ah … Naaga … are all women.'

'Smart boy!' Grampa praised him and eased out a long fart. Then he strained at his bowels once more, making the forest of hair on his back spread out like a peacock showing off its feathers. Rid of his burden, Grampa's taut, black face relaxed and cleared.

Spitting out the sticky sweetness of the ripe red coffee beans, Jithen wiped his fingers on his shorts. Camouflaging themselves as sugarcane clumps, the abundant wild sugarcane grass on the banks of the river whistled when the breeze passed through them. In Jithen's eyes, the fuming brick kiln in the clearing between the wild sugarcane grass and the coffee bushes was Lankapuri set on fire by Hanuman. Those working in the scorching sun were struggling to rescue the Rakshasa babies from the gutted palace.

'Do you know whose poem it is?' Grampa asked, smiling as he held out his hand to take the empty kindi.

Unsure what the question was about, Jithen slyly eyed the yellow snake that Grampa had left behind. Then, crossing the coffee trees, he began to follow his grandfather to his usual ablution spot near the wild sugarcane grass.

Grampa was wearing the mud-coloured loosely woven *thorth* with thin borders that he usually wrapped around his waist while coming out in the open to empty his bowels. After the job was done, the left hand would be stretched behind to ensure that the thin towel was held away from his buttocks. The right hand would be extended forward, holding the spout of the empty kindi. It was a deliberate, slow walk, with the toes of both feet splayed to the sides and pressing into the sand. As he stepped into the river and lowered the kindi into the water, it would say 'bluthm'.

Usually, Ammu, the washerwoman with a mole on her cheek as big as a beetle, would be washing laundry at the river kadavu. It was her regular presence there that made Grampa carry water in the kindi and go behind the wild sugarcane grass reeds, instead of cleaning himself in the river.

Till Grampa returned, Jithen would stand marvelling at the eighth channel of sweat coming down between the milk-mountains of Ammu, who was older than his mother. The lash of the laundry striking the worn-out yellow soap-spot on the washing stone would echo from the other bank, after a moment.

'You didn't answer.' Grampa, cleansed now, came back to poetry: 'Then, let me tell you. It was your great-grandfather, that is my father, who wrote it. Written means not on palm leaf or paper—in his mind!'

'What was Grampa's father's name?' Jithen asked.

'Aaa!' Grampa gestured ignorance with open palms and chuckled. 'To remember the name, shouldn't one at least know what it is? I've not seen him. I know only what Amma has told me. Some naïve chap who came to marry into the Ayyaattumpilli family!' Before starting back, Grampa turned his head to look at Ammu, whose reflection was like a pliant shadow hung upside down from her legs. When he grunted pointedly, Ammu pulled up the corner of her checkered mundu and shoved it into the plunging crevasse between her bubbies.

Revealing his large, tobacco-stained teeth, Grampa laughed out loud. 'Moron!' he said. 'The first to be born in Ayyaattumpilli was Ayyaapilla! My eldest uncle's eldest uncle! Ayyaapilla, who was hanged on the orders of the King of Thiruvithamkoor!'

Looking at the faltering steps of the evil old man and his six-year-old guard, Ammu muttered to herself, 'Hmm, Ayyaattumpilli!'

'PPHO!' Ayyaapilla snapped with terrifying might. A blast of blistering contempt.

On the topmost branch of the ancient tree as tall as the sky, in the crowded thoroughfare, fifty-five-year-old Ayyaapilla lay suspended, incarcerated in the man-shaped iron cage: prey to the wrath of His Majesty of Thiruvithamkoor.

It was now the twenty-seventh day since the sentence had been executed. Ayyaapilla had already transgressed the tradition of the accused giving up and embracing death in the sky, usually within ten or eleven days of being denied food and drink.

It was in the first week of the month of Kumbham that the sentence had been implemented. People from the neighbouring regions of Paravoor and Aalangad—both had acceded to Thiruvithamkoor only a while ago—thronged around the tree, pushing and shoving for a glimpse of the torture chamber made by melding iron slats and contoured to fit a human body. When the limp Ayyaapilla was being hauled up on a hawser slung through a wooden pulley, the fists raised in hailing the king turned into fingers pointed accusingly at the convict.

Ayyaapilla saw the crowd, which had come to watch the hanging, separating and falling back into layered whorls of upwardly tilted heads: in the innermost layer, the minister and other supervisors from the Ananthapuram palace; in the second layer, the local barons and the landlord-chieftains with their lackeys; then came the four castes with the carefully observed norms of untouchability evidenced by their strict observance of ritual distances solicitously kept from one another; and beyond this, his wailing family, with their ululations.

Twirling with the rope, first clockwise and then anti-clockwise,

Ayyaapilla was pulled up till the cage came to rest at its assigned place on the tree. The three men, who had sweated and toiled on the tree until then, climbed down. Only after they finished digging out the earth to make, right below where the accused lay dangling, a two-foot deep circular pit to catch the urine and faeces likely to drop down, did the men wash their limbs and call it a day. Turning to the guards, one of them said: 'That guy up there's robust, but will perish within ten days!'

When darkness began to fall, the lingering crowd broke away and dissolved in different directions. Only the two guards of His Majesty were left behind to wait beneath the suspended Ayyaapilla, left to die of starvation. To avoid getting dunked by human waste, they took up their positions under the tree, taking turns to guard day and night, till Ayyaapilla perished.

The day-sentry suffered no loneliness as long as the steady stream of onlookers, arriving after crossing many miles, stood gawking at Ayyaapilla with open mouths and bulging eyes. However, the night-guard had had enough of sitting sleepless, next to the lighted torch fed with marotti oil. Yawning and scratching his head, he looked up to estimate the height at which Ayyaapilla was hanging in the darkness. Though sorrowful at having to reveal aloud what should have been a secret, he could not resist calling out: 'Wretched sinner, with water and rice having ceased, have you realized the gravity of your crime?'

Disappointed that there was no response from above, the guard raised the torch high, squinting upwards. The luminous spectacle of moonlight in the month of Kumbham, streaming through the foliage, and cradling Ayyaapilla like a stone idol, sent a shudder through him. Aware of the pair of eyes blazing above him, still alive and blinking, he was shaken by the disquieting feeling that he was not watching Ayyaapilla, it was Ayyaapilla who was watching him.

As days went by, the trickling down of urine and faeces dwindled. The two guards, staring up to see if the wish of their venerable Majesty was being fulfilled, became impatient that Ayyaapilla had not succumbed yet. Even inside the torture chamber that would not let him flex his limbs, Ayyaapilla was fiercely indomitable. On the ninth day, when the first vulture was spotted like a dot on the western horizon, he hoped that it would be a pigeon and that it would be holding between its legs a rolled-up missive. He shut his eyes tight—a kindi, a wooden plank-stool for eating and a wide-brimmed uruli, flashed in his mind's eye. The next moment they vanished. Of all the hunger-induced hallucinations, the next one was stranger. An old man, dressed up like a *vidooshakan*, standing in a place that resembled a Koothambalam in a temple, extended a sautéed leaf full of rice, and asked, 'Ayya! Why have you come?'

'On being apprised of the repast being served by the guardians of the temple, methinks perchance I too may partake, wherefore cometh I!' Ayyaapilla replied as if in a trance.

The day-guard was taken aback by Ayyaapilla's strange language. He cocked his head. Ayyaapilla was delirious, and started muttering gibberish, glaring at the vulture: 'Retain the tuft of kuduma hair on your head and shear off the body hair from top and bottom. Don white robes and become a devotee. Embark on the penta-discipline rigour. Loosen the sacred thread over the legs, hold the chopped tuft of hair in hand, and declare, "Off to the nether world!" PPHO!'

The vulture, suspicious at not getting the smell of death, began to circle the tree. Through three days of circling, whenever it tried to approach him, the ferocity of the snapping from inside the iron cage scared it away.

On the twelfth day, the month of Kumbham gave Ayyaapilla another lease of life. Clouds darkened the burning sky and it began to pour. Denied for three days, the vulture landed on the same branch from which Ayyaapilla lay dangling, and perched there staring at its prey.

As the rain thickened and even the trees began to pour down with it, through the corner of his eye, Ayyaapilla could see the vulture's feathers being plastered to its body. Pressing against the loosened hair of his kuduma resting against the metal, he tried to turn his head and failed. Caught in the downpour, he felt his thirst even more acutely. Making use of the length of the chain tied to the shackle around his neck, Ayyaapilla tried to move his body to and fro.

Slowly, he was able to increase the pace into a swing. As the swings became longer, and each time the pitch of oscillations rose, he managed to make his body go horizontal, so that, little by little, he was able to collect water in his open mouth, using his scooped tongue. As moisture slaked ten days of aridity, life writhing inside convulsed his whole body. Touched by rain, the congealed blood—rendered powerless to flow from the abrasions against the iron bars—sketched crimson roots on his drenched skin and diffused. Crazed with thirst, Ayyaapilla drank with his eyes and nose and mouth.

He was beginning to enjoy himself. He drank his fill of not only the Kumbham rain but even of the month that followed—Meenam. After four hours, the rain dwindled, having quenched Ayyaapilla's thirst.

On the eighteenth day, the second vulture arrived. When Ayyaapilla felt that his terrifying glares were not enough to ward off the vultures lusting to eat his flesh through the slits in his cage, he began to bark fiercely with all his remaining strength, 'Pho! Pho!'

The sounds emanating from the soul of the man suspended like a flag fluttering on the mast of sin, continued intermittently day and night. Mothers in the surrounding houses plugged their children's tender ears with balls made from strips of old clothes to prevent them from being frightened by these harsh snaps that sounded like heralds from hell.

Ayyaapilla's snapping did not last beyond Kumbham. The birds in the sky knew of the decaying of his senses and the stilling of his body before the guards on the ground did. As the vultures, impatient with hunger, tried to tear the desiccated skin off his lower abdomen with their beaks, realizing that death sheathed in tickles was kissing his soul, Ayyaapilla let loose his final snap at the birds.

The ferocity of that blistering snap, that 'aattu' named a clan, Ayyaattumpilli.

Ammu made haste to complete the washing and leave the riverbank before the workers from the brick kiln came to wash their hands and legs and sit down to eat their lunch. When they stepped into the river ghat, the water would turn into a milky tea and soil the washed clothes.

By then Sharada of Thandaambat and Bhavaniyamma of Nattukulam arrived, each with a bundle of clothes.

'Eh, Ammu, has that Naraapilla *chettan* left after shitting and washing up?' Sharada asked, scrubbing the newly formed cracks in her rheumatoid heels against the yellow trace of washing soap on the stone that someone had used previously.

'The patriarch of Ayyaattumpilli? There, he just left,' Ammu said.

'That's a relief!' While scrubbing her feet, Sharada removed the pins from her blouse and pulled up her checkered mundu to wrap it around her breasts.

'Wonder what's his problem? Are there no toilets in Ayyaattumpilli?' Bhavaniyamma mouthed an 'aah' as she shrugged, showing her plaque-ridden teeth.

'No, it's not that,' Ammu winked. 'Some people need to be tickled by the grass to unload!'

The laughter of the women, tickled by the double entendre in the words of Ammu with the beetle on her cheek, bubbled over into the river.

TWO

Ancestors

29 March 1999

> ...Want to hear an irony of our times? Among the upper caste 'savarna' lot, even those who call themselves progressive would covertly reveal their castes within the first five sentences that they utter as soon as they make a new acquaintance. Do you know? With no claim to any distinctive qualities as an individual, he will manage to jump onstage with his caste superiority. Whatever I may lack, am I not from the upper caste, the feckless man will claim. Our land is going to be overrun with such imbeciles. Haven't you written that I seem to be a Nair, from my manners and ways? With all my love for you, let me tell you that I hate myself for having made you assume so.

Everyone called Narayana Pillai of Ayyaattumpilli, Naraapilla.

Even as he was hailed all over Thachanakkara as the Naraapilla who measured his money with a *para*, the brass-trimmed, big, measuring vessel for paddy, he was not past his formative years. Brimming youth, overflowing money. Even so, living through the loneliness that his mother had bequeathed her only son through her premature death, there were certain things Naraapilla could not reach or grasp—things impervious to termites.

In 1925, when Mahatma Gandhi arrived at Sree Narayana Guru's Advaithaashramam at Shivagiri, Naraapilla was only twenty-seven. People from Varappuzha, Aalangad, and Kalady-Kaanjoor-Manjapra rushed to the banks of the Aluva river to see the Mahatma. Intoxicated by the whiff of the word freedom that wafted in from afar, the Nairs of Thachanakkara sprinted barefoot towards Aluva. Coming down through the Kaniyaan hill, a number of students, led by their teachers from Union Christian College, sought a shortcut to the ashram through Thachanakkara.

Even before Gandhiji could be seen in the flesh, myths were born. One among the rumours that reached Naraapilla via Appu Nair was that Gandhiji's entourage included four wrestlers from Haryana, one of whom, enraged when he came to know that the tea served to Gandhiji in the waiting room of Aluva railway station was made without the goat's milk he preferred, took the glass tumbler and crushed it in his fist. Appu Nair also claimed that an eyewitness had told him that when Gandhiji alighted from the train, he was wearing a black mask with eye slits of the kind that brigands sport, to avoid the smoke from the locomotive that would cause him to sneeze endlessly—and seeing that apparition with its entourage of wrestlers, the people who had come to receive him had flung down their garlands and fled. Still, Naraapilla did not budge. That he was untouched by the frenzy that the independence struggle had awakened in the youth of the land was not the sole reason for that indifference.

'Why is he on parade here to meet a low-caste Ezhava sanyaasi?' Naraapilla taunted Appu Nair, his voice echoing the vanity of his caste. 'And that too after crossing forests and fording rivers? Where this Nanu sat to meditate, not even a mushroom has sprouted! Hee, hee!'

To the west of Thachanakkara, it was harvest time in the fields of Nedumaali. The thorth-clad Appu Nair was throwing into the adjacent fields, haystacks which were tied in the middle, and resembled women who had their waists tightly girdled.

Naraapilla stood on a ridge of the paddy field, watching the rhythmic movements of the Pulaya women as they bent over the rice, hooking and cutting the stalks with their sickles. The heat of the Meenam sun beat down mercilessly. Naraapilla's bald head and the hairy forest on his back were slick with sweat. With a masculinity at odds with his youth, Naraapilla was by then the owner of not only Kainikkulam in Varappuzha, but also Puththankandam in Paanaayikkulam, and the three-and-a-half acre arid field of Muppathadam.

'People are thronging from as far away as the kadavu near the market.' Gandhi was still effervescent on Appu Nair's lips, even as he was stacking the hay. Wiping his hands on his worn thorth, and stepping onto the ridge, Appu Nair cried: 'The Aluva beach is buzzing as if on Shivaraathri. One can't help marvelling "hari hara", watching the crowds being ferried across to the ashram by the hunchback Velu in his boat!'

Mohandas Karamchand Gandhi was the biggest catch of his lifetime for Appu Nair of Peechamkurichi, who was adept at giving eyewitness accounts of events not witnessed by him. The author of the many myths circulating in the locality about Naraapilla was also the very same Appu Nair, the alter ego of Naraapilla. Nevertheless, this time he erred in gauging Naraapilla's emotions.

'Oho, have you also joined the Ezhavas?' The sweat had enhanced the swarthiness of his brow, and made his bloodshot eyes glow. 'What do these lot think? Didn't they hold an all-religion meeting last year? Weren't you the one who told me about the big board that was displayed in front of it?'

'Yesyesyes!' Appu Nair sidestepped quickly when he saw Naraapilla's change of mood: 'I can still see it in my mind's eye.

"Not to argue or win, but to learn and inform" displayed in front of the tent like a big pumpkin!'

'Ah, that's what I'm saying too! Who will they inform? And what'll they instruct?' Naraapilla's voice rose. A dark-skinned baby, sleeping in its lungi-cradle hung from the small mango tree on the far side of the field, woke up with a start and began crying.

'Aww! Whose is this?' Appu Nair enquired, hoping to change the topic.

'Not mine,' Naraapilla said with a lewd smile. 'Take it if it's yours!'

Appu Nair had learnt from their proximity that laughing aloud at Naraapilla's jokes would fetch him an extra gulp of toddy at noon. So he guffawed loudly. Hearing the baby's cries and Appu Nair's laughter, Kaalippennu put down her sickle and came up from the field.

Casting a beseeching glance at Naraapilla, she scooped up the baby. Appu Nair, the father of four children, was pained to see the breast milk had spilled and mixed with sweat on Kaali's sarong of mill cloth wound tightly around her chest. For the unmarried Naraapilla, it caused tumescence.

The sickles, cutting at the base, frizzled.

The noon was aflame. Passing through two creeper-ridden plots and a narrow alley, they made for Raghavan's toddy shop. A vacuous, loopy grin still lingered on Appu Nair's face.

As a worshipping public—who bestowed on him more devotion than on their resident god, the Aluva thevar—stood gazing at Gandhiji in conversation with a white man under the mango tree in the Advaithaashramam, Naraapilla and Appu Nair belligerently wallowed in toddy.

'What, Rahavaa, didn't you go to see *your* swami?' Naraapilla mocked Raghavan, who was bringing a pewter bowl filled with fish curry.

Missing the barb in Naraapilla's question, Raghavan ventured: 'I heard that Swami is not in Aluva today. Shutting the shop only to go see Gandhi is not going to work for us!'

Hearing this, one of the regulars at the shop laughed gleefully and asked: 'Will Naraapilla chettan answer truthfully if I ask a question?' Eagerly, he came and sat next to Naraapilla and Appu Nair. 'For us Indians, isn't Gandhiji the greatest man? If that great one has come to Aluva to see Nanu Guru, what does that tell us? Pray, what does that mean? '

'You tell me!' Naraapilla spat on the thatched palm-leaf wall of the toddy shop and wiped his lips.

'Isn't it clear? That this Nanu swami is a bigger deal than this Gandhi!' the customer asserted, banging on the long table to make it sound like a fine-strung drum.

Naraapilla's limbs trembled when he heard that. Scared that he would stop drinking and leave, Raghavan interjected slyly, 'But I've also heard that our swami hates toddy tappers more than thieves.' Scratching the nape of his neck, he added: 'I just didn't mention it till now. What are we to do after giving up the toddy business? Become swamis?'

That shut up the regular. Invigorated, Naraapilla and Appu Nair ordered more toddy.

'If it helps sell more of his toddy, our scoundrel Raghavan will renounce even his own mother!' Naraapilla said, patting Raghavan on his shoulder as he paid for the meal. Raghavan bore the touch with pride, aware that it was the intoxication from his toddy that made a Nair touch a Thiyya like him, obliterating the lines of untouchability.

At that moment, with the hand that had blessed the historic Vaikkom Sathyagraha against Hindu untouchability, Gandhiji was signing an accord at the Advaithaashramam. The mango tree on the riverbank, which had given shade to Narayana Guru years ago, shielded one more great man from the unrelenting Meenam heat.

When the paper was handed over to the Thiruvithamkoor Police Commissioner Pitt, seated on a wicker chair under the mango tree, an onlooker, intoxicated by two kinds of devotion, shouted: 'Gandhiji-Pittji pact kii…'

'Jai!' the folk of Aluva-Kaaladi-Kaanjooru-Manjapra took it up.

By the time the news about the Gandhi-Pitt pact tumbled across and reached Appu Nair's ears, it had been abbreviated to 'pickpocket'; a hoax played by a nephew, a student of English at Aluva Union Christian College, abbreviated by all as UC College.

'In the hustle and bustle, someone picked the pocket of Gandhi!' Appu Nair interpreted.

'But does Gandhi have pockets? Doesn't he walk around with just a *mundu* around his shoulders?' pondered Swadeshabhimani Kuttan Pilla,* one of those few old denizens of Thachanakkara who owned a shirt with a pocket.

'So, that's how it is. That is the truth.' Appu Nair brightened like one who has had an epiphany. 'Someone must have played a trick on my nephew; what if he's educated, he's still an idiot!'

Naraapilla's days continued to darken and brighten through Appu Nair. The fear generated by a childhood accident and his own sense of caution stopped Naraapilla from taking a dip in the Periyar river which bounded Thachanakkara on the south. He also remained oblivious to the upheavals of his times. Thus, the

* The real Swadeshabhimani K. Ramakrishna Pillai was a writer, editor-journalist, and political activist, famed for his brave stance against the atrocities of the Diwan and the King of the erstwhile princely state of Travancore. He was known by the name of the newspaper *Swadeshabhimani* he edited. He was arrested, exiled and his newspaper and press confiscated jointly by the officers of the British Raj and the King.

Periyar on the south and Indian history on the north kept flowing, keeping Narayana Pillai at an untouchable's distance.

Naraapilla was a drunkard. Naraapilla was stocky. Naraapilla's skin was the colour of Indian rosewood. The baldness that had crept in during his youth was now the shining crown God had designed for his strange form.

It was to this Naraapilla that Kunjuamma, whose goodness could shame a crepe jasmine, ended up as wife. The effort of trying to find Naraapilla a wife from amongst the numerous Nair tharavaadus in Thachanakkara and neighbouring lands had brought Appu Nair to his knees.

One day, Naraapilla suggested: 'Don't you have a younger sister? The girl who's like an anchovy? What if I marry her?'

'My Thachanakkarappaaa ... Why this brainwave now?' A white bolt of lightning struck Appu Nair's innards. For Naraapilla, it really was an epiphanic moment. Nobody from the Ayyaattumpilli family even partook of lunch after attending weddings in the Peechamkurichi family. It was not that Naraapilla was unaware that the absurd era of the convenience marriages of the *sambandham*, or cohabitation with Nair women without the contractual obligations of marriage, was over. Much time had passed since the matrilineal system of marumakkathaayam had been legally abolished in Thiruvithamkoor. Yet, the apparition of Goddess Lakshmi, the goddess of wealth, personified as the orphaned Naraapilla, preparing to step into the poverty-stricken Peechamkurichi household, fuelled more apprehensions than happiness in Appu Nair.

'The Second Regulation...' Thinking that it would be a sin on his part not to remind Naraapilla of the changed times, Appu Nair tried to say something.

'Don't say anything.' Naraapilla stopped him. 'Go and ask her once! If there are no objections, give your sister to me!'

'If so…' Struggling to hide the blush that had crept up his face as if his kid sister had sprouted a moustache, he took hold of Naraapilla's hand. 'Here, I give you Kunju!'

In 1928, in the month of Kanni, which witnessed the departure of Sree Narayana Guru from this earth, Naraapilla gave Kunju the wedding *pudava*, and brought her to Ayyaattumpilli. Time had gathered and kept in abeyance a few embers to chastize Naraapilla for making fun of Sree Narayana Guru. On their first night in the month of Kanni, resounding with the appalling mating howls of dogs, mingled intermittently with the pitiful moans of bitches repeatedly ravished, Naraapilla conjured up an amorous expression on his inauspicious face, moved a finger to touch his bride, who looked alluring wearing the gold medallion chain that he had bought for her, and asked: 'Kunju, other than my money, do I have anything that Kunju likes?'

Sitting on the cot, with her hands covering her eyes, Kunju answered immediately: 'Um, yes.'

'What's it?' Hardly able to contain his anticipation, Naraapilla took both her hands in his, and held them in his lap.

Kunjuamma blushed. Her voice turned tender: 'Your name!'

'Which? Naraapilla?'

'No, the full name.' Kunjuamma's face suffused with pride for her husband, as she completed her statement, 'Narayanan—Isn't that the real name of the Gurudevan who relinquished his life last week?'

Naraapilla was stunned. As Appu Nair would have said, Naraapilla went hari hara.

However, greater shocks were yet to strike.

THREE

Thachanakkara

15 April 1999

...I have started compromising with everything here. When I see my betel-chewing boss, I am reminded of all the rulers of the world. Have you noticed a ruler's face from close quarters? Not only will it not have a trace of God in it, but will, many a time, have the concealed smile of the devil. Will this same eyeless mask, which is applicable to the heads of families as much as to the American president, appear on my face too when I become your husband tomorrow?

Let it be. Here is a joke that may help you in your Public Services Commission exam alone: our jolly comrade Nayanar has become the chief minister who has ruled Kerala for the longest spell. Our naïve, humorous minister!

Read in the paper that the president, hailing from Uzhavoor, has advised the Central Government to face a no-confidence motion. Do you read the papers? The hoary Nairs of Thachanakkara must be cursing that Uzhavoor man now. But the government will fall. At least by one vote. Do you know that that decisive vote will be mine—the vote of an Indian dejected about the country going to the dogs.

Parashuraman is the lord or thevar of Thachanakkara.

For cleaving Bhoomi Malayalam with his axe from the sea, and measuring and apportioning it as a gift amongst the upper castes, they worship Parashuraman. Like the contours of the animal-skin laid out for Parashuraman to rest, Thachanakkara lay coiled around its temple. To the south of it were Elookkara and Kayintikkara, where the Muslims lived. Unaware of these religious differences, the Periyar flowed past these three villages, sketching their eastern borders, and emptying into the Varappuzha Lake.

On the other side of the river was Uliyanoor, the land of Perumthachchan, the legendary master craftsman—the ooru or land of the uliyan or the chisel-wielder. Thachanakkara is the land that sent that chisel-wielder to *akkare*, or the other bank.

However, for the people of Thachanakkara, 'to go akkare', was not to cross over to the rustic village of Uliyanoor, but to cross the ghat at Kamari to go to Aluva town. For the bridge linking Kamari kadavu to Aluva town to be built, it would take another decade. Rani Sethu Lakshmi Bai was ruling as the regent, as Chithirathirunnal Balarama Varma was still a minor. When Balarama Varma would ascend to the throne, the wave-shaped Marthaanda Varma Bridge would appear over the Kamari kadavu. Linked by the bridge, Aluva would then cease to be akkare or the other side for the people of Thachanakkara. That the first non-Hindu Diwan of Thiruvithamkoor—Watt Sahib, whose name reminded one of hydro-electricity—existed farther south, was not known to the residents of Thachanakkara then.

The topography that Thachanakkara's people learnt, running left-right-front-back, was simple: the mud road that ran along Thachanakkara thevar's line of sight, and extending as far as his vision, creates a crossroad at Thottakkattukara. Turn right and cross Kamari kadavu, you arrive at Aluva town. Turn left, and after two miles of brisk walking up to the Mangala river, you land in the kadavu wriggling with crocodiles that yanked young men towards advaitham; cross that and you are in Adi Sankara's Kalady. Beyond that was Angamaly, starting to teem with the followers of the Nazarene. From Thottakkattukara, walk straight without turning left or right, cross the street and you reach the riverine beach of Aluva, where the solitary Aluva thevar abides, yearning for the Shivaraathri festival.

Though the Raja of Kochi was right next door, Thachanakkara was ruled by the kings of Thiruvithamkoor, residing somewhere in the remote, faraway south. The erstwhile Venad, exalted by Marthaanda Varma as Thiruvithamkoor, had the districts of Paravoor and Aalangad girdling Thachanakkara in the north; they were the central knots in the rope used in the tug of war that went on for centuries, pulled from the south by Thiruvithamkoor and from the north by the Zamorin. The Rama Varmas of Kochi stood in the middle, looking with childlike curiosity at this tug of war. Finally, Marthaanda Varma won. Though located right under Kochi Raja's Adam's apple, Thachanakkara folk began to offer their prayers turning southwards, and learnt to trade with the chakram coins of Sree Padmanabhan of Thiruvithamkoor.

For their understanding of history and civics, the commoners of Thachanakkara were indebted to Swadeshabhimani Kuttan Pillai, who was the only one in Thachanakkara to sport an upper garment with pockets. He had come over ages ago from Thiruvananthapuram, got married in Thachanakkara, and settled down there. Despite a Pillai attached to his name, during his initial years at Thachanakkara, the common folk had secretly believed him to be an Ezhava. However, everyone became certain that he was of Nair stock when they heard him establish his relationship to the celebrated editor Swadeshabhimani Ramakrishna Pillai, whom the Travancore king, Sreemoolam Thirunal, had exiled for criticizing his royal rule.

'Oh, I cannot erase that last scene from my mind,' Kuttan Pillai sighed every day, obviously reliving that scene, sitting in Pooshaappi's shop.

The shop—owned by Poovamparampath Shashwathan Pillai, whose name was elided by familiarity into 'Pooshaappi'—was a thatched hut straining to explode in shame with all the gossip of Thachanakkara. It was a shop from where you could get groceries, vegetables, and basket-loads of gossip. For a long while, it was the stage on which Appu Nair practised his brand of koothu performance, his version of stand-up comedy, satirizing events and targeting people. However, ever since he had become the brother-in-law of Naraapilla of Ayyaattumpilli, he had lost touch with the general public. Imitating Naraapilla, people began to call him 'Appoliyan'—aliyan being brother-in-law—as if it were a titular name. After the change in his status, the Bonaparte of Thachanakkara drastically cut down the number of times he held court on the shop patio, and Kuttan Pillai duly took on the mantle of chief gossip disburser, and became his successor.

Setting up the original Swadeshabhimani, who had died of consumption, as his bosom friend, Kuttan Pillai would set off on his embellished flights of fancy: 'That midnight, as he was getting into the horse carriage accompanied by the police, he turned to look at me once. I must have been forty or forty-one then. Between us, we hardly had an age difference of six or eight, that's all. On that day, blinded by tears, I couldn't see anything. "Do look after my printing press and pen, and give me leave, my Kuttan Pilla chettaa," he had appealed, after which he tumbled right into the carriage!'

The first recipient of the oral circulation of this Swadeshabhimani saga aattakatha was Pooshaappi himself.

Quoting Swadeshabhimani repeatedly, for anything and everything, the outsider Kuttan Pillai turned into Swadeshabhimani Kuttan Pilla.

'But, what about the police, then?' Pooshaappi asked, all anxiety, as he lifted and carefully placed his testicles, swollen like pomelos, on the termite-eaten stool pulled up closer to be in front of his chair.

'Would they dare touch me? Who was the Diwan then? Wasn't it our Rao Bahadur Rajagopalachari? Heh! The very same Madrasi who was the Diwan here in Kochi as well. What do you think is this Achari? It's nothing but our carpenter caste—Ashari! So, that means that surely there will be a certain *this* for people like us. What say you?'

It was that moment which revealed to Pooshaappi that Kuttan Pilla was indeed a Nair. At that point, the washerwoman Thaamara, carrying her baby girl, called out from below the laterite steps, 'Will there be an anna worth of washing soda to take?'

Gingerly moving aside the stool that bore his burden, Pooshaappi got up and opened the soda tin, mentally bookmarking where Kuttan Pilla had left off his tale. Kuttan Pilla's gaze lingered on Thaamara, the eponymous lotus in bloom.

'What's your kid's name, lass?' Kuttan Pilla asked, looking at the snot-nosed girl, a lotus bud, sitting snugly on Thaamara's waist. The little one looked uncomprehendingly at Kuttan Pilla, her hand playing absently with a mole as big as a beetle on her cheek.

'Ammu,' replied Thaamara, as she turned to walk back after paying for the washing soda packet.

The knowledge that this Ammu, now sitting on the waist of Thaamara, was to be the very same Ammu whom Naraapilla's grandson would see forty-eight years later in the form of the middle-aged woman who washed the clothes of the villagers on the stone at the kadavu, made the thevar of Thachanakkara let out a deep sigh that sent scraps of paper lying on the mud road flying and scattering in the air.

The youthful voluptuousness of Thaamara, spilling over like pots of toddy in her checkered mundu, elicited a sigh in the sixty-plus Kuttan Pilla. However, what he said was something else, 'Didn't you hear the name of that washerwoman kid? Ammu, I believe! Look at how far fashion has come, as time goes by!'

'And then?' fascinated by history, again Pooshaappi settled on the two stools, ready to hear the rest of the tale.

'What was I saying? Ah, even the Diwan knew that actually I was the brain behind Ramakrishna Pillai. But then, his Majesty did harbour a distinct animosity towards Ramakrishna Pillai. Who wouldn't get furious when you argue for lower castes like Ezhavas and Pulayars? As for me, though I am progressive and everything, I will not compromise when it comes to caste, as everyone knows! So, they let go of me, in some ingenious manner. But could I rejoice? Was it not the real Swadeshabhimani, who lay prostrate at the feet of that *inspettor* Pichu Iyengar, at midnight, gibbering and weeping? Hey, what's this? Why're you sweating? Is your hydrocele hurting?' Kuttan Pilla's glance fell between Pooshaappi's legs.

'Nah, not that!' Pooshaappi shook his head, still sweating. Whenever he listened to historical tales, invariably the massive double-bundles that he had been bearing for the past sixteen years would start to throb and ache; especially if they were tales about royal wrath. Ensconced on two stools, he was one of those whose hearts would simply cease working and collapse if they were ever to be confronted by the disapproving frown of a ruler whom he may have crossed.

'Whither was he exiled to?' the trembling Pooshaappi prodded.

Kuttan Pilla halted for a moment. If he were to be truthful and say Madras, it was certain that the gravitas of the story would be lost. Madras was a place where even the useless youngsters of Thiruvananthapuram, who ran away from home, ended up in. The memory of a poor eatery in Madras, where he had to eke out a living as a cleaning boy, flashed in Kuttan Pilla's mind.

'Have you heard of Harappajadaro?' The name that he tried to recollect was Andaman and Nicobar. Because it didn't come to his tongue on time, Kuttan Pilla had to make up a name at that very instant.

'Yeah, yesyes,' Pooshaappi agreed, putting on a sombre air, though it was indeed the first time he was hearing it.

'Yeah, that's where he was exiled to. Don't you know that it's a place teeming with barbarians who would eat men in the raw? But, hmm, wasn't it Ramakrishna Pillai after all? He put up a fight there too. Retaining the honour of us Nairs, he killed three, four barbarians as well!'

When he heard that, Pooshaappi's pain lessened a bit. Inspired, Kuttan Pilla was about to add something else. But as quickly as he had opened his mouth, he shut it. Winding up his history rendition abruptly, Kuttan Pilla scrambled out, hastily scooping up the half pound of jaggery that had been kept wrapped in a teak leaf for him.

After a long gap, Appu Nair was seen coming towards the shop.

After the disaster of the first night, Naraapilla had not touched Kunjuamma. The punishment for arrogance. For the first time, Naraapilla was seeing a Nair woman express respect for Narayana Guru, the guru of Ezhavas and Thiyyas; he was touching such a one for the first time. The first touch itself had scorched him. All his inferiority complexes from childhood woke up with a start, swelled rapidly, and unfurled their dark branches over him. In the span of a moment, Naraapilla who measured money with a para, was turned into something worth not even a miserly half-chakra.

He fumed with the thirst for vengeance. His mouth welled up with saliva when he thought of catching and crushing her like a nit. He went around without food for four days. The fourth day, he confronted his wife, who was preparing to go to bed as if unaware of him being angry, and announced dramatically: 'I've brought something for you to eat!'

Kunjuamma was a tad upset that the past few nights her husband had slept alone in the anteroom. She had even amused herself with the thought that the unattractive Naraapilla was trying to lure her into a lover's tiff. Apart from the chain made of sovereigns that he had gifted her on the first night, it looked like he was now offering something more.

Kunjuamma raised the wick of the chimney lamp and stood waiting with blazing anticipation.

'It's underneath the bed! Grab and eat it!' Naraapilla spat in a choleric rage, as he went into the anteroom.

Kunjuamma was startled for a moment. Then, she gathered her hair into a bun at the back of her head and bent down to look under the bed with the chimney lamp.

Under the bed was one of the three laterite bricks that were usually left in front of the pounding shed, and used as the makeshift stove on which water for heated up for Naraapilla's evening bath. How did Naraapilla come to know that Kunjuamma had the habit of eating pieces of burnt laterite stones?

'Pray! How did he come to know of that?' a panting Appu Nair challenged Pooshaappi, as soon as he arrived at the store. 'Achuttan Vaidyan had said long ago that it's because of a deficiency as she didn't have any good nutrients while growing up, eh Pooshaappi ... She got cured of it when she went into a family that could afford to eat and sleep well. But, now, how did he come to know? Tell me, I've told only you. Thachanakkara thevar won't forgive anyone who has done this to betray my Kunju!' Appu Nair couldn't control his sorrow and punched his own throat as he uttered the word Thachanakkara thevar, sighing expansively.

That heartfelt curse came from a crushed soul. Pooshaappi jumped up as if he had been slapped, worried that if he were to endure it further, it may set his shop afire, burning him along with it.

'Ha! What's the point of you acting like this; all loose-tongued and hysterical like women?' Pooshaappi consoled him, holding on to Appu Nair's sweating shoulders, primarily for balancing himself. 'Tell me this first! How did you come to know what happened on a night in Naraapilla's bedroom? Was it your sister who told you?'

Appu Nair's sorrow lessened somewhat when he heard that. '*Cheyy*, will she say that?' Appu Nair pushed away Pooshaappi's hand and sat on the entrance step, gazing towards the road. Pooshaappi almost fell when his support was taken away unexpectedly. He quickly got hold of the shop pillar made of the chopped trunk of an Indian tulip tree.

'Say, will the bitterness of the poison-nut tree disappear if it were to be irrigated with honey?' Appu Nair continued in frustration. 'When I went to Ayyaattumpilli today, the man asked me if it was right to feed grass to a girl used to eating stone!'

When the story reached that stage, Pooshaappi could not help laughing, forgetting the solemnity of the occasion. However, the next moment, he checked himself.

'I do remember,' said Pooshaappi, 'when you were talking about Kunju's stone-eating habit, there were a few others here. One was indeed our Swadeshabhimani Kuttan Pilla. Because you can be certain of that, there's no need to find out about the others. There's also no point in you pouncing on Kuttan Pilla in this regard!'

'Then?' Appu Nair turned his neck to look at Pooshaappi.

'We'll find a way for all that!' Pooshaappi took out his statesmanship. 'I promise that I'll tackle your brother-in-law, advise him to discriminate between right and wrong. Now, is there anything you need to buy?'

Appu Nair made a sound with his mouth that could be taken as a no. Then, Pooshaappi once again used Appu Nair's shoulder as support to bend down, and enquired with a mischievous smile, 'Forget all that. You tell me this now. Did Kunju actually eat the stone that Naraapilla gave her?'

At first, Kunjuamma did not recognize Naraapilla's evil intent. The virgin had just completed eighteen, in the month of Kanni. Keeping the chimney lamp on the floor, Kunjuamma pushed the stone left and right and searched all around it with her right hand. While she was surprised at not finding anything, the tempting smell of burnt stone rushed into her nose. For the first time, Kunjuamma felt some affection for her husband. Kunjuamma marvelled as to how she would have, earlier, finished off the stone at one go.

'Not now,' Kunjuamma told herself. 'It's no fun for the stove not to have all the three stones!'

That night, Parashuraman, who had slashed his mother's throat to let his father's obstinacy win, rolled his eyes as he sat looking at Kunjuamma from within the Thachanakkara temple.

FOUR

Glorious Mother

17 April 1999

...How many astounding fortuities occur behind every man's birth? This bond of ours too is only a coincidence for certain other births in the offing. That's how it is going to be, however we romanticize it. Upset? It's not because I cannot wait till I receive the reply for the letter sent day before yesterday that I am writing yet another long letter. Only if I put this too down on paper for you, today itself, will I be able to sleep.

What did you feel when the government fell by a deficit of one vote? Or, did you not come to know of it? See how prophetic my words were. Anyway, I feel rather peaceful today. Now, shall I tell you something I have not told you so far? My mother was stunned when she heard that the girl I was planning to marry was a Christian. The same shock that my grandfather had felt, half a century ago, when Uncle Govindan decided to marry a lower-caste Thiyya woman from Cherai!

The eighteen-year-old Kunjuamma, whom Naraapilla married and brought home, was the first female braveheart in Thachanakkara to pronounce openly that her husband had bad breath. More than boldness, it was the new bride's naïve enthusiasm that made Kunjuamma say so.

It was indeed Swadeshabhimani Kuttan Pilla who informed Naraapilla of his wife's fetish for burnt laterite. But it was not after the marriage, as surmised by Appu Nair.

A month before, Naraapilla had stepped into the temple pond of Thachanakkara thevar for his regular morning bath. Usually, at that hour, apart from Naraapilla, only the bulbous frogs would be on the wet steps, their ballooning throats cursing the light breaking in the east. From the thoroughly chilled green hue, fine layers of mist would be wafting up. Around the square walls of the pool, the coconut palms would stand unmoving, in daunting silence. At that hour, when everything stood frozen, beyond the shoulder-high wall separating the women's side of the pool, someone entered the water, setting off widening ripples in the water. The sound of a female mouth gargling and spitting out water could be heard. Naraapilla raised his head above the half-wall and peered. On the women's side of the steps, the faint light of dawn framed for Naraapilla the sculpted curves of a female form, clad in a single wet, clinging mundu. He wondered if the sounds of the frogs jumping en masse into the water, after they wound up their music practice, was actually coming from somewhere inside him. Naraapilla dried himself quickly and got out.

Usually, women did not bathe in the carefully preserved temple pond of Thachanakkara, in which soap and oil were not allowed. For them to wash, bathe, and gossip, Punneli kadavu in the Aluva river was deemed perfect. The Nair men and women of Thachanakkara bathed there—except Naraapilla. For Naraapilla, who bathed twice a day, the morning bath was always at the temple pond. Without soap or oil. The yard in front of his grain-pounding house provided the stage for his elaborate second bath of the day in the evenings, with an oil massage, washed off with bath water heated in the copper vat set on the laterite stone stove fired by dried coconut flower spathes.

He too had bathed in the Punneli ghat in his childhood with his mother. Once, his mother was scrubbing away the dirt from the back of his black body with a shikakai scrub. The kadavu was empty. To keep the boy still, she kept singing and annotating a couplet his father—whom he had never seen—had composed. The poem was about the seven mountains that gave birth to the Periyar river. The pepper-infused coconut oil on the boy's unruly hair had started warming up in the midday sun. Letting him get into the river to take a dip by himself, Pappiyamma—left a lonely widow in Ayyaattumpilli, with a single child and hectares of landed property—took ten seconds to wash and wring the thorth dry. She shook the wrinkles out of the thorth and turned, but the lad had vanished! He had gone under, weighted down by the history-laden waters of Aluva river that he had gulped down involuntarily when the sand bank had given way beneath his feet. The first time his head bobbed up, the oiled hair slipped out of Pappiyamma's grasp. The current was slow that day. The next time he surfaced, the mother's grip on the clump of his hair was stronger and surer, fortunately. After she yanked him up to the shore in one strong swing, she found a handful of hair stuck to her palm, and washed it off in the river. From that day onwards, the twelve-year-old Narayanan began to lose hair. If he got into the river, he began to get fits remembering his floundering in the vortex. That is how Naraapilla came to bathe in Thachanakkara thevar's algae-bloom-green pond instead.

If the flowing river tried to drag him away from his mother and steal his life, the still waters of the temple pond gave him life, luring him in the form of Kunjuamma—in his thirtieth year, in the midst of his bath at dawn, Naraapilla recognized the woman who captivated him. The youngest sibling of his dearest friend Appu Nair, the young girl of Peechamkurichi, where they could not afford even a decent midday meal, had blossomed into a full-breasted woman! As he walked, Naraapilla turned back to look at her, and the second toe on his right foot hit the oblation stone on the temple floor and started bleeding.

Early in the morning, he reached Pooshaappi's shop; the wound in his toe was clotted by then. Pooshaappi was just opening the shop, putting away the wooden slats. Kuttan Pilla too had reached, sans his pocket-shirt, yawning and scratching his head. Sidling under the awning of the shop, and moving into the shade, both his injured right toe and the granite-like head with its forehead smeared with sandal-paste from the temple visit early that morning, Naraapilla launched a crafty probe, 'Isn't there a lassie at Peechamkurichi? Appu Nair's younger sibling. Does it have any illness, eh, Pooshaappi? Looks rather odd!'

'Heeeyy, no way!' With a sound resembling a ram's snort, Pooshaappi, who held the statistics of the entire female population of Thachanakkara in his palm, dismissed it, 'The one Naraapilla saw couldn't have been the girl from Peechamkurichi. Though food is scarce, she is of plump stock. Anyone seeing her would yearn for her! But, hasn't Naraapilla seen Appu Nair's sister so far?'

That was all that remained to be discovered. Naraapilla came away before Pooshaappi could even finish opening his shop. But, as he was walking back, he overheard Swadeshabhimani asking Pooshaappi, 'Eh, Pooshaappi, didn't Appu Nair say the other day that she had a fetish for eating stones?'

Naraapilla didn't find anything odd about that. Unpolished rice with adequate curries was sure to put an end to Kunjuamma's stone consumption. If not, and even if it was a disease, the coffers of Ayyaattumpilli had enough money to treat it.

From the street paved with fist-sized granite chunks, Naraapilla entered the alley leading to Ayyaattumpilli. Next to the medicinal herb plants, he saw in the early morning light, the moovandan mango trees, known for giving fruits from the third year onwards, thus earning its name for the species, in blossom and apparently doing their workouts in the breeze.

The breeze, tangy with the smell of mango sap, presaged spring in that month of Dhanu. As the vision of the drenched Kunjuamma in the temple pond appeared before his eyes, Naraapilla's injured toe struck a protruding root.

'Aww!' Naraapilla's mouth opened wide.

There was a reason why Appu Nair's sister Kunjuamma went to bathe in Thachanakkara thevar's pond. Appu Nair had gone west to meet the senior astrologer of Kaniyankunnu to ascertain the root cause and remedy for the tribulations that seemed to plague the family. After the partition, his old parents and younger sister of marriageable age had become part of Appu Nair's inheritance. As far as Appu Nair was concerned, the so-called self-acquired assets mentioned in the new legislation for Nairs were only these. It did not end there—there was also his wife, stooped over from four consecutive pregnancies and deliveries that resulted in four children, whose shapes resembled scooped-out coconut shells and empty measuring naazhis, the smallest paddy measures. After the death of his parents, he stood to inherit the dilapidated, about-to-collapse Peechamkurichi house too. All things considered, a visit to the elder astrologer was overdue.

The senior astrologer of Kaniyankunnu does not spread the cowrie shells to read the future; does not ask the name or the star under which one is born; nor does he ask for the native place or the caste. The person who comes to his front yard, he believed, invariably brings a portent with him. Kittan, his youngest son, who was chopping wood, spotted Appu Nair and called out to his father: 'Father, someone's here!'

When the senior astrologer—his pock-marked face rendered fiercer with the ash smeared on it—stepped out on to the portal, the first thing he saw was his youngest son standing with the axe, drenched in sweat. Behind him was Appu Nair, who had come to seek a remedy. Youngest son, axe, and sweat ... The senior astrologer had no difficulty reading it altogether.

'Instruct the youngest in the family to bathe and offer prayers at Parashuraman's temple for forty-one days. Let it be before daybreak, and before changing out of wet clothes. Problems will be solved,' the senior astrologer shut his eyes and told Appu Nair, his eyeballs almost rolling up into his eyebrows.

Appu Nair was relieved. The remedial action was uncomplicated. In Thiruvithamkoor, there was only one temple for Parashuraman, as far as he knew. That was in Thachanakkara itself. What could he have done if it was as far away as Thripprayaar or Guruvayoor?

The senior astrologer's prophecy did not go wrong. On the very first day of bathing in the temple pond, a soaked Kunjuamma was spotted by Naraapilla. Before the forty-first day, Appu Nair's family was able to come ashore.

What happened on Naraapilla's first night was the crescendo-like climax of all these happenings. When Kunjuamma uttered the name of Narayana Guru, Naraapilla was only momentarily shaken. The next minute he forgot that. As a prelude to the consecration of the goddess whom he had espied at the temple pond, now seated on his rope-bound cot covered with fresh linen, Naraapilla blew out the chimney lamp. Gagging at the foul stench emanating from his mouth, the chimney lamp held its nose and died out. Then he tried to hold Kunjuamma close and kiss her. When the fetid smell, that even his own mother could not have endured, reached her nostrils, the chaste wife shoved aside her husband and said, 'Ayyo, Naraapilla chettan's mouth stinks awfully!'

Naraapilla sank without a trace.

His vow of silence started thus from that day and extended to four days, at the end of which he suddenly divined the only flaw in Kunjuamma—the allegation he had overheard Kuttan Pilla make at Pooshaappi's shop, which he had disregarded then. If he had flaws, so did she! Evading his wife's gaze, and under cover of twilight, he went to the front yard of the pounding room, lifted a burnt stone off the brick stove used for heating water for his evening bath and pushed it surreptitiously under the rope-bound cot. Then he spent his day relishing the thought of his wife being shattered by the dramatic scenes his plan was to set off.

However, things did not go strictly according to Naraapilla's plan. The stone bait could not sway Kunjuamma at all, except for stirring a minor regret in her that she could not consume it then and there, as by that time she was too full with the sumptuous repast she had had for dinner. Naraapilla's effort to bring things to a boil by telling Appu Nair the next day about his sister's flaw too found little success, and on the fifth day, as a compromise formula, he started chewing pan. That was Pooshaappi's masterstroke. To uphold the promise he had given to Appu Nair, from then on, Pooshaappi regularly stored in his shop for Naraapilla, scented arecanut, flavoured tobacco, and fine tender betel leaves that rivalled even the softness of Kunjuamma's underbelly—all procured from Aluva market. Seduced by the potent fragrance of flavoured tobacco, Kunjuamma gave birth to six children in the span of a decade, with strictly-observed intervals of one and three quarter years.

When Kunjuamma spent the period from 1930 to 1940 dutifully producing heirs, Naraapilla too did not remain idle. He immersed himself in building a beautiful house in the plot north of Ayyaattumpilli. The stones that arrived by boat at Punneli kadavu were carried as headloads by the workers till Ayyaattumpilli. The jackfruit tree and teak trees on the eastern boundary, and the jujube tree for the rafters, were cut down. The wood of the white ironwood tree, more durable than teak, had been sourced in advance through the carpenter Gopalan. To prevent the limestone sacks from hardening from contact with rain water, Appu Nair helped stack them in the anteroom.

For pre-natal and post-partum oil baths and massage treatments, a hot-water bathroom, with a roof of coconut leaf-thatch, had stood in the yard for nearly twelve years. The new house coming up was to the north of that too. Unable to resist the lure of the mineral vapours emanating from the stacked stones meditating to be transformed into the house, on some nights, unknown to Naraapilla, the hugely-pregnant Kunjuamma staggered out to the plot on the north side. The hacked-out laterite stones, coated with the honey of moonlight, smiled at Kunjuamma; overcome by irresistible pregnancy cravings, she devoured the pieces she broke off from the edges and corners of the laterite stones. Before going to sleep, she drank water and let out a satisfied burp.

Before the sixth delivery, they shifted to the house that would later be referred to as the New House. Naraapilla entrusted Appu Nair with the onus of ensuring that termites did not attack the old house. Appu Nair led the war against termites by sprinkling the house with herbal infusions. But the empty house in which termites had entrenched themselves, defeated him. He scampered everywhere looking for a tenant. Eventually, the small family of a wife, son and a school master from the government school in Aluva, fell into Appu Nair's net. Sweeping the old house clean, Menon Master and family, who would gain attention in Thachanakkara later as the tenants of Ayyaattumpilli, started living there.

The phrase commonly used by the folk of Thachanakkara later to describe the passage of the years—'Much water has flown under Aluva bridge'—was invalid in describing those years that followed Naraapilla's marriage. Because, it was only when Kunjuamma's belly was swollen with her sixth baby and laterite dust, that the new bridge to Aluva town unfurled like a wave at Kamari kadavu.

As the evening sun warmed the yard of the New House, Kunjuamma, convulsing with labour pangs, paced there from north to south and back, accompanied by the midwife Kalyani. Padminiyamma, the wife of Menon Master, joined them, holding rags torn off old cloth. Govindan, Kunjuamma's eldest boy, sat sweating on the parapet, looking at her. His three younger brothers with snotty noses, stood around him, puzzled. Menon Master's son, the eleven-year-old Achyuthan, with large, intelligent eyes, stood near the fence, gazing at his new friend's mother pacing up and down with her distended tummy. Looking at her son, Padminiyamma spoke to all the boys, 'Well, what're you boys standing here to see? Um, go, go! Go and play somewhere else!'

Despondent that they didn't even feel like playing though it was a school holiday, the boys moved away under the leadership of Govindan, occasionally stealing backward glances. Only a girl child seated on Naraapilla's lap bawled with an open mouth, thrashing her limbs with hands extended towards her mother. Naraapilla kept cursing and whacking her thigh. Suddenly, Appu Nair stormed in, all excitement. 'Brother-in-law, I went and saw the new bridge inaugurated yesterday. Aww! You will go hari hara! Looks as if the Malayalam letter "ga ga" is written repeatedly. On the southern end there is a plaque etched with the name of His Majesty!' He took the thorth from his shoulders, fanned himself with it, and sat on the parapet.

Kunjuamma and the midwife eyed him with irritation. Aware that it was one of the occasions which gave her special privileges, the midwife took on a pointed, peremptory voice and said, 'Here a woman is in labour and waiting for delivery. That's when a brother pops in with his bridge-vidge news! Just shut up, Appu chettaa!'

Naraapilla's hand shut the mouth of the crying baby on his lap and he said, 'Kunju, it's going to be easy to remember the year of birth for our sixth child. The year of the new bridge!'

'For that, let the sixth baby arrive first!' the midwife smouldered, still irritated.

At that point, holding her lower back, Kunjuamma ran inside screaming, 'Ammae.' The midwife Kalyani ran after her, screaming even louder, 'It's time, Naraapilla chettaa!' Hesitating for a moment, Padminiyamma with the experience of only one delivery of her own, joined them, still clutching the rags. A flash of worry about his sister shot through Appu Nair when he saw Naraapilla grinning at him with betel-stained teeth. From inside, a shriek 'O, my Thachanakkara thevare!' soared and subsided.

When the air from the New House hit her face, the sixth offspring of Ayyaattumpilli, a female replica of Naraapilla with the same face and a complexion as dark as Indian rosewood, cried out loud with the same mouth, as the little finger of the midwife wiped blood off it.

This bawling newborn was the one who would deliver Jithendran three decades later.

FIVE

Two Kinds of Rivers

10 April 1999

...I have once seen Thakazhi Sivasankara Pillai in person. I had gone to a friend's place in Changanacherry. Hearing of an award ceremony, for a collection of poems by the thespian Premji, being attended by Thakazhi Sivasankara Pillai and the first chief minister of Kerala, we went there. Now I recall, the book was called *Mattamma*. Having reached early, we took our seats right in the front. Premji and Thakazhi came onstage before others. Just as the programme was about to start, the audience rose to their feet, with a buzz. The cheering was for the leader of the people. He and Thakazhi greeted each other with folded hands. Both of them were aged. Tears of the times past seemed to sparkle in their eyes. In their mutual respect, there wasn't an iota of pretence.

Today, when I heard of the demise of Thakazhi, that scene came to my mind.

'Marthaanda Varma bridge ... Prince of Travancore ... on 14 June 1940 ... umm ... one thousand one hundred and fifteen ... ingineers ... gi bi ee truss coat, yem yess duraiswami ayyengar ... contract ... jay cee ga ... gammon el ti di.'

Govindan, the eldest son of Naraapilla, and Achyuthan, the

only son of Menon Master, jointly read the letters on the plaque of the bridge, etched in Roman script right below the royal emblem of the silver-trimmed conch shell.

On their way back from school in the evening, they were entering the pedestrian walkway on the left side of the Marthaanda Varma Bridge. As they left the plaque behind and reached the midsection of the bridge, the children peered at the river—flowing on the right, caressing the Shivaraathri grounds, going past the bridge to split against a small green isle on the left, to branch off into two—appearing as the forked armrests of a hermit's rod. They laughed in mirth, when the cool breeze, which was tracing strange scripts on the surface of the water, blew over the expanse of the river, making their shirts balloon. The bridge was redolent with the smell of freshly-roasted snacks.

Till now, every school-goer on his way to school in the ferry had his eyes trained on the bridge under construction. They now knew the name of the haughty, jacket-clad sayipp who stood under the wavy arches of the bridge, showering the workers with invectives—G.B.E. Truscott! The avaricious-looking *pattar* with red sandal paste on his forehead, the person seen with him must have been the same Duraiswamy Iyengar, the name now etched on the plaque.

Govindan and Achyuthan ran along the narrow walkway trying to outpace an evil-faced lorry that drove across the bridge, trembling and praying. Stacked to the brim with rice bags and a scrawny lad perched on top of the mound, the lorry drove past the boys, mocking them with its black fumes. The dark lad on the top, holding on to the ropes and preening, made faces at the beaten contemporaries trailing behind, and displaying the rictus of the winner, let out a whoop of victory. The next moment, the vehicle ground to a halt. A herd of cattle headed for the market was crossing the Thottakkattukara junction. Govindan and Achyuthan caught up and ran ahead of the lorry, not forgetting to return, with interest, the grimaces and hoots to the lad atop the vehicle.

Normally, Achyuthan's father would have been with them at that hour. If Menon Master was with them, all this frolicking would not have been be possible. Today, he had gone to invite some brilliant guy from UC College for the inauguration of the school's annual day. The absence of the father made Achyuthan feel more grown up, while the absence of the teacher made Govindan feel more of a kid. Govindan had just joined first standard in the Aluva Government School, after completing class fifth at Aalungal School. Achyuthan was in the second standard at the same school. The son who was fortunate enough to be in his father's class!

Govindan's two brothers, Padmanabhan and Parameswaran, were studying in the fourth and second classes at Aalungal School in Thachanakkara. Chandran, their four-year-old younger brother, and their two sisters, constituted a triumvirate of mouths battling for their mother's two teats. To wean Chandran, Kunjuamma had procured the bitter extract of aloe vera. But if she were to apply it on her breasts, it would get ingested by the two-year-old Thankamma and the infant Chinnamma.

Passing through the bridge, via Thottakkattukara junction, and along the long gravel road watched by Thachanakkara thevar, they reached Pooshaappi's shop, when Kuttan Pilla climbed down the steps and detained Achyuthan to enquire, 'Who, son, is the new arrival at your house?'

Achyuthan opened his palms in a non-verbal 'Aaa' to indicate ignorance. Catching hold of Govindan's arm and pulling him along, he speeded up his pace in anticipation.

Swadeshabhimani Kuttan Pilla found it a struggle to mount the steps back to reach Pooshaappi's sanctorum. Pooshaappi's eldest son, Parameswaran, who was commonly called Kochu Parashu, had made some recent improvements to the shop. Pooshaappi was now installed in a room which had limestone plaster over laterite stones and numbered wooden planks for its opening. The roof had premium tiles, which Kochu Parashu himself had fetched, covered in hay, from Angamaly on his bullock cart. Extending the veranda, and thatching it with palm leaves, he had created an annexe to vend sarsaparilla sherbet and spiced buttermilk. Pooshaappi's testicles inside his mud-coloured single mundu now resembled yams, mature enough to be dug up and yanked from the soil. As Kochu Parashu was there in the shop most of the time, Swadeshabhimani Kuttan Pilla's presence was rarer nowadays. During the gossip sessions, since he was on the wane and his shots lacked their punch, he had started fading. He was also gradually getting on in years. However, his nose for gossip had not diminished.

That day, sipping his jaggery-sweetened coffee from a copper tumbler as he ambled out to the yard, Govindan noticed on their tenant's doorsteps, an attractive pair of plastic footwear in addition to the slippers of Menon Master and Achyuthan.

The footwear of someone with large feet.

Menon Master was sitting on the parapet, having seated the guest in the armchair.

He was almost bursting with joy and pride. He had been nervous when he went to invite him for the school annual day. Would his old friend recognize him? Even if he remembered, would he be shown due consideration? However, when they met in person, all misgivings had disappeared. Not only did he agree to grace the occasion, he even accompanied his old friend to visit his newly-rented house. All the way to Thachanakkara, coming down the college hill and walking up Kaniyankunnu, they reforged the links of their friendship that time had sundered. Still not convinced, Menon Master looked again at the man, whom the whole of Kerala venerated, lolling on his soiled easy chair!

Menon Master recollected how they had gone to talk about a raise in their salary, on the day the Guru arrived at the Sanskrit school of the Advaithaashramam.

'After I came away from the school, never did I manage to see Swami again,' Menon Master mused, overwhelmed by regret.

The visitor picked up the fan made from arecanut spathe, fanned himself, and remained silent for a while. The eyes behind the glasses shut themselves into the many memories that refused to die down; then, after letting out a long sigh, he said in a heavy, grave voice, 'I came away to the college the year he relinquished the mortal coils in samaadhi. I had visited and met him during his final moments too. How quickly have ten years gone by. I can still recall that careworn face. Oh, in the end, he was not at all the radiant Gurudevan whom we had met. Great men shouldn't ever die old, Menon.'

'Oh, was it that bad?' Menon Master asked, as he felt the image of Gurudevan lighting up inside him, with his knowing smile that held within it all answers.

'Really pitiable. I understood the honest ethos of Asan's "Veenapoovu", only twenty years after reading it—when I was witness to the last moments of Gurudevan. Such misery! pathetic!! Now I have come across the news that even the other Gurudevan in Shantiniketan is awaiting imminent death. Wonder if that great poet's character itself has changed in his final days! Did you read about it, Menon?'

Menon Master frowned, indicating that he was not getting the drift. Then his friend continued, 'The great poet is supposed to have made some statements against Gandhiji! Tagore has even stated that the recent Bihar earthquake was a retribution for Gandhiji arraying the Harijans behind him.'

When Menon Master heard his pained laughter, he felt disquiet smoulder within him. 'I have been pondering over what you have written beautifully in one of your recent articles: genius alone cannot make a man great. The words are not exactly the same. But the thought touched me deeply, sir. Your implication seemed to be that a heartless intellectual is no better than an efficient machine.'

He didn't appear to notice that praise. He was still thinking about the finales. 'What impelled me to join rationalist organizations, I think now, was my witnessing the final moments of Gurudevan. Neither Vedanta nor Rationalism has the answer to one question, Menon. That question is, at the end of it all, what is the meaning of our lives?'

The weight of that question left even Menon Master feeling suffocated for a moment. But the duty of the host to lighten the heart of the guest came to the forefront of his mind. 'Let it be,' Menon Master said. 'Sir, you must be past forty now. When I was coming to the college, I had thought you may have married and started a family. My son will be eleven this Dhanu. Why are you delaying it? That there isn't a woman worthy of you in Thiruvithamkoor and Kochi, everyone knows. Even then…'

The guest only laughed in a non-committal manner. By then, Padminiyamma had come and placed coffee and steamed rice dumplings, stuffed with jaggery and grated coconut, on the parapet. Realizing that the talk of marriage was in the air, she too stood there, wiping her hands. Menon Master took the cup and offered it to the guest. Sipping the coffee with the lingering smile, he said, 'It is not being delayed; the decision is not to marry.' After tasting the stuffed dumplings offered by Padminiyamma and acknowledging her culinary skills with his eyes, he continued, 'See, coffee, rice balls, and meals, again coffee, rice balls and meals … Ha ha, you should also take into account that it is also in consideration of why someone should be brought home only to be tethered to our kitchen.'

Menon Master joined Padminiyamma in her laughter. The

presence of the lady of the house swiftly lightened the atmosphere. The master told his wife, 'Listen, Pappini, even though he is a teacher in the college, he is still a student. He has joined the Bachelor of Law course as a private student in Madras University. It's when I heard that, that I invited him home. Ah, we have enough income to invite a student for tea, don't we?'

This time the guest also laughed heartily. 'I don't know if Padminiyamma has been told this by this worthy. When we were students as well as when we were teaching in the Gurudevan's school, he too used to write. Poems and astute articles that hit the bull's eye. Menon, do you remember the special issue of *Yuvajanamithram* in which your poem and my article appeared together?' he asked, leaning forward in the easy chair.

It was Padminiyamma who answered, 'What are you saying! That *Yuvajanamithram* is guarded here like a treasure. When we move house, my son and I may be left behind, but the magazines and books will not be forgotten. That's how he is!' Emboldened by the familiarity that developed during the conversation, Padminiyamma offered one more rice dumpling to the guest.

Menon took that allegation as a compliment. 'I have quite a few issues of *Athmaposhini* with me. Wasn't it in *Athmaposhini* that your article about the ultimate purpose of literature appeared? I had heard about the great poet being thrilled after reading it and how he made you write the foreword to his *Sahithyamanjari*.'

A surfeit of admiration sapped Menon Master's body of its strength. The hand placed on the parapet slipped, and he almost fell.

From the big moovandan mango tree in the yard, a mango fell. Two boys sprinted, fought noisily with each other for the mango, and ran off with it. 'The house-owner's children,' Menon Master said, watching them. 'Six kids like these with a gap each of just one to one-and-a-half years.'

'So, there must be land large enough to partition among the six!' said the visitor, gazing from the portal at the yard and surroundings rendered picturesque by the evening sun.

Padminiyamma offered the water-filled kindi from the porch and went in to fetch a fresh thorth for the visitor.

'Why did you let go of poesy and confine yourself to your profession and the family?' asked the guest softly, taking advantage of the short absence of Padminiyamma, who was inside; he gargled and spat out the water far into the yard. The answer to that question alone was what the master's wife heard when she came out.

'What do I say about that?' said Menon Master. 'To be honest, when I read those poems of the Edappally guys, most of my confidence evaporated. Besides, there was another, more important, reason.' Looking back at Padminiyamma, and as if seeking permission for something, Master continued, 'After marriage and kids and domestic worries, if one must write, sir, one must be a genuine poet. Others will meet the same fate as mine. Either they will scorn writing altogether, or stay away out of respect. In my case, it was the second that happened. Isn't that the reason why I was scared to even call home the old friend who had made a name as a writer? Ha, ha, ha!'

When it became apparent that the guest was getting ready to leave, Menon Master looked in the direction of the gate and said, 'Hasn't the boy come in yet? It's started getting dark.'

'He came long ago,' Padminiyamma said. 'Seeing the new sandals at the portal, he came in through the kitchen door. Despite my telling him, he had his coffee there!'

'Hah, that's not bad!' Menon Master laughed and turning in the direction of the house, called, 'Hey boy, Achyuthaa…'

Achyuthan came out to the porch, scratching his head with his left hand. With his head bowed, and using the eyebrows to hide his eyes partially, he peeked at the guest, who was wearing white and white like his father.

Stroking his sweaty head, the guest said, 'Achyuthan! Nice name. You are studying well, aren't you?'

Achyuthan stood there, abashed. Then, accompanying his parents, he too went up to the gate to see off the guest. At that time, Naraapilla was stepping over the stile to enter the compound, carrying a bunch of arecanuts. Sighting a gentleman with Menon Master, he frowned, and held aloft a shield of unfamiliarity to hide behind.

'Sir, this is my house-owner.' Menon Master introduced one to the other. 'Narayana Pilla chettaa, he is a lecturer at the UC College. One can also say he's my friend.'

'What's the name?' trying to make it sound as if he knew all the teaching faculty at the college, Naraapilla asked, shrinking within himself.

'Krishnapilla,' the guest said.

'You may have heard, he is a renowned author,' Menon Master added.

'Oh yeah, I have heard aplenty! Changampazha, right?' With an interjection of scorn, he continued, 'So, this is the guy! I've heard a ragtag group of kids sitting and singing in Raghavan's shop—a whole lot of songs and poetry, ha ha… As for me, hearing these things itself gets on my nerves. So, that's what… This guy is now a tutor in the college and teaching kids, ay? Harrumph!'

Before Menon Master could utter anything, many things happened together. Though it was not his wont to fold up his mundu and tuck it in, impelled by some strange impetus, Naraapilla did exactly that then. As if it was not enough, he expectorated as if exorcising and brought up non-existent phlegm from inside him and spat it out ostentatiously at the crepe jasmine flowers on the edge of the yard. Menon Master and his wife stood helpless, at a loss as to how to handle the situation. By that time, Kunjuamma, carrying the infant girl and accompanied by Govindan, had reached there. Seeing her husband's stance and his guttural, insulting spitting, Kunjuamma pleaded with the guest, 'Please don't take this amiss, please think nothing of this.'

'But he is not railing at me.' Smiling, the guest said, 'I am not the Changampuzha Krishna Pilla that you are thinking of. This is another Krishna Pilla. Another puzha. Another terribly muddied river of which people like you may have never heard of.'

As the guest passed through the gate, everyone else except Naraapilla stood immobilized, seared by the feeling of having been partners in a great crime. Naraapilla was in denial and gave no impression of having carried out any misconduct. As the disorientation of the moment passed, Menon Master jumped over the stile and ran to catch up with his friend.

Naraapilla wiped his mouth. He thrust the bunch of arecanuts into the hands of Govindan. Then sniping also at his female tenant standing stunned, he told Kunjuamma, 'Where men are talking, what's your business there? Go, go, scram! See what's to be done for supper!'

Being certain that Kunjuamma was not going to obey him, he went inside the house, without glancing back. Kunjuamma, in a low voice, hesitatingly asked Padminiyamma, who was still standing in the yard with a bowed head, 'Pappinichechi, who's that?'

Holding Achyuthan close to her, Padminiyamma, in a voice on the verge of breaking, said, 'Kuttippuzha Krishnapilla sir!'

That name, unheard of till now, affected no one. However, for a long time, the children carried in their minds the memory of a gentleman insulted in that yard with crepe jasmines standing as mute witnesses.

For Naraapilla, the issue was closed the moment he spat it out.

SIX

Casteism

14 May 1999

...The last guru who was capable of leading the Malayali to enlightenment has bid adieu to this world today. I have never been to Fern Hill. However, during my adolescence in Thachanakkara, I had read most of his books at the Vijnanaposhini library. I had noted him down in my diary as the Eternal Spirit of Knowledge. He departed hearing the sounds of the twenty-first century knocking on his doors. Would you believe it, that even in these last decades of the twentieth century, there is no dearth of petty-minded people in Thachanakkara. There was a time when a relative of mine, who noticed that I was reading the Guru's books all the time, told me in a voice that was more frigid than death: 'However much he may write, he's piffle and can come nowhere near our Chinmayaanandan!' I know he hasn't read Chinmayaanandan either!

Our Chinmayaanandan!

And who is this 'us' and 'our'?

Nedumpilli Mana, the manor that housed the pot-bellied and thin-limbed Nampoothiris, was to the north of Parashuraman's temple.

Penury, fatuousness, and casteist vanity were the only contents of the granary of that illam. No amount of scrubbing would rid them of it. The Thachanakkara denizen in general, much less the inhabitants of the illam in particular, had not even heard of institutions such as the Nampoothiri Welfare Society, Nampoothiri Youth Society, etc. After they had started staying at Ayyaattumpilli as tenants, and once when they had gone en famille to the temple on Achyuthan's birthday, Menon Master saw the head priest just once. As he was leaving after circumambulating the deity and collecting the oblation, he saw an old Brahmin headed for the kitchen of the temple and smiled at him. Curious to see the new visitor to the temple, who was accompanied by his comely wife, the priest paused for a chat. But it did not last for long. As Menon Master started talking of the anti-caste dramatist V.T. Bhattathirippad, perplexed as to whether the reference was to mahogany or teak—the initials 'V.T.' sounding like 'veetti' or mahogany in the vernacular—the priest beat a hasty retreat to the sanctum sanctorum. He was Parameswaran Nampoothiri of Nedumpilli Mana. The elderly man was respectfully called Parameswaran Thirumeni to his face and Parashunampoori behind his back by the public. Though, for whatever reason, no one had named their sons Parashuraman, those who were named Parameswaran had Parashu as their pet name. Thachanakkara residents continued the humorous practice of abbreviating the lord (eswaran) into an axe (parashu). Among all the Parashus, after Thachanakkara thevar, Parameswaran Thirumeni was the most prominent one. The presence of such an eminent Parashu was the reason why Pooshaappi's eldest son Parameswaran ended up with the pet name of 'little' or Kochu Parashu.

The women of Nedumpilli Mana, under the patriarch Parashunampoori, were hardly seen by the populace of Thachanakkara. Till Naraapilla married his sister, Appu Nair used to go around saying that Naraapilla had had a tryst with an *antharjanam*, who had come out surreptitiously to take the oblational rice from the temple. It was said that this lady, with a killer smile and ankle-length hair, had a right breast the size of a tender coconut and left breast the size of an arecanut. Because of that, Naraapilla could not guess the age of this lady who supposedly also wore a brass bangle. 'Could be anywhere between twelve and thirty-six' was how Naraapilla had indicated her age to Appu Nair. 'Perhaps one of them may have ballooned abruptly.' Naraapilla gestured with both his hands. 'Or maybe one got stunted around her tenth or twelfth year.'

After giving his sister's hand in marriage to Naraapilla, Appu Nair had stopped discussing such matters with him. Apart from that, he also stopped the practice of spreading stories, both fictional and not-so-fictional, about Naraapilla's conquests. He was gradually reduced to being a mere lackey to do the bidding of Naraapilla, whenever Naraapilla summoned him with a long 'Appoliyyo…' The liaison Naraapilla continued with Kaalippennu, who used to come for harvesting in the field and threshing at the yard, was conveniently shelved by Appu Nair. She was a luckless, dark beauty who had lost her husband immediately following childbirth. In Naraapilla's words, 'The lass whose pulayan* is defunct.' Appu Nair remembered how she used to leave her infant in the cloth cradle suspended from the branch of the mango tree beside the field during harvesting. That small mango tree is now a tall, heavily-branched one. That kid, three years older than Govindan, Naraapilla's eldest, used to visit his mother in the anteroom of the rented house in the Ayyaattumpilli compound. Once the threshing season was on, Naraapilla would get the small

* For Naraapilla, her Pulayan was a generic non-existence, and was not even worthy of having a name.

anteroom, attached to the granary in the house rented by Menon Master, converted into a bedroom for Kaalippennu. Even if she was barred from entering his kitchen, at every opportunity, he would slink into the anteroom that Kaalippennu slept in. He had already recognized that Kaalippennu was highly skilled in some of the arts for which Kunjuamma showed no talent.

'There's some truth in what our master says.' One day, out of nowhere, Naraapilla praised Menon Master to Kunjuamma. 'If we keep sticking to castes, we'll only be doomed.'

Kunjuamma was not surprised by her husband showing uncharacteristic humanity. That chaste woman could divine the bull-like rompings that Naraapilla played out in the anteroom of her tenants, with Kaalippennu as the heroine. She cried on her own.

Five years had passed since the Temple Entry Edict was decreed by Chiththirathirunaal of Travancore, abolishing the ban on lower castes entering temples. The day Kochu Parashu went to town for supplies, an extended conclave took place at Pooshaappi's shop after a long gap, in the thatched annexe added on by Parashu.

It was the rainy season. Sleet and wind created a racket on the newly woven thatches. The sight of the rain falling on the red-hot roof tiles of the temple assuaged Pooshaappi. A grey, stray cat, mewing sceptically at the rain pounding the red soil on the path, had managed to slink close to the edge of the thatch. It sat there listless and uninterested, looking at a yellow-legged crab stepping sideways on to the stairs from its noisy burrow. A soaked, dark child, running in the rain, paused for a moment doubtfully in front of the shop, and then continued to run.

Knowing that Kochu Parashu was absent, Kuttan Pilla had reached the shop early. Naraapilla, who had come to buy his flavoured tobacco, got stuck there, trapped by the rain. Menon Master, on his way out without an umbrella, was caught in the downpour that dimmed his vision as water streamed down his spectacles, and stepped into the shop's patio. Since Naraapilla had been detained there for a while, as could be expected by anyone, Appu Nair also arrived. His kuduma, worn in the front, had come loose and the wet hair tailed into his face. He threw out the wide leaf of colocasia that he had used as an umbrella, pulled his wet hair back, and shook his body like a wet dog.

'Haww!' Kuttan Pilla jumped back as the spray hit his clothes. That set the stage for a discussion on untouchability and the casteist pollution.

'Well, I have been wanting to ask you this, Master. One needn't be afraid to ask people like you with education and good sense,' Kuttan Pilla asked Menon Master in a voice tremulous with age. 'What is your opinion about this Temple Entry issue?'

As if he was expecting an antithetical reply, he sat with a frown fixed on his face.

'That...' Menon Master took off his spectacles, dried them with the edge of the *melmundu* that covered his upper body, and started with a query: 'It's now four or five years since the edict has come. Why has this doubt struck Kuttan Pilla chettan now of all times?'

But this is the first time you have stepped into this shop!' Kuttan Pilla said, also to curry favour with Pooshaappi. 'Indeed, I know that you pick up everything you need from Aluva, on your way back from school ... Nonetheless, isn't it desirable that you fraternize a little with the folks of this place? Yes, isn't it?'

Menon Master smiled. 'Where did you say your native place is, Kuttan Pilla chettaa?' the master asked, replacing his spectacles on his face and looking unwaveringly into his eyes.

Kuttan Pilla became uneasy for a moment. Then, displaying all of his remaining eight teeth, he laughed out loud and said, 'Come to think of it, I am also an outsider like you. Ha ha, but I still didn't get your opinion. So, about the edict, what...?'

In a quick glance, Menon Master took in the conclave of savants adorning Pooshaappi's shop. There were quite a few things that he had nursed in his mind for unleashing on Naraapilla in person. He realized this was a favourable occasion to include those too in his reply.

'I do not know if I have the expertise to reply to Kuttan Pilla chettan's question. Still, I shall speak within my limited knowledge.' Menon Master's low voice was hardly audible to Pooshaappi seated inside the shop. He got up, holding his burden that he removed from the stool in front of his chair, placed the stool outside his room, and offered, 'Here, sit on this and talk, Master.'

Appu Nair took the stool and placed it in front of the master. As a mark of politeness, Master extended that kindness to Naraapilla, 'Narayana Pillai chettan may please sit. I will leave as soon as the rain lets up.'

It took only a moment for the unabashed Naraapilla to accept the stool and sit beaming on it. 'Try telling us! Make an attempt. Let's hear!' he said.

Suppressing a smile that came up like a belch, Menon Master said, 'Isn't the brouhaha that is happening the handiwork of a guy who thinks he is the greatest of all men?'

Naraapilla had a feeling that the master was mocking him. Then, shifting his gaze from Naraapilla, the master continued, 'I was referring to Hitler. He is leading a battle. What is the use? On his own, he has decided that the race he is born in is the best and the rest are inferior. And then? The runt is out to wipe out the Jewish race in which were born great worthies from Jesus Christ to Einstein. Aren't we also suffering from its effects in the form of scarcity and black marketeering?'

When he heard the word Christ, Naraapilla twisted his lips in a grimace and said, 'Isn't that an old tale?'

'Narayana Pillai chettaa, it is no old story. Now, it is about here,

I am talking about this thing now being referred to as the World War.' Menon Master let out the laughter, which was bursting out anyway.

Appu Nair, to protect the honour of his brother-in-law, interjected, 'No, what Naraapilla meant was the connection between the War and the temple entry here…'

Drawing the cat—which was getting wet in the sleet as it was afraid to go into the shop because of the people—closer towards him, with his leg, Menon Master explained, 'That's war, this is peace. It is bad to discriminate between people, to see them as two kinds, Appu chettaa, wherever it may happen. In our land, this division is not just into two, but into four and eight … Therefore, our cruelty is four or eight-fold worse than Hitler's!'

'Well, perhaps he too has his own rationalizations,' Appu Nair said. 'Or else, would other nations join his side in the war? How can it become a world war this way? So let's drop that claim! What Kuttan Pilla chettan was asking was about the Temple Entry Edi—'

Holding up his hand to halt him from continuing, Menon Master said, 'Understood. But if justice reaches everywhere simultaneously, how does it become injustice? In 1932, when the paper allowing voting rights to those who were paying a land tax of five rupees was passed, only the land-owning Nairs and Brahmins would have found that just, right? And then in 1936 when Sir C.P. came and made that amount one rupee, it would have appeared just for a few others too! This is also true in the case of the temple entry, which happened the same year.'

'So you're saying that it's cent percent just, aren't you, Master?' Kuttan Pilla said.

'What's the doubt?' Menon Master said, 'Human beings can be divided into men and women. If you divide them as wise men and fools also, it is acceptable. We can have both in the same house. But this arrangement along castes, that's outrageous! That is where the greatness of the Edict lies. But that is still not enough at all. There, haven't you read about ladies such as Akkamma Cherian coming to the forefront? Does Narayana Pillai chettan recognize who is it?' When Menon Master asked that, Naraapilla twisted his head towards the top dome of the Thachanakkara thevar and sat there as if he was pondering over something. Menon Master had expected that. It was the seventy-year-old Kuttan Pilla who came to the rescue at that point, 'Don't you know, Naraapilla? She's State Kangress's dittaa … or something … what's it that you call it?'

'Exactly! The dictator of the State Congress—Akkamma Cherian!' Menon Master filled in the gap, gladly. 'The warmonger Hitler is also called the same by the English press. But as I clarified earlier, that is the dictator of war; this one is of peace!'

'I have heard of her,' Kuttan Pilla said. 'The Nazrani woman from Kanjirappally, isn't it? But how in the world could a woman who has led a procession protesting against the Maharaja be a pacifist, Master?'

At that point, Naraapilla re-entered the debate with a discernibly special interest. 'Hooom,' he said suddenly, coming back from some other world, 'give four slaps on the cheek and any woman'd stop in her tracks!'

'That is a wrong reading! A time will come when our land will be proud of her, Narayana Pilla chettaa.' He suppressed the urge to say more, reminding himself that he was after all a tenant of Naraapilla. 'Honestly speaking, these are all variations of the same misunderstanding. The Nazis to the Jews, the upper caste for the low caste, Narayana Pillai chettan for women … It is amusing to think of it that way!'

'But all this a law of nature, Master,' Kuttan Pilla, with the mien of a sage, told Menon Master who was about his son's age. 'What's the use of us talking so much about progressiveness? Look at it, even now, not a single Pulaya gets into the Thachanakkara thevar's temple to worship. Why? They are scared despite the decree! That's what we call God's will, God's will!'

'What you said now is utter blasphemy!' As Menon Master felt a twinge of sadness inside him, his voice rose for the first time when he said, 'The only people left to learn of Harijans entering temples are the denizens of Thachanakkara. All the downtrodden people in this land of Kerala are elated at having won a right. It did not happen one fine morning; this majestic event is the consummation of days and nights of the intense efforts on the part of many great souls!'

Naraapilla was hearing the word consummation for the first time. He brought on a sarcastic smile on his face and declared, 'Whatever you may blandish as justification—these are not going to last forever. This Narayana Pillai is positive that His Majesty is going to have a change of mind and will withdraw the decree.' He cracked the knuckles of his right hand twice.

'Yesyes,' Pooshaappi, who was only a spectator till then, energized suddenly by Naraapilla's statement, said in support, 'What Naraapilla said is what is, it's right! I too feel that way!'

Menon Master abruptly turned to look at Pooshaappi. The look Menon Master gave him hurt him in his testicles. 'My Shashwathampilla chettaa,' he addressed him, reminding Pooshaappi of his real name after a long, long time, 'our land is rushing towards a bright future; the whole of India is undergoing a big transformation. If we win independence under the leadership of Gandhiji, a new India will be born. There, now great efforts are on for a united Kerala too. The next meeting for that is to be here in our own Aluva. If Thiruvithamkoor, Kochi, and Malabar unite, monarchy itself will abdicate! Why are you laughing? The educated and worldly-wise youth of ours will restore the glory of our nation. As dreamt by Narayana Guru, we will become ideal human beings with one caste, one religion, and one God!'

Hope made Menon Master's eyes sparkle. When he heard Narayana Guru's name, Naraapilla was enraged. He got up from his seat and said, 'Here, this is what I can't stand! Even educated and sensible youth among Nairs will start to lionize that Nanuguru. I'm asking you because I fail to understand. Why can't guys like you treat our other swami…' As no name came to his tongue, he looked plaintively at Appu Nair.

'Chattambiswamikal!' Appu Nair made a timely contribution.

'Ah, yes, Chattambiswamikal! Why're you people not talking about him? Isn't he better than Nanuguru? As you get ahead, have you teachers also started behaving like kids who can't distinguish between a Chinese potato and a turd?' Naraapilla bellowed, glaring at Menon Master's glasses. The cat, which had been nuzzling against the legs of Menon Master, jumped into the rain and ran away.

'Chattambiswami is also a great soul,' Menon Master said. 'There is no debate. But to establish that jaggery is sweet, why should we say that sugar isn't?'

Kuttan Pilla stared at Naraapilla, open-mouthed.

'Worshipping Chattambiswami is definitely good,' Menon Master continued respectfully, 'but if it is because he is a Nair, then that is not worship, it is an insult. You have not paid heed to what Narayana Guru said about caste. Fine. But, neither have you listened to what the reverend Chattambiswamikal has said! Have you? There is a book he has written castigating our Kalady man, Shankaran. It would be edifying if people like Narayana Pillai chettan could read it. The name of the book is *Vedaadhikaaraniroopanam*. I shall give it you. It must be in my cupboard. Then, when one talks of Chattambiswamikal, one should also talk of Ayyankaali, shouldn't one? The same Ayyankaali, whom Gandhiji came to meet at Vengaanoor, is not great in the eyes of Narayana Pilla chettan because he is not a Nair?

You may not have heard what he has accomplished, right. Have you at least heard of his demise last month?'

The rain was coming down in torrents. The master did not realize that his voice had risen in tandem with the rain.

'Oho, has he too conked out?' Covering up his inability to counter the argument, Naraapilla responded with sarcasm, as he got up and extended his hand out to measure the strength of the rain. His second son, Padmanabhan, was coming towards the shop bearing the umbrella sent by Kunjuamma. Naraapilla jumped down into the canopy of the umbrella and holding close both his son and the flavoured tobacco, he walked fast.

Retrieving his stool, Pooshaappi resumed his usual eight-legged posture. The rest of the people remained in the shop till the rain subsided, not uttering another word.

The rain kept beating its tattoo on the newly-made thatch.

SEVEN

The Vortex

1 April 1999

...In book-reading, there is a kind of nit-picking. A habit that got stuck in our souls long, long ago, from the time we were monkeys, awakens atavistically when we read a book. Take another look at the open book. You can see a head with hair parted in the centre. The black strands chart the lines to either sides from the middle. Amidst them, are word meanings that are alive and scurrying about, trying to escape and hide from you. A vibrant thought, an attractive plump word, a figure of speech that races on six legs, a blood-sucking black emotion, catch our eyes. And then? No peace until we catch and finish it. Therefore, I am certain—even if the world will be filled with television and computers, books are here to stay. Are there lice in your head? My mouth wells up with saliva when I see a louse. This is no April Fool's joke. That too is a habit from that ancestral monkey!

There was a bookshelf in Achyuthan's house. Menon Master's wealth. Jacketed tomes sat inside, enigmatically, like idols in sarppakaavu, the sacred grove for snake-worship.

The bookshelf could be opened on the days when Menon Master was around. So, Govindan waited impatiently for Sundays, cracking his knuckles. In the same room, there was a lidless crate made out of black cedar, the colour of burnt brick, full of magazines and weeklies. Since it was open and accessible at all times, it didn't catch Govindan's fancy.

As he stood in front of the cupboard filled with books, Govindan could feel some mysterious corner of his heart filling up with light. He would forget his father. He would forget his detestable bawl. Instead, a pleasantly cool, comfortable silence, an invaluable tranquillity in which even his own breath resounded, would enfold him. His whole body would tremble in ineluctable admiration of the writer his father had insulted two years ago. When Menon Master would open the bookshelf, Govindan would be assailed by a greater sense of divinity than that was felt when the doors of the sanctum sanctorum of Thachanakkara thevar's temple opened after the lamp-lit pooja at dusk.

Into the names of some of the books, the impressionable age of Govindan lowered its anchor of curiosity. Many a time his tongue twisted when he read titles such as *Arthavuadasootrashathakoti* and *Nivaathakavachakaalakeyavadham*. Inclining his head to read the titles on the books arranged in a slant, he would pull one out with his middle finger. One book retrieved thus was called *Mangkigeetha*, but, Menon Master explained, it had nothing to do with monkeys as he had expected.

'Listen, Achyutha,' bidding his son also to come closer, as he explained about the poet who had written the book, 'remember his name, V.C. Balakrishna Panicker! He died when he was just twenty-three. But what had he achieved in the meantime? Unimaginable! When he was sixteen, that is barely two or three years older than you, he was the editor of a newspaper called *Keralachinthaamani*. In addition, he was responsible for the *Malabari* weekly published from Malabar. Eventually, he came to British Kochi and took care of a newspaper called *Chakravarthi* for a long time. In between, he brought out about fifteen books. One of them is this *Mangkigeetha*. The *mangki* is no monkey! The chap is a maharshi in the Puranas who had amassed illicit wealth. Look, this is Panicker's translation. What is a translation?'

'From one language to another language...' When Achyuthan started to answer as if in class, the master laughed and gestured with his palm to stop him. 'Enough, enough. But this is not his poem,' Master said, searching for something amidst the books. 'You should read an elegy of his. It must be here. Then an excellent poem about Swadeshabhimani Ramakrishna Pillai ... *ngaa ... Thiruvithaamkoorilae Mahadheeran* or something is its title; that too must be here.'

'Then what about the Kuttan Pilla chettan who comes to Pooshaappi's store? Don't people call him Swadeshabhimani too?' Govindan asked.

Menon Master replied with a sweet smile, 'That is the Swadeshabhimani of you Thachanakkara residents. I have also listened to that fellow's bombast. From his accent, it doesn't appear if he has even seen southern Thiruvithamkoor!'

From the second row, Govindan pulled out another, far thicker book. The handwritten name on the spine of the paper-covered book caught his fancy, *Aangalasaamraajyam*.

But when he pulled it out and opened it, though the title said it was about the British Empire, he recognized it as written in Sanskrit. When Master explained that it was an epic poem by A.R. Rajaraja Varma to commemorate the diamond jubilee celebrations of the ascension of Queen Victoria to the throne, which took him two years to write, Achyuthan asked him, 'Father, has no one written an epic poem about our Gandhiji?'

Menon Master said, 'Those will have to be written by you all! Right, Govindaa?'

'Yes!' said Govindan. 'Let Bapuji's diamond jubilee come. I shall pen one!'

All of them laughed.

It was morning. The fresh air that entered the bookshelf as Menon Master opened it, infused a liveliness amongst the closely-packed books.

Padminiyamma and Kunjuamma were seated on the steps of the back veranda of the rented house. Kunjuamma sat on the lower step, her back between Padminiyamma's legs. Padminiyamma was drawing the sandal-coloured nit-comb through Kunjuamma's thick tresses and pulling out the nits. Each time she crushed a nit caught between the long teeth of the nit-comb, she let out a long, '*esshh…!*'

Chinnamma, the youngest, with the same complexion and features as Naraapilla, was covered in dust from below the belly-thread, as she squatted below the breadfruit tree and strained to defecate, her eyes bulging and mouth open.

It was a Sunday. Naraapilla had set apart some coconuts and about twenty fronds for Padminiyamma during the routine harvesting. Menon Master had separated the leaflets from the midribs of the fronds. tied them up and stacked them, and was splitting the midribs and flinging them in the sun for drying. Snot-nosed Chandran, who was standing by, heard the green midribs wailing *riii riii* as the sharpness of the machete split them vertically. He had also joined Aalungal School. Because of his perpetually snotty, runny nose, his brothers had nick-named him 'Snot-champion'. As he was twirling a play-snake made from the palm leaflets by Menon Master, he amused himself by blowing and bursting yellowish snotty bubbles through his nose. To wean Chandran, Kunjuamma finally had to use the aloe vera paste she had preserved for two years. Though he had been weaned, he always stuck close to his mother.

The nit-comb was purchased from Aluva beach. The two families—except Naraapilla and the youngest child—had gone together for Shivaraathri. They were not fasting. Padminiyamma needed to buy some household things. On a whim, Kunjuamma also got ready to go with her. Even after delivering six children, Naraapilla had never taken her for the Shivaraathri at Aluva beach. This time around, she was determined to go. She left her two-year-old youngest daughter with her sister-in-law at Peechamkurichi and she and her other children roamed the beach along with the family of Menon Master. Naraapilla had ordered that they should be back home before it was dark.

Except for Achyuthan, Govindan, and Padmanabhan, the others were amazed by the novelty of the Marthaanda Varma Bridge, which could be seen from the beach. Govindan's younger brother Padmanabhan also had left Aalungal School and already joined Aluva school in the first standard. He had also started using the bridge to go across. Padmanabhan's younger siblings, Pankajaakshan and Chandran, stood looking at the bridge for a long time with their mouths agape. When they heard a whistle behind, they looked towards the other end of the river. At a distance, over a parallel bridge with no wavy arches, a train was moving, belching large clouds of black smoke into the reddening sky.

'Lo, in the water, another *chug-chug*,' the four-year-old Thankamma clapped her mouth shut with both hands, amazed at the reflection of the train chugging along upside down in the water. Everyone laughed looking at her sitting wonderstruck on her mother's hip.

Menon Master pointed out the Advaithaashramam across the river to Kunjuamma. Turning in that direction, Kunjuamma instinctively joined her hands and bowed in prayer. Chandran, who had started sneezing continuously due to the dust from the beach, followed his mom in bowing to the ashramam, unaware of the significance.

Promising that they would return to the thevar's portals before dark, Achyuthan, Govindan, and Padmanabhan ran, holding hands, towards the north end of the beach to inspect the stalls and shops there. Padminiyamma held Pankajaakshan's hand so that he would not be lost in the crowd. Carrying Thankamma on her hip and holding Chandran by his hand, Kunjuamma kept pace with her. Both the women, and the children hanging on to them, were barefoot. When Kunjuamma saw Menon Master walking with his malmal mundu folded up and tucked in to save it from the dust, and the curly hair on his calves gleaming in the evening light, she remembered Naraapilla in panic.

Padminiyamma was remarkably skilled in bargaining with the vendors. She bought at cheap prices two stone vessels, one wooden ladle, and one wooden board used for decanting cooked rice. Kunjuamma was also tempted to buy a few things. But after buying only black bangles and kohl for her daughters, a tiny box of bindi powder for herself, and sugarcane and some puffed rice for Naraapilla, the little money she had managed to prise out of Naraapilla was over. In order to hide her shame, she kept scolding the children who were pointing out and demanding various things. On their return, when they reached the steps leading to the path from the beach, and she saw the lice- and nit-combs in the tray of the chetti-woman selling combs, she tarried as if her legs were aching. Her face filled with longing, like it had when she saw the laterite stones bathed in moonlight at the time when the New House was under construction.

Padminiyamma understood the situation. Offering the coin that was left over in her cloth purse to Kunjuamma, she said, 'Buy the lice- and nit-combs, Kunjommo! My head's also teeming, and I too can do with one!'

They went up from the beach before dark. Talking of the magician they had seen in the north end of the beach, Achyuthan, Govindan, and Padmanabhan made the younger children envious. To pacify them, Menon Master bought the children sarsaparilla sherbet. Only Chandran's sherbet tasted salty; he drank the beverage mixed with the phlegm and snot that flowed into the glass from his nose.

In the afternoons, with the lice- and nit-combs in hand, Kunjuamma would reach the backyard of the tenants' house. On the very first day of this joint lice-hunt, she had realized that Padminiyamma's claim that her head was teeming with lice was a fib. She had seen that each strand of her hair, which smelt of daisy and shoe flower shampoo, was worthy of being pampered individually for their cleanliness. Whereas in Kunjuamma's hair, lice, nits and dermal excrescence flourished in abundance: like the nets hoisted during a rich piscean harvest, a *chaakara*, the lice comb would froth and spill over each time it was passed through her hair.

'Kunjuo!' Naraapilla's voice boomed from the north. 'Where's that damned woman? Oblation to the manes!'

Kunjuamma didn't budge; Naraapilla screamed her name once more on a louder note. Before Kunjuamma could straighten up after dusting her behind, he appeared in the backyard.

'Where's Govindan, eh?' Naraapilla addressed the question half to his wife and half to Menon Master who was splitting coconut tree midribs. Before he got an answer, he saw his daughter squatting and straining beneath the breadfruit tree, which caused his nostrils to flare further: 'Damn! Take her from there. Otherwise the breadfruit will fall on her head and kill her. Oblations to the manes!'

When angry, Naraapilla's every sentence would spew oblation to the manes. As his rage went up, he would make everyone eat his corpse. 'Watch out, I will make y'all eat my gorpse,' is how he would put it.

'Where is he? WHERE?' Naraapilla was hopping mad. In reality, he knew where Govindan was; he was aware that he and Achyuthan, bearing books, had gone to Punneli kadavu, tipped off as he was by Padmanabhan who had carried to Naraapilla the grievance of him being excluded from the gang. He told him that the boys would go to the river to swim and frolic on the pretext of going to read books there. In truth, Naraapilla was unmoved by this piece of news. But he remembered Kunjuamma the next instant. His evil mind imagined the scenario of their eldest son falling into the river and drowning, while the mother was listening to Menon Master's conversation. He prayed for that tragedy to happen, fervently thumping his chest, unseen by anyone.

Menon Master recollected the children asking his permission to go to the river. But fearing that the word river might enrage Naraapilla further, he did not mention it. 'In the morning he had come to check the books,' he said. 'After taking the books, Achyuthan and Govindan then went to the compound or someplace!'

'*Hraa*,' spewing the remnants of masticated betel leaf from his throat, without letting it touch the lips, Naraapilla said, 'Cursed brat! Today, today, today, I will kill him!'

Trembling all over, he ran back. Lifting up her youngest daughter and running after him, the overwrought Kunjuamma cried, 'My Pappinichechi, if that man says he will kill, he will!'

Going past Punneli kadavu, where women bathed, Govindan and Achyuthan walked along the river. Parting the tall stalks of the halfa grass, the children stood on the ridge jutting into the river under golden shower trees in full bloom. The Aluva river kept tempting the boy, who was a tenant and an emigrant from another place, to forget the books he was carrying. Before leaving home, Achyuthan had wound a thorth around his shorts, under the shirt. He undressed and draped the thorth and got ready. His swimming coach, Govindan, younger by a year, took the first plunge breaking the sheet glass-like surface of the still river water.

With his hair plastered and appearance altered, he bobbed up a short distance away and called to his friend, 'Come, Achu. There is no current. Jump!'

Gingerly, as if climbing down from an elephant, Achyuthan slipped into the water, sliding over the ridge and breaking it, while still holding onto the halfa grass. The Periyar embraced the outsider and tickled him. The thorth, fastened around his waist, ballooned up in a circle above his waist-thread. Female fish peeped between the thighs of the guest and floated in a circle.

The green expanse of the river touching Achyuthan's chin rose up and down. Right in front of him, Govindan's head broke the surface of water. Spouting water from his mouth towards the sky in a spray, he pointed to Uliyanoor across the river and said, 'Perumthachchan's house is there. Shall we swim across and take a look?'

Govindan, who turned around to ask permission, saw over his friend's head, the shape of his father descending into the water from the ridge. Following the path suggested by the women in Punneli kadavu, a seething Naraapilla was advancing with a branch broken off a golden shower tree.

'Achan!' after mixing in the water as much terror those two syllables could conjure up, Govindan scrambled up on to the bank. Searing the drenched skin on his back, the leafless stick struck him left, right, and centre. Mortified by seeing his friend being beaten up, an agitated Achyuthan clambered out of the water, bleating.

When his hand grew tired after beating his son like a man possessed, Naraapilla threw down the stick. Govindan didn't even let out a whimper through the thrashing, defeating Naraapilla. That was when he saw the two books near the clothes left by the children. He did something about which he himself had no sentience: he grabbed the two books and flung them far out into river, with an imprecation, 'To damnation!'

Like two decapitated and dismembered white birds, the two books flew, thrashing about. The books, which Menon Master had given in trust, floated for a moment on the surface of the water and then sank and disappeared.

Then something unexpected happened. In a rage born from sorrow, Govindan opened the mouth he had pursed shut. He screamed. Then with the all the strength a fourteen-year-old could muster, he beat his father with the stick retrieved from the ground.

He hit him again and again and again.

EIGHT

Outsider

26 May 1999

...Amma has written that property prices in Thachanakkara are rising rapidly. Only the day before, the president commissioned an international airport just a twenty-minute drive away. With this, the price for the land will shoot up.

However, here villages exist cheek-by-jowl with the city. In the city square, smiling, stands the beautiful statue of the renowned writer who became famous writing about his land, though he was a globetrotter. Yes, it is not that of any Zamorin, but that of a writer! His statue defines the character of this town. Not only to the indigenous locals, this land will extend affection to strangers too. There is a magnet in this soil that attracts those aliens who are on the lookout for newer shores. That Gama's Portuguese ship reached Kappad was certainly no accident, is something that I know now. In the long line of outsiders starting from Gama, at the other end is this poor me. The difference is that the distance traversed is short, the sea crossed is of tears and the ship used was that of loneliness. When you come here, what would you be called? Outsider? Foreigner? This term was damaging enough to hurt a woman in Delhi, enough to make her resign from the position of the leader of the opposition party six days ago.

In that Thulam month, in which Menon Master decided to finally move from Thachanakkara, there was an unexpected death in Ayyaattumpilli—a very small, unsung death.

It was a time when Naraapilla's six children and Menon Master's Achyuthan were afflicted by a debilitating whooping cough. Both the houses of Ayyaattumpilli rang with cough day and night. The kids coughed incessantly and vomited many times with their hands clutching their tummies. The illness broke first with Padmanabhan, the second son after Govindan. When he came back from school, coughing as if his throat was about to rent itself, Kunjuamma spotted urine spots in his shorts and sensed danger.

'*Ey*, listen...' Choosing a favourable moment, Kunjuamma told Naraapilla, 'Our Pappanaavan seems to have a bad cough!'

Naraapilla, who was busy scraping the outer skin of an arecanut with the sharp edge of a nutcracker, squinted his eyes to look at the boy coughing and leaning limp against his mother's body.

'If they go and gambol in the sun in the guise of going to study, they will cough, fart, everything,' Naraapilla said with dismissive indifference.

'This is not that.' Kunjuamma heaved in agitation, as she held Padmanabhan close and massaged his chest. 'The boy's miserable. While coughing, he's passing urine too.'

When Naraapilla continued to chop arecanut in silence, Kunjuamma sharpened her voice and added, 'If you give me money, I'll take him to Achuttan Vaidyan!'

'You can take or kill or whatever!' said Naraapilla, sending the arecanut pieces and the nutcracker with the brass handles flying with a sweep of his hand. 'If you want, take that outsider next door too! But you won't get even a quarter from me!'

Peering inside, he made his voice tremble to a crescendo, 'Good-fo'-nothings that strike their mother 'n father will only die coughing and shitting. What's the point of them recovering from illnesses after all? To do my oblation to the manes?'

By dusk, Padmanabhan's illness intensified. When the children were washing their hands and feet to sit before the lamp and pray in the evening, Padmanabhan vomited a mouthful of yellow liquid on the front step. Naraapilla stood looking sympathetically at Kaalippennu who was washing the steps. Before he could hurl curses at Kunjuamma, Kaalippennu intervened, 'So wh't, master, don't I too 've a boy of the same age!'

Kaali's smile and enthusiasm cooled Naraapilla.

In the night, Kunjuamma gave Padmanabhan hot coffee laced with dried ginger and pepper. Pleased with such consideration that came rarely, he hugged his mother's cold tummy and lay coughing. 'Next time when you go to the beach…' Pausing after a cough that seemed to wring out his soul, he piped up, '…'ll Amma buy me a thing?'

'Surely. What does Amma's Pappanaavan want? Tell me, my dear!' Kunjuamma stroked his forehead.

Padmanabhan smiled a mischievous smile. 'That…' He tried teasing his mother, 'That's something. A thing!' Because he started coughing again, he could not finish telling her.

More than her concern for her son's cough, Kunjuamma felt the weight of her husband's irresponsibility acutely on her chest, and somehow managed to pass the night. By daybreak, the two younger ones, who were sleeping on a mat on the floor beside the cot, had also started coughing. When the five-year-old Chinnamma puckered her mouth and her eyes bulged as she coughed, Kunjuamma glimpsed on her small face an expression akin to that of her husband in his angry moments, and felt a little cross. Then Pankajaakshan coughed. By the time the rasping drumming was on the ascendant, Chandran also joined in. By evening, all six of them, including Govindan, had started coughing and spitting out phlegm, pushing their ribcages forward.

Fed up with Appu Nair's efforts to douse Naraapilla's unbridled misadventures through affectionate reasoning, Naraapilla had been keeping his distance from Appu Nair. Kunjuamma was also banned from visiting her brother and sister-in-law at Peechamkurichi. Clinging to his last fistful of dignity, Appu Nair had also stopped going to Ayyaattumpilli and being Naraapilla's lackey. Appu Nair had on his side reasons that would be found justifiable by anyone who cared to listen: even after the harvesting, threshing and the filling of the granary were over, Kaalippennu had not vacated the love-nest of the tenant's anteroom. Naraapilla was making Kaalippennu stay, scarcely bothering to get Menon Master's consent.

That night, while lying with Kaalippennu to unload the weight of his lust, and listening to the coughs of his children breaking through the confines of the New House, Naraapilla recollected his wedding night: remembering the bitterness of that night in the month of Kanni fifteen years ago, Naraapilla told Kaalippennu in the darkness, 'Oh, the entire lot has caught a terminal cough! Don't they sound like dogs in heat in Kanni?'

Menon Master and Padminiyamma heard from their bedroom the suppressed moans of Kaalippennu and the growls of Naraapilla in the middle of the night. The door of the anteroom opened to the outside. Fearing that a murder was being committed in their house, the couple stood trembling with fear, ears pressed to the wall. It took them a long time to understand that inside were two bodies competing with each other in unimaginable sexual acrobatics, in utter disregard of all norms of untouchability and castiest pollution. After making sure that the sixteen-year-old Achyuthan was asleep, Menon Master retreated with his wife.

Till the door was shut, the rhythmic panting of a female voice moaning 'Master, Master' and the growling throatiness of a male voice's underplayed amorous cuss words could be heard from the anteroom.

'*Ayye*, why does it sound that way?' Padminiyamma, who couldn't sleep, asked Menon Master in his ear.

'Who knows?' Making a determined decision to leave Thachanakkara with his family, Menon Master said, 'I know only of things related to human beings!'

Right after the children of the New House caught the bug, Achyuthan also started to cough. As soon as he reached home from school, Menon Master got ready to take him to Achuttan Vaidyan of Kaniyankunnu. When Padminiyamma came to the New House kitchen to tell Kunjuamma, she too went inside, changed her mundu and came out with her children as well. Though they were all coughing non-stop, the little children began to laugh with joy, as if going together for a festival.

Chinnamma, who was to join Aalungal school next June, was the worst affected by the cough. The whooping cough's intensity was in inverse relation to age. Govindan and Menon Master's Achyuthan, who were on the verge passing their childhood, coughed only a little. Crossing the ledges and alleys shadowed by beleric trees, the children walked upto Achuttan Vaidyan's clinic, walking in a procession with a cough as its slogan. During the examination, when Achuttan Vaidyan asked them to demonstrate their cough, Govindan and Achyuthan couldn't cough. But the kids obeyed the order. Like the early morning frog-orchestra at the Thachanakkara thevar's pond, Padmanabhan, Pankajaakshan, Chandran, Thankamma, and Chinnamma on the hip of Kunjuamma, began to cough with little respite.

'Enough, enough!' Achuttan Vaidyan scolded, gesturing with

the penknife with which he was sharpening the pencil butt to write the prescription. In a moment, all of them went silent together. When the suppressed cough behind the forcefully pressed mouths began to push and bubble in their kiddy throats and started to redden the capillaries in their popping eyes, Achuttan Vaidyan's heart melted and he said, 'Ah, go ahead and cough a little!'

Permission granted, the group started coughing with renewed strength.

Their examination over, Achyuthan and Govindan were standing on their toes to peer at the thick tomes in the top shelf of Achuttan Vaidyan's medicine shelf. Amongst the sheaves of paper sheets between the moth-eaten covers, oily with use, lay an ocean of knowledge about wellness and longevity. With the experience gathered from Menon Master's bookshelf, and holding his head cocked to the side, Govindan began to read some of their names: '*Pharmacographia Indica, Materia Medica of Hindus, Siddhaprayogalathika, Dravyagunavijnanam*…' But even as he was uttering the words, without letting his friend notice, his eye was hovering around his mother. After the prescriptions were written and medicines handed over, who would pay Achuttan Vaidyan? He knew his mother was sweating in dread of that moment.

In his left ear, Achuttan Vaidyan's voice rang, 'For the little ones, the illness is a little bad. Would there be Malabar nut herb in your yard? You may be able to identify it. Didn't you say you were a schoolmaster? Ah, then tell me, in *Ramayana*, to slay the demoness Thaadaka, Sage Vishwamithran had recruited Raman and Lakshmanan; then, the sage taught unto them two mantras to enhance their strength. Which ones?'

Master smiled. With affection for the old apothecary, he replied, 'Bala and athibala, if my memory is right.'

'Bravo! Exactly!' Achuttan Vaidyan's face reflected his happiness at having met a worthy man after a long time. 'So, like me, you too are not from this place, isn't it? Okay, then tell us this too, what actually are bala and athibala?'

Kunjuamma shifted the coughing child on her hip, without disturbing their conversation. Feeling guilty, Master reminded the vaidyan, 'The children are coughing badly. If we leave now we can start them on their medicines!'

'Ah! If you don't know, here, listen. The arrow leaf *sida* plant, ubiquitous in our yards, is what is called this bala! In the same family, athibala is the one with greater potency! Understood?'

Revealing his dark gums, Achuttan Vaidyan laughed loudly.

Pointing at Achyuthan and Govindan standing near the almirah, Achuttan Vaidyan said, '*Ngaa*, let's leave Raman's medicines and come to our case. For the elder boys—there, for those Rama-Lakshmanans—fenugreek decoction will do. For the little ones, sweet flag should be ground and given in the honey of stingless bees twice daily. Didn't I mention Malabar nut sometime ago? Its leaf and seeds, roasted and powdered, and mixed with pepper, dry ginger, and sugar crystals can be given to the babies. This guy in between, what's his name? Ah, I don't think his is a case of whooping cough alone! How old is he now? Ten or eleven?'

Govindan stood up from the bookshelf, and moved closer to his brother. Padmanabhan was sitting shirtless in front of the Vaidyan, exhausted and resembling a wilted colocasia stem.

'Will be fourteen this *Medam*!' said Kunjuamma, stroking Padmanabhan's chest.

'*Ooh*!' Achuttan Vaidyan was stunned. 'Then…' he said, frowning, 'Tell that Naraapilla to come up here when he is free!'

Before receiving the prescription, when Master's hand was going into his pocket, Achuttan Vaidyan stopped him and said, '*Nhum, nhumm*! Keep it with you; first visit, right? It can be the next time!'

Helping the children button up, Kunjuamma got out, holding them all close together. Govindan and Achyuthan walked in the front. Menon Master took the youngest from Kunjuamma. Kunjuamma picked up the tired Padmanabhan, the fourteen-year-old who looked only eleven.

Then, Govindan turned back and took his brother off his mother. That this walk from Kaniyankunnu to Ayyaattumpilli carrying his brother, who was only one-and-a-half years younger, would be a lifelong memory for Govindan, was a fact he did not know at the time.

Of the children of Ayyaattumpilli, it was Padmanabhan who stopped coughing first.

Despite Achuttan Vaidyan's orders, his father did not go to the clinic. The Vaidyan's suspicion about the boy's sickness was not misplaced. But, he did not get the time to treat and cure it. Ten days after the cough started, the youngest baby called for her mother when she saw a white thread-like thing emerging from the nostrils of Padmanabhan, who lay with a smile in the early morning cold. Kunjuamma, roasting the leaves and rice of Malabar nut in the kitchen, had to look only once. '*Ayyo*!' with a bellow louder than any that she had ever made during any of her pregnancies, Kunjuamma burst out crying, beating her chest. '*Ayyo* … My Pappanaavan is gone!'

He was gone. Worms emerged not only from his mouth, but also from his nostrils and ears and eyes. In the midst of children who were struggling to both cry and cough at the same time, Kunjuamma hugged Padmanabhan's wasted body and screamed with her wet throat, 'Call that devil, children … Tell him my son is gone!'

Naraapilla came, held the boy's face by the chin and turned it left and right, and twisted his lips. 'My Thachanakkara thevare!'

He pummelled his chest with his closed fists with all his strength and cried, 'You've made me eat my gorpse!'

Then he came out and, forgetting the long-drawn-out hostility, called out to Peechamkurichi: 'Appoliyo!' He coughed up nonexistent sobs and bawled loudly, 'Come here quickly, Appoliyo! One is gone here!'

Hearing the sound, it was Menon Master who came first, with the burnt husk dentifrice still in his mouth and holding in his hand the tongue-cleaner, improvised out of a split coconut leaf spine. When she saw Padminiyamma who followed right behind, Kunjuamma's heart surged into her throat and got constricted. They cried hugging each other. To bear the pain of death, the mourners began to split up in pairs: Kunjuamma and Padminiyamma; the younger daughters beside the dead body now stretched on the floor; leaning against the wall beyond were Pankajaakshan and Chandran, who were younger than Padmanabhan; seated close to each other on the porch were Govindan and Achyuthan; and in the yard, without uttering a word or touching or crying, were Naraapilla and Menon Master...

Before afternoon, not only Appu Nair, but the whole of Thachanakkara had reached Ayyaattumpilli. Because a contagion was suspected, it was suggested that the child's body be cremated on a wood pyre. Though dried cow dung discs and coconut shells had already reached the house, a mango tree yet to bloom was chopped down from the western boundary to turn Padmanabhan into ashes. When the body was taken southwards, shrouded and bound in white, Govindan, who had kept his heart on a leash by holding on tight to Achyuthan's hand, started to roll on the floor and wail.

Govindan was to cry once again after a month and a half. It was when, stuffing household effects in two hand-drawn carts, Menon

Master, Padminiyamma and Achyuthan left, ending their sojourn at Ayyaattumpilli. Padminiyamma and Kunjuamma hugged each other and cried. Govindan and Achyuthan looked into each other's eyes and cried. Menon Master and Naraapilla settled the rent arrears, returned the advance receipt and shook hands and parted.

With leaden feet and unseeing eyes, Govindan walked a long way, aimlessly following the direction that their hired car had taken. Achyuthan kept waving back, sitting in the taxi. First the car, and then the carts drawn by two emaciated coolies, disappeared from sight.

Everything was returning the way it had arrived. Among the household effects in the carts, Master's bookshelf was the biggest. But the heaviest was something that had been added on at Ayyaattumpilli: sorrow.

NINE

Crepe Jasmine

17 July 1999

...I never met my grandmother. Neither did grandmother see the three children my mother gave birth to. So, grandma existed only in the realm of hearsay for me. During my childhood, if anyone contracted conjunctivitis in Thachanakkara, someone would come to Ayyaattumpilli to take some of the crepe jasmine growing in abundance in the southern corner where grandma had been cremated. The Thachanakkara folk believed that the crepe jasmine growing there had more power for restoring human sight than any of the same kind of flowers that sprout elsewhere. Later, when the property had been divided up into smaller plots as inheritances and houses sprung up in them, the luxuriant crepe jasmine disappeared. Even Grampa has forgotten Kunjuamma of Ayyaattumpilli. I am sure that none of this information will be of use to you for the interview on the 21st. Therefore, I will write a factoid I read in the newspaper today: Eileen Collins of America has won the honour of being the first woman to head a space mission.

Kunjuamma, who appeared before Naraapilla in the temple pond, was the tenth child of Paramu Nair of Peechamkurichi.

They were seven girls and three boys, headed by Appu Nair, the eldest son of Paramu Nair. The penury at Peechamkurichi was such that if the land were to be split between the ten siblings, each would not have got even six feet of the ground as burial space for each one of them. But Kunjuamma had inherited something from her mother that her six elder sisters did not: thick tresses which had started touching her small bum even as she was just eight years old. Though Paramu Nair's wife Echuamma was a broken woman after delivering ten children, in her prime she was one of the true beauties of Thachanakkara. During the infamous flood of thousand ninety-nine of Malayalam calender, after she had lost her footing while trying to retrieve a plate that was floating away from the kitchen, she had slipped into the surging waters of the canal, and Paramu Nair, who had swum in pursuit, was able to pull her out of the water only because of her hair. After that, the legend of her hair was elevated to that of the supernatural tales about *yakshis*, who trapped men with the alluring beauty of their tresses. She was only saved by her hair getting caught in the bamboo stems stretching across the waters of the canal, which emptied into the Periyar river. The youngest daughter, Kunjuamma, who had inherited the same bountiful hair from her mother Echuamma, got caught in the flash flood of Naraapilla's lust in her eighteenth year at the Thachanakkara thevar's temple pond.

Two of Kunjuamma's brothers and three of her sisters had fallen prey to various diseases in their childhood and had become one with the soil of Peechamkurichi. Thus, Appu Nair was her only living brother. After their weddings, the three sisters had left for their husbands' houses and, of the ten children, only the eldest, Appu Nair, and the youngest, Kunjuamma, were left behind. After the death of Paramu Nair and Echuamma, apart from his four children, this unmarried youngest sister also became his share in an inheritance. That was when Naraapilla chettan of Ayyaattumpilli had taken him under his wing, though they were unequals; as his lust heaved, Naraapilla had married Appu Nair's sister to sleep with her. However, after being a wife to a man and delivering his six children, in her brief forty-five years of life, Kunjuamma had very few chances of knowing the meaning of the word happiness. Even in the few instances of happiness she had experienced, her husband Naraapilla, who was renowned in Thachanakkara for measuring out money using a para, had no role to play.

Appu Nair's sister's son, Kesavan, who was the same age as Kunjuamma, was the source of the first spring of her life. When Echuamma of Peechamkurichi was pregnant with her tenth child, her eldest daughter was also carrying. When Kunjuamma had occupied the mother's womb, Kesavan occupied the eldest daughter's womb. The daughter gave birth first; two months later, the mother delivered. When the children started talking, Kesavan started calling the girl, who was younger in age but elder in relationship, Vavachitta, or baby-aunt. The well-spread ainee tree in the western corner of Peechamkurichi had a root jutting out of the earth, resembling a crocodile's tail. A circular spot around that root, which had been cleared of grass, was their private haven when they were children.

In her death throes, as she started banging her head against the wall in Ayyaattumpilli, this crocodile-tail root was the first of the three or four visions that flashed through Kunjuamma's mind.

Kesavan, who used burnt rice husk to darken his incipient moustache, was the one who remedied her problems of not being able to continue her education in a school. Kesavan's amma had been married into a family named Peechampadinjaappuram, to the west of Peechamkurichi. From there, he came every day to see *Vavachitta*. He explained to her about the independence struggle, and about Gandhiji whom he had visited in the Advaithaashramam. He instilled in her respect towards social reformers such as Narayana Guru. He explained to her how the world really began outside Thachanakkara.

One Sunday, as they sat squeezing out and eating the flesh of ainee fruit, Kesavan said, 'Vavachittae, you should marry someone who's educated and knowledgeable. And when you have children, send them to big colleges and educate them.'

'Get lost, lad,' said a coyly blushing sixteen-year-old Kunjuamma, leaning against the termite-eaten pillar of Peechamkurichi, and pinching her nephew as she heard the word marriage. Keeping his forearm where he had been pinched close to his nose to smell the ainee, he said again, 'When you have children, don't add a suffix to their names with Nair, Pillai, etc. I feel, in the times to come, such surnames will be out of fashion.'

'Lad, who told you all this?' A piqued Kunjuamma jumped down from the parapet.

'Isn't there a college on the other side of Kaniyankunnu? Didn't I tell you the other day, about how Gandhiji had come there and planted a mango tree? That day, there was a super speech by one of the teachers in the college. As Gandhiji's arrival got delayed, his speech was prolonged. But as I sat listening to him, I wished Gandhiji would be delayed further. So interesting was that speech! His words had this something … what should I say … an illumination. That day, that's what the teacher said.'

'Go, you fibber.' Pinching him once more, Kunjuamma ran into the kitchen. His eyes shone with a chivalry beyond his sixteen years; Kesavan said to himself, 'I am also going to snip my name, Vavachitta. What is the use of this? Kesavan Nair! Kesava Menon, Kesava Pillai! Kesava Kosavan! Pthooo!' He spat.

To escape the dire penury at Peechampadinjaappuram and, more importantly, to know the world outside Thachanakkara, in his seventeenth year, Kesavan ran away from his home, without telling even Kunjuamma. While his flight would not cause anyone else any remarkable pain, Kunjuamma froze, unable to even weep. She developed a pain in her throat which made swallowing her own spit painful. Her mind was hollowed out in a single day. The next day, as she was gathering the scattered ainee seeds from beneath the ainee tree, unknowingly she gathered small stones the size of the seeds and deposited them in the bowl formed out of her skirt. When she ate the roasted ainee seeds, she ate the roasted stones as well. When she realized she was eating stones, she acknowledged those were tastier than anything else she had eaten before. Stones collected from the small clearing around the crocodile-tail root of the ainee tree. How could the others understand the taste? Till Appu Nair discovered it and took her to Achuttan Vaidyan, she continued eating roasted stones regularly.

'It is a lack of nutrients,' Achuttan Vaidyan told Appu Nair, lifting her eyelid and peering. 'When she gets a good husband, your sister's stone-eating and all will stop all by itself.'

It was a misdiagnosis by Achuttan Vaidyan. Kunjuamma's stone-eating habit was related to her psyche, not her body. But as if to prove him right, when she was eating rice and curry to her fill in Ayyaattumpilli for her three meals, her stone-eating did seem to stop for a long while. On the fourth night of her wedding, even when tempted by her husband by his gift of burnt laterite, she was unmoved. Till the pregnancy cravings in her third pregnancy drew her out to come across the stones bathed in moonlight, and stacked up for building the New House, Kunjuamma had forgotten the pleasure of eating stones.

'Pappinichechi.' As she sat on the steps at the back of the tenant's in the afternoon breeze, Kunjuamma would point out to Padmanabhan, who was too small for his age, and say, 'If I tell you, you will not believe me. When I was pregnant with this Pappanaavan, my tummy had more laterite stones than the child.'

When she heard that, Padminiyamma would feel a fondness

that breached the levees of all indulgent affection for Kunjuamma's innocence. As she gazed at the flat tummy which six pregnancies hadn't made flabby, she would tease, 'It is no wonder it is a hard-as-stone abdomen.'

When all her four boys were registered in the school, Kunjuamma had used a trick to ensure that their names were not tagged with Nair or Pillai surnames.

'As per tradition, shouldn't we keep Nair for our children, like in their uncles' names?' Kunjuamma asked once when Appu Nair had come to Ayyaattumpilli.

'Nah!' Appu Nair interjected, 'Hasn't the matrilineal system moved on? For your kids, use Pillai! Isn't it, Naraapilla chettaa?'

Unaware whether Nair or Pillai was more eminent, Naraapilla was perplexed. Using that opportunity, Kunjuamma said, 'But if we go against tradition and add one or the other, what if there is some problem? Let's now admit them as mere humans without surnames. All the suffixing can be done later, no?'

Thus, after finding out some names which were in fashion then and using them for her sons without a surname, envisioning a reformation, Kunjuamma repaid her debt to the playmate of her childhood.

The second owner of Kunjuamma's joys was Padminiyamma who stayed as a tenant for many years at Ayyaattumpilli. The one instance that gave Kunjuamma great happiness was when, just before her last confinement, Padminiyamma secretly carried out a strange procedure practiced solely where the latter came from.

It was the month of Thulam. Those were the days when Naraapilla remained obsessed with banana plantations, and most of the time, he was tending to the one-and-half acres of land in Paanaayikkulam and grappling with green leaf manure and fresh cow dung. Though there was Appu Nair to attend to these matters, a restless Naraapilla could not sit tight at home.

'Owner's supervision is the primary manure.' Thus turning his presence at the fields into a philosophy, Naraapilla would rush to Paanaayikkulam every morning.

One day, when Naraapilla was not at home, Padminiyamma made Kunjuamma sit in the lotus position facing east, in the portico of the New House. In her womb, her sixth child had already started the kicking and punching of the ninth month. Since it was afternoon, the surroundings were in a somnolent state. Padminiyamma had extracted juice out of the hog plum—which she had got Achyuthan and Govindan to gather from the compound the previous day—by crushing it on the grindstone and collecting the juice in a coconut shell. Chandran, who had not yet joined school, was despatched to fetch the knife from the kitchen. She let the sour juice drip on to the knife, held pointing north and above the face of Kunjuamma; Kunjuamma started to lap up the juice falling and scattering off the tip of the knife.

'Oh my Pappinichechi,' Kunjuamma expostulated with a contorted face. 'OH! what sourness! Enough to kill the lice on one's head!'

Her facial expression was mirrored on the face of Chandran, who was standing to the side.

'Thus our sour-juice drinking ritual is over,' said Padminiyamma after throwing out the coconut shell and wiping the knife clean. 'Now you watch, this next child of yours; it will be like a battering ram!'

Those were the few sparkling moments of real happiness that Kunjuamma received as her meagre share in her petty life. She used to grieve over the lack of education of her husband and herself with the tenant couple repeatedly. She would try to imitate with her own husband how Padminiyamma would behave with Menon Master, only to meet with chagrin. She would burn up inside with the realization that, unless undressed, her husband was incapable of showing any affection. When in her forty-fifth year, she hit menopause when menarche had still not set in for her sixteen-year-old youngest daughter. During those last months of hers, she used to have a same dream repeat itself early in the morning. In her entire life, this was the strangest and most dismaying dream.

In that nightmare, the Ayyaattumpilli house was slipping under water, which had risen to roof level, flooded from torrential rains and the Periyar river in spate. All the men of Thachanakkara were running towards Kaniyankunnu, carrying their wives and children. Under the grey skies, in the vast floodwaters, seeing her six children, whom she had been clutching close to her, slip away one by one from her grasp and drowning and disappearing, she started bawling. The water was lapping against the last row of the roof tiles. She crawled up the slippery tiles using her cold, trembling legs, towards the top of the roof. Naraapilla was standing astride the inverted V-shaped top tiles, as if on an elephant. He was wearing only a loin cloth. He was telling her, as she pleaded to be saved with stretched hands, 'Kunjo, it is easy for me to remember the year you died—the year of the floods.'

Then, when he would start his attempt to throw her off, flinging at her fist-sized laterite stones from inside his bulging loin cloth, she would wake up with palpitations loud enough to echo off the walls of Ayyaattumpilli.

During the initial days of her marriage, just on one night, she had seen a light dream, which had made her happy enough to remember it till her death.

'Kunjo,' running his fingers through her hair, Naraapilla asked her in the dream, 'which is my Kunju's favourite colour?'

'The green of the tender plantain inflorescence.'

'Favourite bird?'

'Parrot.'

'Then who's the most favourite person?'

'Who else?' She hugged and kissed him and said, 'This Narayanan himself.'

Preserving the sweet smile gifted by that dream, Kunjuamma found the match box, lit the chimney lamp, and gazed at her sleeping husband. She smiled bitterly looking at the reality—with the sweat pouring off him and the snores causing his cheeks and jowl to tremble.

During day time, the eternally love-starved Kunjuamma would be regaled by Padminiyamma, who would retell the tales of uxorious love that she had heard from Menon Master. That is how she came to know of a writer called Chandumenon writing a long tale for his wife to read and be entertained. She found out through Govindan that that book was not available in Menon Master's book shelf. For a long time she thought that the Menon who had woven a story for amusing his wife was their Menon Master himself, the husband of Padminiyamma. When he heard of that mistaken identity and had laughed for a long time, he narrated to her, in person, a more amusing episode. Menon Master went in and fetched the handwritten edition of an *aattakatha*, written by a gifted writer, Kottayathu Thampuran.

He searched for a particular page and handed over the book to Padminiyamma. In a nasal voice, Padminiyamma started reciting the poem:

> Reveal thy provenance to me,
> Ye pretty-face who comes in war!
> Are you Kamadeva, Vishnu, ye exalted one,
> Or Shiva, or a mere human being?

When she saw Padminiyamma gaze at her husband with love, after finishing the recital without any stutter or spit-spraying, Kunjuamma felt a flash in the pit of her stomach.

'Kunjuamma has understood the meaning, no?' asked Menon Master. 'Nivaathakavachan, an asura is asking this question of Arjunan, who has come to kill him. Did you find any anomaly in this question?'

Kunjuamma stood in a stupor, looking at the sky.

'Ayyae, I thought they were the words of some woman,' Padminiyamma said.

'That is the joke!' Menon Master said. 'Actually, these lines in the aattakatha were not written by Kottayathuthampuran.' As if afraid that Thampuran's spirit may be hovering around, Menon Master looked around and lowered his voice and said, 'His wife, Kaitheri Maakkam, is the author of these four lines! She was reportedly very erudite. When Thampuran had got up from his writing and had gone away, possibly to pass urine, Maakkam came and added these four lines. The words which came out of the asura Nivaathakavachan's mouth became that of a woman's, filled with desire for the accomplished archer!'

Kunjuamma and Padminiyamma laughed heartily.

'Kunjuo.' The next moment, Naraapilla's summons came.

'Nivaathakavachan has come!' saying so, as Kunjuamma stood up, Menon Master and Padminiyamma continued their laughter.

That was the only occasion when Kunjuamma had laughed with abandon. When she heard, in 1947, that the white men had left India, though she didn't laugh open-mouthed, she had felt very happy in her heart. In 1948, when she heard of Gandhiji being shot and killed, she was in the midst of her household chores and felt so weak in the legs that she had to sit down. Staring at the cracked floor of the kitchen, she cried thinking of her nephew Kesavan.

In 1955, when her daughter, who resembled Naraapilla in form and features, turned sixteen, Kunjuamma fell prey to an undiagnosed condition that troubled her badly. Showing signs of prolonged insanity, she kept circling her room and hitting her head against the walls, leaving bloodstains there.

'Where is that? There was a door here!' Every time she hit her head against the wall, she said, with her eyes rolling. 'Menon Master … Pappinichechi … Keshavaa … my Pappanaavaa…' she wailed, invoking names that would never return, having departed many years ago.

It was the Thiruvaathira day in the month of Dhanu. As was usual, when Appu Nair came in the morning to see his sister and check on her condition, Ayyaattumpilli appeared unusually gloomy. Rubbing his cataract-dimmed eyes, he called Chinnamma, raising his voice. His youngest niece appeared before him yawning after scrambling up from her mat, rheum in her eyes and dried drool at the corners of her lips. Appu Nair peered once more, rubbing his eyes. He started feeling as if a bank of dark clouds had descended into the atmosphere, as would in the monsoon month of Karkkadakam. When he felt his ancient heart beating with uncharacteristic loudness, he ran into her room, shouting his youngest sibling's name.

Kunjuamma was lying prone on the bare floor, close to the wall. Most part of her body was covered with her still dark and luxurious hair. When he knelt by her side and touched her oily hair, his fingers touched the oilier-than-oil fresh blood. Wiping his hand above the blood marks on the wall left by her untied hair strands, he started sobbing like a child.

Seeing that and sensing danger, the sixteen-year-old Chinnamma started wailing loud enough to be heard over Thachanakkara and to bring people running.

When Kunjuamma of Ayyaattumpilli fell for the last time, smashing her head against the wall, as a representative of a thousand unremembered and unsung mothers and grandmothers, respectfully joining her hands towards to the brilliant radiance that came from within, neither the five surviving children of the six she gave birth to, nor Naraapilla was by her side. Because of that, none of them could hear the last word she had spoken.

Looking at the receding form of Naraapilla, headed to the temple pond for his morning bath in the grey light, and slamming her head into the wall with all her might, her last word was:

'Killer.'

TEN

The Circle

2 October 1999

It is Gandhiji's birthday today. The hapless Mohandas who can't be found anywhere else in India other than on the five-hundred-rupee currency note. Nevertheless, I feel this year is more important than this day. Because this year is the fifty-first death anniversary of Gandhiji. Our nation has already completed half a century of living, racked by guilt over the patricide. As we wait for the results of the Lok Sabha elections, such a day of funereal remembrance has more relevance. And along with that, for this question as well: who will win? Even children will know the answer: on whose head the crown of the prime minister will sit, when all around us resound the invisible celebrations of the jubilee of Godse's triumph.

When Time completes drawing a circle in fifty years, on the pages of history, a filthy zero appears.

Though no one expected it, on hearing of the death of Kunjuamma, Govindan reached Ayyaattumpilli with his wife and child by afternoon. Appu Nair had despatched his eldest son to Cherai in the morning to inform Govindan of the death. When he arrived there, Govindan Master and Sulochana Teacher were at the school, giving lessons. So, their fingers were still coated with chalk powder when they reached Ayyaattumpilli.

In that funereal milieu, Govindan's wife, Sulochana, was distraught as she realized that her person was drawing more attention than the corpse. She could guess what everyone was murmuring about her from the time they passed the stile.

Kunjuamma had discovered about his love from Govindan's single-line notebook. He had a secret passion for writing poetry. When she found time from her chores, she would read the spring-scented words in his notebooks without his knowledge. Those handwritten books helped her imagine some similarities between her son and Menon Master. She recognized that in him—unlike in the nature of her other sons, Pankajaakshan, Chandran and the deceased Padmanabhan—every breath was kindling an ember.

From the day at the riverside, when he had beaten his father with the same branch of the golden shower tree with which his father had beaten him mercilessly, he had stopped all communication with Naraapilla forever. With the death of his immediate younger brother, Padmanabhan, he became more withdrawn. Each time he heard Naraapilla refer emotionlessly to 'the year our Pappanaavan died', in unrelated contexts, he felt like killing his father and then stabbing himself to death. But as in the case of his mother's life, Menon Master and his family lightened the burden of his life at Ayyaattumpilli. He completed reading the last book in Menon Master's bookshelf. The bright- and wide-eyed Achyuthan was not a mere friend, but the warrior hero who drove out the stifling air from Ayyaattumpilli. When he considered himself a supporting actor in a play in which Achyuthan was the protagonist, Govindan felt more joy than any feeling of inferiority. Many a time, during the eighty years of his life, Govindan used to muse about the evening, blessed by a cool breeze and slanted golden rays, when he and Achyuthan, happy and laughing, had raced along the pedestrian path against the rice-laden lorry on the freshly-painted Marthaanda Varma Bridge. Every time, the heart-rending anguish of not being able to find that friendship ever again would assail him, as when he remembered when he had to beat his own father by the riverside.

In an exquisite hand, Govindan had jotted down all these as poems in the empty pages of his notebooks. With a passion imbibed from Padminiyamma, Kunjuamma used to pore over the pain expressed in poetry and try to understand it, without Govindan's knowledge. In a notebook with rain-smudged words, right below a poem by Govindan, she saw a handwriting different from his, which had written this and signed off:

> I cannot condone tears shed in remembrance of lost springs
> that turn one blind to the beautiful flower in front of him.
>
> Yours, Sulochana.

Though she floundered over the meaning of a cryptic word used in that couplet, with the key of feminine observation, Kunjuamma managed to open the secret vault of her son's romance before the rainy season was over.

It was during their intermediate course that Sulochana won the love of Govindan, two years elder to her. They had both won prizes in a poetry contest held to discover young poets, organized by *Kavyachandrika*, a magazine published from Thripunithura that ceased publication without notice after the third edition. The names and addresses of the prize winners came out in the third edition. With that, the magazine discontinued. Though it was announced that the prizes would be sent to them, neither of them ever got any. Instead, a letter reached Ayyaattumpilli for the first time. The letter with small flowers in faint blue ink drawn around the address was from her—Sulochana, the first-prize winner. The reply he sent and the response he received from her had more poetry in them than the poems that won them prizes in the contest. Their fate lines were being redrawn by love as their correspondence progressed, and the smart girl, who possessed both beauty and knowledge, moved to her aunt's house near Kaniyankunnu, to continue her studies at UC College. Wearing a yellow long skirt and blouse with big green leaves and a light-yellow half-saree, one Monday, on the pretext of worshipping at the Thachanakkara thevar's temple, she came to meet Kunjuamma along with her aunt. With her heart aflutter as she waited near the sacrificial chamber for the first sight of her future daughter-in-law, Kunjuamma sent her gaze unconsciously towards the temple pond. She tried to recollect that eighteen-year-old who had been instructed to bathe in the temple pond for forty-one days, as per the prescription of the senior astrologer. If she had to believe that girl was her, she should have had the dreadful habit of believing nightmares were reality.

At that moment, looking like a yellow-clothed reincarnation of her own past, a girl, accompanied by a middle-aged woman wearing thick glasses, came out. A glance was enough for her to recognize her son's love interest. Standing outside the temple, and through the bars of the sacrificial chamber, Govindan saw his mother holding in her hand his beloved's right hand, sanctified by holy water. While she was applying the sandal paste from the leaf in her hand above the holy ash smear on the girl's forehead, Govindan could lip-read his mother mouthing, 'My daughter!'

Impetuously, Kunjuamma gave her word that she would bring Sulochana to Ayyaattumpilli by the time the clouds of the monsoon rains would have moved on. The truth was that in those moments of indulgent love and affection, she had completely forgotten Naraapilla. Going by the traditions of the land, though her son had not reached marriageable age, she recognized that his girl, being only two years younger than him, was already ripe for marriage and would be soon seen as too shop-soiled. In the face of the aunt who seemed to be capable only of smiling, Kunjuamma saw the reflection of her future daughter-in-law. Though she was not educated or sagacious, an inner enlightenment gave her right hand the strength to bless a Nair-Ezhava alliance, which was going to shake all of Thachanakkara. It manifested itself on Sulochana's forehead in the form of the sandal-paste mark.

The monsoon was not over yet.

On an evening when the younger children were reciting their prayers, Appu Nair, who had come as usual to collect paddy at the end of the month, became the first person to hear about this alliance from Kunjuamma. Busy moving the paddy in the granary with the bushel, Appu Nair laughed out loud when he heard of the proposal. Kunjuamma only hid the fact that the girl selected by her son was an Ezhava. After gathering enough paddy in the round basket and covering its mouth with a plantain leaf, Appu Nair stepped into the yard in the light rain, and laughed again at the mischief of his sister proposing to get her twenty-three-year-old son married. In the interval between a flash of lightning and thunder that followed, Kunjuamma asked, 'Will you please make enquiries?'

The clap of thunder followed. The dried fruits of the achiote plant, which stood on the way to the gate, caught fire and started to burn.

'Look at the omen,' Appu Nair said, looking at the burning bush, 'looks like we should not proceed with this proposal, Kunjo.'

Since the time he had visited the senior astrologer, Appu Nair had been giving shape to his version of a science of omen-reading. He did not spare anything that remotely resembled a presage or portent. But even when the achiote plant had caught fire, Kunjuamma did not relent. Finally, he gave his word that he would go to Cherai and enquire after the girl's family. He was on his way out when he saw Naraapilla come out of the anteroom of the old house and pee in the open.

'Hasn't that slut left yet?' Muttering to himself, Appu Nair went away in search of another route to Peechamkurichi.

Three days later, when Naraapilla was away in the afternoon, Appu Nair came to his sister after having made his enquiries in Cherai, and for the first time in his life, berated his sister: 'What's wrong with you, Kunjo? The girl that your darling son has identified for marriage is excellent! A first-rate Ezhava! Is he raving mad to marry Ezhava and Pulaya women? If Naraapilla comes to know of this, would he spare you or your son?' Swabbing his sweat, he looked up and said, 'I don't know what, my Thachanakkara thevare!'

He gave her the rest of the information he had gathered during his visit to Cherai: except in the matter of caste, the family was above Ayyaattumpilli in every sense. She was the eldest of the three daughters of Anandan Master, well respected in that area, for his opposition to toddy tapping… After narrating what he had learnt faithfully, he despaired, 'But, what is the point? Isn't everything useless because they are Ezhava?'

'What do you mean useless?' Kunjuamma challenged him for the first time in a voice full of determination. 'Say that my son has found a girl who has everything, Appu chettaa.'

Appu Nair froze. Without uttering another word, he drank a glass of diluted buttermilk in one gulp and returned to Peechamkurichi.

In the yard, Naraapilla was drying himself after his hot water bath of the evening. This was the time when he was seen at his most peaceable. The time when he enjoyed being clean, after the hot water had washed away all the sweat and grime of the day. Kunjuamma was gathering spathe and midribs fallen beneath the coconut trees and waiting for his bath to get over. Going to him as gently as she could, she started to talk diplomatically about their son's wedding. Glossing over his lack of income and that he was yet to turn twenty-three, she started to stutter over the matter of the girl's caste, and Naraapilla flung away his thorth and shouted, 'If he dares to marry some Ezhava girl he chances upon…' He bounded to where Kunjuamma was standing and bellowed, 'No way will I Iet them enter these premises.'

At that moment, with a smile which could render any man numb, Kunjuamma asked her husband, 'So, what about the Pulaya woman in the anteroom? What shall I do with her?'

Stumped for an answer, he grimaced. Picking up the thorth from the ground and dusting it, he flung it on his shoulder and went inside.

The wedding of the eldest son of Ayyaattumpilli happened without even Pooshaappi getting wind of it. There was no wedding tent or feast. No musical band or ululation was called for. Naraapilla raised his hand to strike Govindan who had brought Sulochana from her house. Holding down Naraapilla, who was hopping mad, his brothers, barely out of their adolescence, beseeched Govindan: 'Chettaa, please go wherever you can. If you stay back, one of you will die. That's for sure.'

Anticipating such a scene, Sulochana's father and two relatives were waiting with two hired cycle-rickshaws beyond the stile of Ayyaattumpilli. Kunjuamma wept seeing her son leave with his bride. Her daughters wept. When he was able to free his right hand from the grip of his sons, Naraapilla screamed, 'You, you, you, you…' After searching for the appropriate phrase to bless the marriage of his first-born and stuttering, he finally exploded,

'You'll be damned forever. You'll be so destitute that you will dig up and sell the cornerstone of your abode. You'll go begging with a spathe. This is Naraapilla's oath … nghaaa!'

Govindan did not meet damnation. Nor did he dig up his abode's foundation stone. He joined a school in Cherai as a teacher, stayed in his wife's house, which had a framed photograph of Narayana Guru, and became the Govindan Master that the local people respected. After Sulochana too got a job as a teacher in the same school, they shifted to a small house built in that same compound.

Govindan Master and Sulochana Teacher hung the photos of Narayana Guru and Chattambiswamikal side by side in their portico. The house was blessed by the two great souls.

Those were the final few months of Kunjuamma's life. In the month of Medam, when the hoisted flag announced the start of the festival of the Thachanakkara thevar's temple, Govindan and Sulochana, bearing their infant, came to the temple to meet the mother and daughters. Through Appu Nair's youngest son, whom he met at the temple grounds, Govindan sent word to his mother that he and his family were waiting for her in the temple premises. Kunjuamma and the youngest daughter, Chinnamma, came running. The mother and son stood looking at each other for a long time without uttering a word. Their hearts beat louder than the drums in the temple nearing their crescendo.

Sulochana had brought a set of a high-quality mundu and neryathu woven on Chendamangalam looms for Kunjuamma, and silk skirts for the sisters. Gathering Govindan's one-and-half-year-old daughter in her arms and pinching her cheek, Chinnamma asked Govindan, 'Looks exactly like our mother, no, Vallyettaa?'

'She resembles her, but hasn't got our mother's hair and beauty,' Govindan Master replied.

The mother and the daughter-in-law had a lot of news to exchange. Govindan's brother Pankajaakshan joining the police; the younger one Chandran fighting with his father over Govindan and leaving the house; an alliance in the offing for Thankamma, elder to Chinnamma; Thankamma's disappointment at not being able to come to the temple and meet her brother as she was menstruating—Kunjuamma narrated all this in one breath. Seeing the manner in which her fifteen-year-old sister-in-law was talking to the street vendor selling spin tops, Sulochana whispered the question in her mother-in-law's ear, 'Has menarche set in for her?'

Kunjuamma contorted her face and shrugged her shoulders to indicate that it had not. 'If it goes on like this,' she whispered back to her daughter-in-law, 'I am afraid that she won't start menstruating even after I am dead.'

Kunjuamma invited her son and daughter-in-law for lunch at Ayyaattumpilli.

'Some other time,' Govindan said.

'When?' Kunjuamma asked, 'For the oblation rite on the sixteenth day of my death?'

The last two things Kunjuamma said to Govindan turned out to be prophetic: she did not live to see Chinnamma menstruating. The next time Govindan and family came to Ayyaattumpilli was on hearing of her death.

Kunjuamma, who was carrying the new mundu and neryathu, given to her by her son as *Vishukaineettam*, close to her chest, as fondly as she would carry an infant, was waylaid at the stile by Naraapilla. Someone had reported to Naraapilla about seeing his son, daughter-in-law, and the grandchild in the company of Kunjuamma. Naraapilla snatched the new set of clothes gifted to her out of her hands and flung it away into the compound. As his youngest daughter started to make a dash for the packet, suddenly recalling that the dot-patterned material for her skirt was also in the packet, Naraapilla slapped her on her back, and hollered, 'Phaa, daughter of a mongrel! Did you also go to receive the gift of that Ezhava woman? Sister of the father-beater!'

Kunjuamma was next in line. Yanking her by her hair and dragging her along the yard, Naraapilla dumped her on the steps of the New House. 'Misbegotten bitch.' Letting the leg raised to kick her remain suspended in air for an instant, he said, 'If you try to defeat Naraapilla, I will make you eat my gorpse.' Then, yearning to smash her head between the hardness of the burnt bricks of the steps and his equally hard heel, he landed a violent kick to her head.

'Chechiii ... our Amma's being killed!' Chinnamma ran screaming into the house. When Naraapilla quit the arena after his rage was spent, the sisters carried their mother into the house.

With that kick, Naraapilla made his last physical contact with Kunjuamma. Though the news scarcely percolated beyond the boundaries of Ayyaattumpilli, with that kick Kunjuamma had entered her last days. She found pleasure in bloodying herself by hitting her head against the walls, leaving crimson patches on them. After one-and-a-half months of suffering, till she finally collapsed dead by voluntarily ramming her head for one last time into the Ayyaattumpilli wall, Kunjuamma did not step out of the room with its walls filled with murals in blood.

By the time Govindan and his family arrived, Kunjuamma had already been moved out to the southern boundary for cremation. In the absence of his elder three brothers, the youngest son, Chandran, had lit the pyre. Unable to endure the sight of his mother burning, as Govindan turned to leave, Naraapilla came rushing out of the house. In a voice that made comprehension difficult even to himself, he lashed out at Govindan in front of the assembled mourners. 'Satisfied? After making that poor woman suffer to her death, aren't you satisfied now?'

After a long while, much after his reputation as a soft-natured teacher had been set, once again Govindan's heart heaved with a burst of murderous intent. Sensing that, Sulochana squeezed his arm and held on to it. Perceiving the amazing phenomenon of the surge of a force potent enough to kill a savage beast with a single blow coursing through a man's hand, once again, Sulochana left Ayyaattumpilli in the company of her husband.

Having completed the ritual bath after sixteen days of sequestration following Kunjuamma's death, Naraapilla returned to the temple pond for his usual early morning bath. When he lowered his fifty-seven-year-old feet into the glass-like surface of the water lying still on the steps, he wondered if he was hallucinating: it seemed that the water in the pond was flowing rapidly! From the women's kadavu, sounds were heard of someone gargling and spitting out gutturally! Realizing that old age had come to get acquainted with him with a handshake in his fifty-seventh year, he felt faint. He scrambled up and sat panting on the dry, upper steps. After the sixteen days of sequestration, untrammelled by the corporeal form, Kunjuamma had returned to follow her husband till his death.

The year was 1955. Naraapilla was already a grandfather. But it was only after his third daughter Chinnamma would have her menarche the next year, get married the year after, undergo the sorrow of being childless for ten years and then have three children with a gap of two years between each, that Naraapilla would become the grandfather of her third child, Jithendran.

For that he would have to wait till 1972. Not on the steps of the pond that seemed to be flowing; but on the much more immense, much more slippery, much more merciless steps of Time.

Part Two

Artha

'The writer may very well serve a movement of history as its mouthpiece, but he cannot of course create it.'

—Karl Marx

ONE

Transformation

5 June 1999

…Yesterday I had a strange dream; really a nightmare. The dream, set at least two centuries earlier, in times of yore, started with me in the role of a sentry at a palace. Though I was not guarding the ramparts of the palace but a more imposing darkness. I believe that some of the words we utter randomly during our waking hours are seized swiftly by our hearts, held, and transferred to our brain in the night. I had told you yesterday about my accompanying my grandfather during his trips into the open for defecating. In order to embellish it, I may have referred to it as my 'sentry duty'. Just imagine, that word, which extends its roots beyond so many centuries, and its embers, were adopted by my mind the moment I uttered it. Then, once its ashes were blown away, it was handed over to my brain to let it grow potent enough to burn down forests in dreams! The dream went like this: I was standing as a night sentry holding a flaming torch in one hand and a spear in the other under a large tree, which had many desiccated roots bursting out of the ground and hovering like serpents about to strike. I didn't know whom was I guarding. The heat and the smoke from the flambeau were unbearable. An ache, which could be described as agreeable, was building up in my legs. Through the shadows of the branches of that mammoth

> tree, a full moon of startling size could be seen. My head had started getting wet from the drops of moonlight falling on it. All of a sudden, dark clouds blanketed the moon. A terrific bolt of lightning struck the torch out of my hand and then struck the earth. For a moment, the world lay luminously before my eyes with a strange and profound beauty. Then, thunder crashed, deafening the ears of the pitch-blackness. As the torch had been extinguished as it fell from my hand, I could not locate it. Then, seeing an extraordinary flame of light high above in the tree, I looked up, tilting my head. Something heavy came down like a meteor, fell beside me and caught fire. It was a vulture with its wings aflame! With a burning heart, and trembling with fear, again I looked up into the tree. Horrified by the vision of a human shape burning from the lightning strike, wearing an iron torture chamber fitted like body armour and swinging slowly to and fro on the tree from which it was hanging, I woke up…

When Kunjuamma died, Chinnamma cried the loudest. However, those were not tears from a heart evolved enough to feel racked by the pain of bereavement. She bawled only as if to sustain the validity of a saying amongst the Thachanakkara folk: 'Ayyaattumpilli bawls its throat out'; that was all. Other than stealing glances at the gathered mourners, as she was bawling, and fearing that she would die of hunger during the prolonged and stultifying rituals, she was not capable of recognizing the unbearable emptiness created by the loss of the person who lay dead. More than her immaturity, the problem was the blood of Naraapilla, which flowed raucously through her heart and veins. In this matter, her brother Pankajaakshan, who had joined the police, was her male version—an arrant wild tree that had sprouted and ripened in the soil of Ayyaattumpilli. It was constable Raman Pillai, who was their neighbour on the east side, who had told Pankajaakshan about the physical tests for recruitment to the police that were taking place at the government school grounds at Aluva. Raman Pillai had returned to Thachanakkara after having served in many places at various times in the Thiru-Kochi state. Since 'Raambillapolice' was more feared than respected by the denizens of Thachanakkara, Pankajaakshan was nervous at the sight of him coming across as if he wanted to talk to him.

'Aren't you Naraapilla's son?' Raambilla, with bloodshot eyes and a twirled-up moustache, asked Pankajaakshan, surveying him from head to toe.

Pankajaakshan stood without confirming or denying, scratching the nape of his neck.

'Why? Aren't you sure?' Even in mufti, Raambilla retained his police manners.

'Yes,' Pankajaakshan was vexed with a suddenly dry mouth.

'What yes? That you are not sure, or that you are indeed the seed of Naraapilla?'

The dryness now reached Pankajaakshan's throat.

'Then you listen,' Raambilla said. 'They are recruiting policemen at Aluva School. Go with the papers of your educational qualifications, if you have any! Looking at your height and girth, it looks like you can wear khaki!'

Taking along a friend called Shankunni, Pankajaakshan went immediately to Aluva Government School and stood in queue for the physical tests of running and jumping. Unable to bear the heat of the sun and the weight of his own expectations simultaneously, and feeling faint, the friend retreated before the name Shankunni Nair could even be called out. However, in the shade of his enticing daydreams of wearing the khaki police uniform and thrashing all and sundry, Pankajaakshan held on without wilting. As per their instructions he ran, leaped, and won the imprimatur of the police. Thus, after Raambillapolice, Thachanakkara got a second policeman—Pankajaakshanpolice.

It was immediately after Govindan had moved residence to Cherai along with his girl that Pankajaakshan went to Kochi for his training following his recruitment. When he returned after his six-month training, on reaching the stile, he called out to Kunjuamma, 'Ammae, there's someone with me.'

'Who is it, your friend?' Kunjuamma asked seeing a flash of red through the gap in the fence.

'No, no,' Pankajaakshanpolice said, 'it's a female friend. My wife.'

The next person to speak was Naraapilla, who came out of the house, 'Do not enter! Both can go back the same way you came!'

'But then we're not two, there're three,' said Pankajaakshan bravely, climbing over the stile. 'The third person is here, in her womb.'

A comely girl wearing a silk saree appeared from behind the fence. That sight softened Naraapilla somewhat. 'Oh ho, now which genus is this one? Ezhava or Pulaya?'

'Nair from an aristocratic family. Genuine Menons from Kochi!' Holding her hand, Pankajaakshan entered Ayyaattumpilli.

When Kunjuamma died, Pankajaakshan and his wife Kalyanikuttyamma were not at Ayyaattumpilli. His father-in-law knew the manager of a tea plantation at Munnar. Enticed by the word honeymoon, which was gaining currency in Kochi lately, taking a week's leave, Pankajaakshan along with his wife gallivanted about in Munnar, abetted by the manager. In the house with a white door and window frames, and more glass windows than granite, arranged by the manager whose snuff-tinged reddish moustache and sprightliness belied his years, Pankajaakshan lay panting from his exertions of many hours of lovemaking, provoked by his wrong notion that his wife could be impressed by his staying powers—while his youngest brother, Chandran, was setting alight the pyre of Kunjuamma. At the very same moment, when the flames started to eat into his mother's left flank, unaware of all that and lost in the pleasure of the cool climate of Munnar, Pankajaakshan assured his new bride, 'When it comes to this feat, I am the real son of Naraapilla of Ayyaattumpilli!'

After all the efforts of Appu Nair to inform Pankajaakshan and bring him to Thachanakkara had failed, everyone concurred in the decision to cremate the body before it started to decay. Since they had left for Munnar without even bothering to say goodbye to his mother, who had started smashing her head against the walls and muttering deliriously, her death was the cause for a lifelong guilt for Pankajaakshan and his wife. The day he and his wife got back was the day of Sanchayanam, the day for the ritual of gathering the bones from the ashes. With his brow touching the burnt pyre, which looked tinier than his mother, Pankajaakshan cursed his wife silently. Kalyanikuttyamma, who knew how to pander to her husband, gradually survived those curses. Persuaded by the only daughter-in-law to move into Ayyaattumpilli, soon, Pankajaakshan moved to a small house built in the southern corner of the compound and started living there.

Thankamma, younger than the runaway Chandran, and older than Chinnamma, was married to Appu Nair's second son, Kumaran. Naraapilla bequeathed to Thankamma the old house that Menon Master and his family used to rent.

Kumaran had found a job in the FACT company in Eloor. After hearing that the company was hiring, he had gone there to try his luck, and returned proud with the title of the first company employee from Thachanakkara. It was to celebrate the news of his new job that he had come to Ayyaattumpilli along with his father, with toffees bought from Pooshaappi's shop. While describing his job, he tried to impress Naraapilla with words such as nitrate and ammonium sulphate.

'Which means real good fertilizers!' Appu Nair added with gravitas.

'But what's there in it to rejoice so much?' Naraapilla asked. 'Does it behove Nairs like us to work for wages for some third party?'

Appu Nair and his son looked at each other with misgivings.

'Umm, all right,' Naraapilla told Appu Nair. 'Go and check at Kaniyankunnu. Let's not delay his and Thankamma's wedding!'

Hearing that, Thankamma, who was watching her cousin through the gap in the window, laughed shyly with her toffee-smeared mouth. Feeling amazed at an unusual sweetness in those toffees, she pinched her younger sister.

In front of the shop in the name of Poovamparampath Shashvathanpilla alias Pooshaappi, his reformist son Kochu Parashu had put up a new board: 'Poovamparampath Stores'.

The board was painted by Artist Krishnan, the son of the local barber Aandi, who plied his trade making the rounds of all the houses in Thachanakkara. Not only did Krishnan not follow his father's trade, he also wore his hair long and planted a small board in front of his house that said 'Artist Krishnan'. The artist declared that he was not ready to go around houses cutting hair and cleaning up the armpits of all and sundry.

The new board painted by Artist Krishnan hid the dome of the sanctum sanctorum of the Thachanakkara temple from Pooshaappi's view. That gave him an indescribable relief. During afternoons bereft of customers, the sight of the round top pointed skywards, and the dome underneath that seemed to bulge out bigger and bigger every moment in the heat of the sun, used to discomfit him. As he sat on his two stools, he used to feel that the dome of the Thachanakkara thevar was withering his solitudes in the sun.

Two decades had passed after the Temple Entry Edict had come into force. Even then, the *avarnar* hesitated to enter the Thachanakkara temple and worship Parashuraman, the deity. Instead, they continued their practice of taking their sorrows to the Muthappan deity of the kavu at Kaniyankunnu to the west of Thachanakkara, where he had confined himself in maintaining a non-polluting distance from Parashuraman, whose axe he kept clear of. In front of the Muthappan kavu was Madhavachon's grocery store. Muthappan provided for the spiritual needs of the avarnar; Madhavachon looked after their physical needs. They were, like in the case of the Thachanakkara thevar's temple, afraid to enter Poovamparampath Shashvathanpilla's store as well. Only washerwoman Thaamara bought things from his store on cash and credit, though she had to stand at the bottom of the steps for that. Used as she was to washing the dirty laundry of the savarnar, Thaamara knew that in the matter of dirt and beauty, people were the same. The next one to come was indeed Artist Krishnan. As a voice inside him had been whispering to him that the status of an artist is one between God and man, he was untouched by fear.

When he heard that Artist Krishnan was going to Ernakulam to buy brushes, Kochu Parashu also accompanied him to procure high-quality fragrant soaps for the shop. As he was getting out after buying ten cakes each of Wellington and Rose of Kerala Soap Company, and twelve cakes of Chaavi brand soap of Godrej, the brown board on the building across caught Kochu Parashu's eye. Kochu Parashu felt he should capitalize on the opportunity—a chance to shock the young barber with his ability to read English.

Kochu Parashu read aloud: 'The National Furniture Co., Ernakulam, south India. For superior works in timber and metal, supplying electric materials, commission agents, ee tee cee, ee tee cee.'

'Et cetera, et cetera.' When Krishnan corrected Parashu's pronunciation of the last two words, Kochu Parashu was shocked. Barber Aandi's son was correcting his English!

'Shall we also keep one like this in front of your shop?' Krishnan asked. 'I will paint it for you; just give me the cost of the paint and the board.'

Kochu Parashu thought that it was a great idea. In future, that would serve him better, having something Madhavachon's did not have.

Writing the name of Pooshaappi's shop took up a whole Sunday. Till the last letter was written, a big gang of children hovered around Artist Krishnan, whose left thumb sported a nail as long as a magnolia petal. It was in large yellow letters that Krishnan wrote 'Poovamparampath Stores'. On his own accord, he had drawn a rooster's comb in red, right over the letter P, which came first. Kochu Parashu frowned in displeasure, assuming it was a spelling error, but was placated by the smiling Krishnan. 'That's the emblem of our shop. Haven't you seen the silver-trimmed conch on the Marthaanda Varma Bridge? Like that.'

After writing PRO followed by a colon, underneath the name, he asked, 'Now the proprietor's name. Whose name shall I write, yours or Pooshaappi chettan's?'

Kochu Parashu stood there, scratching his head. The children around him did not comprehend the dilemma that was going on inside that head. When he looked at his father sitting inside the shop, nodding off, suddenly the lighthouse of his childhood swirled in his head, providing illumination. It was not him alone, there were six other children who were clinging to his father's hand. His father's self-acquired wealth, in addition to the house and the shop.

'Let it be father's name,' Kochu Parashu said, 'Poovamparampath Shashwathan Pilla—write it fully.'

After writing the name split into three sections in white paint, Krishnan changed the initial letters alone into yellow. The children read only those: Poo … Sha … Pi.

They felt for Artist Krishnan the kind of veneration and feeling of distance that they felt only for the priest in the Thachanakkara thevar's temple.

By the time the board was taken up for hanging after the paint had dried, it was already afternoon. As it was being lifted up, spotting washerwoman Thaamara's daughter Ammu coming alone to the shop for the first time, Kochu Parashu paused for a moment and asked, 'What, lass, where is your mother today?'

'Amma has gone to Vettungal where that Kuttambilla chettan died,' Ammu said.

'Who, our Swadeshabhimani?' Setting the board down, Kochu Parashu shouted into the interior of the shop, 'Father, it seems our Kuttanpilla chettan is dead.'

After instructing Artist Krishnan to look after the shop, Kochu Parashu helped his father up and supported him down the steps to head towards the deceased's house.

Artist Krishnan got in and sat inside the shop. As Ammu stood at the bottom of the steps imitating her mother and called out for washing soda and 501 bar soap, Krishnan said, 'Come up and stand here, lass. Those days are over.'

With hands dotted with yellow and white paint, Krishnan gave her a bar of soap and a matching quantity of washing soda. The artist in him saw sweat painting dark blue peacock feathers in the arm pits of that beauty's light blue blouse.

'One day I'll paint you, including this birthmark on your face,' said Krishnan, while taking and putting the money into the till.

Inside that sweet seventeen-year-old, a drum ensemble rolled. She staggered when she heard Krishnan ask, 'Do you hear a sound?'

But Krishnan was listening to something in the distance. 'Can't you hear?' he asked again. 'Oh, today is the first of November. That must be the procession celebrating the founding day of our Kerala state. They may have reached the bridge now. They may come this way too. Do you want to see?'

Without replying to that, Ammu got out with the soap and washing soda. It was not that she did not want to see the celebrations of the changing times. But waiting for her at the riverbank was dirty laundry that was much more than what her mother could handle.

TWO

Seed

19 September 1999

...It's after ages that I am seeing a movie. When this art form, capable of depicting human form and genius at its acme, is being reduced to a farce with comedians who crack jokes indiscriminately, I am unable to enjoy the humour. If I sit and cry amidst people roaring with laughter, it would be even more farcical. But yesterday's film was not like that. Undoubtedly, he is one of the greatest actors of our times. This man, who seems very ordinary when he is standing, creates sheer poetry when he starts moving or when he delivers his dialogue. The story was that of a bond between the protagonist and his greying mother. But I could not enjoy it even a bit.

I don't know why I hate that actress who walks around with an eternal expression of maternal affection on her face, now frozen into a mask.

Only one child born to Kunjuamma was a spitting image of Naraapilla—that was their sixth child, Chinnamma. While the four boys, including the deceased Padmanabhan, and Thankamma were more or less an amalgam of the diversities of Kunjuamma and Naraapilla in varying degrees, the youngest daughter, Chinnamma, was cent per cent Naraapilla. The eldest son, Govindan, was the closest to his mother in nature and appearance. From there on, in the children, increasingly there was less of Kunjuamma and more of Naraapilla. In the sixth one, Chinnamma, Naraapilla was complete and Kunjuamma was missing.

Before a year had gone by after the death of Kunjuamma, an incident—which had been anticipated for long and for which all hope had been abandoned—occurred in Ayyaattumpilli: in her sixteenth year, Chinnamma experienced the onset of menarche.

It was four years since she had stopped going to school, troubled as she was with a persistent issue of her endemic worm attacks. It was Naraapilla himself who had named the child—with knobbly forehead, a large head, bulbous nose, and missing eyebrows—Chinnamma, on her twenty-eighth day, after ritually tying around her waist five beads made of gold, silver, copper, iron, and lead. At the time of her admission in Aalungal School, the headmaster Karunakara Menon, while entering her name in the attendance register, lifted up his head from the writing and told Naraapilla, 'A Christian child with the same name also has been admitted yesterday.'

'Oho,' said Naraapilla, 'then tell its father to change its name quickly.'

Initially, when everyone used to say that the child resembled him, Naraapilla used to misconstrue that as a compliment to his looks. On such occasions, with a fondness not bestowed on his other offspring, he used to gather up his youngest daughter in his arms indulgently and utter, with a loopy grin, a phrase—which had obscure origins and which could be taken to mean 'my youngest'—'embilla elava'.

Chinnamma traversed the tricky terrains of female adolescence like a champion. Govindan, who was beaten by Naraapilla for swimming in the Periyar river and had hit him back, had unknowingly seized from his father a right for his younger siblings—the right to cavort in the Aluva river to their hearts' content. Naraapilla did not beat his children for the crime of bathing in the river again. Because of that, before she turned nine, Chinnamma had acquired the prowess to swim across the river to Uliyanoor and swim back even before she managed to get her breath back. Once she tried to clamber aboard a houseboat headed for Varappuzha, which was moving with the help of sails and was loaded with vegetables. Finding a favourable wind unexpectedly after a long stint at punting the boat, the boatmen had just hoisted the patched sail. After laying down the long bamboo punts in the boat, the young men were smoking beedis and chatting, sitting on the edge of the plank on which banana bunches had been stacked. One of them, while dipping the small oar in the water to steer the boat, saw someone trying to board the boat from one side. It was Chinnamma. As he rushed along the length of the boat to push the intruder off using the oar, Chinnamma yanked the oar along with him and pulled them both into the water. The enraged man managed to swim to the oar, catch hold of it and shove it into the boat, before he turned to face the intruder in the water. In the struggle that ensued, the opponent lost her thorth, the only piece of cloth on her, alarming the astonished young man who let go of her in panic and clambered back into the boat, to warn his fellow boatman at the sail. 'Ayye, that's a woman, Mammad!'

Making up for the arrears of her father, who had avoided the waters of the river for an inordinate length of time, Chinnamma continued to bathe in Punneli kadavu. With the death of Kunjuamma, the reins on Chinnamma had come undone completely. Her fellow water-maiden was Leela of the Muringaattil family, who lived five houses away from Ayyaattumpilli. In the company of Leela, a stick-like emaciated figure with the face of an owl and a voice like a cracked bell, Chinnamma swam to the land of Perumthachchan countless times.

It was the day that they brought home bundles of red spinach stolen from Uliyanoor, planted and tended by unknown Mappila Muslims. As they walked down the alley, to those who looked at them and the spinach bunches in their hands suspiciously, Chinnamma and Leela said, 'A Mappila threw this for us from the other bank. If you go quickly, all of you will also get some!'

'Which Mappila flings them this far?' the washerwoman Thaamara wondered aloud, while she was walking towards the kadavu, with soiled clothes in light red plastic buckets and a washing soap bar with the 777 brand prominently written on it. With her was Ammu with the beetle on her cheek, a nubile seventeen-year-old.

As the flushed, drenched girls ran with effort, they laughed and made up a name on a lark, 'Perumthachchan Mappila.'

While Muringaattil Leela had lunch with spinach curry that afternoon, what awaited Chinnamma was the fury of Naraapilla. After grinding the stolen spinach underfoot, Naraapilla broke off a branch from the tamarind tree and whipped Chinnamma brutally. The tamarind stick landed on the wet skirt with the sound of crackers going off. Embilla elava writhed in pain. Naraapilla's eyes bulged; he gnashed his teeth; he trembled in his rage. 'You good-for-nothing!' he said. 'Do you think you can do anything just because your mother is dead?'

It was the first time Chinnamma was getting a beating from her father after her mother's death. As she was bawling, recognizing the truth that she had become an orphan, she felt miserable. When the tamarind stick broke, Naraapilla threw it away and stomped off in fury. Alarmed at the fear of her father flowing down her thighs, she ran to the latrine at the southern end of the compound. Her youth was emerging, breaking free of the cocoon of adolescence. The tender and colourful wings of femininity were unfurling painfully. Her womanhood, delayed by years, was squeezing her tight so as to extract the last drop. Trembling and standing with her legs apart, she screamed loud enough to be heard in the old house, 'Chechi, please come quickly…' Bending and peering down between her legs once more, she leant her head against the latrine wall and shouted again, 'It looks as if the damned thing has come!'

Rushed by her sister's shouts, Thankamma reached the New House, and the first thing she saw was the red spinach on the floor crushed into a pulp by her father. From there, on the beaten path in the grass winding southward, she saw droplets of blood scattered like seeds of the coral bead tree. Following their trail, she reached the latrine.

'Don't crow!' Though she was older by only two years, with a maturity forced on her by her married life, Thankamma scolded her sister, 'Crowing and announcing are for the hens.'

Chinnamma sat in the latrine for the next three hours. When Thankamma checked on her every now and then as her sister sat straining with the unending flow, she spied on her dark thighs and buttocks the welts left by the tamarind branch.

'So that was what was lacking for her all this while,' Thankamma mused to herself.

Informed by Thankamma, by evening Appu Nair and his wife arrived from Peechamkurichi and made a few arrangements for the *therandukalyanam*, the menarche ceremony. In the room in the southern corner of the New House, on a rug folded in four and covered with a starched white sheet, the maiden was seated like an accused, holding a brass handheld mirror. Her face wore an inscrutable expression those days, due the persistence of the painful spasms on the one hand and the excitement of unexpectedly becoming the centre of everyone's attention on the other. Her upper lip appeared to be smiling even as her lower lip seemed to weep. Muringaattil Leela, mourning the break in water games in Punneli kadavu, and a brass pot filled with paddy in which a coconut flower had been planted, sat beside Chinnamma as her constant companion for the next four days. As per the tradition, the women in the neighbourhood visited, carrying beaten rice and plantains. Hearing of a girl attaining menarche in Thachanakkara, the velathi women from Muppaththadam arrived on the third day, with a change of clothes for the menstruating girl, and to sing the song of menarche. An innocuous couplet sung by these washerwomen, through teeth that protruded as if by their constant singing, got stuck in Chinnamma's mind.

...Aren't Mother and Step-mother listening
We are singing glories of your daughter dearest!

Chinnamma was drinking a tumbler full of warm milk after a long time. When the song reached this couplet, she wiped her mouth, belched, handed the tumbler back to Thankamma and said, 'Our mother too should've been here now, no, chechi?'

At that moment, the spirit of Kunjuamma possessed Thankamma. Holding her younger sister close, the elder sister said, 'Am I not there for you? Am I not your mother?'

Though Thankamma, from the standpoint of a mother, had instructed Chinnamma on accepted feminine ways, Chinnamma broke them at every possible turn. When she climbed the tree on the sly to pluck hog plums, the tender branch broke and she fell down. With no second thoughts, she left blood-stained menstrual cloth on top of the heap of the dirty linen waiting to be given to the washerwoman. On the day she frolicked till dusk in Punneli kadavu, an otter bit the calf of her leg. Anxious months went by. As her biological clock was fickle, her monthly periods were irregular. It was Thankamma who felt all the pressure.

She shared her anxiety about her sister with her husband: 'Her therandukalyanam got delayed anyway,' said Thankamma one night. 'There's nothing we can do about it. But at least we should get her married off without further delay!'

Kumaran smiled in the dark thinking of an amazing coincidence. He remembered the dark and slim Shankaran who was with him in the Communist Party study class in a room in the primary school in Eloor, which was still under construction. Kannan Master who was taking the class, spraying his spittle everywhere, was talking of a country called Cuba, its ruler Batista, and a brave young man called Fidel Castro who had declared total war against Batista. As he was wiping the back of his neck with his thorth, while insisting that the first election in Kerala was a war akin to that, Kannan Master saw the face of a young man sitting at the back contorting with pain. Shankaran stood up holding the bandaged middle finger of his trembling right hand with his left fist. After first scolding him for ignoring the finger that had been caught in a machine, Kannan Master sent him off to the hospital, instructing Shankaran and another comrade—Kumaran—to accompany him.

Returning from the hospital after the finger was stitched up and bandaged, Shankaran gave Kumaran a précis of his life story. Meanwhile, a brown colour secretion that smelt like a millipede was oozing from within and turning the white bandage dark. That was the beginning of a close relationship between Kumaran and Shankaran, which was to stretch into many years in the future. When they were finally wrapping up the day and getting ready to go their separate ways, realizing it was necessary, Kumaran asked him a question which workers engaged in a class struggle would normally not ask each other: 'Not that it matters, but what caste are you? Nair?'

Shankaran smiled. 'I don't know my caste. But I am sure that my father and mother are Nairs!'

Lying beside Thankamma in the dark, Kumaran was marvelling at that day. Though he did not have the wisdom to appreciate the astonishing process chosen by Time to blend two strains of blood, unwittingly, he became the catalyst for such a merger. Three weeks later, an impromptu ceremony of seeing the prospective bride took place in Ayyaattumpilli, without anyone's foreknowledge. Pointing to Chinnamma, who had come out at dusk to sweep the yard of the New House with a broom made of the spines of coconut leaflets, Kumaran urged his friend, 'Take a good look. That's the girl.'

As she was serving steamed banana cuts and jaggery-sweetened coffee to the guest, Thankamma's heart was beating wildly. Looking through the window at Chinnamma, who was cursing herself as she swept the yard of the neighbouring house, the impoverished young man popped a piece of steamed banana into his mouth and said indistinctly, 'Not as bad as I imagined!'

Kumaran and Thankamma were in the forefront to get Naraapilla's permission and to invite the Thachanakkara folk for the wedding. Except for going to Cherai to invite Govindan, Naraapilla assented to everything. Thus in 1957, in front of Thachanakkara thevar, the communist Shankaran married Chinnamma, who stood wearing eight sovereigns of gold. Under the tent put up in Ayyaattumpilli was a feast for all the folk of Thachanakkara. The paayasam for the feast was made with jaggery. The groom's emaciated mother and younger sister, with elephantiasis on her right leg, stood on either side of the bride, holding her hands throughout the ceremony. Unaware of what was expected of them during such ceremonies, this was an escape route to which the hapless women had clung. To accept the wedding puduva which Shankaran was extending towards her on a brass plate, Chinnamma shook off both their hands, protesting, 'Can you let go now? Let me accept this. How else!' As if its continuation, Naraapilla, apparently to make conversation with them, bent down low and told the mother who was fanning her mouth with pappadam to assuage the heat of the chilli, and her daughter who was licking the curry made with sweet bananas, 'Shovel in and eat your fill! I don't have another daughter to hold a marriage feast for!'

The tent held many people willing to laugh at the misery of those distressed women.

In the month of Dhanu that year, under the aegis of Thankamma, a *poothiruvaathira*, which is the first thiruvaathira celebration of a bride after her wedding, was held in Ayyaattumpilli. All the women of Thachanakkara took part in the dance performed for attaining everlasting marital bliss, in which women danced moving in a circular pattern while clapping hands and singing, for twelve nights starting from the day of *thiruvonam* and lasting till *thiruvaathira*. On the portico of the New House, Naraapilla's two communist sons-in-law sat watching the performance without demurring. Though Appu Nair's son Kumaran had seen thiruvaathirakali performances before, for Chinnamma's husband, Shankaran, this was something new. The sound of the tender palms of the women clapping was closer to the sound that the mature tamarind fruits made, pattering en masse when shaken out of the trees. Kumaran had learnt by heart the names of eight things needed for the offering called *ettangaadi* during the makayiram fasting, which he had to buy from the Aluva market, from the shopping list his wife gave him. But Kochu Parashu, Pooshaappi's son, surprised him one day, appearing with a bursting gunny bag, before the dance began. As yam, greater yam, lesser yam, long beans, coleus, and colocasia tumbled out of the gunny bag when Kochu Parashu emptied it, he told the women, 'Here is the stuff for the ettangaadi. It's all on me, for my pleasure!'

When compared, the condiments to the list of eight things he had learnt by rote he found some missing, Kumaran queried, 'But then, where are the coconuts and plantains?'

'O.' Kochu Parashu stroked Kumaran's shoulder and laughed. 'Do I have to bring plantains and coconuts for Naraapilla chettan's house?'

As she swayed artlessly to either side along with the other women dancing in a circle around the lighted lamp, to impress her husband, Chinnamma's full-throated voice accompanied the others in the thiruvaathira songs being sung. Next to her, Muringaattil Leela, her mate in water games, was circling the nilavilakku lamp with a face that reflected envy, and as if only to warm herself in the chill of the nights of Dhanu. But her indifference was just an impression. Even as she was physically accompanying the chorus, she was perfecting a new thiruvaathira song within her, which she had learnt over the previous two weeks with great effort, in order to make her friend's poothiruvaathira memorable. As stage fright held her back the first ten nights, and as more songs were necessary to keep everyone awake on the night of thiruvaathira, that unexpected miracle happened.

Eleyelo...
eleyelo, eleyelo, eleyelo
thaam thaka thaam!

The sound rose from within the circle of women as if from a cracked temple bell. That was Muringaattil Leela. The women in the circle, taken aback by this new entrant, nevertheless took up the chorus. Though her inspiration almost drained her, she sang in a fast tempo, impressing her fellow dancers more by her improvised lyrics that tickled her fellow dancers into laughter more than by her singing voice:

Rapid on seas, a mercantile ship
Dropped anchor in eventide

Cutlery-plates-blankets-whisky
Matchboxes-kerosene-mull mull
These and sundries unloaded on shore
Reached the middle of the Atlantic Ocean...

Chinnamma was the one who enjoyed the song the most. She was at the end of her tether after singing the praises of Lord Ganapathi and Goddess Saraswathi continuously. She felt unmoved by the romantic songs that the women of Thachanakkara had always been singing. However, she felt that Leela's song, the provenance and authorship of which were completely unknown, was written specifically for her honeymoon. She also felt as if she and Leela were swimming in an ocean, and overtaking a sailing ship that was leaving behind two lines of white froth in its wake. As the other women were laughing it away as a joke, Chinnamma, immersed in her friend's song, was sweating with the pleasure that the song gave her even in the chill of Dhanu. Another person who enjoyed the song with the same gusto was Naraapilla, who was sitting half asleep on the portico of the New House. Days after the thiruvaathira was over, he continued to remember her every now and then: 'You know, that girl from Muringaattil? She's smart!'

Five months later, Naraapilla had to say the same sentence in past tense. That was the day Muringaattil Leela disappeared, leaving behind a white mildewed dress, a torn green skirt, and a piece of washing soap on the ghat of the Periyar river. Though boats and canoes searched for her up to Varappuzha, her body was never found. As an expert swimmer, a death by drowning seemed unlikely for her. Many had seen the nubile girl, past the age of marriage, going alone for her bath towards the river. Anyone who looked at the tattered relics left by her on the kadavu could easily guess how, with no one to wait for her, no one to want her and no place to anchor in, Leela could have taken her life deep into the recesses of the river.

'All said and done, that girl from Muringaattil was a smart one!' standing on the kadavu, Naraapilla said with a face that seemed to curse the flowing river.

Hugging Shankaran, Chinnamma cried the whole of that night, tearlessly.

THREE

The Decade

10 April 1999

...After the phase of reading children's stories is over and done with, it is by searching for sexual content within the pages that most people begin their reading of serious literature. The literature that is available in the school texts being winnowed and cleaned of all desires, the reader would have scant regard for literature during his school days. As for the history in the educational texts, it would, unfortunately exhibit closer links with mathematics than human life. Except nausea, it can create little. However, for the sake of three or four sentences touching upon the secrets of male and female bodies, scattered randomly in the book, a thirteen-year-old may finish reading a three-hundred-page work of literature in three days' time. And if it is a history book that is given to him? He will start yawning. Scratching his crazed head, he will keep looking around. Someone inside him will keep reminding him that it is only the sexuality of the dead that can be gleaned from history. He will be least interested in unearthing the dead bodies of beautiful damsels from between the lines.

Dearest girl, do not be upset with this repeated use of 'for him, for him, for him'! To write 'for her', some changes will have to take place.

I am writing this by keeping this sheet of paper on a two-day-old newspaper. In it is the picture of President K.R. Narayanan inaugurating the C. Achutha Menon Memorial Study Centre at Poojappura.

From the time of Chinnamma's wedding to the first delivery of her child ten years later, the world outside Thachanakkara was going through stupendous changes. It was in the year that the first communist ministry was formed in Kerala under the leadership of E.M. Sankaran Namboodiripad, popularly known as EMS, when Shankaran Nair entered Ayyaattumpilli as Chinnamma's husband. Ten years later, in 1967, when EMS came to power again, Chinnamma, taken to be a barren woman throughout Thachanakkara for a decade, uttered some new words unheard in lullabies, with her four-cubit-long tongue. From the *Mathrubhumi* newspaper that Kalyanikuttyamma, wife of Pankajaakshan, had started subscribing to, many new words and names had vaulted over the stile of Ayyaattumpilli: the birth of the Kerala state, vimochanasamaram or liberation struggle, Periyar Water Irrigation Project, Sputnik, general election, Khrushchev, Angamaly Crypt, Fidel Castro, Mannathu Padmanabhan and the NSS, President's Rule, Explorer, Baghdad Pact, Kennedy, Atom Bomb, China border, Indira Gandhi, Kantambechcha Coat, R. Shankar, Cuba, old-age pension, Kwame Nkrumah, Armistice, Yuri Gagarin, Kerala Congress, Sirimavo Bandaranaike, and the Communist Party split, were all part of those interesting words. Stuttering on the neologism of 'seven-party coalition', EMS ascended to power for the second time, when with Chinnamma's first delivery, a girl, was born to Shankaran the communist. This was the only remote connection that Naraapilla's Ayyaattumpilli had with Kerala history.

'All babies stay inside the stomach for ten months,' Chinnamma used to say every time she scolded her eldest daughter, Geetha, 'but you alone stayed for ten years, your majesty!'

During those ten years in which she did not conceive, many rumours were being spread about Chinnamma in Thachanakkara. At first, everyone thought that the revulsion or indifference wrought by Muringaattil Leela's death was the reason why her menstrual periods were not halting. But, eventually, her husband Shankaran, and later the rumour-mongers, realized that, apart from letting out an open-mouthed bawl like she had at the death of her mother, she was unaffected by any deep sorrow when she came to know of Leela's death. The people of Thachanakkara saw Chinnamma forcing her apparently unromantic communist husband to learn swimming in the very same river in which the wavelets created by the boats and canoes zipping about in desperate search for Leela had not subsided; and they were surprised at how Chinnamma was laughing heartily, while returning with him, wet and flushed. When Shankaran was ashamed to discover himself cavorting in the river in a manner not befitting a working-class man and tried to escape by reminding her of her best friend Leela, Chinnamma's response debased the memory of her dead friend, quite undeservedly. Pushing out her eyes, which looked as if Indian nightshade had been applied on them, bloodshot from diving with eyes open, she dismissed her old swimming mate. 'What's wrong with you? Those who're dead are dead!'

Muringaattil Leela, who had not been noticed by anyone nor desired by any man in Thachanakkara while she was alive, had begun to reign in the Periyar as a person to reckon with, after her death. Washing clothes one afternoon, washerwoman Thaamara's daughter Ammu felt that something like a woman's finger touched her on the calf of her leg. That touch ignited unprecedented discussions about life after death in Thachanakkara. Waking up from a nap one afternoon, Pooshaappi saw with sleep-startled eyes, the dead Swadeshabhimani Kuttan Pilla weeping as he stood in front of his shop with a torn umbrella and a dented vessel used for carrying rice gruel. But Kochu Parashu, who did not like anyone—even the dead—coming to the shop other than for buying something, insisted that it was a hallucination of his rapidly-aging father. The noteworthy question raised by Kochu Parashu was, if the dead were to visit friends again, how was it possible for Naraapilla's daughter Chinnamma to swim fearlessly in Punneli kadavu, without bumping into Muringaattil Leela? Nevertheless, that interrogation mark, which was bent a little too far, snapped shortly. One by one, accounts were emerging, confirming the popular assumption that Muringaattil Leela, whom Periyar river had consumed without even giving up her body, had started laying hands on unmarried young women bathing at the Punneli kadavu. Women staying near the river began to lose sleep over sounds heard at midnight, echoes of Leela beating her tattered skirt on the washing stone, standing naked in the river. Many housewives clearly heard the song starting with 'eleyelo', which Leela had sung for Chinnamma's first thiruvaathira, even amidst all the din created by the famished and jealous foxes in the bushes near Punneli kadavu who, with howls that went on for hours together on full-moon nights, futilely tried to heckle into submission the moon in its full glory. Swadeshabhimani Kuttan Pilla's granddaughter, the eighteen-year-old Sarala, who had inherited her grandfather's penchant for exaggeration, shuddered at the sight of Leela's face with eyes melting like wax, when she opened her own eyes in the water while bathing in the river. With strands of her hair floating up in the light-green, glassy water, Leela smiled at Sarala.

'Your marriage is fixed, no? Lucky dame!' With each syllable sending up a huge bubble, Leela said with a voice that seemed to resound as if she had spoken into a copper water pot.

'She's even come to know of the news of my marriage,' scrambling out of the river with trembling limbs, Sarala told her aunt who had also come along to bathe. 'Even after she's dead, her jealousy has not lessened! The corpse!'

It was Naraapilla, who did not bathe in the river, who was most vexed by the legends about Muringaattil Leela's post-death antics in the water. Even during his morning bath at the Thachanakkara thevar's pond, he used to go underwater only with his eyes tightly shut. Nevertheless, during those three or four minutes between staying under water and breaking surface, Kunjuamma would appear suddenly in the morass of green algae bloom, smiling with a face which oozed blood drops bubbling up into the boiling mirage above, and tell him a different thing each time: what was to be made for lunch; that Padmanabhan had a bad fever; asking him if he would have some spiced buttermilk; or worrying that their Chinnamma had still not had her menarche. Naraapilla thus came to understand that the thoughts of the dead concerned only those things that took place till the time of their death. To prevent the dead worrying over things that time had solved unknown to them, once again he went to see the senior astrologer, climbing Kaniyankunnu along with Appu Nair. The omen was clear to the senior astrologer as soon as he saw the two sixty-plus men coming towards the house.

'Which wife is making trouble?' The elder astrologer looked into both the faces. 'The living or the dead?'

'The deceased one!' said Appu Nair. 'Wasn't it my younger sister that Naraapilla had married? It's many years since she departed. But he still does see her sometimes!'

'Perhaps the deceased hadn't done enough loving!' said the elder astrologer, rotating his index finger and eyes simultaneously while trying to dig out a tiny blob of ear wax that had been tormenting him, from the depths of his left ear. 'Now what we must do is take good care of the dead one's offspring. Convince the deceased that everything is being looked after well, leaving no stone unturned. Should also completely give up the things that would have displeased the dead when alive. Understood?'

Naraapilla did not understand. Coming down Kaniyankunnu, Appu Nair interpreted the elder diviner's words for Naraapilla. Ahead of them, a herd of buffaloes was moving. Needlessly whipping their shiny backs that looked as if they were oiled, and enjoying it, was a cheruman boy, a low-caste cowherd. Naraapilla, who was listening carefully to Appu Nair's interpretation, patted the boy's back and asked, 'Why are you laughing over it?' Going past the boy, who stood baffled, unable to make out the significance of that friendly gesture, Naraapilla and Appu Nair took the turn towards Thachanakkara.

Following the next harvest and threshing, Kaalippennu did not get permission to stay on in the anteroom. Behind Naraapilla's back, people said that it was because she was ageing. But Naraapilla's communist sons-in-law, Thankamma's husband Kumaran and Chinnamma's husband Shankaran, saw it differently. Thankamma was going through a bad patch, following the loss of her third pregnancy, after delivering two. Her womb had, in the sixth month, ejected a stillborn boy who was supposed to keep company for the elder two daughters. Though she did not get the baby, post-natal care had to be given as per tradition. While eating rice sprinkled with fried onions and turmeric, to heal the inside of the womb and the cervix, baring her yellowed teeth and lips, she found out about things from her husband.

'Your father is cleverer than I thought,' said Kumaran, getting ready to go for the second shift by dabbing Cuticura talcum powder behind his shirt collar. 'He knows that all this fun will end when our party comes to power again. Didn't Kaalippennu build a hut in the corner of the Muttattaali field? By law, that now belongs to Kaalippennu. It's your father's luck that Comrade EMS's government fell within two years, following the *Vimochanasamaram*. Or else, all of Muttattaali field would have gone to Kaalippennu and other low-caste comrades!'

'To our luck, you should say!' Thankamma corrected him, listening to the joyous sounds of her two girls playing a game juggling pebbles on the porch.

'We should have only what is needed to fill our children's tummies. Let those who do not have anything get what is surplus. Isn't it better?' said Kumaran, tucking in his mundu securely before heading out.

'I don't think that's so great. God, don't let this man's Communist Party ever come to power!' said Thankamma.

Next door, at the New House, Thankamma's sister Chinnamma was untouched by such anxieties. As she did not have children yet, Shankaran's salary itself seemed to be a lot for Chinnamma. Imitating her sister-in-law, Kalyanikuttyamma, she began making tea for her husband in the morning and dosa and puttu for breakfast, instead of day-old rice gruel. Hearing that in places such as Kochi, people had begun to make different dishes for breakfast, Chinnamma too decided to introduce those in her house. Waking up at six, she cleared the ash from the stove, sprinkled it with water and pushed in fresh firewood into the stove. She lighted the kerosene-sprinkled dry coconut frond midribs with the pieces of paper that had come as wrapping for groceries from the shop. Blowing through a broken iron pipe that made a sound like that of a damaged conch shell, she made the fire flare. White smoke like clouds about to melt wafted up above the tiles of the New House, which had started to blacken with moss, and began to become visible in the gentle rays of the early morning sun as Chinnamma's kitchen woke up and yawned.

The day Kaalippennu left Ayyaattumpilli for good, Shankaran told his wife with a half-smile, as she pushed firewood into the stove, 'Whatever you might say, that woman was a good match for your father!'

From the time Pankajaakshan's wife, who was from Kochi, began to get the newspaper delivered at Ayyaattumpilli for the first time, the roar of the waves of history from afar began to be heard in Ayyaattumpilli too. For Thankamma and Chinnamma, Kalyanikuttyamma of Kochi was Kalluchechi. Pankajaakshan's plot alone stood in the middle of Ayyaattumpilli with a bamboo fence all around it—another habit imported from Kochi—amongst the other plots that had survived without fences and pales, even though they had already been partitioned. Though she was loved as a sister-in-law, Thankamma thought for a while that everything Kalluchechi said was a flagrant lie. Part of it was that hundreds of Jews, who had lived in central Kerala for centuries, had departed with their children, and other encumbrances, in a ship bound for a country called Israel. As Kalyanikuttyamma insisted that it happened just two years before she was married and brought to Ayyaattumpilli, Thankamma felt that the chances of it being a lie were four-fold. However, since the newspaper began to come to Pankajaakshan's house, Thankamma became certain that things stranger than fiction were happening in the world outside. In the afternoons, Thankamma went to her sister-in-law's and lapped up everything in *Mathrubhumi*. Through Thankamma, Time was taking revenge for something which could not be done through Kunjuamma. She read from the newspaper that Jordan's King Hussein had suppressed the rebels who raised their voices for Egypt, and to help King Hussein, America had sent their sixth naval battalion to the Mediterranean, relishing it like a war story that someone had put together in the days of yore. The newspaper had started to influence her so much that the day after she read about Soviet Union sending a dog to space, she nagged her husband to get her a dog as a pet. After scouring for two weeks, finally Kumaran was able to bring to Ayyaattumpilli a puppy, whisked away from a bitch nursing her litter near the riverbank. The day Naraapilla broke its front legs with one kick for the crime of having licked his feet, Thankamma too had a thorny fence built around her plot to protect her dear possessions from her father.

Fences were chopping up Ayyaattumpilli into several pieces. Except for the dead Padmanabhan and the runaway Chandran, Naraapilla had divided his house plots and fields amongst his surviving four children—including Govindan who had become a resident of Cherai: he had the deeds drawn, and sat smug for having done his duty. Over half an acre of a house plot on the eastern boundary and half of the Kainikkulam field at Paanaayikkulam were set aside for Govindan. It was an act done as per the advice of the elder astrologer of Kaniyankunnu, to please Kunjuamma who kept coming to show her face in the temple pond. But traders like Kochu Parashu of the new generation interpreted this apportioning as a pre-emptive action on the part of Naraapilla, foreseeing the implementation of new laws by the communist government likely to come to power again.

In 1967, when a victory parade marched through Thachanakkara to celebrate the day of ascension of the EMS ministry, at the vanguard were the two sons-in-law of Naraapilla. At that time, Chinnamma who was washing her hair in the Punneli kadavu noticed big bubbles taking turns to come up to the surface and bursting with a sound resembling a cracked bronze bell saying 'Oh God!' She stopped washing her hair to dive underneath to find out about the source of that familiar voice. She recognized the pale form of Muringaattil Leela sitting in the lotus position on the riverbed, chanting the names of gods. With each utterance of 'Oh God', a bubble rolled up from her mouth. Unable to bear the suspense, Chinnamma touched Leela. Leela, who looked the same age she was ten years ago, opened her eyes, grinned to show her broken tooth and said, 'And finally you too have become pregnant, no? Lucky dame!'

When Shankaran arrived late in the night, Chinnamma pressed his hand, which still smelt of firecrackers, to her belly and and told him about her first conception. When she told him that during her afternoon nap she dreamt of bathing in the river and Muringaattil Leela had congratulated her on her pregnancy, Shankaran laughed the laugh of a communist.

However, Chinnamma was right. Shankaran saw that she had vomited out the mouthful of river water she had brought in from her dream during her afternoon nap near the sleeping mat. After misleading Thachanakkara for ten years about being barren, Chinnamma was going to bear a child.

Jithendran's eldest sister, Geetha was in the womb. Time was in a hurry. But only after the delivery of Geetha in sixty-eight, Rema in seventy, and an abortion in seventy-one, could Jithen be born in seventy-two.

FOUR

Siam Weed

1 May 1999

...Hadn't you asked me why I don't write about my father? It is on purpose. A person who regrets that today is a dry day on account of it being May Day, has no right to even reminisce about him, let alone write about him. It has always surprised me that a green plant with the power to heal wounds quickly is called *appa* in our region. (I forgot to ask you: do you call your father appa?) Another, rather interesting, name for appa is Communist Pachcha. This Siam weed, which used to grow abundantly once upon a time in the fallow lands of Thachanakkara, may perhaps appear in tomorrow's markets as a medicine that can keep the cash counters ringing. What was I talking about? Oh, yes, my father. In the first half of the century, following the disappearance of the matrilineal system and the ensuing division of property, when Nair joint families were split up rendering young men rudderless, many ended up as tiller-holders in the communist movement, intoxicated by revolutionary spirit, whereas a few others who were less gifted—like my Siam weed father—thrived on account of being married into families like those in Thachanakkara. Though they had not read the red books, it was the inner calling—that a worker earning his livelihood by himself, merits dignity—that made them lean naturally towards communism. The blood and stool of such savarnars could be tested against the single phrase of 'the dictatorship of the proletariat'.

Poovamparampath Shashwathanpilla alias Pooshaappi didn't live long enough to hear the first radio of Thachanakkara, sitting in his shop, chattering non-stop about the Land Reforms Act. Pooshaappi, whose testicles used to ache while listening to historical tales, died on his son Kochu Parashu's fifty-eighth birthday, when his soul escaped along with a burp after the feast.

'Father had no illness,' Kochu Parashu told all the mourners who had come for the cremation, till his mouth ran dry. 'When he got up to wash after eating to his heart's content, I held his hand. Since he had that problem, he had difficulty walking, no? Saying "I am feeling very sleepy, Kochu Parashuve," he burped with a strange sound. One couldn't tell if it was a burp or a yawn—it was that kind of a noise. To cut the story short, he didn't fall down because I was holding him, fortunately!'

For the last ten years, Pooshaappi had lived in the house built by his son and heir apparent to the shop, Kochu Parashu. He had been the upright trunk of a big family tree with sons for branches and grandchildren for twigs. All his seven children, including the youngest son Phalgunan, who usurped the original tharavaad when the partition of the property was done, had become white-haired. They had started their squabbles over property, cursing their dead mother, challenging their extant father, and living as if they were weighed down by being dragged into some vexing moral struggle. The six younger siblings suffered severe heartburn over the coveted piece of land on which the shop stood, adjacent to the Thachanakkara temple grounds, being given to Kochu Parashu. Those siblings conveniently forgot that it was Kochu Parashu's sweat and efforts that had transformed a tiny grocery store into a shopping complex big enough to let even its premises be known, in later years, as Pooshaappi Corner. It was while old Pooshaappi was still healthy enough to sit in the shop and wrap and tie the condiments, that his wife, Sarojiniamma, younger than him by twenty years, felt dizzy and fell in the kitchen to her death. From that day onwards, the next ten years of his life were spent on the cot in Kochu Parashu's house. In his shrunken, desiccated body, his soul was still blooming. Except for the tremors in his limbs and forgetfulness, and hallucinations about the dead calling on him, his mind was none the worse for the ravages of his geriatric state. Naraapilla and Appu Nair and the other recently-aged folk of Thachanakkara would come occasionally and sit around his bed and chat. In his body, which was withering from the unbearable heat of the fear of death that accompanies old age, his testicles still continued to grow. During his last days, his demeanour was that of a hapless chameleon, beleaguered by peckings received for hiding, between his legs, large eggs that he had filched from some mammoth bird. When Naraapilla and Appu Nair came to visit him four days before his death, he woke up with a start, as if from his previous life, having smelt fragrant tobacco, and looked at them.

'Ayyo, Naraapilla.' With his tongue tremulous in his toothless mouth bereft of saliva, Pooshaappi said, 'I forgot to buy your fragrant tobacco today also!'

'It's sixteen years since I stopped chewing paan, Pooshaappiye,' Naraapilla reminded him. After struggling for some time to make sense of things, and then reading Appu Nair's face suddenly gone gloomy with the thoughts of his youngest sister, Pooshaappi said, 'So, it's so many years since Kunjuamma left us, isn't it? What kind of sleep have I been sleeping?'

The public of Thachanakkara forgot Pooshaappi the moment he let his life escape in the midst of an indeterminate yawn or burp. Instead, they continued calling his son Kochu Parashu 'Pooshaappi', as if it was an inheritable title. Sitting beside Kochu

Parashu on the stool used by Pooshaappi to support his testicles, a radio with big knobby-eyes taught new words to the denizen of Thachanakkara. Some of these words such as K.C. Pant, Ninth Schedule, Land Tribunal, etc., were beyond the understanding of the new generation who came to listen to film songs.

Time was standing like a four-legged creature, swishing its tail and staring at the people of Thachanakkara, with its hind legs planted in memories, and forelegs in hope.

Building two more rooms on either side of the store, Kochu Parashu gave it the wings of progress. Shivan, Aandi's youngest son—and the fourth after Krishnan, who had thrown away the barber's scissors and turned artist—had rented the room at the south end for fifteen rupees and started a barbershop. When Aandi died, Shivan brought the surviving tonsorial implements and a new mirror as big as a winnowing tray, and installed them in the shop. If it was Aandi's eldest son, Artist Krishnan, who had painted the board for Poovamparampath Stores, it was his eldest son, Babu, who repainted that old board appending Pooshaappi Buildings to it after the passage of many years. With the remaining paint, on the front wall of his uncle's shop, he also painted 'Shivan's Barbershop' with the letters vertically arranged. Then, more with artistic freedom than the liberty of a relative, he also painted the picture of Lord Shiva with his matted hair, beneath the lettering.

The big room adjacent to the barbershop fitted with a door at the back and a makeshift kitchen added to it as a lean-to, made up Vengooran Thankappan's teashop. In that shop, inside a glass almirah, about half a dozen each of parippu vada and uzhunnų vada lay at all times like pitiable little orphans. The shop owner was Thankappan, who had migrated from Vengoor and married into a Thachanakkara family. His cross-eyes, which seemed to focus on three people at the same time, would have helped him in his business a lot more, had it been a busy teashop with lots of people to focus on. The public of Thachanakkara thought the name Vengooran had more to do with his cross-eyes than with Vengoor, the land of his origin—so much so that, in later years if any squint-eyed suitor came looking for a bride in Thachanakkara, the words that sprung to their tongues were, 'Oh, here's another Vengooran!'

The Thachanakkara folk's surmise that Vengooran Thankappan could not have been a Nair, being an orphan, was only partially correct. He had come to Thachanakkara by marrying Shantha, the younger sister of Leela of Muringaattil, who had committed suicide by jumping into the river. Kochu Parashu knew that the reason people had doubts about Thankappan's caste was because he showed no false pride by trying to avoid running a teashop in his wife's village. 'If Thankappan were to loiter around like our old Swadeshabhimani Kuttan Pilla, gossiping and doing nothing, I am sure none of you would have any suspicions about his caste!' Kochu Parashu said with conviction, to a few who secretly asked him about Thankappan's caste.

The room on the right side of Kochu Parashu's grocery store had not been let out. Used as a storeroom, it had a large jar for storing salt, closed with a plank, atop which sat a coconut shell scoop darkened by the contact with salt; coir ropes of various thickness; full and partially-empty sacks of chillies, onions, and rice; and stacks of coconut oil tins with their surfaces reflecting all the contents of the room. In between these, baby tit-mice with pencil-line moustaches, scurried about, unmindful of Kochu Parashu's curses. The room beyond this housed the Eagles Club and Reading Room, where the young generation of Thachanakkara met up irrespective of it being day or night. Since the eldest sons of Kochu Parashu—Vishwanathan and Vijayan, who were students of UC College—were the stalwarts of the club, Kochu Parashu did not get any rent from the room. When assailed by the clamour of the tit-mice squeaks, whenever he opened the storeroom to take rice or decant oil, he used to peer into the next room full of silent young readers of that day's newspapers and taunt, 'Hey, smart eagles, instead of wasting your time reading, can't you all kill and eat some of these mice?'

Newspaper reading was not the only activity at the Eagles Club. The young generation of Thachanakkara, inspired by progressive ideas that came along with the light that streaked in through a window on the north side of that small room, were getting to learn of a new world order in which neither caste nor creed built fences, the sweat of the worker was deemed more potent than wine, and which did not make necks sprain trying to hold conversation ensconced on upper and lower levels. When in addition to newspapers, some books too reached them, the dream union of those young men began to grow rapidly. The chief conductor for all these was the junior Nampoothiri from the Nedumpilli Mana, Vasudevan, who had smashed through the mana's walls built with casteist arrogance and incomparable ignorance. Vasudevan Nampoothiri, who graduated in physics from UC College, was the maternal grandson of Parameswaran Nampoothiri, who the folk of Thachanakkara used to call Parashunampoori. Parameswaran Nampoothiri was on his deathbed, watching helplessly as this young scion of the illam, who did not pray at the temple or wear the poonool thread, or maintain the traditional prescriptions of ritual distances to be maintained to avoid getting polluted by lower castes—the gap varied from a distance of twelve feet from Nair, thirty-six feet from Ezhava, and sixty feet from Pulaya—and instead mingled freely with the populace of Thachanakkara. When Parameswaran Nampoothiri, the main priest, heard that the upstart had started demanding that instead of being addressed respectfully as *cheriya thirumeni*, or junior highness, he should be called only Vasudevan, the soiled thread of his sacred poonool stuck to the old man's body trembled just where it passed across his chest.

These were the replays of revolutionary scenes, which had played out elsewhere in Kerala some forty years earlier, being staged in Thachanakkara as if they were new productions. It was undertaken by the youth, not as a farce, but rather as an anxious and panting run to catch up with the train of history that they had missed. Educated Muslim youth of Elookkara and Kayintikkara, which lay to the south of Thachanakkara, came to the Eagles Club and started reading the newspaper, drawn by Vasudevan's sphere of attraction. In their houses, where the arguments used to be only about whether the newborn should be named Kunjumohammed or Abdullakutty, a number of new names were introduced through the newspapers: to make it easier to select from the thousands of names in the Holy Book, news about the many great leaders outside India, who governed their countries, helped. Names such as Nasser, Ayub, Yahya, Faisal, Hussain, etc., thus flowed from history into the new generation of Elookkara and Kayintikkara. The progressive Nair youth of Thachanakkara went a step further. They showed remarkable courage in eschewing names that would reveal the religion and caste of their children at the first instance. Faced with mothers who came to make offerings in the names of Siji, Viji, Mini, Gini, etc., the younger brothers of Parashunampoori, and their sons in the temple, were bewildered. The other Nampoothiris of Nedumpilli were dismayed to know that it was their own Vasudevan—remembered as a child troubled by chronic diarrhoea—who, in the capacity of a guide, was directing the belated wavelets of the giant wave of reformation that had already swept through Kerala, towards the Thachanakkara folk. During the evening poojas of lit lamps, and after closing the door of the sanctum sanctorum when he was alone with God, each Nampoothiri prayed for good sense to be granted to Vasudevan Nampoothiri. Since Thachanakkara thevar did not have sufficient felicity with human language to explain to them that what Vasudevan had now was indeed right sense, the unhappiness of the Nampoothiris continued unmitigated for a long while.

When it was evident that their dreams could not be contained within the small shop-room of Kochu Parashu, the young men shifted their club to a small hut they built from woven coconut palm leaves, in the common poromboke land, which lay unclaimed to the west of the temple, overgrown with goat weed and touch-me-not. Karunakaran Karthaavu, who had been importuning Kochu Parashu for a room on rent, moved into the empty room. He was Thachanakkara's document writer. Karunakaran Karthaavu, who used to take up his pen only once in a while till his middle age, came to be in demand with the coming of the land reforms. He moved into the building of Pooshaappi one Monday, with a small table, a sheaf of papers, and a writing board. On a plank broken off an old clothes box, using a wet chalk, Karunakaran Karthaavu wrote 'Document Writer's Office' in the old winding script and hung it as a board in front of his room. As he was seen busy all the while with his writing, Thachanakkara's youth gave him a nickname—Karunasky.

A new name board was also required for the club, which had been transplanted to the thatched hut. As Babu mixed his paints and got ready, an epiphany that floated in from somewhere made Vasudevan say thus: 'Eagles doesn't seem to be the name we should keep. It's the emblem of America. So, shall we change it?'

'But,' Kochu Parashu's son, Vijayan asked, 'will we get another super name like this?'

'What about Young Challengers?' a new member from Elookkara asked.

Vasudevan stood pondering for some time, chewing on his moustache, which had grown over his upper lip. Opening his naturally large eyes a little wider, he glanced at everyone. 'We'll give it a Malayalam name,' he said. 'Arunodaya Arts Club and Reading Room, what say?'

Everyone agreed on that name, which meant 'red dawn'. The moment he heard the name, a fitting image came to artist Babu's mind. Two hills, resembling the breasts of a supine nude woman, visible when looked at with one's face pressed against her navel, and between them a halved rising sun with wavy flying hair. Before he lost the vision, the artist quickly sketched it on the board.

This sunrise, lying exposed to the elements for eight years, atop the thatched hut-club, was the first painting enjoyed by Jithendran—when he was three years old.

Jithen was on the hip of his eldest sister Geetha, who had gone to the club in search of Venu, the son of Pankajaakshan Uncle. Clawing her face to draw her attention to the picture on the thatched hut, Jithen said in his indistinct words, 'Lo, bubbies.'

It was his off-day. After a hair-cut in Shivan's saloon, drinking tea in Vengooran's teashop and having four parippu vadas packed, and buying two packets of beedis from Kochu Parashu's shop, Shankaran told him, 'Kochu Parashu chettaa, I have been confirmed in my job in the company.'

'That's good. Your child is lucky for you, then. What have you named it?'

'Geetha,' Shankaran said.

'Hai, do the communists name their daughters Geetha and all?' Kochu Parashu asked.

Shankaran did not understand the allusion to the Bhagavad Gita. He had other things to say.

'What I meant was,' Shankaran went on, 'when it is a salary, there won't be money every day in hand. Like you give Kumaran, if you could give me credit from this month onwards...'

Kochu Parashu pondered over it. His merchant's mind was flooded with questions.

'What's the salary date?' Kochu Parashu asked.

'The first,' Shankaran replied.

'Will you pay on time?'

In reply, Shankaran gave him an open, honest smile. That appealed to Kochu Parashu. Handing him a book smaller than his palm, Kochu Parashu said, 'Then keep this. I too shall write in the book here. We'll start with today's beedis, what?'

Shankaran smiled gratefully. As he was stepping down from the shop with the book in hand, he overheard Kochu Parashu say, 'When credit is sought for Ayyaattumpilli, how can I say no? I only hesitated because I'm scared of these Commies.'

Shankaran stopped when he saw a new thatched hut where the temple grounds ended. He walked towards it and stood in front of it. 'Even one like this would be good enough,' he said to himself, thinking of something.

Since he was coming from the barbershop, stray hairs were pricking the nape of his neck and his back. Deciding to take a bath in the river, he turned to go, repeating the word he had read on the board on the thatched hut.

'Arunodaya,' he said. 'Meaningful word.'

FIVE

Meanie

18 March 1999

A meanie—*chetta*—will not waste a single occasion to show his lowliness.

Fear not, this is just a sentence that I wrote down in the diary yesterday transforming the anger I felt towards a colleague. After that, I felt that this sentence stemmed from the worst kind of mental conditioning that Thachanakkara had left in me. When you call a low-thinking, debased person as a chetta, when you deprecate things that lack elegance and finesse as kitsch, you may be unknowingly hurting a few around you. Once upon a time, the word we now use for a meanie, a base person, 'chetta', was also a name for the home of the lower caste, dear to the owner.

No, I was not sentient the day I wrote this sentence in the diary.

After the Land Reforms Bill had prised large tracts of land from Naraapilla, both as fields and plots, the stature of Ayyaattumpilli had come down somewhat. In the lands partitioned among the five children of Naraapilla—except Govindan who had married the woman from Cherai, and Chandran who had run away—houses encircled by thorny bamboo fences abounded: the one in which Naraapilla was born; the one he constructed; the one built by Pankajaakshan; and the thatched hut made by Chinnamma after quarrelling with Naraapilla. Thus, smoke from four kitchens rose in the air.

It was Chinnamma's demand that her father should make out the New House in her name like the old house had been given to her sister Thankamma, which planted the seeds for the rise of the fourth house in the compound. Countering Chinnamma's obstinacy with twisted lips and a wagging forefinger, Naraapilla was dismissive: 'Such tricks won't work with Naraapilla, you damned one! If you want a house, tell your Nair to make one! Listen, I have apportioned the best land. Do what you want! This, I have made for me to sleep in! No upstart need drool, hankering after this!'

The fight between father and daughter lasted till dusk. Though it all started with Chinnamma rebelling ostensibly against Naraapilla, cursing her newborn for wailing, later it emerged that there was a graver reason for Chinnamma to have suddenly moved the demand for the New House. Till Shankaran reached home in the evening, passers-by could hear the uniformly high-pitched, open-throated bellowing of the father and daughter from Ayyaattumpilli. From the other side of the fence, Thankamma and Kalyanikuttyamma, Pankajaakshan's wife, leant over and looked now and then, and went back to their work. That evening, when Thankamma was about to start chanting her evening prayers in front of the lit lamp, Chinnamma came carrying the baby in one hand and dragging her husband behind her with the other, and said, 'Eh chechi, for a few days, we're staying here. Can't stay with that … that … that devil anymore!'

'What're you saying?' Thankamma asked, gathering the infant into her arms, and taking care not to look at Shankaran standing behind her sister with his head bowed.

Sitting sprawled on the floor, Chinnamma said, 'With the

blessings of God, I too have a small plot of land. Even if it's only a pitched tent, we will build something on that land and make do!' She called out to her husband standing in the darkness on the front steps, 'You come here, man. Isn't this my chechi's house? We'll stay here in peace for two days!'

Till Kumaran came home, Shankaran stood there on the steps thinking of this and that. Shankaran was thinking about a small, thatched house he had seen on the western corner of Thachanakkara temple.

Not two days, but two months did Chinnamma stay with her husband and infant in her sister's house. Thankamma, Kumaran, and Kalyanikuttyamma tried to patch things up between the father and daughter and failed. Pankajaakshan, the only son of Naraapilla left in Ayyaattumpilli, did not interfere in these affairs and held court at Vengooran Thankappan's tea stall, boasting loudly about his police days. Informed by his son Kumaran, Appu Nair came from Peechamkurichi on the fourth day to seek a compromise with Chinnamma. Because his vision was glazed over by the cataract, Appu Nair often mistook Chinnamma for Thankamma and vice versa. Appu Nair was shocked to find in the hands of Chinnamma an allegation which was to be a potent weapon to wield against the father.

'Do know, Uncle?' said Chinnamma, laying her baby in the cradle hung for Thankamma's youngest child, and rocking it by pushing her body forward and backward, 'Our New House is kept to be given away as a gift!'

The direction of Chinnamma's allegation was missed by both Thankamma and Appu Nair.

'Gift?' Appu Nair probed. 'For whom?'

'For who else?' Chinnamma raised her voice. 'Isn't there that fair madam at Chammaram, the crone that is out to seduce moneyed old men? For that same one!'

Appu Nair understood what was worrying Chinnamma. After Kaalippennu was ousted from the anteroom, Naraapilla had resumed his old relationship with Amminiyamma of Chammaram house, four houses to the north of Ayyaattumpilli. Amminiyamma, wife of Gangadharan Nair, whom Thachanakkara denizens had nicknamed 'Kamanthan', remained as beautiful as the core of sandalwood, even after delivering seven children. The seven children that she bore were of eight types. That the two middle ones among them resembled Naraapilla was something that was often alleged in Vengooran's teashop by Paanamparampath Nanu, who prided himself on having the lowdown on all the illicit children of Thachanakkara. Kamanthan sat on the porch, swatting mosquitoes, unable to enjoy the many skills of Amminiyamma, with which she used to lure many old lechers with fat purses to Chammaram. Before her death, Kunjuamma was once forced to cross that gate at Chammaram, on which chaste women would spit in disgust. That day, when Naraapilla, who was supposed to be having his bath in the evening in front of the granary, was not to be found, as if guided by an inner voice, Kunjuamma crossed the four houses to the north of Ayyaattumpilli to reach Chammaram, and called out into the house for her husband. Her guess was correct. 'Won't let me be, would you?' Naraapilla screamed, sitting on Amminiyamma's cot, and threw a heavy brass kindi, which missed Kunjuamma standing in the half-light and hit the tulsi plant and broke it. At a loss as to what to do next, Kunjuamma took the tulsi plant and returned home crying in the darkening gloom gaining ground around her, and hid her tears. Neither did she let anyone see them. When the hunchback crone of Naattyol came and stood in front of her like a question mark, Kunjuamma said, 'I'd gone to pluck a sweet tulsi plant!'

When Kamanthan Gangadharan, fed up with sitting on the veranda, fell dead there one day, all of Thachanakkara assembled in front of that house. It was Paanamparampath Nanu, the one who made up limericks about the man-eating ways of Amminiyamma and carried tales throughout Thachanakkara, who was in the lead when it came to overseeing the funeral rites. Nanu brought a wooden chair to the yard from inside for Naraapilla to sit. Though there was only the distance of four houses between them, since the flag had been lowered after their earlier celebrations of lusty unions tapered off, Naraapilla was seeing Amminiyamma again after a gap of many years. Naraapilla thought that Amminiyamma's body, which had crossed half a century, was shining brighter than the lamp near Kamanthan's corpse. Bereft of spouses, they both had become partners in sorrow, and that they had reached certain unspoken decisions, communicated at regular intervals in the midst of the rituals when their eyes met, was something that was not noticed by anyone—except Chinnamma, who was watching her father's changing expressions and mien from a distance. Chinnamma was taken aback to see Amminiyamma's tear-filled eyes often sending looks of coy invitation to her ageing father.

Before the sixteenth day of Kamanthan's death, Naraapilla was sharing the bed at Chammaram in the evenings. Running her fingers through the greying hirsute forest on Naraapilla's back, Amminiyamma promised not to let anyone except Naraapilla into Chammaram house henceforth. Chinnamma's tongue swelled with bitterness when she realized that, after his evening bath, Naraapilla was being tempted by the bed at Chammaram. Chinnamma was not the ilk of Kunjuamma to come back home, feeling crushed by a kindi thrown at her. One Shivaraathri night, as she was having a dip in the river and saw Amminiyamma's face emerging from the water, she spat out the venom of bitterness she had been carrying for long: 'Phthoo, you whoring slut!' Chinnamma threw down the clothes and the soap she was carrying. 'You found only my father with one leg in the grave to fornicate with and lead astray?'

In front of Chinnamma, the maturity that was older than her mother, did not quake. 'Did your father deliver on the road, after I led him astray?' Amminiyamma got out of the water and stood her ground on the bank.

The blasting and basting between two generations lasted for hours. The final challenge that the old-school representative threw at the novice of the newer generation, after she picked up the rinsed clothes and got ready to leave, shocked the younger challenger into silence.

'Does the darling daughter want to see?' said Amminiyamma. 'If I am challenged, I will make your father will the land you now live on as a gift to me. Want to see?'

The same shudder that ran through her at the riverbank when she first heard the threat, flashed again in her mind as she stood rocking the cradle. 'Do you now realize why father kept picking fights with me for the baby crying, shitting, and all that, Uncle?' Chinnamma stopped rocking the cradle, making sure the child was asleep. Thankamma was sitting with her mouth wide open. 'Is there a law that will allow such a gift deed, Uncle?' Thankamma, who was not convinced about the far-sighted vision of her younger sister, asked Appu Nair in a voice that could be barely heard. At that moment, with the shadow of helplessness clouding it, Thankamma's face resembled Kunjuamma's face more than ever. 'As a gift deed…' Appu Nair said without much conviction. 'Don't you worry! Will anyone give away gifts to such women, just like that?'

With a sagacious mien, Thankamma added, 'If so, I would say it was a mistake on your part to have left the house. We should cling on to such people!'

'Tthhu…' Chinnamma shook her head and snapped ferociously. 'My chechi, I say this as a vow, from now on only my dog will go to that house!'

Thus, Gopalan Panickan came to Ayyaattumpilli to drive the stake for a new house. In the land set aside for Chinnamma, a hut began to come up. Chinnamma said that they could start living there after laying the foundation with laterite and using coconut thatch for walls. Shankaran agreed. On loan and against cash, came bricks, thatch, and doors. Loaded on a bullock cart, first-rate thatch and ropes were brought from Aluva by Maniyan pulayan. Within four days, the foundation was raised. On the fifth day, by the time Shankaran came back from work in the evening, Maniyan pulayan had levelled the floor of the foundation using the handheld iron compounder to a smoothness that rivalled the base on which the clay icon of Thrikkakkarappan is installed along with carpets of flower during Onam. The mature flame-of-the-forest trees in the yard were cut down to make pillars for the house. Chopped arecanut palms were split to make the central beam and spliced further to make supporting beams, after their soft innards were removed. Within six weeks, Maniyan's brother Kochayyappan and Kochayyappan's eldest son, Ayyankaali, worked together to finish the work on the hut.

Maniyan pulayan had constructed Chinnamma's house modelled on his own. After making the floor smooth with a paste of powdered charcoal and cow dung, Maniyan pulayan grinned with his yellow teeth at Chinnamma who had come to see the house and told her, 'To tell you the truth, thatched houses are better. We can even take the coconut leaf spine to pick our teeth from the wall!'

On a Wednesday in that month of Midhunam, Chinnamma boiled the milk for the housewarming ceremony. The VIP guests at the housewarming function included Pankajaakshan's three sons, Thankamma's two girls and two boys, and Appu Nair's four grandchildren. When the army of children began to poke holes in the thatched walls and started to compete amongst each other to untie the complicated knots which Maniyan pulayan had used to secure the thatch together, Chinnamma's limbs trembled and she shouted, 'Ho! Finish eating and go back to your houses, children!'

On a stove made with bricks and plastered with mud, the sisters lit a fire with coconut spathes, and let the milk boil over. As per custom, she put sugar in the milk, passed on the cup for everyone to have a mouthful, and throwing the leftover mouthful of milk in the direction of the New House, Chinnamma said, 'This is for all the patriarchs! Though he is evil, we've to do what we've to do, right?'

Without fail, Thankamma sent morning gruel and dinner, covered with a banana leaf, for the sixty-eight-year-old Naraapilla, who was living alone in the New House. His lunch and evening coffee along with some snack, was delivered by Kalyanikuttyamma. Thankamma arranged for old Kotha pulayi to sweep the yard, clean the house, and wash Naraapilla's clothes. Kotha pulayi, who kept smoking beedis to counter her toothache, kept the fire in Naraapilla's kitchen burning. Rather than to heat up the water for Naraapilla's evening bath, the stove in the New House proved more useful for lighting, at her pleasure, the beedi butts that she had collected from various places and kept rolled up safely in the end of her mundu. In the kitchen that had once been maintained like a shrine by Kunjuamma, now Kotha pulayi squatted smoking her beedi butts. The reason she gave for not lighting the stove in front of the granary to heat the water for Naraapilla's evening bath, convinced Naraapilla: 'It is good that the children will bring food and water for the master,' Kotha pulayi had said through the blackened stumps of her incisors. 'Yet, if no fire burns in one's own kitchen, that's inauspicious, Master!'

Chinnamma gradually realized that her fear of Amminiyamma of Chammaram moving into Ayyaattumpilli to light the fire in the kitchen of the New House was scarcely shared by others, and it was an anxiety that bugged her alone. When she saw her sister and sister-in-law gathering fallen coconuts and midribs from the New House as if it was their right, Chinnamma's demeanour changed. With her second child in her womb, Chinnamma rushed to the fence. 'I know how you all are!' Chinnamma thus inaugurated a volley of accusations which escalated into a full-blown verbal battle across the bamboo fence. 'Irrespective of day or night, you sisters-in-law are feeding and mollycoddling the darling father, isn't it? If you will be happy to get that house too, take that too! For that, you needn't have played such a drama to keep me away!'

Kalyanikuttyamma and Thankamma stood rooted on the spot, stupefied, wondering who had staged a play. Taking their silence to be an admission of guilt, Chinnamma began to shake the fence to advance forward, and Kalyanikuttyamma was forced to counter, 'Who was the lazy one who got out on a ruse, to escape looking after father? And now the blame is on others, eh?'

To that question, Chinnamma replied with a freshly-baked snap, 'Phtthu! When our mother lay dying, after banging her head on the walls, wasn't this daughter-in-law enjoying herself with her Nair in Munnar? Don't make me say more!'

Meetings and interactions between the children of Ayyaattumpilli became lesser and lesser. But slinking through the fences, the grandchildren of Naraapilla became bound by friendship. Chinnamma's second child—the first child of Ayyaattumpilli to be born in a thatched house—was also a girl. With the cash they got from selling the field of Nedumaali, which had come to them in the partition, to a Christian from Angamaly, Shankaran knocked down the thatched house and built in its place a house with brick walls and roof tiles that very year. A nazrani from Angamaly called Devassy had rented from Naraapilla a plot called Thekkepallam on the riverbank and had put up a brick kiln. Shankaran raised the walls of his house by buying bricks that were not properly baked, which Devassy sold at discounted rates. From Govindan's land, untended and overgrown with shrubs, and which had become a sanctuary for the foxes, Chinnamma cut jackfruit and ainee trees without telling or asking anyone, and gave them to carpenter Gopalan to make rafters and beams. When Thankamma came to enquire, hearing the sound of trees being felled from the plot belonging to the eldest brother, Chinnamma puffed up her chest in defiance and said loud enough to let Thankamma hear, 'Who's got a complaint? My brother's plot, my brother's trees. If I cut one or two of them, it's no skin off anyone's nose!'

Chinnamma joined the workers to build the house. It was in her third pregnancy. Carrying the three-month-old baby in her womb and a few bricks on a plank on her head, Chinnamma ran around till the walls of the house were built. Many a time, Chinnamma carried bricks and lime all by herself, letting the shrivelled-looking Malli cherumi, who was to do the fetching and carrying, stand as a mute witness. Thus her third pregnancy was aborted, and ended up as a three-month-old lump of flesh ejected prematurely.

In her new house, it was with unusual care that Chinnamma waited for her next pregnancy. She had made an offering to Thachanakkara thevar to give her a boy to keep company for the elder girls. One night, faint from post-coital exhaustion, Chinnamma got up to drink water, and opened the front door, mistaking it for the kitchen door, and took the kindi from the parapet. It was a full moon night. In the eastern side of the yard, where the thatch from the old house was stacked, a champaka flower, with intense fragrance, was in bloom. With the moonlight and fragrance of champaka suffusing the night air, Chinnamma had the delusion that the kindi was filled with some heavenly drink. After drinking her fill from it, she took the rest to the bedroom to give to her husband. Raising the wick of the lantern to look into the pitcher, he smiled and said, 'Silly! The half kindi that you filled yourself with was only moonlight!'

To come back to reality and laugh out loud, Chinnamma took nearly ten seconds. But those ten seconds were completely made use of by a new soul. After being formed in Chinnamma's womb that night, the first nutrient that it got was this:

Half a kindi of moonlight.

SIX

Crescent

6 December 1999

...Today the newspaper says that there will be high-level security checks at the airports, railway stations, and bus stands. Even on this cool day in December, the nation fears an erstwhile sibling that might arrive at the terminals.

Has my nazrani girl heard of this story from *Mahabharatham*? The story of a dog ascending to heaven? Fully aware that despite fighting battles and winning it all, they had lost everything in front of God, the five Pandava siblings and their shared wife had started climbing the mountain to enter heaven in their corporeal forms. Even as the rest of his companions fell behind him, one by one, the eldest continued on his way, justifying his progress. Finally, he and a dog, which had accompanied him all the way, reached heaven. But how deserving was he of that? When he appears morally more depraved than those who fell, by his sole act of proceeding alone without heeding the tragedy that befell his siblings?

This I am telling you in confidence: the version that the dog who accompanied him to heaven was Yamadharman, the lord of death, is a hoax. A ruse planned by the author Vyasan to not dishearten the readers. The moral of the story is this: the chances of a selfish person ascending to heaven are the same as that of a scruffy mongrel.

My nazrani lass, it is in the same India where a mausoleum built by Emperor Shah Jahan is showcased as a matter of pride that a mosque built by Shah Jahan's great-grandfather was razed.

A killer joke about families, no?

The pomelos, which grow in abundance in Chinnamma's plot now, were planted by Chandran who left Thachanakkara fifteen years ago.

Chandran—after the deceased Padmanabhan—was a member of Ayyaattumpilli who was heartlessly forgotten by the denizens of Thachanakkara. The one who stuck to Kunjuamma like her shadow. The one who suckled at her breast the longest. The one who clung to his mother, even after being weaned using aloe vera paste.

Most of the stories he had heard as a child were about his mother's eldest sister's son and her playmate, Kesavan. In his mother's remembrances about this valiant and heroic person, the sword of the past flashed. Kesavan, who had run away without uttering a word to anyone before Kunjuamma's wedding, thus grew into a legend in Chandran's imagination. The young man called Kesavan, who had not even left a photo to remember him from the time he had disappeared like vapour in history, was recreated in Chandran's mind in glowing form like the archer Arjunan, through the tales his mother told of him. Like death, which was the ultimate measure for engendering fond memories in others, running away was the second-best method to make others remember one. This was a feeling that grew in him, blessed by the spirit of Kesavan. He had the far-sighted vision that circumstances would conspire to provide him with reasons to leave on an endless journey, flying on the mast of courage. When he was thirteen, he confessed to Kunjuamma.

'Ammae,' he called her one day in a seemingly mature voice

and said, 'if you find me missing one of these days, you should not feel distressed!'

Kunjuamma was squatting on the bamboo mat, amidst the de-shelled tamarind left in the sun for drying. Busy using the knife-point to do surgery on the tamarind to expel the seeds, she gave Chandran a sharp look. 'If something like that happens,' Kunjuamma said, lifting only her index finger from the handle of the knife, 'I will do that thing which I could not do when Kesavan had left.'

'What thing?' Chandran asked, picking up the tamarind seeds that had to be roasted and de-shelled, and their kernels put in salt water.

'You try running away, then we'll see. Ngaa,' Kunjuamma spoke with flared nostrils.

Though, like all mothers, Kunjuamma was also jesting, it stuck in Chandran's heart. After many years, the drops of breast milk that he had drunk till he was five—and which he had won from the share of his two younger sisters, with the help of his tears, started popping in his veins. He forgot the bitterness of the aloe vera paste.

'Surely not.' Kneeling down and pressing his face against the cool, sandal-smelling tummy of his mother, he said, 'I will never leave my mother and go anywhere!'

That was not a vow. Nor had he attained the age to make vows. His adolescent attempt to flee from his house ended up unsuccessful. It was when he took on Naraapilla, after declaring his intention to visit his brother Govindan in Cherai, that his first running away drama was played out. Two months after spending his days in Poornathrayeeshan Temple in Thripunithura, on the sixty-first night a dream shocked him out of his sleep. In that nightmare, which left him dry-mouthed, Kunjuamma sat with a knife on the stile of Ayyaattumpilli, crying non-stop, calling out his name, 'Chandra ... Chandra.' The next day, when he reached Ayyaattumpilli what awaited him was a reality close to his dream, but more horrific. With a blood-soaked bandage wrapped around her head, Kunjuamma had begun her final days. It did not look as if the mother recognized her son who had come back. Naraapilla had succeeded in creating the impression that it was her son's running away that was responsible for Kunjuamma's condition. Afraid of the accusing looks of his father and siblings, he walked with his head bowed. He wept through the window bars looking at his mother, who had started circling around the room, calling out to people dead and gone. After two months, when he was lighting his mother's pyre, he became completely free from the single thread that was holding him back from his journey. As he stood by to light the pyre, forced by the gap created by his three absent elder brothers—holding behind him the twisted twigs from the mango tree, each cut approximately to the length of a chenda drumstick—he realized that he was also firing open his own liberation. As his mother's body was being baked in a mound made of dried coconut shells and cow dung discs plastered over with river clay, and the flames began first by consuming her luxuriant hair followed by the rest of the body, smiling with tears in his eyes, he asked his wretched mother: 'What would you do Amma, if I run away now?'

On the day after the sanchayanam, Chandran again clashed with Naraapilla for insulting Govindan and his wife in front of the public, when they arrived in the evening. Pankajaakshan stood by guiltily, having reached only on the day of sanchayanam, as he could not be contacted earlier when he was on a pleasure trip to Munnar with his wife. Pankajaakshan realized that it was neither the animosity towards their father nor his love for their eldest brother that was impelling Chandran to raise his rebellion. He was only creating a justification in the eyes of the world for his next flight from home.

'I felt right then that he was making grounds to go away again,' Pankajaakshan said on a later occasion, sitting in Vengooran Thankappan's teashop. 'When one decides to run away, here, there will be two vertical folds on the forehead!' Pankajaakshan said, touching the centre of Vengooran Thankappan's forehead. When the policeman's fingers touched him, Vengooran felt as if the crown of his head was splitting from the touch of Bhasmaasuran.

On the seventeenth day of Kunjuamma's death, after completing the daily oblations to the manes and ensuring that his mother had ascended to heaven, Chandran scribbled his decision to leave, in a complex, curly script that was as illegible as tiny, on Naraapilla's lime-washed bedroom walls with a piece of charcoal taken from the brick stove, and left Thachanakkara. On the floor beneath the wall lay a used charcoal piece like a relic of his life in Ayyaattumpilli. The gist of the lengthy scrawl of ungrammatical sentences written with that piece of charcoal, which had made its way from the kitchen Kunjuamma had used for so many years and into the bedroom of Naraapilla, was simple enough for anyone to guess. It was more or less this: This house is hell. But when mother was there, I could bear it.

This time, Pankajaakshan himself made a missing person's report on behalf of his father. While trying to take his thumb impression, Naraapilla frowned and asked, 'But, what's the benefit in getting him back?'

Reading the charcoal mural on the wall, Thankamma cried loudly. The whole night, she dreamt that her kochettan was running directionless through the dark night, clutching two shirts and two mundus wrapped as a bundle. The next morning, as soon as she woke up, she went seeking him in the narrow space behind the mirror almirah in Naraapilla's room. What prompted the still half-asleep Thankamma to head there, was her thought that like in the old times her brother would be hiding there between the wall and the back of the mirror almirah. Once in their childhood, when Chandran went missing, after searching for a long time, she had found him in that secret place behind the mirror almirah. The sanctuary of the twelve-year-old, for taking refuge after his crime. Kunjuamma had entrusted him to stand guard for the dried red chillies left in the sun, spread out on bamboo mats. In the meanwhile, a mother hen and her chicks came into the yard. They were the darlings of Bhavaniyamma of Naattyol house. As they started pecking, attracted by the bright red colour of the chillies, an immature coconut thrown by Chandran to scare them away took the life of an innocent, sprightly chick. As her yellow brood ran helter skelter, the mother hen stood by the side of the dead chick—lying with its legs pointing up—cocking its head left and right, in a daze. Once again, Chandran heard the echoing wails of his mother calling for her Pappanaavan, holding on to the body of his elder brother, three years ago. His heart trembled. In a quick dash he was inside the house; realizing that the shadow of his amma's clothes box was not large enough to hide him, he stood baffled for a while and finding himself boxed in, he chose to hide behind the mirror almirah in his father's room. Wedged between the lime-washed wall of Ayyaattumpilli and his father's treasury, he spent two-and-a-half hours, afraid that the sound of his heartbeat would give away his hiding place. He could hear four throats calling out 'Chandro' and 'kochetto' in various pitches, looking for him in the various corners of Ayyaattumpilli. Then Thankamma's tilted head stretched into that cob-webby, narrow space and screamed for the whole world to hear: 'Ammae ... here's the venerable chicken-killer!'

He came out ready to accept any punishment for the merciless killing of the neighbour's chick. Kunjuamma embraced him and removed the cobwebs sticking to his head and swabbed the sweat off his face. Then she kissed him on the crown of his head with a vehemence that seemed enough to suck it in. 'How you frightened your mother!' she said with unshed tears.

The corpse of the chicken was missing in the yard. The mother hen and rest of its brood were not there either. His father was not there. None that he feared was there. 'My son needn't tell anyone about the chicken dying,' Kunjuamma said. 'If the fox took it away, how is it my son's fault?'

Not just the fox that stole the chicken of Bhavaniyamma of Naattyol, but another fox which had stolen his elder brother at a tender age was what flashed in Chandran's mind for a moment like a bolt of lightning. That fox which lurked and pounced was called Time. That vision's inspiration was powerful enough to instigate him to leave not only Thachanakkara and Kerala, but even the whole world, and go wandering around. As if to make up for that one life obliterated by him, he planted and watered innumerable saplings all over Ayyaattumpilli—the edges of the yard, the compound, along the fences, everywhere. Not flowering plants, but those bearing fruits and nuts. In that plot of Naraapilla, replete with coconut, mango and jackfruit trees, and plantains, in all the empty spaces, new kinds of trees started to grow and flourish. The new generation of Ayyaattumpilli got to see sapote, Indian almond, and pomegranate only when the saplings planted by Chandran grew into trees. Among those saplings uprooted from his friend's places, one alone, due to its droll name, happened to grow nurtured by everyone's anticipation. When Kunjuamma suspected it to be Key lime, because its smell remotely reminded her of it when she had crushed the tender leaves, Chandran corrected her, 'Nothing of the sort, Amma. This is babloos lime. Babloos. Wait till it grows up and then see. This tree will resemble my mother.'

Kunjuamma waned from Ayyaattumpilli. Chandran, named after the moon, disappeared too. In the plot that was given as

Chinnamma's share, the pomelos or the so-called babloos grew plentiful. It was Geetha, Chinnamma's eldest daughter who spotted the first babloos flower; amongst the shiny, oiled-looking leaves, it stood smiling. As the sunlight that streamed through the foliage was too blinding, Chinnamma could not see the flower pointed out to her by the four-year-old Geetha. That evening, while seated on the hip of Shankaran, the child pointed up once more. This time everyone managed to see the flower. Within the next two or three days, more flowers were seen on the tree. As it grew, initially as big as a lemon, then sweet orange, then Key lime, and finally reached the size of Kunjuamma's breasts that had suckled six children, Chinnamma smiled remembering Chandran and told her husband, 'So, this is what kochettan had meant then, when he said that to our mother!'

'What?' Shankaran queried.

Without answering and donning a faux sadness on her face, Chinnamma said, 'Lord, if only one could hear that he's not dead and is living somewhere!'

Since it was about someone whom he had never met, that prayer did not touch Shankaran.

One afternoon, two months later, as the work on her brick house was going on, following the demolition of the thatched hut, one of the workers plucked the first babloos from the tree. At that time, Aaminumma from Elookkara was also present. Aaminumma was an old lady, with a soiled cloth covering her hair and pierced ears resembling sieves, who used to come to the houses in Ayyaattumpilli to collect rice water with a rimless bucket. Suffering from a condition which made her burp loudly all the time, Aaminumma used to carry news from the outside world to Ayyaattumpilli, as a free service in return for the rice water. One of her favourite subjects was the poverty amongst the Muslim families of Elookkara and Kayintikkara. With her tummy filled with the hunger tales of Elookkara, she journeyed to Thachanakkara and returned with a bucketful of rice water to Elookkara—burping all the while. With the first calving of her cow, which was more desperate than her, Ayyaattumpilli got creamy yoghurt. In return, she mowed the thick-growing grass in the empty plots earmarked for Govindan and Chandran and carried it as a headload back with her.

Those days, Chinnamma and Shankaran and their two daughters were living in a one-room lean-to that resembled a small cowshed, made out of the thatches retrieved from the demolished house, and built adjacent to the laterite foundation of their new house being built. Though Kumaran and Thankamma had come in person overlooking their old tiff, and invited them to stay with them while the new house was being built, Chinnamma did not relent. In a voice untouched by affection, she said, 'Why should we bother you, chechi? To say this and that, and needlessly pick on each other? My children and I can make do with this and sleep here!'

Aaminumma, who visited all the houses in Ayyaattumpilli, collected and took to Elookkara, along with the rice water, the titillating stories of the fights between sisters and sister-in-law and the loneliness of Naraapilla in the New House. She would narrate the tales of the corrupted blood of Naraapilla in front of her own children, their spouses, and neighbours and let out a long burp and declare, 'Lord, even if you didn't give us money, at least you didn't let us be born Nairs, that is enough!'

On her return to Ayyaattumpilli, while decanting the rice water she would tell each housewife, 'Dear, who doesn't have difficulties? Whatever you'd say, can the Nairs let go of their prestige? Tell me!'

That day, while decanting the rice water, Aaminumma saw the building workers sharing something to eat. Leaving the bucket there, she headed towards the gang.

'Bu-u-rr-rrp.' After a burp broken up by inquisitiveness, she frowned and asked: 'What now, what's this new thing?'

Offering one from the crescent-shaped carpels found when they had peeled the moon-shaped pomelo, one of the workers said, 'Here, eat this. If a categorization is needed, it can be taken as a younger uncle of our orange!'

When she peeled the white covering off her carpel, she saw the juice sacs, resembling neatly-stacked pieces of chopped reddish earthworm. Flicking away the yellow seeds stuck on the edge, she started eating it with suspicion. As the sweet-sour juice of the pomelo touched her worn taste buds, the old woman, with eyes tightly shut, said, referring to her hungry grandchildren, 'Give an entire one for Aaminumma, son. My house has a number of sparrows; it's for them.'

So the pomelo too reached Elookkara through Aaminumma. When the Aalungal School closed for the summer holidays, the children from Elookkara came to Chinnamma's house and bought pomelos at thirty paise each. Carrying vessels stacked with peeled carpels on their young shoulders, the little vendors rushed about in Thachanakkara, Elookkara, and Kayintikkara, touting their wares loudly, 'Liiiime caaaarpels…'

By selling each carpel at five paise and getting fifty paise for an entire pomelo, the children became vainly rich. They bought green gram to go with gruel, and buns for the evenings, for their mothers. The mothers were happy. They prayed to Allah for a bountiful harvest of pomelos at Ayyaattumpilli.

When the money from the sale of the paddy field was not enough, Shankaran mortgaged the plot on which the house stood to the Thachanakkara Service Cooperative Society for a loan of seven thousand rupees, and completed the house before Onam. Provided the gestational calculation did not go wrong,

Chinnamma was supposed to deliver her third child on the auspicious day of thiruvonam or the nearby dates. She insisted that, before that, they had to move from the lean-to, which had earthworms and millipedes crawling about. The day she saw a baby rat snake slipping out of the mat she was rolling up, and on which her daughters had slept the previous night, watching the yellow snake slithering away, Chinnamma said, 'At least let this one in the womb be destined to live in a proper house. We'd be lucky if these two do not die of snake or centipede bites by then!'

The innovative design of Pankajaakshan's house, effected by her sister-in-law from Kochi, had entranced Chinnamma. If Chinnamma had not insisted that the rounded drawing room in the front should have a concrete ceiling, after that fashion, the work could have been completed without taking a loan. Using the money remaining in the loan of seven thousand, Shankaran was able to build a laterite compound wall in the front and have a small metal gate with Geethalayam written on it in English with the letters bent and cut with difficulty. It was the first iron gate to appear not just in Ayyaattumpilli, but in all of Thachanakkara. When Pankajaakshan's and Thankamma's children mistook the blue gate for an instrument of entertainment, and during Onam holidays climbed on and started swinging it as if it were a vehicle, the hugely-pregnant Chinnamma screamed at them, 'Go home, brats!' Gathering the four-year-old Geetha and the two-year-old Rema close to her, she frowned at the others. 'Swinging it this way and that way, and spoiling it! Go back to your homes and play ... ummm ... Scram!'

Not old enough to be sentient about boundaries, the children of the other house ran away, signalling to Geetha that they would come back later.

It was Jithendran who provided the children with the opportunity to play on the gate, swinging it like a vehicle for an entire week, without being afraid of Chinnamma. It was the day of Onam when Chinnamma was awaiting labour in the new house, which smelled of fresh lime plaster. Nothing happened on thiruvonam day, contrary to what was expected by Shankaran and feared by Chinnamma. The next day, when the labour started, Chinnamma thought it was due to overeating during the feast the previous day. However, the newbie had marked the beginning of his troubles by getting his oversized head lodged in his mother's pelvis, unable to come out. For three hours, Chinnamma screamed incessantly. Yet he did not come into the grip of the seventy-year-old midwife, Kalyani.

'It is beyond me.' Opening out the hands calloused by aiding countless childbirths, Kalyani told Shankaran.

Madhavan, the grandson of Achuttan Vaidyan of Kaniyankunnu, had joined a new hospital in Aluva, having completed his studies in Western medicine. Shankaran waited on the road that the doctor took to return home for lunch, and signalled down the Premier Padmini car with its red cross sticker on the rear windscreen to a stop, and stated his case. Thus, for the first time, a car arrived at the gate of Geethalayam. Setting aside their long-standing differences, Kalyanikuttyamma and Thankamma rushed to her aid. In her struggle to climb into the car with her distended tummy, Chinnamma stepped on and broke the clay icon of Thrikkakkarappan near the gate. Following Madhavan doctor's car, in which Shankaran and Chinnamma had left, wearing whatever came to their hand, both Thankamma and Kalyanikuttyamma ran to the new hospital in Aluva. The children of Ayyaattumpilli whooped and started to play 'car' on the gate.

It was the avittam day in the month of Chingam. While his youngest grandchild had his head stuck on his way into this world, Naraapilla was straining to reclaim an old wild path in the body of Chammarath Amminiyamma, which had been blocked by landslides.

SEVEN

The Birth

11 August 1999

...Thank you for your curiosity about my birthday. With gifts of flowers and pleasant words, can we lessen anyone's pain for having been born? Those birth pangs that are more sublime than labour pains?

I can see the frown on your face reading these bitter philosophical ruminations in the letter to the girl one is going to marry. It wouldn't be amiss to see the wives of philosophers also as widows, would it? Forgive me for saying that; that was a bit too much. My birthday is in the month of Chingam. Wedged exactly between the remembrance days of the two Malayalis who considered all human beings equal. On the hapless star of avittam, wedged and squeezed between thiruvonam and chathayam. The year when Idukki district came into existence.

Don't you want to know how it is depicted in my book that has little possibility of being completed? See this. Read without besmirching your heart with any stain:

... she looked once more. The new arrival, who tormented her existence with the pain of pulling out the roots and gave pleasure even through the torment. Even after his first bath, something that had enveloped him in the womb still seemed to cling to his body like patches of white film. Like all newborns, he too was ugly. His limbs hung lifeless like cloth. From him, she could get the smell of her own insides. The skin on the tiny knees was shrivelled. Whenever he opened his eyes now and then, seeing the pupils not focusing on anything, she worried that the baby would turn out to be cross-eyed. But what scared her most was the size of the infant's head and penis. That the boy, to be named Jithendran and called Jithen, would have only two choices, was unknown to his mother:

One: to be an extraordinary artist.

Two: to be a world-class criminal.

With a trembling hand, Shankaran signed the consent form to cut open Chinnamma's stomach and handed it to Madhavan doctor. Afterwards, he stood on the hospital veranda, undecided about his next move. The middle toes of both his feet began to ache. Noticing his stricken face, a lady cleaning the mosaic floor with a pungent-smelling liquid, straightened her back and asked, 'The one who died this morning, was that your relative?'

Shankaran shook his head. Suddenly doubtful, he went into Chinnamma's labour ward to ensure she was fine. By then, Thankamma and Kalyanikuttyamma had arrived too, after checking every room on the way. The women were shocked to hear the word operation. Offering a *thulaabharam* of poovan bananas for Thachanakkara thevar in the name of the child about to be born, Thankamma assured her sister, 'Nothing bad'll happen. I've made an offering of thulaabharam. Now you just pray to our mother too!'

Without paying her any heed, Chinnamma said, 'When y'were coming, were those children dangling on the gate? Those rascals will only destroy it!'

Thankamma and Kalyanikuttyamma looked at each other. 'If the gate breaks, let it,' said Kalyanikuttyamma irritably. 'If only these two would come apart as two separate wholes, without much ado!'

'Which two?' Chinnamma's mouth was agape, clueless as to what her sister-in-law was referring to. Two nurses and a middle-aged man with a sandal-mark on his forehead moved Chinnamma onto a wheeled iron bed. In agony, Chinnamma was bawling 'Acho, Acho.' The lady in the next bed with her own distended belly looked at Chinnamma in alarm.

'See, she still likes our father!' surmised Thankamma, gratified.

'Did the children eat something, Chechi?' Chinnamma asked between howls as she was being wheeled away. Walking with her, Thankamma said, 'There's banana curry and rice in closed vessels. I've entrusted my eldest with everything. Thankamani is no longer a child. She's almost fourteen! She'll take care of everything.'

'Will the little ones jump into the river or something, Kalluchechi?' Chinnamma asked her sister-in-law.

'If they jump, let them! What else can we do?' said Kalyanikuttyamma.

The next question was to the nurse pushing the cot, 'This "operasshum" is to be through which one, daughter?'

'Through that itself!' the nurse replied.

When it came to that point, Shankaran retreated. After telling the women that he would be back soon, he walked aimlessly along the road. The sun had started blazing. For a while, he stood looking at a dog dozing on a handcart under the shade of a tree. Then he walked north again. Halting in front of the gate of a house which had the clay icon of Thrikkakkarappan, Shankaran scratched his head. When he heard an aged voice asking from inside 'Who's it?' he convulsed as if scalded, and started to walk again. At Marthaanda Varma Bridge, he saw people jostling, leaning on the railings on both sides and peering down. Climbing on to the bridge, Shankaran too looked down. A black stomach, shining in the sun, could be seen above the water. An eagle, whose talons were plunged into that island of flesh with green algae swirling around it, lifted its head and anxiously surveyed the people on the bridge. Though the current was slow that day, the black thing floated away, swaying in the water. On the bridge, an argument broke out about whether it was an elephant or a pregnant buffalo.

Shankaran chewed on his tongue. Suddenly he consoled himself saying, 'Kochu Parashu chettan will give!'

He crossed the bridge and ran to Thachanakkara.

Karunakaran Karthaavu, who had established himself in one of Kochu Parashu's rooms, was a surveyor capable of measuring and apportioning not only Thachanakkara, but the whole state of Kerala: a second Vamanan with a short body and splayed feet.

On the rare occasions when he did not go out for measuring and allocating, and sat working on the yellowed deed documents of Thachanakkara, Karunakaran Karthaavu resembled one of those writers who keep writing without inspiration. Those days, the members of the Arunodaya Club used to refer to him secretly as Karunasky, echoing the names of some Soviet writers. Whenever he got respite from his writing, after shutting the doors of his writer's office, Karthaavu would come over to sit in Vengooran's teashop and untie the bundle of his amazing knowledge. In his words and looks sparked the still-glowing embers of his experience garnered during his long stint as a lawyer's clerk somewhere in north India. The unmitigated loneliness of the days of his youth, spent in north India, had turned him into an eternal fan of Hindi film actresses. Even after crossing the age of sixty, Karunakaran Karthaavu had enough swashbuckling still left in him to shut his office and go to Ernakulam to watch Hindi movies the moment he heard about a new release playing in the theatres there. He was adept at regaling Vengooran Thankappan and barber Shivan with these film stories, without them having to spend even five rupees. Karthaavu's forte was not the kind of gossip indulged in by Paanamparampath Nanu. Karthaavu never pointed fingers at anyone. Nor did he praise anyone. Kochu Parashu understood that it was possible to speak a lot without taking either of these positions only after Karunakaran Karthaavu set up his writer's office in one of his shops. Barber Shivan was his usual, ardent listener. In the afternoons, when customers would dwindle, Kochu Parashu would also join them to enjoy a change in seating. In the months when he did not go to watch movies, Karunakaran Karthaavu would hold his peer Kochu Parashu spellbound with his rendition of world history and geography, as if they were things he had witnessed firsthand as a child. At times, Karthaavu revealed truths born of the mating between world history and geography: when he divulged the news that all the gold and money that the warrior lords of Thiruvithamkoor had buried in pots and containers, fearing possible looting during Tippu Sultan's military siege of Kerala, were now resurfacing as treasures at different locations when diggings were being done for foundations and wells, barber Shivan, who was listening intently, turned into stone.

'So, these well-diggers must be having a ball!' Shivan exclaimed with a grin displaying chipped incisors from a fall in his childhood. 'If one pot pops up during digging, no need to work at all in this lifetime!'

Kochu Parashu was suddenly assailed by a reckless desire to make Maniyan Pulayan dig up the whole of his eighty-six cents of land within a single night. Vengooran Thankappan sat staring into the daylight of Chingam, lost in a dream, with a mouth he had forgotten to shut after laughing: the dream of him turning into a well-digger after forsaking his teashop.

Two old Muslim men, who were returning to Elookkara from

Aluva, washed their faces in the water kept in front for washing hands, cursed the sun and sighed as they entered the shop. One of them was Anthru Mappila, who had leased a plot to grow nenthran bananas, and had lost the crop to high winds before the bananas could ripen. The other, Adi Mappila, whose skin resembled parched fields, was holding a hen close to his hip. They refused the still-warm banana fritters offered by Vengooran to ease their fatigue, worried that the money in their pockets would not be enough to pay for the sweet temptations. After a two-day holiday at the shop for uthradam and thiruvonam, Vengooran had made fresh banana fritters and vada. Blinking its yellow eyelids at regular intervals, the hen on Adi Mappila's hip kept staring at the glass cupboard containing the banana fritters, lost in thought.

With the entry of the sweating Mappilas, a pleasant smell was crawling along in Vengooran's shop. When Shivan's nose was trying to discern if the smell was of old age or of the hen, Karunakaran Karthaavu continued with his saga about treasure-hunts, 'But you won't find a treasure just by digging anywhere, dear Shiva! At the time it was buried, then and there, Thachanakkara thevar would have decided that after so many years, so-and-so would get it. That's the game the Lord plays!'

Shivan, who leaned forward to ask something else, fell silent, aware of the presence of outsiders. At that moment, Karthaavu gave an example of God's decisions, 'It's not just the case of the unearthed treasures. Isn't it so even in the case of the birth of great men? For instance, take Mahatma Gandhi.'

'What, did Gandhiji also get a treasure?' Vengooran Thankappan asked with a booming sound echoing from inside the well that he had been digging in his dream.

'The one who got the treasure was not Gandhiji, but his father, Karamchand Gandhi,' said Karthaavu as he shooed away the Chingam heat with his veshti. 'How many times do you think our

Gandhi's father married? Not just one or two, but FOUR! Do you understand?' Detracting one finger from the palm raised as if to bless, Karthaavu showed four fingers. The old men of Elookkara looked yearningly at that and slurped their tea loudly.

The stunned Kochu Parashu needed further explanation. 'Really?' he asked.

'Then what?' said Karthaavu, pleased with his own knowledge. 'Karamchand Gandhi, that is the father of the Father of our Nation, married four times, one after the other. One, when one wife passed away; another, when she died; yet another, when that one also died; and so on. Then what happened? The first three delivered only girls. The fourth one ... that ... ssho, what was her name? Aah, Putthaleebai, she too delivered four. Our Gandhiji was the last among them!'

'But then, you said he got a treasure?' Vengooran convulsed for the denouement.

'Mahatma Gandhi is the name of that treasure!' said Karthaavu, taking a vada from Vengooran's glass cabinet, breaking it into two, and offering one half to Kochu Parashu. 'What was I saying? Yes, that Gandhiji had to be born was the decision of someone sitting above. That's it! We buy a piece of land. We dig a well in it, build a house, and live there for a time. Then we sell it and buy another one. Then, after moving on like that three or four times, in the well dug in the fourth piece of land, lo and behold, we chance upon the treasure! So, what's the meaning of it? Isn't it that there is some power that leads us towards that treasure? This is what happened in our Gandhi's case too. If the first wife hadn't died, or if the second hadn't, or the third hadn't, or if the fourth had stopped after her third delivery, imagine, what would have happened to our country?'

'Then,' said Vengooran Thankappan, 'then, you Kongress fellows would have had it!'

As if looking at Fate's magical chessboard in front of him, barber Shivan's mouth remained open. Floundering for a while as he was not able to come up with a fitting adjective for God, he said, 'Oh, one must hand it to this devil whom we call God!' That acclamation also included his anger for Karthaavu, who did not offer him even a single tidbit of the vada.

When the old men of Elookkara were leaving the shop, after paying for the tea, Kochu Parashu chatted with them, 'Where are you off to with this hen, eh, Adi Mappila? Bought or going to sell?'

Adi Mappila turned and smiled, his pitiful state reflected in his toothless gums, and said, 'Neither, my son! When I went to borrow some cash from a relative, he appeared to be in a state worse than mine! Finally, they gave me this egg-laying hen. I brought it with me, thinking that if a hen, then at least that!'

Anthru Mappila had already started walking. Following him briskly to catch up with him, Adi Mappila wondered aloud, 'Now, from where'll I find the feed for this?'

The Mappilas stopped when they spotted Shankaran hurrying towards them, drenched in sweat. Shankaran's daily commute to the aluminium company was through Elookkara, after which it was Kayintikkara by foot and then crossing over to Eloor by ferry. So, the eyes of Elookkara recognized Shankaran from afar.

'What happened, Nair? This haste doesn't bode well!' Anthru Mappila questioned Shankaran with a frown.

Without replying, Shankaran climbed the steps to the shop, beckoned Kochu Parashu closer, and whispered something into his ears. After standing with his head bowed, stroking his chin and chest, Kochu Parashu asked something in return. Satisfied with the reply he got, Kochu Parashu went into the shop and counted quite a few notes from the cash box and handed them over to Shankaran. Directing an affectionate smile at the Mappilas, Shankaran said: 'An elephant's carcass is floating in the Aluva river.

The bridge is full of people. After some time, it will reach the bend at our Punneli kadavu. If you wanna see, just wait there!'

Shankaran did not forget to say this also to the bewildered old men: 'A small operation for the wife. I'm not familiar with these things, you know?' He held his pocket with his left palm and ran.

After Anthru Mappila and Adi Mappila were farther away, barber Shivan asked Karthaavu the question that he had been keeping in check for quite some time: 'Chettaa, imagine we sold our land to a Mappila. Imagine he got a treasure while digging a well. If so, would the god who kept the treasure in the well be our god or theirs?'

After looking at him pointedly, Karunakaran Karthaavu walked up to Kochu Parashu. 'There isn't any problem with that girl from Ayyaattumpilli?' he asked.

'Hey,' Kochu Parashu denied, 'the problem's with poor Shankaran. He doesn't have a single paisa in his hand. If someone from Ayyaattumpilli asks for money, how can one say no?'

While he was talking, Kochu Parashu switched on the radio. As the long marker on its glass forehead began to move left and right, varied music and human voices were heard, intermittently. Disappointed at not finding what he wanted, Kochu Parashu switched off the radio, and called out, 'Shivo! The corpse of an elephant is floating in Aluva river! You can catch it if you go to Punneli kadavu quickly. If you get at least one tusk, your fortune is made!'

'It can't be that of an elephant, my Kochu Parashu chettaa,' barber Shivan called out as he was getting into his den, continuing to have his doubts about gods. 'Must be some ox or buffalo that has died and is now bloated. Communists like our Shankaran chettan will think elephant even when they see a buffalo!'

Sitting in the teashop, Vengooran Thankappan laughed heartily. Kochu Parashu and Karthaavu smiled.

The children of Ayyaattumpilli milled and jostled around the hospital bed to see the baby. All of them had arrived together in the evening to visit Chinnamma and the new born. For their second visit, Thankamma and Kalyanikuttyamma were wearing new sarees. When the children began to circle around the oranges and Chinese pears, a kilo each of which Pankajaakshan had brought, Chinnamma said, 'Chechi, whatever it is, peel and give to the children!'

Shankaran had gone with the prescription for medicines. Thankamma's husband, Kumaran, looked at the baby snuggling beside Chinnamma, and remarked to his brother-in-law: '*Aliyaa*, look at its ears. Truly elephant ears!'

Removing the white cloth covering the baby from waist down, Pankajaakshan added, 'Not just the ears, see *this*!'

To ward off her brother's evil eye, Chinnamma pulled the baby's cloth back in place. The blood from the umbilical cord began to form a red flower on the white sheet, like the lotus growing out of Lord Vishnu's navel. Rolling his eyes, the baby looked in wonder at all the faces around him. Nine children, from Thankamani, the fourteen-year-old daughter of Thankamma, to the two-year-old Rema, a little elder to him, were peering down at him. Beyond that circle of little faces, the faces of Thankamma, Kumaran, Kalyanikuttyamma, and Pankajaakshan hovered. His unfocused pupils got stuck on another peeping face that had joined them just then: Shankaran, who had come back after fetching the medicines. Like the iron particles in sand vibrating in front of a magnet, every tender cell of the newborn vacillated towards that face. His soul, not yet matured to use language, tried to hail this man who had kindled for him ten months ago, the light, the sound, the touch, the sweetness and smell of amma's milk, and also all the joys, sorrows, desires, and rejections of life on earth that were yet to come.

The syllable 'chha' of achchan—father—sprouted in his soul,

and knocked on all of his nine orifices, bewildered at not being able to find an outlet.

'Chchoo,' sneezed the newborn, through the nose through which life's breath had cleared its path to the outside.

The story of how an elephant come to drink water lost its footing in a slippery stream high up in the Western Ghats, tumbled six or seven times, slammed its head against the rocks, and, being ripped of its life and ivory, got carried in swiftly flowing water without getting struck in the bunds and dams, came under the public gaze for the first time beneath the Marthaanda Varma Bridge, floating through the stares of the unblinking eyes of amazed children on both sides of the river before rotting and becoming an apology for an elephant, till it finally got stuck for three weeks in the mangroves at Punneli kadavu, was a story that grew into an elephantine lie, which Shankaran would tell his son much later. Told by the elder children of Ayyaattumpilli that the carcass found in the river on his birthday was that of a buffalo, Jithen made up a story that other children could not dream of: the story of how the God of Death, Kaalan, who was lurking near the hospital on his buffalo to take the lives of his mother and his own the day after Onam, was scared off by Thachanakkara thevar, who also killed Kaalan's buffalo and threw it in the river, and how that buffalo, as big as an elephant, had floated all along Aluva river till it reached its final resting place among the mangroves at Punneli kadavu for all of the Thachanakkara folk to see.

EIGHT

Progeny

8 May 1999

...I have been sending you at least one letter a week since I came here in March upon getting this job. I know a lot of this must be boring you. However, as this is my sole means of tiding over this infernal loneliness, you will have to bear with my letters. When I sit down to write, even if it is only a letter to you, I am in God's lap. To say a little more harshly, in God's den!

Write something readable about life; or else, live in a way fit for others to write about you—these are the only two ways to escape death.

Undoubtedly, these are not my words. I am not old enough to state things of such gravitas. Nevertheless, I know one fact: all those who attempt to write about life must suffer failure at one point. That is, when trying to render human childhood into language. Which wordsmith of a fisherman can net the free-swimming goldfish of childhood from the great ocean of the unconscious mind?

I am not continuing with this concept. There is a more important thing. A writer not being able to write only goes on to show that he is a genuine writer. A dilemma remains: how does a person who is struggling, on the one hand, in not being able to bring real art into one's writings, and on the other hand, is not able to live life in all its realness, survive his own death?

The ten grandchildren of Naraapilla kept extending the empire of their childhood by pulling up the pales and fences of the four houses of Ayyaattumpilli. The fort and battlements of the tiny empire was the laterite wall built only along the front yard of Chinnamma's house that stood in the seventy-eight-cent plot of land. During the summer holidays, the Muslim children of Elookkara and Kaintikkara breached the ramparts to pluck and take away the pomelos. The young ones with yeast infection and warts, and an eye for profit clambered up the pomelo trees, braving the crawling fire ants with acid sacs on their backsides. Except Thankamani, who had started feeling that looking up at the clambering kids wearing only shorts was something of a sin, all the other children of Ayyaattumpilli stood around looking up with their mouths agape.

With no defence against old age and cataract, Naraapilla had started to flounder in the New House. Yet, he hadn't stopped his early morning baths in the temple pond of Thachanakkara thevar. Sitting on the last row of the broken stone steps of the pond covered in algae bloom, he bathed, using a bowl to pour water on himself. His advanced age was not the only thing keeping him from going waist-deep into the water, holding his nose and immersing himself completely. The remedies prescribed by the senior astrologer in Kaniyankunnu to stop him from having visions of Kunjuamma when he immersed himself in the pond, had not removed his dread completely. Appu Nair, who understood that the temple pond also had started giving Naraapilla the jitters like the waters of Aluva river used to, was fobbed off by Naraapilla. 'After all, it's also water, isn't it? Whether in the river or the pond or in the well, one can't trust it, Appoliyo!'

Naraapilla could not identify the children of varying ages—who ran about in the yard of the New House where he was living alone—as the offspring of their respective parents. He would not make a mistake with only Thankamani, the eldest daughter of Thankamma. She had long tresses and had inherited Kunjuamma's looks. When the other children would appear as shadows on the portico, he would ask, 'Whose are you, Pankajaakshan's or Thankamma's or that accursed one's?'

If the children of the eldest son, Govindan, who anyway were being brought up in Cherai, were to be excluded, the first grandchild that should have been born in Ayyaattumpilli was the one in Kalyanikuttyamma's womb, when she had walked in with Pankajaakshan. However, caught in the heat of a honeymoon celebrated in Munnar, that child had forfeited the honour and departed from this world as a stillborn. As she was being carried for burial at the southern boundary of his plot, seeing the dark curly hair of that six-month-old baby, Pankajaakshan remembered his mother. When Kalyanikuttyamma did not conceive for the next two years, Pankajaakshan was convinced that it was retribution for leaving his sinking mother and going for his honeymoon. When his sister gave birth the same year to a child resembling his own, who was buried, Pankajaakshan was overwhelmed. She had been named Thankamani by Kumaran and Thankamma, but in order to remember his own mother, Pankajaakshan gave her a pet name: Kunjikunjomma. She, in return, called him Pankaachammavan. Thus, Pankajaakshanpolice became Pankaachammavan for the children of Thankamma and Chinnamma.

Thankamma gave birth to another girl after Thankamani—Radha, the singer who was afflicted with polio and ended up with a limp—followed by two boys, Vijayan and Vidyadharan. Kalyanikuttyamma, Pankajaakshan's wife, after the loss of the curly-haired stillborn, gave birth to three boys with an interval of two years each between them: Venu, Shashi, and Soman, who had all inherited their father's features and the Ayyaattumpilli bawl. It was after four plus three, i.e., seven children in the neighbourhood and his two sisters—Geetha whose name that graced the iron gate, and Rema who at two had started making noises like Chinnamma—filled Ayyaattumpilli, that Jithendran's incarnation happened. The Tenth One. The first child to be born in a hospital in the Ayyaattumpilli lineage. The first one to be taken out with a scalpel. The baby with a huge head and big genitals. The first grandchild to affectionately touch Naraapilla, who was turning fetid like a corpse. Despite being given a name which meant 'he who has triumphed over Lord Indra', a hapless Jithendran could not even triumph over himself.

The wonder of coincidences worked even in the selection of his name, which the Thachanakkara denizens had thought to be rather strange when they first heard it. The name, Jithendran, took shape the day the eldest son of Pankajaakshan, Venu, fell off the bicycle and broke his leg.

The anniversary celebrations of Arunodaya Club had taken place in the temple grounds, along with the Onam festivities. Using the surplus amount remaining from the donations collected by moving from house to house in Thachanakkara, Muppaththadam, and Panaayikkulam in the hot sun, the club bought a new cycle for general use. Reading out loud the shiny red lettering on the iron pipe, which extended below, emerging underneath the seat and shining like a black beetle, which said Raleigh Cycle, Vasudevan the club president said, 'It's the number one company. If we keep the cycle in the club, it's for certain that thieves would take it away, breaking in through the thatch.'

Entranced by the smell of the new tyre and the reflections on the oily dome of the bell, which transformed every skinny member into a pot-bellied giant, the members standing around the cycle looked at each other with fear-tinged surmise. The solution also came from Vasudevan: 'There's one thing we can do. Each day, it can be taken to a different member's house. Those who do not know how to ride a cycle can also practise in the morning in the temple grounds.'

Thus, taken by turns to the members' houses, on the twenty-fourth day, it finally reached Ayyaattumpilli. Venu, the eldest son of Pankajaakshan, was the youngest member of the Club. It was by virtue of being the son of Pankajaakshanpolice that he got in as a member though not out of his adolescence yet. In order to impress his mother, seating his younger brothers Soman and Shashi in the front and back, he started circling his home on the cycle. By the third round, Soman, who was sitting astride the pipe in front, felt his hardly-ten-year-old tender testicles inside his knickers getting crushed. As he lifted his bum off the pipe to give a little relief to the aching testicles, the rider lost his balance and the cycle fell. Bearing the weight of both his brothers, Venu's right leg got caught under the cycle and was crushed. The fourteen-year-old's bone was fractured below the knee.

That evening Paanamparampath Nanu reached Vengooran Thankappan's teashop with the tale of Pankajaakshanpolice's son falling off the cycle and fracturing his leg. It was when the discussion, which started with Nanu's declamation that reposing faith in a tyre as thin as a rat snake—that too, a tyre in motion—and riding on it, was not for intelligent people, moved on to motorized two-wheelers, that Karunakaran Karthaavu joined in, after closing the door of his Writer's Office. That set the stage for Karunakaran Karthaavu to narrate the story, taking care not to compromise one bit on its entertainment quotient, of the Hindi movie he had seen the previous week in a talkies in Ernakulam.

'Amongst the actors to date, who's the most accomplished in riding motorcycles?' Karthaavu entered into a direct quiz. Not just Nanu, Vengooran, Thankappan, Shivan barber, and Kochu

Parashu, but even Shankaran who had just reached to pay his credit amount, shrank back in front of that question. Who is the best rider of a motorcycle was a question they had not asked themselves before!

'That's our Sivaji Ganesan,' said Nanu, a staunch fan of Sivaji, the thespian actor of Tamil movies.

'Haeey, what good are Tamilians other than for driving lorries?' Karthaavu dismissed it contemptuously. 'If you don't know, listen, it is Hindi's Jeetendra!' Enjoying the frown on everyone's brow occasioned by that name, Karthaavu continued, 'Ho, last week I had been to Ernaa'lum and saw that guy's movie. Parichay.'

'Parichai! The Tamil name of the parichaa thingy we use to block blows by the sword?' Nanu asked innocently.

'That it is NOT.' Karthaavu was cross. 'This is "parichay" in Hindi. What we call *parichayam*, or acquaintance.'

'What is its story?' queried an eager Barber Shivan, angling to hear the story of a Hindi movie without spending money.

'That's fun!' Karthaavu started off with his typical laugh that made him shut his eyes, which was how he always set off his narration of the story of a movie. In the five listeners, five inner silver screens began to come alive with five different movies based on a single story. In them, a grandfather called Pran, his son and a music lover, Sanjeev Kumar, his five children, the eldest of which was Jaya Bhaduri, flickered and grew in clarity. With the death of their parents, the brats reached their grandfather's house and began to indulge in much mischief. One by one, the masters who came to tutor them failed. Finally, the very smart Jeetendra turns up at their bungalow, and succeeds in taming the children. The eldest child, Jaya Bhaduri, falls in love with Jeetendra. On the assurance that their wedding will happen, on each of the five screens 'The End' flashed in Malayalam as shubham, as the Hindi movie played out.

When he realized that Shankaran had come to pay his credit amount, Kochu Parashu got up from his inner cinema and came out. Shankaran had come also to invite Kochu Parashu for the next day's naming ceremony of his third child. After taking the money, marking the entry, and returning the notebook, Kochu Parashu asked the usual question, 'What are you naming your son?'

'Not decided yet,' Shankaran said. 'Do you have any good names?'

After thinking about something for a while, Kochu Parashu switched on the radio. The needle which runs over stations tickled many places. Finally, Kochu Parashu's search ended on a wavy film song. That was a Malayalam song which emanated from Ceylon, which had recently renamed itself Sri Lanka. 'Haven't people used up most of the names?' Kochu Parashu spoke without turning his head away from the radio. 'Now the kids will have to be named Jeetendra, Jaya Bhaduri, and the like.'

While at that time his opinion appeared to be in jest, next day, by the time the five ceremonial beads were to be tied on his child, it had brought Shankaran to a state of dilemma. Though he had told Kochu Parashu that no name had been decided on, an eminent name was glowing inside him. The name of a comrade who had been dismissed for unionizing the workers in the aluminium factory: Balaanandan. But when only hours were left for the naming ceremony, Chinnamma protested against the name.

'You could find only this oldie's name?' Chinnamma asked, powdering the navel of the child. 'We should give him a modern name. Something like Surendran or Rajendran … It's that kind of name I am thinking of.'

Shankaran tried in vain to recall the name of the hero in Karthaavu's movie. On the pretext of going to get turmeric paste for applying on the string of beads, he got out and asked Karthaavu the name of the hero whose motorcycle-riding skills were exemplary.

'His real name is Ravi,' Karunakaran Karthaavu explained about that baptism while he was opening his Document Office. 'Ravi Kapoor who used to peddle gold jewellery to cinema actors. When he started acting, Jeetendra was the name given to him by Director Shantaram.'

'Jithendra,' Shankaran repeated that name many times, as he was walking back. By the time he reached home, the name had grown a tail of half a syllable. As it is typical of Malayali names, Jithendra lengthened into Jithendran. In the circumstance in which her sister-in-law's son was down with a broken leg falling off a bicycle, Chinnamma heartily approved naming her son after a skilled motorcycle rider.

For the naming ceremony, there were only two invitees other than the Ayyaattumpilli family members. Kochu Parashu, who came exactly around lunchtime after locking up his shop, and the policeman Raman Pilla, who attended the function but did not stay for lunch. To register his protest at his wife not being invited, Raambillapolice left the moment the beads were tied on. Shankaran had gone two days ago to the New House and invited Naraapilla. After he had delayed so long to see his grandson, no one expected Naraapilla to turn up for the twenty-eighth day ceremony. As the time drew close for the ceremony, Geethalayam was filled with Ayyaattumpilli members. As the baby to be named had a cold and was sneezing since morning, Chinnamma refused to give him a head bath; instead, she lay him on a spathe and washed his body with lukewarm water. After shaking out and spreading a grass mat, Shankaran sat with the baby, facing East. Two-year-old Rema stood close, touching him. Applying kohl on his bulbous eyes, dabbing the snot with his own mundu, and tying the turmeric-encrusted string with the five-metal beads on the baby's waist, Shankaran reinforced his recall of the chosen name. Closing the right ear of his son with a tender betel leaf, into the left ear he whispered 'Shreeparameswaran' thrice. Then, blocking the left ear, in the right ear he called his son thrice: 'Jithendran … Jithendra … Jithendro!'

Tickled by the syllables, Jithendran laughed. In various pitches, in various sounds, amazingly bereft of love…

Can you see his roguish smile?

Hey, have a look at Remakutty's face … as if stung by a hornet!

For that, praise our Geetha! Her brother is her life.

Move over! Let me see the kiddo.

Havooo! Where was Pankaachammavan till now?

Is there any need to ask? Can't you see he's coming after a tipple?

After the kohl has been applied, doesn't he resemble our father, Chinnammae?

Shush, kunjetta … my son is not that repulsive!

Isn't it so, Kalloo? You take a look.

I felt it before. Grampa's features mean that of you all as well.

Haii, why have you come here now with your broken leg?

I am going mad lying there all by myself, ammae. You want to hear something? When I was coming here, achchachan asked if there was a feast.

I see! He didn't ask what has happened to your leg?

Fancy! When I came away without answering, he was cursing me to a shortened life!

Thankamani, take some rice and curry for father in a vessel.

I won't go. If you want, you go yourself.

What, you are leaving, Raambillachettaa? Have something and go.

No, no. She'll be waiting there to eat with me. Shankaro, my friend, let me leave then!

Shush … he's coming, leaning on the stick!

My God, dee, Chinnamma, look, father's coming this side!

What should I do? Should I light a lamp with buttermilk? Whoever has to come will come. There's enough to eat his fill. Let him eat. And go.

Where's the baby? All the kids go out. Shankaro, where's the baby?

Why call Shankaran? I'll tell you. Here, this is the baby. You haven't come all these days. Take a good look!

Shush ... sis-in-law, this is not the time to talk this way.

Why have you put charcoal on his face?

That isn't charcoal. It's kohl! Today's his twenty-eighth day, no?

Eh?

His twenty-eighth day! Don't you know?

That's why I came. What have you called him?

Jithendran...

Eh?

Jithendran.

What kind of name is that?

I am also asking the same thing!

She'll do that and worse. She's always done what she wants.

I am living in my home with my kid! Chechiye, if he's hungry feed him and send him away. Let me hold my peace.

Phthooo! Who needs your feed? Naraapilla hasn't come to eat your food. That accursed corpse of a woman came when I was nodding and asked if I wasn't going to see her grandson. He's a boy like our Govindan, she said. Go and take a look, and she wept. That's why I came ... not for your rice ... phthooo!

Don't go, Father, because she said things mindlessly. Come, sit here. Dee Thankamaniye, cut a plantain leaf!

I don't think he's going to sit down, Kumaro!

Shankara, hold him please. If he falls on the steps, that'd be it!

How old is uncle?

Seventy-four. Was born in ninety-eight.

Son, why are you in the midst of this throng with your bandaged leg?

Right, let me move away. If achchachan sees me, he'll begin cursing.

Chinnammae, did you hear what father said? That Amma came to him in his sleep and told him that the baby resembles our vallyettan! When I look at him now, I too feel so.

Lies. I don't want to listen to all this.

No. Take a look. Really. Etta, here, you take a look. See if he resembles vallyettan.

Aavo! I don't feel anything. Well, hasn't anyone informed Govindettan? After the surgery and all that happened here?

Who's there to inform him? Let my tummy heal. I am going to Cherai with my kids. Sulu sister-in-law dotes on me. Isn't it this accursed father who kept that poor thing away?

Aw! Will you keep quiet, Chinnammae? You shouldn't be shouting like this now, do you understand?

In that case, lay the plantain leaves for everyone. Everyone go back home after food. Boys, cut a few plantain leaves. Not from the New House. Can't start a fight for that!

Looks like this ruckus has frightened the baby, look at its face!

Now he really resembles vallyettan. He too left after being fed up with the shouting.

Jithendra … monae, Jithendrakutta … don't worry. When you can walk and run, you too escape to someplace else!

NINE

Iconoclasm

13 June 1999

...Have you noticed that all the schoolchildren in uniforms nowadays have the same face. Same eyebrows, same nose, same mouths that have been pressed down with wires to remove all resemblances to Dravidian looks ... like the most popular toy manufactured in our toy factory—a monkey playing a drum. Same attire, same facial expression, same drum, even the sound it makes is homophonic...

But each child at Aalungal School, where I went, was different. Each smile and each soul was different.

Why did I remember this now?

Yesterday, a friend in my office bought a mobile phone. A young man from a rich family. He said that this thing which can be carried in the pocket is going to become very common in our country too, like it is abroad. Since both our houses don't even have land phones, we don't have to bother about it, do we? Will the time come when all will carry such mobile phones? Should we have been born a little late in time? No. Let's love now and live now and die now itself. It will be terrifying to live at a time in which letters written by dipping in love will be supplanted with something else. An instrument that is an accomplice in destroying words will defile human life tomorrow. Oh God, has that time come?

There used to be a mad Nampoothiri in the Thachanakkara of my childhood who would walk around with an old telephone receiver with its wires cut, talking earnestly to important people not present at the other end of the line. On our way to school, we used to run and hide after calling him by some nickname. When father told me that he was once the president of the youngsters' club in Thachanakkara, and was exceptionally smart, I stopped joining the kids' army that harassed that poor soul.

During the time she was breastfeeding her youngest child, Chinnamma had shifted her bath from Periyar river to the irrigation bund.

It was after the asphalt layers had blackened the mud road that ran caressing Kochu Parashu's shop, that the new irrigation bund, which came as part of the Water Authority scheme, drew parallel lines through the green fields of Thachanakkara. Beyond the temple, on the border of the land on which Arunodaya Club stood, the road passed over a culvert to cross the irrigation bund. The waters of the Periyar, sucked up and spat out by a gigantic machine that wheezed from insufficient horsepower, lost control and kept gushing through the cemented channel of the eight-feet-wide irrigation canal. The first things that floated like ripened yellow mango leaves, in the water surging through the channels gone dry in the heat of the summer mornings, were human faeces. Before the crack of dawn, the children from the houses anchored close to the edges of the bund, moved like sleepwalkers towards the bund to empty their bowels. Turning the dry bund into an endless snake boat, they squatted here and there. When they would hear the clog-like sounds of water approaching from afar, they would clutch the floor of the bund, clawing their toes in as a precaution against losing their balance in the onrush of water. When the warmth of the first surge of water hit their bottoms, the children's mouths would open in primordial pleasure. And, when the water, flowing just above the floor for a long while at the beginning, would begin to rise, the children's turn would be over. By then the women, who had learnt to bathe in the bund without losing their balance and to stand perched in the water like monkeys, would start arriving with their bundles of dirty linen. The irrigation bund was a refuge from the Aluva river in which Muringaattil Leela still romped. Forgetting the *advaitham* that both the waters were the same, some silly women said, 'It's not at all like the river water, there's this something special in bund water!'

Of the soiled clothes of Ayyaattumpilli, now, only Naraapilla's single mundus took their trips to Punneli kadavu, passing through the hands of washerwoman Ammu. Ammu's mother Thaamara had stopped washing, after her right hand had become paralyzed. Out of the habit of having washed the dirty laundry of Thachanakkara, the old Thaamara still fancied that she had in her right hand, which had become limp like a wrung mundu, an impulse that felt like the one just before she raised the cloth to hit the washing stone. Thaamara's life had began to fold in, sighing at how the Thachanakkara women had started washing their clothes, and gave only a small share of their soiled linen to Ammu with the beetle on her cheek. By then, the Thachanakkara women had realized that it was better to stand in the sunlight and wash their clothes in the irrigation bund, rather than give ten paisa each for shirts and mundus to Ammu as washing charges. Kalyanikuttyamma, the wife of Pankajaakshan of Ayyaattumpilli, had begun washing her family's clothes by beating them on the washing stone fixed near the well in her house, following the trend she had picked up from Kochi. Thankamma on the other hand, went to the bund just to wash clothes, after the sun's heat retreated a little. To be one up on her sister, Chinnamma went to the bund in the scorching heat, wrapped in a single mundu covering her breasts and torso, and washed and wrung dry all the clothes and stacked them on the dry upper steps. Then, she scrubbed herself with coir fibre and leftover washing soap, before she returned home around the turn of noon, with a sunburnt hide. She would scorn her sister and sister-in-law who wouldn't go with her to have a bath in the daytime. 'Won't the madams become dark if they were to bathe in the daytime? For us people since there's nothing left to darken, if it's the bund, then it shall be the bund!'

Chinnamma used to go for her baths, leaving Geetha and Rema at Thankamma's and the younger one, who had started to crawl, in the house of Raambillapolice. This was the same Raman Pillai, who remained as Thachanakkara's Raambillapolice even after his retirement, and whose virtue of having informed Pankajaakshan that recruitment to the police force was taking place on the grounds of Aluva School, was later turned into a lie when he claimed that it was he who got the job for Pankajaakshan. Due to some mysterious reason, even the shadow of Raambillapolice was detested by Pankajaakshan's wife Kalyanikuttyamma. She forbade her three sons from going to his house. Raambillapolice's house, with its corroded pillars on the half wall, was just across the small road in front of the laterite wall of Geethalayam. The three children of Chinnamma called him Granpa Rambilla. Each time that tall dark man, who was marking time in his childless life with a wife who looked older than him, heard himself addressed so by Chinnamma's children, he would experience a surge of happiness not befitting the policemen of his era. Chinnamma's younger son, Jithen, peed on Granpa Rambilla's chest, and tried to pull out the lush grey hair on his umbrella-like ears. When the boy was lifted up into the air, he kicked his nose and forehead with baby feet. Raambilla would laugh uproariously, taking care to not let his two protruding front teeth hurt the child. Jithen stole from Granpa Rambilla. who was merely a neighbour, the sum total of all the affection due to the nine grandchildren of Ayyaattumpilli from the patriarch Naraapilla, but was never received by any.

When Vasudevan of Nedumpilli Mana was being taken away by policemen, charged with trying to dump the minor deity of the Thachanakkara temple into the temple pond, Granpa Raambilla warned Jithen, who was bouncing on his waist and watching the scene innocently, 'If you misbehave, I will make policemen catch you too like that, ngaa!'

Jithen was then not old enough to understand how the childless Raambillapolice had turned an innocent young man of Thachanakkara into a madman. By the time he heard, for the first time, about how the youngest Nampoothiri of Nedumpilli Mana had evolved into a madman named Alamboori, he had grown up. Granpa Raambilla, who had gifted Alamboori to Thachanakkara, had expired.

The story begins with Vishwanathan, the eldest son of Kochu Parashu, the most important trader of Thachanakkara.

Vishwanathan's selfishness was behind the decision to shift the club from the confines of the small shop next to Poovamparampath Stores. Not many knew that it was Lalitha, the youngest daughter of Amminiyamma of Chammaram and the deceased Kamanthan Gangadharan Nair, who was the reason for transplanting the club. At the very onset of her youth, Lalitha who was smoothly rounded like a spout-less kindi, had gone way ahead of her mother in mastering certain techniques of sexual combat. Vishwanathan, who once happened to glance accidentally at the bathing ghat at the irrigation bund in the killing heat of the month of Kumbham, was struck by lightning when Lalitha opened her sarong and retied it with a sweeping swish. Though it looked totally unintentional then, it was actually a very clever ploy on her part to trap into her mundu the more-than-capable son of Kochu Parashu who always had cash in his cash box. Vishwanathan, who had been sent by his father to check the flow of water from the bund to his field, was hurled upside down by that fleeting vision of temptation that he had witnessed.

It was the time when he had been sending applications and waiting for a job, after having completed his bachelor's degree from UC College. It was he, along with his brother Vijayan, two years younger than him, and Vasudevan of Nedumpilli Mana, who had established the Eagles Arts Club in one of the unused shops owned by his father. When the increasing membership made the functioning of the Eagles Club difficult within the confines of Pooshaappi's shop, Lalitha's enticing figure, revealed when her lungi was flung open, flashed again in Vishwanathan's mind. He was beckoned by a place that would not be accessible to his father's eyes, so that he could worship that idol during the unengaged afternoons at the club. With that, the club moved from the shop to the unused plot near the irrigation bund. Into the afternoons of the hermitage of the club, renamed Arunodaya, Lalitha turned up, wet and plump, like a goddess strutting out of the irrigation bund. Vishwanathan began to experience from top to toe, the complexities of her short body which was taut like a tightly strung udukku drum.

When Vijayan, Vishwanathan's younger brother and a club member, found a correlation between money disappearing unaccountably from his father's cash box and Vishwanathan's club visits in the afternoons, there was a new turn for the secret rendezvous. It was left to the club president, Vasudevan, to deliver the final words of the chastisement to Vishwanathan after summoning him alone to the club: 'In my opinion, the ill-repute to the club would only be secondary. What about channelling your father's hard-earned money to flow freely to Chammaram? You should realize one thing. She is not Lalitha. She's a man-eater, a pucca Poothana, Poothana!'

After that, there was a temporary hiatus in Chammaram Lalitha siphoning off cash from Kochu Parashu's cash box, with Vishwanathan as the key. But she did not stay idle. Since her mother had started ageing, there had been a substantial decrease in the income at Chammaram. When Vishwanathan could find no new place to meet her, as Vasudevan had forbidden him from opening the Arunodaya Club in the afternoons, Lalitha guided him to the little temple that was constructed for the minor deity on the north-western corner of the Thachanakkara temple yard. The isolation of the temple yard, the small temple surrounded by thickets of Siam weed plants, was no doubt an ideal place for secret sex. The deity there was a small Vishnu idol, with a hand wrecked in a fall during Tippu's military occupation of Kerala. Circling the small temple of red laterite stones, was a narrow mud path made by the footfalls of the devotees who went around it, as if in sympathy for those who came without fail in the morning and evening to bow before Thachanakkara thevar. Lalitha assured him that except for the two or three cows and the crows that came to eat the insects on their backs, in the frightening silence of the temple yard reposing in the afternoon, there would be no one around. As he had imbibed enough atheism from Vasudevan, Vishwanathan did not have any qualms in picking up the kid-sized idol of the small temple from its place to lay it on the floor, and to spread the lungi in that empty space to gambol with Lalitha. Due more out of womanly greed than fear of God, for each ten-rupee note that smelt of tea and coconut oil that Kochu Parashu's son Vishwanathan had filched for her, an adequate performance was presented by Lalitha in her sanctuary. Though he was frightened by the sounds of the hooves of cows occasionally, Vishwanathan panted with elation at the return of the joyous days of Arunodaya Club that he had thought were over for good.

However, those happy days too were short-lived.

Raambillapolice, who had come to the temple yard to graze his newly-acquired cow in the temple lands, frowned seeing a movement in the isolation of the small temple further ahead. Letting the cow graze among the touch-me-not plants, with a leftover gusto from his old khaki days, he walked with sure steps towards the temple. At that point, inside the little temple, the last rendezvous between Lalitha and Vishwanathan was reaching its crescendo. Spotting a greying head near the clumps of Siam weed plants, Lalitha broke the prolonged union and pushed Vishwanathan away, saying, 'There, somebody's coming! Just give that money and run, son!'

She disappeared into the thickets around the temple with the ten-rupee note. Holding in his hand the red shirt he had draped around the idol, Vishwanathan jumped out and ran towards Arunodaya Club. In their hurry, the lovers had forgotten to return the granite Vishnu to his place.

As soon he was able to adjust his vision after the initial blindness upon entering from the glare of the sunlit yard, Raambillapolice, casting his eye around, deduced what had happened. He went directly to Aluva Police Station to report in person about how his timely intervention had prevented the uprooting and throwing of the deity into the temple pond by two young men who had run for their lives into Arunodaya Club. Raambillapolice pointedly stressed to the young sub-inspector—who had joined service only after his retirement—that though the faces of the young men were not distinct, the man who ran behind had a red flag in his hand. Before evening, a police jeep reached Arunodaya Club. When Vasudevan asked the three policemen what the matter was as they threw out all the magazines and newspapers in the club, one policeman demanded, 'Where're the pamphlets?'

Right in front of the club, the policemen in peaked caps began to bash the president who was perspiring, unable to answer them.

Vishwanathan fainted seeing Vasudevan being taken away in the jeep.

In the lock-up of the Aluva Police Station, after smashing in Vasudevan's right eye, the sub-inspector bellowed, with his upturned moustache trembling, 'Son of a bitch! Are you all playing Naxalism in my territory?'

They did not listen to anything Vasudevan said. After writing down his name and his house name, with one yank they tore off his shirt buttons and stripped him. They kicked him in his navel, scorning him for being a Nampoothiri without his sacred thread. They regretted that they could not conveniently bash his head against the wall, as their hold on his oily hair kept slipping. Blood squirted from the broken bridge of his nose and forehead. Poked by the hard bamboo baton, his ribs broke. The torture increased. With their kicks, faeces spurted out. Their containers wrecked, the seeds of this descendant of an ancient lineage that venerated the deity for centuries, lay scattered.

'Arunodaya Club! That means red dawn, doesn't it? Yeah, yeah, you will have many bloodied, "red" dawns!' mocked a policeman, as he broke Vasudevan's cheekbones with a knuckleduster. Vasudevan silently cursed the moment when the name of the club was changed for no reason. They continued their punishment, demanding the name of his companion who had helped remove the idol to install the revolutionary flag instead. Before he lost consciousness, they had inscribed in blood many new names in his mind. After vomiting a mouthful of blood on his naked thighs and fainting in front of the khaki figures melting in the air, the young lord of Nedumpilli Mana heard this too: 'You will dump the icon in the pond, chop off the heads of feudal lords! Right, you bastard son of a dog?'

That year, the re-installation of the idol of Vishnu was celebrated with great zeal by the Thachanakkara folk. As part of it, *lakshaarchana* pooja and *udayasthamana* pooja were celebrated for the first time in Thachanakkara. In the *thaamboola prashnam*, or soothsaying using betel leaves, it came to be revealed that the Vishnu of the little temple was more powerful than Thachanakkara thevar, who was the avatar of Parashuraman. The young man, despite being brilliant and a Brahmin, who was turned into a madman the very instant he thought of dumping Vishnu's idol into the temple pond, was acclaimed as the living example of the maya of Vishnu. An extra elephant was added for Vishnu of the small temple for that year's festival in the month of Medam. To add to the gaiety of the children's festivities, apart from balloon sellers and ice fruit vendors, a new lunatic too appeared on the temple land. It was Vasudevan of Nedumpilli Mana, whose life was totally crushed. By the time his innocence was established in the trial court, he was unable to remember anything from his prior life. He had started walking around with a chunky black telephone receiver that he had found from somewhere, which he kept pressed to his ear. Instead of the sacred thread he had discarded in his saner days, he had a yellow plastic thread tied across his torso, with which he had done his initiation ritual into a boiling insanity, all by himself. He walked busily through the temple ground, deep in conversation through his wrecked phone, with the strangers planted in his shattered consciousness as mere names. Often, he was troubled with a breakdown in communication, saying, 'Hello, isn't this Kanu Sanyal? This is me, Vasudevan! Hah, don't you remember? The one who operated that idol case … Hello, Choman Mooppan? Hello, is this Mandakini chechi? Hello … 'allo … 'allo…'

Children honoured him by calling him Hello Nampoothiri. As time went by, Hello Nampoothiri got abbreviated to Alomboori, and then to Alamboori. Kochu Parashu's son Vishwanathan began to take different routes, scared by Alamboori's stare which, like that of a beaten cat, would not lose any of its sharpness even after nine lives. To endorse her vaunted charity, for which she was known throughout Thachanakkara in those days, on every Vishu of the month of Medam, Lalitha used to give Alamboori a one-rupee coin and bow before him. Accepting the coin and touching it to his blinded right eye, each time the erstwhile young lord of Nedumpilli Mana held his yellow plastic thread ritually with his left hand, and gave his blessings extending his right hand. 'Always, only good will happen to you!'

The first man in Thachanakkara who started bathing in the irrigation bund was Alamboori. Those who would pass by before the crack of dawn would see a piteous figure, a silhouetted idol standing smiling on the culvert, praying with raised hands, for the good of the entire world to the sun god emerging from the east.

Someone's sin.

Someone's sin.

Someone's grievous sin.

TEN

Treasure Chest

24 December 1999

...Tomorrow being a postal holiday, this letter may reach you late. There is no point in me now requesting you to remember me on this Christmas eve. Tomorrow is the last Christmas of our pre-nuptial life. Ann Marie, my patron saint of love, from tonight I will be writing about my childhood. While you will be praying on this night of the Nativity, I will be able to recall the furthest extent of my childhood.

Oh, childhood! In that is the brotherhood of all creatures of this world. A young cobra breaking out of an egg and a plant emerging from the seed into the light with its leafy eyes, are similar not just visually. One should not be surprised if God and the Devil were exchanged at birth and brought up by unsuspecting parents. The essence of childish innocence cannot be influenced by time-space differences. Religion or caste or gender have little to do with it. But the misfortune is this: even if insignificant, everyone must outgrow that exalted state.

There is only one job in which, with every promotion, one has a feeling of self-deprecation: Life.

Kunthi, who had elephantiasis in her right leg, stayed for twelve days at Geethalayam during that year's Onam. Shankaran's younger sister used to catch a bus from Thaayikkattukara to Thachanakkara, once a month, keeping his salary date in her calculation. The sister-in-law usually returned on the second or the third day, by which time the displeasure on Chinnamma's face would be evident. For the children, she was Kunthi'mmayi.

Till his mother's death, once a month, Shankaran used to travel from Thachanakkara to Thaayikkattukara. He had to look after not only his mother, but also his sister, who was forsaken on the third day of her wedding for the crime of having hidden her elephantiasis. The prophecy of an old, radiant astrologer that her name also would contribute to her failure in life was coming true. When he swore that other than a river in the north, the name Kunthi was not prevalent anywhere on the earth for girls, it devastated her. 'It's not auspicious for girls to be named after rivers,' said the old man, who had tied a yellow scarf over his matted hair. 'You will see; the lives of girls who have names of rivers, will flow through misfortune!'

Grieving for her divorced daughter, the mother died. For Kunthi, who was left alone in the small house in Thaayikkattukara, only her elephantiasis-affected leg kept her company. Hearing that her husband had divorced her, fearing that he too would get infected with elephantiasis if he slept with her, the young men of Thaayikkattukara gave her a wide berth, and avoided her house.

She always spoke about her husband, who had abandoned her, with pride. 'Listen, edathiammae,' keeping her left leg folded in and stretching and stroking her right leg, she would tell Chinnamma, 'at least three days he stayed with me? Had it been someone else, wouldn't he have left me the first night itself, seeing my leg? That is what I said, he was humane.'

Oiling her leg, Kunthi nurtured her elephantiasis. Every time before leaving Geethalayam she would come to Shankaran and show her pustule-ridden leg and say, 'Look, pappae, when I applied the oil pappa gave me, it started shining!'

Looking indulgently at the leg which resembled a yam yanked out of the soil, Shankaran would say, 'It has come down.' Then, digging out some coins from the little money in his pocket, he would hand them to her and say, 'Don't stop the oil. Here, keep this with you.'

From the time Aunt Kunthi would disembark at the bus stop in front of the temple, the other children of Ayyaattumpilli would stop coming anywhere near Geethalayam, fearing infection from her leg. But it was their loss. Only Chinnamma's daughters had the good fortune to enjoy her folk tales that did not lose their charm even if heard a hundred times, find small contrivances to locate the source of smelly farts, and chant potent mantras for driving away minor ailments like head and tummy aches—all learnt first-hand from their aunt.

The five-year-old Geetha would plead with Kunthi, lisping, 'Pleeesh Kunthi'mmayi, say, no, Kunthi'mmayi?'

'What should I say?'

'The mantra that takes away headaches,' Geetha, carrying her younger brother on her hip, would crow to her with anticipation.

'I'll say this only once more. Everyone, listen carefully.' Then putting on a grave face, Aunt Kunthi would clear her throat and start her staccato recitation:

Kudukudu mathra, kudukudumanthra,
that is going to cure you tomorrow
and cure you completely day after tomorrow, UUSVAA!

As soon as the powerful mantra recitation was over, Geetha's sister Rema would pull out a coconut leaf spine from the broom and stretching it towards Kunthi, start her sniffle, 'Kunthi'mmayi, Kunthi'mmayi, can you please make me the device for identifying the kid who farts?'

'Ayye.' Aunt Kunthi would turn her head away to hide her laughter.

'Why Kunthi'mmayi, you are our dearest, no? Please make us that "oochankkol" to catch farts.' Geetha would advocate her sister's cause.

Aunt Kunthi would screw up her nose and take the coconut leaf spine. She would break it into a piece the size of a finger and fold one half like an arm and holding the other half between her palms, start turning it as if spinning a wick for the lamp and then recite the mantra to make it point in the right direction:

Oochankolae, thirukolae,
Oh wand of fart, thou divine wand
show me the farting smarty-pants

The device would stop spinning upon hearing the request for pointing out the person who had passed wind. It would always point towards baby Jithen. Looking at the little miscreant, Geetha and Radha would roar with laughter.

Seeing her sister-in-law's antics, Chinnamma would fly into a rage, 'What are you doing, Kunthi? Oho, worse than children. Don't spoil the children with your inanities. Come and scrape this coconut for me. Or … Never mind, as if you can sit on the scraper with that leg! Dee, Geethae, here, take and scrape this. You are not a baby. At your age I had started draining boiled rice!'

The children waited for each visit, And not only did they not fear her leg with elephantiasis, they even felt sympathy for the one without elephantiasis. 'If our Kunthi'mmayi had elephantiasis on her other leg too, what fun it would be!' Geetha told Rema, awaiting Aunt Kunthi's next visit.

'Ouw, shut up, will you, you wicked girl,' Chinnamma would scold Geetha. Unable to comprehend how her wish could be wickedness, Geetha would stare at her sister, open-mouthed.

Though she had only joined the first standard in Aalungal School, even as a child she had attained an elder-sister aura, taking after her eldest cousin Thankamani. 'Dee Remae,' she would order about her sister peremptorily, 'don't stand in the sun; go inside. If you are disobedient, Alamboori will take you away, ngaa!'

Thankamani, elder to Geetha by ten years, had completed her tenth standard and passed out from the St Francis Girls' High School, Aluva, and thoughts of her marriage were weighing heavily on the mind of Thankamma in the old house. Thankamani had inherited the thick curly hair of her grandmother; she wanted to be a dancer. She had joined the dance school started by a dance teacher called Sadanandan in a room in front of the Thachanakkara temple, which had been used as a free lodge previously. During the temple festival that year, on the second day when the dance by new dancers was staged, she won applause for her performance of *Kaaliyamardhanam*. However, Ayyaattumpilli was not fated to have a danseuse in the family. Her guru eloped with another student who had shown great promise in Mohiniyaattam. For many years, Guru Sadanandan's yellow board hung askew, covered in cobwebs with the faded 'Parashurama Nritta Vidyaalayam' still visible on it. With the elopement of the guru, Thankamani started taking primary lessons in culinary skills from her mother in preparation for her marital life. Her debut in Thachanakkara temple thus became her farewell show as well. The large serpent cut-out painted by artist Babu on double thick paper as the show's backdrop, lay in the attic of the old house in a crumpled heap till it disintegrated. She gave the accoutrements she wore on her hair when performing *Kaaliyamardhanam*, to her cousin Geetha. The five-year-old carried around the *kunjalam*, made of gilt, velvet, and black string, with more veneration than it deserved. Tying the kunjalam to her hair, which was yet to reach below her neck, she happily enacted *Kaaliyamardhanam* in front of the mirror almirah her father had bought recently.

Only Chinnamma did not have a well of her own in Ayyaattumpilli. Through the fence dividing Geethalayam and the New House, she had an opening to go through and fetch water. She was in a hurry to have a clean break with her father and stop drawing water from the well in the New House. 'If only we had used the money and dug a well instead of the damned wall and gate,' she would often curse herself.

During those Onam days, carrying Jithen on her hip, Kunthi paced the front yard of Geethalayam, hampered by her leg. Walking like her aunt's shadow, Rema kept tickling Jithen's silver anklet-clad leg. When she saw Kunthi standing, carrying her son, near the break in the fence leading to the New House, Chinnamma shouted, 'Kunthiyye, come here with my son.'

Naraapilla and Kunthi were two souls who were isolated for different reasons in their houses in Thachanakkara and Thaayikkattukara, respectively. Because of that, despite knowing all the vile tales about Naraapilla, Kunthi felt sympathy for the old man. Naraapilla reminded her of her own father, who had died when she was still a baby. When she would calculate that it was sixteen years since her brother had moved to Ayyaattumpilli, she would wonder that, after the episode of Naraapilla ridiculing her during the wedding feast for scraping the curry off the plantain leaf, he had never talked to her!

In normal circumstances, Chinnamma would not have had any misgivings about Kunthi who stood near the breach in the fence, pondering. However, she had become vigilant ever since Appu Nair had called her and had given her a timely warning. 'That he has become old, he alone doesn't know,' Appu Nair had told his niece. 'Listen, Chinnammae. He may find even the elephantiasis attractive.'

But despite Appu Nair's anxiety, Chinnamma once herself had to send Kunthi to Naraapilla's side. Jithen was completing two years on avittam day in the month of Chingam. Kunthi, who reached a day before aththam, stayed at Geethalayam for twelve days to attend Jithen's birthday. Though there was leftover wheat paayasam made for Thiruvonam, the next day Chinnamma made parippu paayasam for her son's birthday. After all of them had eaten it, there was a lot of paayasam left over. Chinnamma poured it into three vessels. Then, after thinking for some time, one portion she sent with Geetha to Pankajaakshan's house, and one with Rema to Thankamma's house. Though she went out carrying the third vessel, she did not go forward. She called Kunthi after some time and told her, 'Kunthiye, take this to that side. I have a pile of clothes to wash.'

Chinnamma left to wash clothes in the irrigation bund in the blazing sun; the forty-year-old Kunthi, with the birthday boy Jithen on her hip and the paayasam vessel in her hand, headed towards the seventy-five-year-old Naraapilla.

Eight years later, one of the two women to wail loudly on seeing the white-cloth-swathed body of Naraapilla in the New House would be Kunthi, Shankaran's sister. On that day, Appu Nair, who had known Naraapilla for close to eight decades, would use his ultimate powers to be astonished one more time and bring out, and dust up one of his forgotten old usages. 'When I saw that Shankaran's sister cry out so loud, I went hari hara,' he would say. 'Why was she crying? I am still not able to understand that.'

Though he was only about ten years old that day, since a very hazy picture from the past kept rising in his mind, for Jithendran alone the wails of his Aunt Kunthi would not appear aberrant. Instead, he would feel an unexplained dread towards the thoroughly sodden body of his grandfather, which took a long time to burn up, having been lying in the algae bloom-filled temple pond for a long time.

Remembering how he had tried not to fall off a bouncing cot bound with coir, looking alternately at an unopened vessel of paayasam and a swollen foot of a woman which repeatedly kept coming close to it, a two-year-old boy inside him started crying again.

For the ten grandchildren of Naraapilla, except Govindan's kids, Aunt Kunthi gave a descriptor: the first one was favourite; the second one, sovereign; the third, a thechi flower; the fourth one, a fine lemon; the fifth, a five-colour parrot; the sixth one, an axe thief; the seventh one, a sacred script; the eighth, a weighty pot; the ninth one, a nincompoop; and for the tenth, cometh the treasure chest.

On those ten descriptors, Aunt Kunthi imposed the traits of everyone from Thankamma's daughter Thankamani to Chinnamma's son Jithen. In the chronological order, thus Jithen who was the last, became the treasure chest.

The treasure chest. The collections in the chest were the memories from the beginning of childhood. Memories had roots. They had branches and twigs. Memories would flower and bud. Sometimes they would get mixed up and create new flowers and fruits, never seen by anyone before.

On the riverbank where the wild sugarcane grass was hissing, with a bell metal kindi in his hand, the six-year-old Jithen was standing guard for Naraapilla. When he heard about the seven mountains that had given birth to Periyar river from his grandfather, a stream of words, which he had heard from Aunt Kunthi, began to be reborn as a story through him:

A devatha rose up from the ocean and accosted Parashuraman,

who was waiting after having flung his axe into the sea to create Kerala. She had a gleaming silver axe in her hand.

'Is this the axe that you threw?' the devatha asked him.

Parashuraman replied in the negative. After going back to the deep, she resurfaced and this time she had a golden axe in her hand. 'Is this your axe?'

'No, no.' Rubbing his beard, Parashuraman fought temptation.

The third time, the devatha returned with the original axe. Though it was lying deep in the salt water, the blood from his mother's neck was congealed dark on its edge.

'This is mine,' Parashuraman said, taking the axe in his hand and examining the blood stains. 'But I had thrown it into the sea to lose it.'

'And I gave it back to counsel you,' the devatha said. 'Where can you get rid of the axe with which you killed your own mother? Without the parashu or axe, won't you become a mere Raman?'

The devatha vanished. Giving up his plan, Parashuraman came to Thachanakkara temple and installed himself as the deity. He held the axe in his right hand as if about to swing it.

Naraapilla roared with laughter.

Imagining the squatting Naraapilla in the midst of the coffee bushes, beyond the wild sugarcane grass and beyond the brick kiln, washerwoman Ammu, who was washing dirty laundry in Punneli kadavu, was startled, and froze.

Part Three

Kaama

'Men are more moral than they think and far more immoral than they can imagine.'

—Sigmund Freud

ONE

Sequel

25 December 1999

...As usual, I am abandoning halfway what I started writing yesterday. This time I am not throwing it into the wastebasket anyway. This useless piece of paper is also enclosed with yesterday's letter. I know very well that there is nothing valuable in this paper for you to preserve it. Yet, before you throw it away do not forget to read it thoroughly! It's the farthest point of my memories, the awakening of my senses:

Resounding light. The shadows that emerge from it. The many forms born as they firm up to become bodies. Everything in constant motion. Some come close, are enlarged, and become clearer. Some dissolve in the flicker of a moment. Bodies with faces stuck on top come closer, with firm steps. Eyes stuck on unfamiliar faces begin to blink and sway alarmingly. Below the glass eyes, small clamorous burrows full of white teeth. Many kinds of hands. If they came closer, baby trips to the cradle, or cot, or the baby bath in the spathe of areca palm. On the oiled tummy, warm water keeps sliding. In the nose and eyes, the sting and aroma of soap bubbles. When his mother blows a mouthful of air on the top of the head to dry his hair after bathing him, the momentary shudder and loss of breath. The bubbies that ooze milk when given a kiss. Suckling drowsily, forgetting even to breathe. Waking up startled, sighing, and diving back into slumber. Then, the odours of shoulders and necks. The yucky tastes of many sweats and blouses. Sounds kept boiling over. Suspended in them, many emotions. Screeching caws of crows in the scorching sun. Songs of indeterminate birds that lose out to the cawing. The soft tone asking where my son is, where my little son is, while tickling the face with his stubble, is Father. Glancing often to check if asleep, and singing loud lullabies that don't allow sleep is Amma: '*Omanakuttan govindan balaramanae koode koottathe, malinimaniyamma thannannga seemani chennu.*' 'Geethae, deee, Geethae … oh, oh, oh … where's this accursed girl?' The swinging cradle. The squeaky cry of the cradle's rope. The swaying beams and cobwebby roof tiles. The rope that goes around the beam under the attic-less roof and hangs down double-tailed; the rod of the cradle at its end, bisecting the vision. The rattle hung on the rhythmically swinging rod, tinkling on.

Except for the New House that Naraapilla stayed in, the other three houses in Ayyaattumpilli got electricity that year.

That was the time when four government servants scampered about in Thachanakkara, enthusiastic and sunburnt, planting wooden poles resembling stretched crucifixes at regular distances and pulling shining double cables through them. It was Pankajaakshan's wife, Kalyanikuttyamma, who educated Thankamma and Chinnamma on the greatness of electricity and filled and submitted the three applications for Ayyaattumpilli. She repeated the new word 'connection' often. It was with awe that Chinnamma and Thankamma uttered words such as wiring, plug and main switch.

Kalyanikuttyamma, who had gone that year with new clothes as Onam gifts for her parents in Kochi, returned with two paper parcels. After a fight over the disappearance of ripe pineapples from the plants near the fence, the sisters-in-law had just started talking to each other again. Making her youngest son Soman summon both Thankamma and Chinnamma, Kalyanikuttyamma took out the parcels to open them. Into the line of vision of her waiting sisters-in-law, who expected to see either the sweetened rice balls or high-quality tea she usually brought from Kochi, she displayed something resembling the piriform head of a mace, lifting it out with some difficulty from the first package. By then Soman had pulled out, one after the other from the second package, three big yellowing steel petals that he handed to his mother. By the time Kalyanikuttyamma had arranged the three petals equidistant around the dome, as if making a floral decoration for Onam, everyone had more or less made out what it was. The twelve-year-old Soman asked loudly, 'Hey, isn't this our fan in Kochi?'

Looking at her sisters-in-law, Kalyanikuttyamma said with pride, 'Our old fan, my father gave it to us to use when we get the connection!'

Envisaging the fan suspended from the ceiling like a bunch of bananas, Chinnamma had a start. What Kalyanikuttyamma had brought to Ayyaattumpilli, all wrapped up, was the monster which had robbed her of her sleep through all the four nights that she spent in the hospital after delivering Jithen! Those days, she had complained repeatedly to the nurses about the dangers posed by it, spinning and swinging with an alarming noise, directly above her and her days-old child. Unsatisfied with their assurances, on the fourth day, when Dr Madhavan came to discharge her and score out her name from the patients' list, pointing at the fan overhead, she said, 'Before that damned spinning thing falls on our heads and kills my baby, I just want to be home, dottr!'

Madhavan Doctor laughed. 'The fan won't cause any problem.' Lifting the sheet covering the child with his pen, and peering at the navel, he said, 'as long as Chinnamma won't go and attack it!'

Not only did the doctor's words not make her fears disappear, but it also instilled a belief in her unconscious mind that the fan was a strange animal without a sentient mind. But when she saw her sister-in-law from Kochi treating it like a toy sent by her father, Chinnamma lost her fear. 'Oh,' she said shifting Jithen from her left hip to the right side of her waist, 'we too have a so-called father!'

There was some substance in that grouse. Naraapilla's concept of electricity itself was something else. When Kalyanikuttyamma approached him with the application form, his response was, 'To get electricity? For what? Is there anything in the night life of humans that can be done in the presence of light?'

On the country roads and alleys forking off the tarred main road, cables slithered. With great devotion, the housewives living on either side of the alleyways offered containers filled with ginger-laced buttermilk and pickle-laced gruel to the workers. The folk of Thachanakkara were left open-mouthed as they stood looking up at the workers who were busy atop the just-installed poles, to which they were secured with the yellow nylon ropes tied around their middles. The children were spellbound at how easily these workers caught, with their hands, the small implements for cutting and joining that were thrown up to them. On the day the pole was planted in front of Geethalayam, Geetha, with baby Jithen at her waist and her sister Rema by her side, stood watching them the whole day.

'Now,' Geetha asked one of the workers, 'why're you uncles burying these poles and stretching the rope across them?'

'It's for drying our wet clothes!' he replied without batting an eyelid.

'Ayyo! But for that, why do you need to string up the clothesline so high?' Rema asked.

Patting Jithen's cheeks, he changed his style to suit the children. 'Only we males know the secret of this, isn't it so, son? The clothes that we are going to hang on this, are God's clothes! Humungous dresses which only boys can see!'

When she realized the brother she was carrying on her hip was a male, for the first time, she felt envious of him. Unaware that they were talking about lengthy loincloths, that was also the first moment when she felt sad about being born a girl.

Electricity had reached more than half the houses in Thachanakkara. When a street light was put up on the extant pole near Pooshaappi Junction, Thachanakkara stayed illumined even after sunset. The houses that had indicated their presence earlier by the twinkle of their chimney lamps seen through the dark shadows of the fences, now appeared here and there like painted backdrops with walls and tiles used as stage curtains. Delivered from the smoky chimney lamps that made the hair of their nostrils sooty, children sat beneath the new incandescent bulbs and read their lessons loudly, late into the night. Arecanut spathes, replaced by electric fans, reincarnated as containers for drying marinated and salted vegetables and rice paste in the yards. Those Nairs who still had considerable landed property left—even after being stripped by Land Reforms and partitioning of family wealth—in which they grew coconuts palm and plantains, installed water pumps on the wells overrun by Siam weed. As the elephant-trunk-like hoses of the pumps spewed the crystal slivers of water into the canals hacked in the dry earth, even the grown-ups were amazed. Coconut palms and plantains sucked in water upto the tip of their buds and belched.

Atop the external portal of the Thachanakkara thevar's temple, two spittoons facing east and west appeared. Morning and evening, they sang hymns from *Jnaanappana* and *Harinaamakeerthanam* to the Thachanakkara denizen, in a veteran female voice. On hearing that the lady melodiously reciting the hymns sitting squeezed inside the spittoon-shaped loudspeakers was called Leela, at least some of the women of Thachanakkara genuinely believed that it was Leela of Muringaattil, who committed suicide at Punneli kadavu. It was so imbued with the voice and music of the supernatural. Before they left the temple grounds after finishing the circumambulation, some of the old women stood in worshipful devotion in front of the blue loudspeakers, which were the source of the disembodied voice, with the same reverence with which they bowed before the oblation stones and the banyan tree.

The folks of Thachanakkara were dumbfounded by the sight of the brilliant light from the ripening glass bubbles on the vines suspended from the ceiling, which outshone bell metal oil lamps and camphor lights.

Naraapilla had leased about seventy-five cents of land on the riverbank adjacent to Punneli kadavu, to Devassy from Angamaly for putting up a brick kiln. That place, where the brick kiln now stood, looking like the ruins of a riparian civilization, could not easily be included in deed documents, being an extension of the riverbank. Hence, Naraapilla had not included it in the property to be divided amongst his children. Pankajaakshan who was whiling away his time as he was suspended from police service, had an eye on that land, unaware of its status. Devassy, who had come to Thachanakkara on the lookout for a suitable place to set up his brick kiln, had to undergo greater ordeals than the fire in a brick kiln. Because he was a Christian, his entrance test into Thachanakkara itself proved to be a trying one. When the rumour went around that the men and women who were coming to work at the kiln were all Christians from Angamaly, the Nairs of Thachanakkara were livid. Advancing as a group, they waylaid Devassy and in the middle of a one-sided squabble, toppled his bicycle which had a box on its carrier.

Devassy, who had remained silent till then, set his cycle right and asked with a smile, 'We can employ anyone at the brick kiln. But tell me, how many of you Nairs will come to knead the clay for making bricks?'

Faced with that question, the Nairs looked at each other, swallowed their saliva and left one by one. Thus, with Christian women from Angamaly and able-bodied Muslim men from Elookkara, Devassy started the kiln. In between, Paanamparampath Nanu tried to spread an allegation that in the name of the kiln, Devassy was actually digging up the riverbank looking for treasure, but it did not hold water even with Naraapilla. Devassy quickly improved his image when he sold half-priced bricks—even though they were only half-baked—to Shankaran when he was building Geethalayam at Ayyaattumpilli. On top of all that, by rescuing a boy from Chammaram, accepted as lost when he nearly drowned while learning to swim, Devassy—who dived headlong without even taking off his shirt—gained such eminence that he was, from then on, affectionately referred to by the Thachanakkara folk as 'Achaayan'.

Pankajaakshan, who was trying his best to curry favour with Naraapilla ever since he got dismissed from the police service, finally succeeded in getting Naraapilla's permission to collect the rent from the kiln. Pankajaakshan was aided by Kalyanikuttyamma's shrewdness and regularity in sending one meal a day to the New House for Naraapilla without fail.

In the surplus land beyond the kiln, Pankajaakshan planted some coffee saplings on his own. A friend of Kalyanikuttyamma's father, that same estate manager in Munnar who had once arranged for them a cottage that had more glass than bricks to enjoy their honeymoon days in, had sent thirty of those saplings. Though he had to suffer a lot of ridicule initially for transplanting the coffee saplings from the cold climate of Munnar, the trees stumped the critics by growing quickly and growing in girth on the riverbank.

The Christian women who came early in the morning to work at Devassy's kiln, changed from their sarees into their husband's shirts and lungis behind the coffee trees as soon as they got there. They put the sarees and blouses into soiled plastic bags, which they left hanging on the branches of the dwarfish coffee trees till they wound up work in the evening. One of the workers, Rebecca, easily identified because of her shapely figure and fair skin, once discovered an adolescent boy standing under the coffee tree, smelling the faultless yellow saree that she had hung on the coffee tree and trembling as if struck by electricity. From that day, the women gave up the practice of hanging the plastic bags from the branches. The adolescent boy who stood trembling was Shashi, Pankajaakshan's second son. During twenty-six days of that summer vacation, every day he used to search and smell only Rebecca's clothes, and run home when he could not stand the ecstasy anymore. On the twenty-sixth day, Rebecca, who had come to pee under the coffee tree, unexpectedly saw that sight.

'Jesus Christ!' Looking at the fourteen-year-old, she called out to everyone, 'Is this fellow going to be one up on his father and grandfather?'

The toilet at the New House overflowed.

Though Appu Nair searched in all directions for scavengers, he could not find anyone. Appu Nair was unable to search and persuade people like old times. Cataract had congealed like a film of rice water in his pupils. Though he advised his brother-in-law to finish the job in either Thankamma's or Pankajaakshan's toilet, Naraapilla did not listen. As he felt that it was not proper to ask him to go to Chinnamma's from where he would not eat anything, Appu Nair did not mention her name at all. But, Chinnamma was aware of her father's dilemma. She was also planning countermoves to Pankajaakshan's secret moves to wrest the Puzhampallath land. She had initiated the first phase of that plan, when she pushed Kunthi to take the paayasam to the New House, the day after Onam the previous year. The birthday boy, who accompanied her, had grown two years older now and had started running and jumping. Whether because he had accompanied Kunthi that day, or because Kunjuamma kept talking about him often in his dreams—it was difficult to determine—Naraapilla had started feeling an intense fondness for Jithen. Thus, even if temporarily, Jithen's days were transplanted from Granpa Raambilla's house to Naraapilla's sombre presence. Once the initial unfamiliarity was over, Jithen must have recognized in his own grandfather, a stronger magnetism pulling him from Granpa Raambilla. Chinnamma too felt that it was better that this bond of affection continued, at least till the heir to the New House was revealed. As soon as he woke up, Jithen would cross the fence and go over to Grampa's. Despite seeing the hairy forest on Grampa's back and his silvery stubble innumerable times, Jithen's fascination did not abate. His favourite toys were the wooden holy ash basket hung on the porch of the New House and the latches fixed on the inside of the front door. He was the first among the grandchildren of Ayyaattumpilli who touched Naraapilla. When Naraapilla went behind the cover of the coffee trees at Puzhampallath to escape from his overflowing toilets, Jithen accompanied him, hanging on to his finger. When he became strong enough to lift the kindi, which Naraapilla used to fill water from the river, Jithen carried it as he walked with him. From his momentary inspirations, he blended the many stories his tiny ears had heard to spin new ones and narrated them to his Grampa. In return, he had only one tale left to tell his grandson. The tale of the Periyar originating from the seven mighty hills of the Western Ghats. Squatting under the coffee trees, he tried to recollect a couplet he had heard from his mother at least three-quarters of a century ago.

'*Chokkaampetti ... Paachi ... Sundaram ...*' Unable to remember the rest of it, he kept straining.

In the grey forest of hair on his back a thrill spread. 'Got it!' Laughing like a child, he began to recite it in full:

> '*And these were the names of those mighty hills:*
> *Chokkaampetti, Paachi, Kaali, Sundar, Naaga, Ko, and Valli.*'

The seventy-seven-year old Naraapilla did not have an option. Hanging on to his thumb was a marvelling childhood in the form of Jithen, which transformed the wind-swept njaanganna clusters into sugarcane fields and the brick kilns emitting smoke into the sky of Lankapuri that had been turned to ashes by Hanuman.

When referring to the youngest among his grandchildren, Naraapilla began to repeat the same phrase that he had affectionately used for the youngest among his six children, three decades ago:

Embilla elava!

TWO

Maternal Uncle

20 June 1999

...Do not know if this is happy news; for the time being, let's call it a curious piece of news: after many years of legal battles, my Pankachammaavan has started getting a pension. The same Pankajaakshan who was chucked out of police service a quarter century ago. The one who ran, along with his friend, to the Aluva School grounds, heeding the words of Raambillapolice. The official who brought two new words—Suspend and Dismiss—to Thachanakkara. The hero who gave Vengooran Thankappan goose pimples by averring that if he were to meet the then Home Minister, a geriatric who later became the chief minister, he would spit on his face. I intend to add my first memories of Pankaachammavan in the novel; I have already written a bit. As I am too lazy to transcribe it, I am sending that sheet in its original form with this letter. Barely a paragraph, that's all. Please don't forget to send this back to me along with your reply.

An uncle intervenes in Jithen's confrontations with the sensuality of the visual:

The uncle is drinking buttermilk standing on the veranda. A sloka in Kalidasa's *Kumarasambhavam* describes how a raindrop falling on the eyelids of Parvathi, slides down her lips and bosom and wells up in her navel before spilling over. Here, when the buttermilk, mixed with crushed ginger and bird's-eye chilli, is poured into uncle's mouth from the tumbler, a spillover from that mimics the path of that streamlet in the poem. As the buttermilk hasn't got anything to do with uncle's eyelashes, it is bypassed. Starting from his mouth, in accordance with the sloka, striking his lips, slipping and losing its foothold somewhat on the hair on his chest and abdomen, the buttermilk reaches his navel. His is a bung navel with a finger like protuberance—a result of the careless snipping of his umbilical cord by the midwife who used a sickle. Uncle tightens the mundu below the navel where his potbelly declines. The complete route of the buttermilk is not visible to Jithen, standing below the veranda. All that is visible is the string of buttermilk bouncing off the bung navel. The Fount of Buttermilk!

Jithen's mouth remained open in amazement. Here's a magical man with a hole in his tummy. Half of the buttermilk he was drinking was leaking from that! He ran to inform his mother of this naked truth. Seeing it from another angle of view, as he sat on the hip of his mother rocking with laughter, he saw that truncated version of Kalidasa's image of the journey of the fount from start to finish. He was utterly disappointed. Nine years later, when Remadevi teacher was teaching the translation of *Kumarasambhavam* in the Malayalam class, and about the mesmerizing beauty of a similar journey, Jithen would remember this scene with revulsion. He would imagine the midwife who snipped the umbilical cord. He would realize that the navel of a woman is not an erotic sight, but merely the reminder of the connection with the mother.

Do not be shocked. It is no different from a male navel; or like the stem of an apple or a lime.

In 1974, the day after his fortieth birthday, Pankajaakshan received the paper dismissing him from police service. Freed from the burden of a job, he spent his time alternating between his home and Vengooran Thankappan's teashop, and hence, when the news of the death of his sister-in-law came after two years, he found ample time to lead a troupe of mourners from Ayyaattumpilli to Cherai. Thus, he repaid the debt of not reaching Thachanakkara at the time of his mother's death, by being in Cherai on the day of his sister-in-law's death.

For a long time, Pankajaakshan had been under suspension for taking a bribe of seventeen rupees. In the interim, many cases had come up against him with evidence and witnesses. He was not a member of the khaki-clad gang that had battered the junior Nampoothiri of Nedumpilli Mana for the crime of trying to throw the deity's idol in the pond. That occured during the time he was stationed at Muvattupuzha, where he had been transferred for having disrespected the new Sub-Inspector who had taken charge recently; he had sat with his legs on the table, inebriated. Constable Pankajaakshan had seen Vasudevan Nampoothiri in his original form for the last time in his life the day he was waiting for the bus to Aluva in front of the temple, with the plastic bag into which Kalyanikuttyamma had bundled his clothes. Vasudevan was running in the direction of the Arunodaya Club in the light rain, with the right palm shielding his head and the left hand holding a book under his shirt to keep the water away.

'It's raining. Didn't Venu's father take an umbrella?' he asked Pankajaakshan who was standing under the tree. As the rain was getting stronger, Vasudevan went away without waiting for the answer.

By the time Pankajaakshan returned to Thachanakkara, Vasudevan Nampoothiri had become a lunatic, walking around with a phone receiver in his hand. After alighting from the bus, as he was walking towards Ayyaattumpilli, Pankajaakshan did not realize that the strange creature coming towards him was Vasudevan Nampoothiri. The moment he saw Pankajaakshan, his eyes rolled up as if he was getting an epileptic attack, and he slid down to the ground, writhing in convulsions.

'Venu's father didn't take an umbrella. But who got wet? Who fell ill? This me!' he said, looking up at the skies and then at the ground, with a laughter verging on tears.

After standing bemused for some time, he shouted at Vasudevan, who was only old enough to be his son, 'Daa, Vasudeva, edaa! You rascal ... you have started drinking, haven't you?'

As Paanamparampath Nanu reached there in time, Pankajaakshan had to withdraw the hand he had raised to slap Vasudevan. Touching his head with his finger, Nanu made a circular motion, and winked at Pankajaakshan.

'He's got that you-know-what, sir,' said Nanu, displaying his teeth with gossip's verdigris on them.

Pankajaakshan swore that if he had been around he could have proven that Arunodaya Club, of which his own eldest son Venu was a member, had no links to the revolutionary movement and he could have saved Vasudevan from his unfortunate fate. He extended his leave for three days and stayed on in Thachanakkara. He took the initiative to get the Nampoothiris of Nedumpilli Mana to file a complaint against the young sub-inspector of Aluva police station. With that, his days in the service were numbered. Charges for sins that he did not commit, and which were blown out of proportion, were foisted on him. It was the blood of Naraapilla that flowed in his veins, which made him misconstrue each of those charges against him as a feather in the cap of his masculinity. When, all that was required was an unconditional apology on the part of Pankajaakshan to exonerate himself from the charges of disrespecting a senior officer, and for sitting with his legs extended on the table in front of the Sub-Inspector who was ten years younger, that he could not bring himself to do it was also due to this lineage to Naraapilla. When there was an enquiry by the senior officers, his defence was that he was afraid of vermin, and had lifted his leg seeing one of them sitting next to his table—which was a clever exercise in double entendre, directed against the young inspector. Avaraan, who had joined the force at the same time as Pankajaakshan and, having won regular promotions, was now his superior, made a last-ditch attempt to solve the problem. Avaraanpolice was an old-fashioned gent who believed that people could be reformed through counselling.

'Mr Pankajaakshan,' Circle Inspector Avaraan told him when they were alone together, 'we entered the service together. If you weren't a drunkard, you too would have got promoted to the grade of a circle inspector, like me!'

Avaraan's formal diction was countered in typical Ayyaattumpilli style by Pankajaakshan. 'Loser! You've been serving them, bound hand and foot, afraid to exhale, and still you have become just a circle?' Taking off his pointed cap, and smacking himself on his pot belly with his palm, Pankajaakshan preened, 'But when I gulp in two hundred millilitres, at that moment, I am an IG, my Avaraan, an Inspector General of Police!'

Seated in Vengooran Thankappan's teashop, Pankajaakshan used to elaborate on his outrageous and rash behaviour that had cost him his job, regaling his audience with dramatic gestures. Each time he described the same incident, he sprinkled them with his fantasy and welded on new scenes. Having started to identify himself dangerously with the narration style of Pankajaakshan from the repeated hearings, Paanamparampath Nanu started to weave his own stories on the occasions when Pankajaakshan was not around. Nanu alleged that corruption and disrespect to seniors were not the only reasons behind Pankajaakshan losing his job. Once, at noon, as he entered Thankappan's teashop, a story arose in Nanu's mind, as if in a revelation.

Closing his eyes as if he had lost sight from the inspiration, he started on his story. 'Listen, Shiva, after he has lost his job, Pankajaakshanpolice has been saying so many things. But only we know the cambleet story.'

Sitting down on the bench, opening his eyes and peering to make sure Pankajaakshan was not in the company, he continued, 'Once, some rowdies tried to finish off one of this man's superior police officers on the road. That sir escaped death since Pankajaakshan reached there in time. He was in a hurry to go somewhere. So, our man could not treat Pankajaakshan in a befitting manner. But, he had a steel bangle, much the same as the kind used by policemen to hit offenders. He took it off and presented it to Pankajaakshan, along with a note on a sheet of paper. And what was written in the note?'

'What?' barber Shivan questioned him in return.

Paanamparampath extended the open left palm towards his right side. Then, writing on it with an imaginary pen he said, 'I am indebted to this man for my whole life. Therefore, you are also indebted. Wherefore, for this day you shall treat him like how you treat me and give him all considerations, thus! It is Pankajaakshanpolice, no? The seed of Naraapilla chettan! Carrying the letter, he reached the officer's house directly. The wife of that sir was a fair, buxom stunner, reportedly! The rest can be imagined?'

Nanu paused the story there, rubbed his thigh, and laughed leeringly. 'If he had accomplished things with tact, all these problems wouldn't have cropped up for sure! But our Pankajaakshanpolice had to show some vigour. Things changed then, what?'

When Paanamparampath Nanu finished the story, Vengooran Thankappan asked him, 'Who told you all this?'

'Does one have to be told all this?' looking at a stranger who had entered just then, Nanu said, 'With some common sense all these can be found out.'

Seeing the young man in a white mundu and faded blue shirt, who had let down his folded mundu as a mark of respect, heading towards Kochu Parashu on the other side, Nanu jumped up from his place. Frowning, he left the teashop and made for Kochu Parashu's shop. Looking alternately at Kochu Parashu and Nanu, the newcomer asked, 'Chettaa, which is this house called Ayyaattupallee here?'

'It is not Ayyaattupallee, but Ayyaattumpilli,' Kochu Parashu said, immersed in his debtor's ledger. The rest was said by Nanu: 'It's close by. Who do you want to see?'

With the relief of one who has found what he was looking for, the man wiped his face hard with the edge of his mundu and said, 'Can be anyone. It's to inform them about a death!'

Kochu Parashu raised his face with a start and looked at him. He closed the ledger marking the place with the pen and stood up. 'Where are you from?'

'From Cherai. Which is this Ayyaattumpilli?' The newcomer was getting impatient.

'Come, I'll show you,' Paanamparampath Nanu went down the steps. Vengooran Thankappan and barber Shivan stood with their senses sharpened. Closing the door of his shop, Karunakaran Karthaavu also joined them. Kochu Parashu beckoned from behind the man from Cherai, who was following Nanu. 'There, stop a moment. Who died? Govindan…' the sentence got truncated by the anxiety.

'The wife of Govindan Master,' the young man said hurriedly, 'Sulochana teacher.'

Unsure of which of the four houses of Ayyaattumpilli he should enter first, Paanamparampath Nanu stopped. The young man with him asked, 'Which of these is Ayyaattumpilli?'

'All of them are,' said Nanu. 'You may tell any one of them. You may not tell any one of them too.'

Not understanding the riddle in that sentence, the young man headed to the closest house. That was Thankamma's house. Radha, who was on the porch playing discs with her younger brothers, limped back into the house, seeing the stranger. Thankamani came out, tying up her hair.

'Who's it?' she asked.

He gave the news. Then he drank buttermilk, sitting on the portico. The news of the death spread to the four houses. Since Shankaran and Kumaran were at their workplaces, Ayyaattumpilli got ready to leave without them for Cherai, under the leadership of Pankajaakshan. Venu, Pankajaakshan's eldest, rushed to Aluva by cycle and summoned a taxi. Chinnamma got in first, carrying Jithen. Then Thankamma and Kalyanikuttyamma followed. Thankamani was given the responsibility of supervising the three houses in their absence. As he was getting in to sit beside the young man in the front seat, Pankajaakshan had an inner prompt and jumped out and went towards the New House.

'Father, are you coming in the car?' Pankajaakshan called in.

There was no response from inside.

'Father, I am asking if you are coming to Cherai,' Pankajaakshan asked again.

The door, which had been ajar, was shut completely.

'But, it isn't him who's dead! Isn't it her?' he heard his father's voice from inside.

Paanamparampath Nanu, who was witness to all this, standing by the fence, sighed, and ran towards Pooshappi Stores.

That was a Sunday. The nine grandchildren of Naraapilla, except Jithen who was inside, crowded around the car. After Pankajaakshan also managed to sqeeze in, possessed by a sorrow from some unknown source, Chinnamma let out a loud wail: 'My Suluchedathiyammae! Ayyo!' making Jithen jump out of his skin.

The car bearing the siblings of Govindan Master started towards the first daughter-in-law of Ayyaattumpilli.

THREE

Mixed Breed

8 September 1999

Every ideal wife prays that her husband should die before she does.

From your enraged response to the sentence that I wrote in the last letter, I understood that it had vexed you quite deeply. So, listen: I had written that about spouses who would have started smouldering with old age; not about newly-weds, like how you have surmised. If she were to die first, who will look after her husband is something that every ageing Malayali woman worries about (On this count, I am not generalizing. To say also that all Malayali women are like that would be foolish. There may also be women who, for a different reason, desire the death of their husbands).

My grandfather became a widower before his sixtieth birthday. With my grandfather's eldest son, the same dreadful fate befell him before he was fifty. I never saw my grandmother. The first time I saw Uncle Govindan's wife, she was dead. I have not heard anyone mention that grandfather mourned grandmother's death. But I saw Uncle Govindan cry the day my aunt died. I still remember that day. I too was seeing him for the first time. Yes, that great man entered my life, crying. Now I know that it was the entry of a real man. My girl, I think that the generation of real men started and ended there. Perhaps, this may be purely my feeling.

There were people to tell me about the relationship between Granma and Grampa. But between Uncle Govindan and his wife? No one knows. Neither could anyone imagine it.

But one thing I know. A woman's tears have always been used by men as a lubricant for intercourse. Everywhere; always.

In the times to come, Sulochana would agitate the heart of Govindan Master, like a poem read in one's dreams: though sure that the content was excellent, one was unable to recollect details or to reclaim, in memory, the enticing turns of phrase and figures of speech.

Sulochana, who was the eldest of the three children of Anandan Master of Cherai, and the wife of Govindan of Ayyaattumpilli, was not old enough to think about death, least of all to die. When Sulochana died, her parents were still alive. The marriage of her elder daughter Chandrika, cuddled by Kunjuamma and Chinnamma eighteen years ago on the day of the festival of Thachanakkara thevar, had already been fixed. Her son, the eighteen-year-old Narayanan, who bore an incredible resemblance to Naraapilla of Ayyaattumpilli, in both looks and nature, had stopped going to college and had started idling at home and loitering around in the village. Narayanan, who was called Kannan by his family and the public, abandoned his education midway, due to adolescent alopecia and epileptic fits set off by the slightest emotional incident, causing him to fall down with convulsions.

The cohabitation of many years had entwined the souls of Govindan Master and Sulochana teacher so inseparably that it was not possible to discern whose influence went deeper. Time had given Govindan the strength to remember the scenes of his life dispassionately, as if it were somebody else's life story—how after bringing them together from two distant places through a poetry contest, the magazine called *Kavyachandrika*, published from Thripunithura, after which they named their firstborn Chandrika, had closed down after three issues; how a letter had come to Ayyaattumpilli as its first ever postal article, with the address written in light-blue ink with tiny flowers adorning it; how she came to stay at her aunt's place to study at Aluva UC College only for winning over the second-prize winner of the poetry contest; how she had gone to meet his mother near the oblation stone at Thachanakkara thevar's temple, wearing a yellow full skirt with green leaves and a light-yellow half saree; how after a half-consented wedding, the curses of Naraapilla had descended on their heads bowed for receiving blessings; and how the son and wife had left Thachanakkara for good, insulted by the father, in the presence of Kunjuamma burning in the pyre.

In a marriage that lasted only for twenty years, Sulochana had quarrelled with Govindan Master just once. It started as a discussion and ended without raised voices: it was about the naming of their son, while Sulochana was having her post-partum recuperation. It was when Govindan Master insisted on naming the baby Narayanan.

'Narayanan!' Sulochana lifted her head and looked at her husband. 'Understood! The full name of the man who cursed and banished us that day, right?' she asked with displeasure.

'It can be taken that way too,' Govindan Master said. 'There's a small debt to be repaid. Narayanan was the one who created this Govindan. Govindan repays it by creating another Narayanan!'

For a moment, Sulochana felt an unreasonable hatred towards the ebony-dark infant lying next to her. With no resemblance to either her or Govindan in complexion or looks, the boy lay with a big head and thin body, like a stone-cutting axe that Naraapilla had hurled afar from Thachanakkara to Cherai. Her first born, Chandrika, who resembled Kunjuamma so much like a sapling sprouted from the hacked root of Kunjuamma, stood near the cot and said, 'Shall I say what I've named the li'l baby? Kannan, the nickname of Lord Krishna! See, isn't he as dark as Lord Krishna?'

With that, the name the baby would have at home was set, but the argument about what should be his name on the records continued between the parents. Sulochana suggested many names that sounded close to Chandrika. Govindan Master was stuck on Narayanan. When he felt that the name was hated only because it was a reminder of his father, from Govindan Master's mouth popped out a statement that took him by shock.

'Don't consider it my father's name,' Govindan Master said in a voice unfamiliar to Sulochana. 'It can be considered the name of your Guru as well. Yes?'

When he realized that Sulochana, who was on her delivery bed, was looking at him with fuming eyes, Govindan Master cast his eyes down. He discerned within himself a dimmed shore of casteist pride. Hearing from within him the surging sound of the blood of Ayyaattumpilli advancing as a wave and shattering against a mammoth rock inscribed with the name of Naraapilla in large, ungainly letters, Govindan Master was mortified. As if to stop losing his balance in that wave, he held his three-year-old daughter close to him.

'Oh.' Sulochana pulled her nipple from the child's mouth and lay on her back. 'Your guru! That's what you said now, isn't it? That is, the guru of Ezhavas, no? How pathetic!'

One look from Sulochana had vaporized the flood tide of polluted blood in Govindan Master's veins. He went near her bed, and caressing her cheek tenderly, said, 'Forgive me, Sulu. I said that with not a bit of...' and jerking his hand away, he rolled it into a fist, and smashing it on his forehead, he said, '*Chchey*. So dreadful!'

When Chandrika, standing between father and mother, began to cry looking at her baby brother, the clash that had flowered by drawing water through roots that extended deep into remote time, hastily folded its petals and subsided.

Whether it was in memory of the ebony-coloured Naraapilla or the world-renowned great guru, finally, Govindan Master's son was named Narayanan. At home, he was called Kannan. He grew up with certain characteristics not usually seen among the children of teacher couples, and it was evident from the first glance that he was a soul that harboured unusual emotional torment. After he showed signs of epilepsy in his sixth year, Govindan Master was compelled to bring him up without letting him come under any mental stress. Seeing in his son standing next to him, an image of the one from whom he had tried to run and hide, a bitter smile became a permanent feature on Govindan Master's face. Returning from school, he lay in the armchair, immersed in some book from one of the three glass cupboards full of neatly-arranged books in his room. At times, he leaned towards a board balanced on the arms of the chair and scribbled something. His greying hair, thick glasses, and white clothes had gifted him the signs of premature ageing when he was just past forty.

Narayanan hated his father and his book cabinets. He hated his name and roots too. His nights were hell from the knowledge that not far from his place, lived an old devil with his name and likeness. In the daytime, he carried his adolescent body like the flesh of some wild beast impaled on the trident of inferiority. He fled from the presence of women, even as he lusted after them. He was deeply devoted to his mother and sister. One late evening, he thrashed a youth in an alleyway in Cherai, who was foolish enough to make the mistake of thinking that it would be easier to give a love letter to Chandrika by getting into the good books of her younger brother. Had he himself not fallen down in an epileptic fit, Narayanan would have ended up a murderer on that occasion. Without bothering for the permission of his father, he removed the two glass-framed pictures—of Narayana Guru and Chattambi Swamikal that Govindan Master had hung on the porch—which, attacked by hornets and termites, had begun to look like the map of hell, and hung in their place a painter friend's rendering of the sunset at Cherai beach and a picture of the silhouette of Vladimir Lenin. Though he was not good in studies, that he was gifted with a remarkable memory was something that Govindan Master could make out even as he was a small child. Govindan Master was stunned when he realized that, during Narayanan's epileptic fits, often he would blabber about events that happened prior to his birth, as if he were recollecting them from memory. It was on the day he declared that he had stopped going to college, and at the end of the long and heated exchange of words that ensued, that Govindan Master came to know of his son's ability in all its potency. At one point, when he could not stand his backtalk, Govindan Master raised his hand. Stopping his father with his left hand, with a voice slurred because he was frothing at his mouth, Narayanan lifted his right hand and said, 'Do you want to get from me what you gave your father in Thachanakkara long back? Do you want to?' Trying and failing to repeat that question once again, he fell with his eyes popping out; from that eighteen-year-old's mouth spewed the lava of epilepsy, like the wrath held in check by a volcano for centuries.

That night when she witnessed her son raising his hand to hit her husband, Sulochana had her first episode of chest pain. After a detailed examination, the specialist doctor from Ernakulam told Govindan Master that her condition was not mild enough to be ignored. Her heart, once brimming with poetry, was on its last legs. Govindan Master had already been warned about the inevitable solitude looming over him. He began to look quickly for alliances for his daughter, who was trying for a job after completing her bachelor's degree. To find a groom for a girl born of a Nair-Ezhava marriage was not as difficult as he had expected. However, on the day of the engagement of his daughter with a progressive-minded school teacher at Paravoor School, Govindan Master was not able to introduce the girl's brother to the boy's relatives. That whole day, Narayanan was whiling away time, sitting under a coconut palm on Cherai beach. He had started becoming unreasonably disturbed even as alliances were being weighed up for his sister. Anyway, Sulochana did not live to see the greater complications that were to happen on Chandrika's wedding day. Sulochana and Govindan Master were leaving for Ernakulam to buy gold ornaments and dresses for their daughter's wedding. She was on long-leave from school. When she insisted on going to shop for her daughter's wedding dress, Govindan Master agreed, despite her condition. When they were about to get into the bus from Cherai to Vypin, Sulochana's legs gave away and she sat down on the ground.

To her husband, who rushed out of the back door through which he had boarded the bus, tried to lift her up, when she lifted her sweat-drenched face and said, 'How sudden, isn't it? Oh, how altogether sudden!'

The hospital was quite near. As if it was meant to take her there, a cycle-rickshaw was standing near the bus stop. But nothing was of use. Govindan Master felt faint as he realized that it was his sanctuary of twenty years that was now lying insensate on his arm. He, by then, had recognized the full significance of what she meant by 'how sudden'. Certain things that shine from an illusion of conferred immortality suddenly get extinguished and dissolve into nothingness: the irreplaceable security of mutual trust; a radiant love that no one else can extend in this world anymore; a pure affection that could not be polluted by caste, religion, or gender differences…

In one's journey, everything falls by the wayside.

At the point of time when the sun's heat was abating, on the mud road in front of Govindan Master's house, some unexpected visitors arrived in a taxi. Except the boy who had gone to Thachanakkara to inform them of the death, none of the mourners congregated in the house where the death had occurred could recognize any of the visitors. Opening the front door of the car, a man with protruding eyes and a thick, upturned moustache was the first to get out. Giving the house a once-over, he opened the back door. Three women, who showed no resemblance whatsoever to each other, looked askance at the surroundings before they got out. Hanging on to the hand of the last woman to get out, a little boy too appeared.

The car doors shut loudly. Govindan Master, who sat near the dead body, turned his head to look at them and informed his aged father-in-law seated near him, 'It's them!'

People made way for the group to enter. Letting go of the child, Chinnamma reached first. Freed from his mother, the little one began to explore a house in mourning for the first time. With pillars made from arecanut palm and mud-coloured tarpaulin, a tent had been erected in the yard with potted plants on both sides. Seated around in circles here and there on rented steel chairs, people were murmuring. The first daughter-in-law of Ayyaattumpilli lay shrouded in white, on a banana leaf spread across the length of the dining table placed to the right of the sacred fount for the holy basil plant.

A family infamous for their open-throated wailing stood silent around the corpse. To Govindan Master, the silence began to feel frighteningly lethal. When Govindan Master lifted the cloth from Sulochana's face, a scream loud enough to startle the dead person broke out. 'My Sulu chettathiamme!'

That was Chinnamma. It was taken up by Thankamma and Kalyanikuttyamma. Noticing Kalyanikuttyamma crying near the corpse of a person she had never met before, Pankajaakshan touched his brother on his shoulder, after a gap of many years. 'Chettaa…' He pointed to his wife, and bowed down to be level with his brother's ear and said, 'This is my…'

The mourners who stood around, began to deduce the identity of the visitors. Govindan Master's daughter, Chandrika, held on to the fingers of the aunties she was seeing for the first time, one after the other. Thankamma cried, hugging her.

After a round of crying, Chinnamma queried in the ear of her niece, 'Where to urinate a little, daughter?'

This urge, which she had been holding back during the long trip, was troubling her more than the sadness of death. Chandrika took her inside.

That's when it happened. From inside, came a roar potent enough to shock the Ayyaattumpilli stock. A young man, clad in only a saffron mundu, rushed out towards the visitors, stamping his feet and screaming, 'Who is it who wants to see my mother's corpse? Tell me, who?'

In an astonishing upending of time, as if the youth of Naraapilla of Ayyaattumpilli was being re-enacted with little deviation, Govindan Master's son, Narayanan, jumped into the yard. Like the possessed oracle in the temple of some evil spirits, unable to curb himself from insulting the folk from Ayyaattumpilli, he verbally challenged the relatives around his mother's dead body. 'For whose oblation to the manes have all of you come uninvited? Eh?' Trying to rush forward and break free from the hold of the two younger brothers of Sulochana, he looked at Pankajaakshan's face and asked, 'What, do you too want to eat my mother's corpse? Eh? Get out all, this moment! Or else … or else…' At the corner of Narayanan's mouth, froth began to form a channel. His eyes vanished into his forehead. The explosion of emotion inside made the nerves in the neck and forehead of that young man bulge.

The very next moment, he slipped out of his uncles' hold and down onto the floor, unconscious.

After a long while, when everything except the still-blazing pyre had abated somewhat, happy at the melting of twenty years' of frosty distances and forgetting that she was in a house in mourning, Chinnamma uttered impulsively, 'Whatever it is, we got to see our chettan, at least on this excuse!'

Then, aware that it was time to return, she started looking for her child. Away from all the hullabaloo, Jithen was standing near Govindan Master's bookshelves. From the time he let go of his mother's hand, he had taken refuge in that deserted room. Govindan Master searched for Jithen, calling out his name and coming across the child standing with his face stuck to the glass of the bookshelf, he gathered him into his arms and kissed him.

Jithen did not know that the salt he tasted when he licked the wetness on his lips was from tears. He also didn't realize that, seeing the boy standing alone among the books, Govindan Master had wept suddenly, remembering his childhood.

Dusk was approaching. Jithen was also not old enough to understand that the smouldering light, which could be seen through the window, was the waning of the solace that had come into that man's life twenty years ago.

FOUR

The Well

30 August 1999

...Since returning after our meeting last week, it felt as if I was caught in a whirl. The day I reached here, it rained well. When I say well, I mean terrifyingly. When I entered the house at night, it was full of water and stinking! It was with great difficulty that I had found this house for a rent of a thousand rupees, for us to live here after our wedding. This is one half of a tiled house occupied by an aged couple. There was no power because of the rain. After opening the door and getting hold of a candle and lighting it, I understood that the water from the drainage outside had flowed in. The foundation of this house is below the level of the gutter! The aged owner of the house came in stumbling and apologized. He is as old as my father. How many nights have the moans of his ailing wife troubled me! Abandoned by their children, their only source of income is the rent I pay. To bail out the muck inside, he too joined me with a bucket. As the rain became stronger again, I sent him away, wishing him a good night. I feel like crying. From the time I remember, I have not cried aloud. Tears of twenty-seven years have welled up like a pool in my soul. Twenty-seven multiplied by three hundred and sixty-five. Are you able to comprehend? I lay there, fully dressed, listening to the gutter water lapping into my room. For no reason, I dreamt about a tortoise which had fallen into our well in my childhood and which was rescued by my father who climbed down into the well.

Together, the ten grandchildren of Ayyaattumpilli built a cowshed in Pankajaakshan's plot.

It was Pankajaakshan who cut down the arecanut palms in the plots kept aside for Govindan and Chandran. Everyone, including the polio-affected Radha, took part in the funeral procession of the arecanut trees. The rear was brought up by Jithen and Rema, holding on to the dark green fronds of the arecanut palm. After Pankajaakshan decapitated the palms with his machete, sharpened on the edges of Kalyanikuttyamma's washing stone, the youngest children got bunches of wonderful arecanut flowers. The arecanut tree had been saving these for them all this while, ensconcing them in their attractive yellow and green spathes. When the spathes were separated, they saw the arecanuts in their infancy, stacked one upon the other. As the flower bunch was liberated from the spathe, the tenderness of the flowers thrilled Jithen's palm. Attracted by the smell, he chewed on the tips of those tender flowers.

Pankajaakshan's son Venu and Thankamma's son Vijayan made a square-shaped clearing in the plot, overgrown by touch-me-nots interspersed with crepe jasmines. Thankamma's youngest son, Vidyadharan, and the younger sons of Pankajaakshan, Shashi and Soman, helped Pankajaakshan split the trunks using an axe and crowbar. Making the foundation a single laterite stone high, filling it with soil, watering, and then compacting it into a smooth floor was done by Thankamani and Radha. As Radha moved up smoothening the floor, dragging her polio-affected leg, she created complex patterns behind her, which looked like music notations. Fearing the distress of the handicapped, no one excluded Radha from any activity. Since she had a talent for singing, after her tenth standard, she had joined the music school in The Alwaye

Sangeetha Sabha, better known by its abbreviation, TASS, and had progressed to mastering many ragas. Having taken an oath to win recognition through music, which her sister could not do with her dancing, she used to walk, her lame leg notwithstanding, cross the Marthaanda Varma Bridge, and take the short cut in front of the Aluva Market and reach the Sangeetha Sabha for her music lessons.

When he looked at his nieces daubing the floor with mud for the cowshed, for some reason, Pankajaakshan was touched by the past.

'Hey, Thankamani.' Reminded of his mother as he saw the tip of Thankamani's hair touch the floor, Pankajaakshan asked, 'do you know where we are making this cowshed?'

'Of course!' Thankamani said, shifting her hair with the back of her hand, 'Pankaachammavan's property.'

'No dee, my Kunjikunjommae.' Calling her by her pet name after a long time, Pankajaakshan said, 'this is where your grandma was cremated.'

'Ayyo.' Getting up with a start, Thankamani said, 'are you serious?'

'Then what! It was fortunate that we didn't build a memorial for her here. Or else where would we have found the place to make this cowshed now?' Pankajaakshan said with an expression unique to Ayyaattumpilli stock.

Thankamani and Radha gazed with melancholy at the chopped crepe jasmine plants lying on the side. Despite their bodies being slashed and flung on the bed of arrows made by the thorny touch-me-nots, their flowers had not wilted and were now turned smilingly towards Naraapilla's grandchildren.

'O my mother!' Pankajaakshan howled as a splinter from the arecanut trunk pierced his hand. Grimacing, he pulled out the splinter, and blood began to flow freely. As it was noon, and the tide had started affecting his father's hand to bleed more, the frightened Soman called out for his mother. By the time Kalyanikuttyamma came running, her hands smeared with rice dough, Pankajaakshan had pulled out some cobweb from between the midribs of a young coconut tree and covered his wound with that.

'Nothing,' Pankajaakshan told his wife, 'it's only a reminder from Mother.'

By the time it was evening, the cowshed was ready with all the work completed, except the thatching of the roof. The woven coconut fronds, brought by Maniyan pulayan in his handcart, were stacked on the yard. He had been instructed to come the next day to fix them on the roof.

When Naraapilla's grandchildren were splitting up, having washed their limbs and cleaned up, Geetha asked, 'So the cowshed is ready. When will the cow come, Pankaachammava?'

The rays of the setting sun and anticipation had reddened the faces of the younger children.

'Day after tomorrow,' Pankajaakshan said, pouring water on the congealed blood on his wound. 'If not, then the day after. If it doesn't come even then, we can tie this Kunjukunjomma inside the shed and feed her the grass. She is overdue for getting married, anyway, no?'

'Pankachchamma, stop it,' Thankamani protested coyly and ran to her home. Head bowed, Radha limped behind her.

Looking at Radha, Kalyanikuttyamma said, 'Poor girl, she's also of the age to get married!'

'Oh-ho!' said Pankajaakshan. 'Then we can tie her up as well in our cowshed!'

Chinnamma scolded her children severely for going to build the cowshed in her brother's plot and, since she took her younger siblings with her, Geetha was beaten with a piece of the midrib of a coconut tree. Kalyanikuttyamma also heard Chinnamma shouting above Geetha's cries, 'She, she, she ... She's gone to build a cowshed in someone's house.'

On the other side, Thankamma did not even scold her children for helping build the cowshed. Instead, she said, 'That was a good thing, children. After the cow comes and a calf follows, sister-in-law will surely give us some milk.'

After three days, a Jersey cow arrived in Pankajaakshan's cowshed. She, who came with sorrel colour maps on the body, eyelids that seemed to droop with tiredness and shyness competing with each other, and a ring the size of a copper coin in her left ear, started her life in the cowshed, which had sprung up at the spot where Kunjuamma had been cremated. On the pretext of chewing hay, she began to masticate on the cud of memories that went back to Time immemorial.

Kothappulakkalli, who used to sit and smoke beedis in Naraapilla's kitchen, got a friend to kill time in the afternoons: a creature which fell into the well in the New House, having lost its way when riding the floodwaters. A tortoise, which was tired of circling along the laterite wall of the well.

Hearing Naraapilla's snores in the afternoon, the tortoise would surface from the depths of the well. Staring at the gleaming white clouds seen above the ring of the well, broken only by the cement pillar on which the pulley was hung, and the branch of a jackfruit tree pointing at the pillar from the opposite direction, the tortoise lay suspended in the water with a terrifying stillness. Looking at the thousands of clouds passing every moment through its circle of vision, it filled its longevity with wonder.

One afternoon, an old woman's face, framed by hair as white as the clouds, came into its circle of vision. Before it could dive and hide, a tender voice of love penetrated its shell and touched it.

'When did this come and fall into this well? My son, won't you die of starvation?' Kotha asked.

The tortoise was not amenable to words of love or the invitation to climb on board the spathe-bucket guided by the rope from above. When the spathe-bucket touched its shell, hardened from centuries of primordial fear, the tortoise dove down to the bottom of the well, paved with gooseberry planks.

Gradually its fear faded. Its neck started hurting from stretching out and looking up at the sky to see if Kothappulakkalli was coming for their afternoon parley.

Without Naraapilla's knowledge, without the knowledge of the Ayyaattumpilli neighbourhood, Kothappulakkalli started scattering cooked rice into the well. Pressing her flaccid abdomen, made soft and loose by bearing eight children, against the coolness of the well's parapet wall and bending over, the old woman enjoyed talking and singing to the solitary creature inside. In a voice deprived of its femininity by beedi smoke, she emptied into the well the only ditty she had learnt in her childhood, about the story of Rama and Seetha, who in her dialect were Cheetha and Ramachan:

Cheetha the daughter of Chanaka,
For her Ramachan offered the wedding sari,
Wasn't it her that Ravana swiped away
Because of which the monkey roasted Lanka too.

As she could not remember the rest of the lines, she repeated them. Her attempts to lengthen the recital by adding a line of her own succeeded finally. With a voice laced with pain that lessened from sharing, and bending further into the well, Kotha sang the fifth line: '*Did you know any of these, tortoise-sir?*'

Each time the ditty was sung, she laughed loudly, tickled by her own creative genius. The like-hearted fellow in the well swam around helplessly, inscribing a zero in the water. This was repeated till the next flood came along.

Chinnamma did not have to go to Kalyanikuttyamma's house to read about the death of A.K. Gopalan, the renowned communist leader. By that time, the newspaper boy had started shoving the eight-folded *Mathrubhumi* newspaper into the gate of Geethalayam. As the subscription to the newspaper had started before the annual exams of Geetha and Rema, news of A.K. Gopalan's death and the resignation of the Achutha Menon ministry, which had ruled for seven years, reached Geethalayam the next day itself. At the beginning of April, Chinnamma was to be astonished by the detailed news of Karunakaran taking over as chief minister, only to be followed by a youngster called A.K. Antony, in a few days' time. The reading of newspapers those days created a strange impression in Chinnamma: a feeling that time was rushing past.

'Listen,' Chinnamma told Shankaran, who was keeping her company while she was drawing water from her father's well in the night, 'this coming June we have to enrol the boy in school. Shouldn't we dig a well before that?'

As the husband stood trying to make the connection between the school and the well, she continued, 'The rains will start in June. If we dig the well before that, well, that'd be over with!'

Four days later, Paanamparampath Nanu and Karunakaran Karthaavu prospected the location for the well and marked the spot with a stake. Apart from document-writing and narrating film stories, Karthaavu also had powers of water-divining. The unemployed Paanamparampath Nanu accompanied Karthaavu in his water-divining forays. After Karthaavu had selected the spot, Nanu would linger at the site, lazing around the mouth of the well, till the well-diggers finished their work. As the workers' pickaxe or spade struck something solid and gave out a metallic ring, with a palpitating heart Nanu would say, 'Easy, easy, if it is some treasure pot, we split half-half!'

However, when he accompanied Karthaavu to site the well in Chinnamma's land, Paanamparampath Nanu had more than just treasure-prospecting as his purpose. Nanu had been yearning to follow the story of what happened after the Ayyaattumpilli team left in a car for Cherai, upon hearing of Govindan Master's wife's demise. There was a physical ache in the pit of his stomach to know of the rest of the story, and though he had created many denouements for that story in his imagination, Nanu was dissatisfied with all of them, and scratched his head in frustration, sitting in Vengooran's teashop. Since the stories he had created about Pankajaakshan's dismissal had gained more currency than he had expected, Nanu was spending his days dreading meeting him. When he heard of the planned well in Chinnamma's plot, his stomachache vanished completely.

As Karunakaran Karthaavu and Nanu were entering Geethalayam, Shankaran and Chinnamma, carrying their youngest child, were leaving for somewhere. Looking at the weakened child, lying with his head on Chinnamma's shoulder and leaving snot stains there, Karthaavu and Nanu had misgivings.

'You get the site fixed. I'll take the boy to the doctor,' Chinnamma told her husband.

'What happened to him?' Nanu asked, touching Jithen's limp palm.

'Oh, the less said the better, my Nanu,' Chinnamma replied, stuffing the currency notes given by her husband into her blouse. 'It's a disease he's had since birth. He's been wheezing and wheezing! This morning I lay him on his back on the mat. I thought, if he has to die, at least let him die lying down properly.'

'Okay then, you go and come.' Not allowing his wife to get

ahead further, Shankaran interrupted, 'go to the government clinic! Won't you take care while boarding the bus?'

'Oh, aren't I still wet behind the ears!' With a sarcastic laugh, Chinnamma walked into the alley. As he walked back, unbuttoning his shirt, Shankaran told Karthaavu, 'All the smoke which the companies in Eloor are belching out is proliferating in the air. It's not just our kid, lots of children now have this ailment!'

'Only air?' Nanu added a lie come to him at that instant. 'What about water? My wife has broken out in rashes after bathing in Punneli kadavu!'

'Haeey!' Karthaavu intervened. 'That cannot be true. Aren't the Eloor companies so far down the river from Punneli kadavu? From there, can the pollutants come up river, against the flow?'

'It will, it will,' Nanu said with conviction, 'it's poison, isn't it? It'll come up the river like migrating fish do.'

All three walked towards the northeast corner of the plot. He noticed two types of trees dominant there, Karthaavu's intuition woke up and started functioning. Holding a forked stick ahead of him, resembling a catapult, and of unrevealed origin, Karthaavu walked among the trees along an imaginary line over and over. The yearning of the branch to be a tree growing from the earth made the hands of Karthaavu shiver when it reached the place where the presence of water was strong. 'Here, you can dig here,' Karthaavu told Shankaran after spiking the branch into the soil. 'It's a dead certainty that you'll find water here.'

The work on the well started the next day. Jithen, standing on the windowsill, saw workers making many trips, bringing in cement rings on their handcarts. His attempt to piddle into the grey ciphers lying scattered on the yard failed. He was worn-out from the bitter medicines and tablets, which looked like tiny idlis cooked only to feed birds.

On the third day, when Kochchayyappan and Kandankaali

had come to dig the well, Jithen was granted permission to leave the house. He also stood in wonderment near the pit by the side of which endless dialogues were taking place between Paanamparampath Nanu and his own mother. To view the well being made by lowering cement rings, instead of traditional wells with angle-measured laterite-lined walls, sometimes passers-by also came in. Jithen felt frightened as the pit deepened further and he felt that the workers inside, who were lowering and stacking the cement rings tied with ropes, resembled Thachanakkara thevar. The laughter of Kochchayyappan and Kandankaali from deep down inside, joyful at the sight of the spring, echoed off the cement rings and rose up and made Jithen peer inside, stretching towards the mouth of the well and holding his mother's hand tightly.

'Ayyo,' he asked, 'how will you climb up now?'

'Don't worry, little master,' came the reply from below, the incomprehensibility of which troubled him for a long time. 'First I will bend down, and he will climb up stepping on me,' Kandankaali said looking up, 'then when he bends down, I will climb up stepping on his back!'

Jithen did not see how they came up that evening, after their backbreaking work.

That year, the rains came down hard, before the school opened.

The dark clouds enveloped Thachanakkara and beat down on it. Fiery sparks flashed in suppressed melancholy. The rumbling thunder frightened the small children. The rain blew a different tone inside covered ears. The fallen arecanut trees turned into multiplication symbols. The sky, which let in threads of light like wicks of the chimney lamp through the cracks in the tiles in summer, now used the same cracks to insert the fingers of rain to catch the residents. The big vessels and pots, which had been arrayed in a line to catch the water falling off the eaves, floated a while on the yard and settled down and got filled with water. The children of Thachanakkara, who rinsed their mouths after the meals with that water, felt the taste of the rain along with its chill that made their teeth sensitive. The children had goose pimples from their skin brushing against the damp clothes, which had suddenly started appearing on the clotheslines inside. The soles of their feet, which were wet all the time, had become paper white. The tortoise, which had been fed cooked rice by Kothappulakkalli, broke out of his decades' long incarceration and escaped from the well.

As the rains ceased, the water drained and skies cleared, Geetha saw a tortoise near the gate of Geethalayam.

'Ayyo, poor thing,' she said standing on its hard shell. All the children came to Geethalayam to see the tortoise. They flipped it on its back to prevent it from escaping.

It disappeared the next day. No one knew that Soman, the youngest son of Pankajaakshan, had got up early in the morning, slipped out surreptitiously, and put the tortoise in the new well at Geethalayam.

Kothappulakkalli had no idea that her new friend, after escaping from his old well, had ended up in the well of Geethalayam and was to spend the rest of his days there.

FIVE

The Old Man

21 November 1999

...Yesterday, I dreamt of you again. Our first night. Before you sat on the bed, you touched my feet and placed your finger on the crown of your head, in that traditional way of showing deference. For this lusty man, the desire was to see the scenes after that. But, from that point, the dream vanished.

Kisses for the Anasooya and Priyamvada on your bosom; on the softness of the tautened skin like a drum top, seen through the rounded low-cut back of your blouse; on the last vertebra of the spine; on the webbing of your toes ; and then, on each of your seven pores...

Girl, snuggle under my wings. Stay close to my shade. Get wet in my rain. Now I am a red-hot iron idol in the smithy of lust. Inside me smoulder those seeds held in reserve for you.

Yes, as you know, I am living with a lust lit from the stars. When I am ablaze, struck by the lightning of lust, I burn with enough hunger to consume a cow elephant in the raw.

Then, hear this too, in moments of love, I need only the tender heart of a doe to feel satiated as with a feast.

Naraapilla was informed by Paanamparampath Nanu, that a sanyaasi with divine powers had taken up residence in the standalone single room called the 'lodge' by the local people. It was adjacent to the low platform built around the banyan tree in front of Thachanakkara thevar, where once a dance master from Paravoor called Sadanandan had run a dance school.

It was the time when the well at Chinnamma's was being dug. Nanu had began to thrive, loitering with ears cocked around the wide open mouth of the well till the workers broke for lunch, and squeezing out as many secrets about Ayyaattumpilli as he could from Chinnamma. Rightaway Chinnamma revealed how they were amazed to hear the eighteen-year-old Narayanan of Cherai, who had not seen Naraapilla even once, brandish usages exclusively used by his grandfather, like 'oblation to the manes' and 'eating the corpse'. She kept harping on how Chandrika resembled Kunjuamma more than Thankamma's daughter, Thankamani, did.

'That can't be otherwise!' Nanu brought up a proverb, 'the point of the thorn and the aroma of sweet basil are innate!'

When Chinnamma told Nanu about how no one except Pankajaakshan went for Chandrika's marriage, which had been postponed for a long time on account of Sulochana's death, miffed that they had not been invited in person, and almost as a punishment to Pankajaakshan for not keeping his own dignity, how Narayanan had insulted him more virulently than on the day of his mother's funeral, Nanu gnashed his teeth in a pretence that his blood was boiling.

'And our Pankajaakshanpolice just stood there?' Nanu asked, frowning and making his eyes bulge.

'What could chettan do? If chettan were to just swing his hand won't that weakling die?' Chinnamma retorted.

Nanu quaked inside. Imagining Pankajaakshan aiming a swipe at him for spreading concocted rumours about him and feeling as if his head was cleaving, Nanu shut his eyes tight. Quickly, he changed the topic to the greatness of the new types of wells. Feeling a little jaded at the realization that Nanu had a lot to say about wells dug with concrete rings lowered into them, to stand her ground, Chinnamma looked left and right and said with a lowered voice, 'When I went for sister-in-law's funeral, unfortunately, I felt like peeing. When that girl took me into the bedroom, I thought maybe there'd be some outlet to a urinal. My Nanu, you won't believe it when I say this; though it's a nice house and everything, their latrine is inside the house! Oh, I found it repulsive! From big brother's room there's a door directly to the latrine! Hau! But then, if one is dying to urinate, can we refrain from passing urine? What's the point of big brother having so much education and knowledge?' Chinnamma lowered her voice further, making sure that the workers in the well could not hear. 'Perhaps these Ezhavas don't mind these things, no, Nanu?'

Nanu's hood for gossip lost its venom. Nanu had heard the latest fad was to have toilets inside houses. Nanu also knew that it had a name beginning with Europe or America. But now, when he heard that the house of Sulochana of Cherai had that amenity, he sweated briefly, helpless in supporting it. Glancing quickly into the well, he winked and swerved his head, saying, 'Shh … let's discuss it later!'

That moment, he felt like seeing Naraapilla. It was months since Naraapilla had asked Nanu to find a person to empty the latrine. When he saw that the well-diggers were getting out for their lunch, he quickly went through the fence into the next house. Taking a quick glance at Pankajaakshan's house and making sure there was no one there, he went over to Naraapilla's house.

Hesitating at the threshold for some time, he cleared his throat. Then he called out, 'Listen, Naraapilla chettaa.'

'Who's that?' Naraapilla asked from inside.

'It's poor me, Nanu!' He entered the house boldly.

Nanu saw Naraapilla, seated on the coir-wound cot, stuffing

some papers folded in the middle and which looked like deeds, into a wooden box, only slightly bigger than the box used for carrying betel leaves and arecanuts. Before closing the box with brass adornments in its corners, Naraapilla took out a paper from it, offered it to Nanu, and said, 'You couldn't find a scavenger till now, no? I don't need him either now! I find defecating in the open at the riverbank more comfortable. It couldn't have been for no reason that earlier generations built their houses so close to the river. Anyway, let that be, but you read what is written on this paper. Read it silently. There are children around.'

Nanu opened the yellowed paper that was tearing at the creases and smelled remotely of medicinal concoctions. Since a bunch of what looked like deeds on stamp paper had already caught his eye earlier, assuming them to be of great importance for Ayyaattumpilli, he looked at them with reverence and anxiety. However, it was only a sloka using small words written laterally. Holding it against the light from the open window, he started reading the Sanskrit words on it: '*Dasha vaidya sama patni, dasha patni sama ravi, dasha soorya sama mathaa, dasha mathru hareethiki*.'

'Do you know whose handwriting that is?' Naraapilla asked Nanu, who was staring uncomprehendingly at him after reading it.

Not getting the riddle, Nanu was perplexed. After taking back the paper and putting it in the box, Naraapilla said, with a smile borrowed from his youth, 'Do you remember that Achuttan Vaidyan of Kaniyankunnu who is dead? It's his script. One can also say that this is the only bit of poetry I have with me. When I went to him for consultation once, he recited this and told me the meaning too. I got him to write it down and took it. Then, keeping it between the deeds, I forgot all about it! Dey, I just got it back!' Naraapilla stood up, opened the tied mundu, shook it, and tied it back. Nanu espied his full-blown masculinity bulging out through the loincloth like a small bag of sand.

Fanning himself with the arecanut spathe fan, Naraapilla walked to the portico. Nanu walked with servile deference behind him.

'Listen to its meaning,' Naraapilla said, 'ten vaidyas equal one wife, ten wives equal the sun, ten suns equal one mother, ten mothers equal one *hareethiki*. What is this hareethiki? Here, like you now, I too stared with my mouth open that day, till Vaidyan explained it to me. *Hareethiki* means the gall nut. Understood?'

Nanu understood more than necessary. When he imagined what could be the ailment for which Naraapilla had gone to Achuttan Vaidyan that day, a tale of great potential started to gnaw inside Nanu, given that gall nut was known to be an aphrodisiac.

'That kind of…' Nanu probed, with hesitation and coyness. 'Does Naraapilla chettan have such feelings even now?'

'Even though I am close to eighty, I can still see well, can't I?' Naraapilla said, 'I can hear with my ears, smell with my nose, eat with my mouth. No? Then why should there be a problem with that alone?'

'Absolutely,' Nanu toed the line. 'Now there is only one doubt left. If it's like this even now, why did you then go and ask Achuttan Vaidyan for the gall nut?'

'Eh?'

Nanu rephrased the question and made it more direct. Reproducing one of his simpers from the past, Naraapilla said, 'You moron, who asked for gall nut? Achuttan Vaidyan prescribed gall nut for me. When he started reciting the sloka, I asked him to write it down. Then I locked it up in the box. Other than that, what gall nut or gully nut for Naraapilla?'

It occurred to Nanu that Naraapilla, whose vision and hearing were getting weaker, might live on for another hundred years. That much fire, still remnant in the old man, scorched Nanu.

'Shouldn't we then admire people who become ascetics in their youth?' Nanu asked. 'What all they must be suppressing to live as sanyaasis? Aw!'

'Idiot,' Naraapilla said, 'who says they are repressing? If so, they must be impotent, for sure!'

At that point, Nanu suddenly remembered the sanyaasi who was camping in the lodge under the banyan tree of the Thachanakkara thevar. As he realized that the topic of conversation was taking a new turn, forgetting even his hunger he said, 'Its only now I remembered. Did Naraapilla chettan come to know of a sanyaasi who has been staying in Thachanakkara temple? In the lodge under the banyan tree? A noble guy by his looks. Hair and beard, here, this long! Takes little food; he's meditating all the time, meditating!'

'Is that so?' Naraapilla's rheumy eyes widened. 'In that case, I'd also like to meet that worthy. When I'll go for Pooshaappi's son's sixtieth birthday, I'll make a detour via the lodge. I have certain things pending that the sanyaasis can help with.'

'The sixtieth birthday of which son of Pooshaappi? Radhikeshan's, the one younger to Kochu Parashu?' Nanu blinked.

'Heyy, the second youngest after him,' Naraapilla said.

It was late afternoon. Seeing Kalyanikuttyamma coming with two vessels covered with plantain leaf, Nanu climbed down the steps of the New House and said, 'Then you have your lunch; I will go home quickly and come back!'

Paanamparampath Nanu still had a lot of things to discover. The sight of the frown between the arched eyebrows of Kalyanikuttyamma made his stomach uneasy. Wondering how the long cohabitation had made the features of her husband appear in Kalyanikuttyamma as well, Nanu passed through the fence.

Poovamparampath Puththanveettil Prabhakaran Nair, the sixth son of Pooshaappi, and sibling of Kochu Parashu, and the one who kicked up the worst racket with his own father for bequeathing the shop to Kochu Parashu when the partitioning was done, was celebrating his sixtieth birthday with a feast where all of Thachanakkara was invited. Since the month of Medam was drawing to a close and there could be unexpected showers, a huge tent had been put up covering their entire yard. People had come even from Muppathadath and Paanaayikkulam. His glee at being elected as the new president of the local unit of the Nair Service Society, as well as his eternal loathing for his brother Kochu Parashu, had worked equally behind the holding of the celebrations. While even Devassy of Angamaly, who ran the brick kiln, was invited to the *shashtipoorthi* celebration marking the completion of sixty years, Kochu Parashu and his family were not. The shashtipoorthi became memorable as the first feast where two kinds of paayasam were served. That was also the last celebration and feast that Naraapilla of Ayyaattumpilli took part in.

When Jithen started to play with his friends behind the tent, having not found a place in the first sitting in the feast, someone uttered that word: shashtipoorthi.

He did not understand the importance of the celebrations and the crowd. After making his mother let go of her hold on his hand, he was walking with the other, older children from Ayyaattumpilli; but when he found an opportunity, he gave them the slip and started walking in the compound alone. He had fallen prey to the thrill of fantasizing about hitherto unseen lands as forests and traversing through them all alone. He would fantasize about a rogue elephant appearing from behind the tree just ahead of him. A wild, white-water stream, huge trees on its banks covered with giant vines, and if possible, a leafy bower in the midst, an aborigine hunter, with his arrow at the ready, in pursuit of his game … Jithen would start anticipating such sights. He went past the compound of the Poovamparampath Puththanveettil, which had been cleared of undergrowth for the occasion. Blowing up flowers of berries and popping them on his forehead and eating its yellow fruit, he walked. When he reached a small channel, which carried the rainwater into Periyar river, he saw a man standing like an angler. That was Alamboori. The fishing rod in his hand was just a bamboo stick pulled out of the fence. Jithen did not feel any fear. He did not realize that the name Alamboori, which was taken at least once a day by his sisters to frighten him, belonged to the man who stood ahead of him.

Hearing the crackle of dry leaves underfoot, Alamboori turned back and looked. He threw the bamboo stick into the water, took up the phone receiver lying on the ground, and spoke into it, 'No, it isn't the police. Policemen can never take on the disguise of a child. No, no, no. Okay. The rest I shall inform you later.'

Jithen walked up to Alamboori and looked at the wondrous thing in his hand. The word shashtipoorthi came from inside him like a hiccup. Without being conscious of it, the question came out of him, 'Tell me, what's this thingy called shashtipoorthi?'

Alamboori gazed intently at the kid in shorts who had to come to ask a valid question.

Making sure they were alone, Alamboori came closer to Jithen and kneeled in front of him. Jithen could only stand in front of him with his eyes glazed, as if hypnotized. Alamboori started to say with a beatific smile blossoming inside his matted beard:

'God has given all the creatures in the world seeds to bring forth the next generation. Pollen to the flowers, seeds to the jackfruit tree, coconuts to the coconut palms ... Do you understand? In the same way, men also have a pouch full of seeds. Move closer. Now, take off your shorts. Good boy. This thingy is used to pee. What is this thing which hangs in between like a skin-sack? Ha! ha! This is the thingy I told you about. A super pouch of skin containing the seeds! A boon from God! But do you know what scoundrels humans are? Many live as misers, without spending these fully. And when they keep living like that, and when they are sixty years old, God would play a trick on them. This sac, which would have dried like dry ginger by then, would drop these nuts just like that!'

Jithen was breathless. He pulled apart Alamboori's hands by force and pulled up his trousers.

Soman and Geetha were coming towards the channel in search of Jithen. He gazed down, impelled by an unknown fear. Alamboori completed his oration, 'What is fallen on the ground is retrieved immediately and placed in the pooja room on a plantain leaf. Black sesame, flowers, and sandal paste are kept along with it. Then that sixty-year-old rascal will sit and pray along. He will invite all the people and give them a feast. They won't have the courage to call dignified people like me. Ha! ha! ha!'

Geetha screamed in alarm recognizing the person kneeling in front of her brother, 'Ayyo, my brother has been caught by Alamboori.'

Alamboori was more shocked than Jithen hearing her scream. He stood up in one breath, turned, and running away, disappeared.

Running towards Jithen, Soman asked him, panting, 'What did he do to you?'

That was when Jithen understood that the person who ran away hearing Geetha's scream was Alamboori. He laughed once like a retard. Then giving the feint to Geetha and Soman, he ran towards the tent.

Before lunch, Jithen went to Prabhakaran Nair's pooja room and peeped in. There was something brown there on a plantain leaf. It was that—resembling beaten rice mixed with jaggery and coconut. Perhaps, it may have been mashed by someone using a ladle.

Protecting his own seed pouch with his right hand, Jithen ran from the pooja room towards his mother. While he was running, he prayed to Thachanakkara thevar that he should die before he was sixty.

As he was stepping out of the tent after the feast, Thankamma came running to hold Naraapilla's hand to steady him. Slapping away her hand, Naraapilla said, 'No one need hold me. Naraapilla knows how to go back the way he came.'

The Thachanakkara folk were seeing Naraapilla in a shirt after a long time. Though he was sweating in the hot and humid Medam, his shirt did not touch his body due to his thick body hair. He was holding a walking stick, which he himself had fashioned out of a big wild persimmon stick. With the help of that, he walked without missing a step.

'Appoliyo!' he called into the crowd behind him.

On their return, Naraapilla and Appu Nair stopped in front of the lodge in front of the temple. Like a riddle confronted by imbeciles, the lodge remained closed. With the pointed tip of the umbrella, Appu Nair began to spike the fallen banyan leaves, scattered around. It was clear that the person was inside. Appu Nair also was curious to see the sanyaasi who had taken up residence in the lodge. But the door remained shut despite their repeated knocks.

'He may be meditating,' Appu Nair said.

'Then let's not disturb him,' Naraapilla said.

The old men walked back, their umbrellas open in the scorching heat. Above the dome of the greying cloth, strewn on the tip of the umbrella, the yellow leaves were still present, like prior deeds.

For Naraapilla, it was not yet time for the rendezvous.

SIX

Oxen

3 July 1999

...If the plan is to wear jewellery bought with borrowed money on our wedding day, I'll kill you! A girl covered in jewellery is a pitiable sight, like a tortoise turned on its back. Neither God, nor the Devil, nor I would like to stand beside such a bride as the groom. Then the question of dowry: tell your mother that I don't want that either, since I know for sure that you will not be able to give as much gold and money as I may ask for. Now something for your knowledge alone: real men do not notice a woman's jewellery— unless he is a jewellery thief. A man may, at the most, notice a woman's nose stud; and it will end there. If it is a pretty nose, even better than a nose stud would be a God-given mole in its place. Therefore, my girl, come without jewellery, without garments, and if possible, forfeit your body and come.

I remembered when I wrote this—we children of Ayyaattumpilli had developed a craving for rings. If we were to give goldsmith Chellappan a twenty-paisa copper coin, with the lotus emblem stamped on it, he would beat it into the shape of a ring. I would like to write about that in my novel. Since I remembered it suddenly, if there is time, I will try to write that section alone and attach it. If so, I will send you that sheet as well.

My girl, after sitting up for one-and-a-half hours, I could

write only eight sentences, that too with much difficulty. I don't think they are of any worth. Throw away this sheet after you read it. I am not adding it to the novel:

When Grampa used to go out to defecate, I was the one who always accompanied him. The riverbank in that area was full of coffee plants. Till he selected the spot among the coffee plants, which were greedy to grow into trees, but were cursed to be bushes, one had to walk with the bell metal kindi in the right hand and the left hand holding onto Grampa's middle finger. When he defecated, the stench was of solidified misdeeds. There was a small reward for suffering through it. A copper disc with a lotus stamped on one side. Those days, we children as well as some of the grown-ups, used to convert this copper disc into a ring, with the help of the goldsmith. Thus, Grampa's prehistorical stench provided rings to adorn the fingers of us boys.

When Geetha and Rema were returning happily from school, after finishing their terminal examinations in March, a new word dropped down from the decorated truck which came against them, full of whooping and hurrahs: Murdabad!

Shankaran had tutored his two daughters, who were writing their terminal examinations, especially Geetha who was hoping to go to Upper Primary by clearing her fourth standard examination, with some general questions.

'The great Chinese communist leader who expired last year?' Shankaran asked Geetha on the previous day of her Social Studies examination.

Geetha, scratching her head, ventured, 'Jimmy Carter?'

'My blooming idiot,' Shankaran said, 'isn't that the name of the new American president? That isn't an important question. But this they may ask. Write it without forgetting. Mao Tse Tung. What? Mao...'

'Se thoong!' Geetha said.

If her Social Studies exam were after two days, Shankaran could have taught her the answer to a more important question. Shankaran firmly believed that that question about A.K. Gopalan, the great communist stalwart of Kerala, had not been included because the question paper was set earlier. Unfazed by the question on Mao not being asked, Shankaran said, 'Let it be; but remember the one I am telling you now. It's going to be asked in the next year's examination, for sure.'

He opened that day's newspaper and showed an obituary in big bold letters on the first page to Geetha, who was standing despondent that the questions were not ceasing even after the exams had.

'A... K... G...' Geetha and Rema picked out the letters.

The girls remembered the new word that they had heard that day while returning from the exam. 'Father,' Geetha asked, 'what's the meaning of this *inniraanthi moordabad*?'

'Haven't you heard Inquilab Zindabad?' Taking his eyes off AKG's photo and looking at a female's picture on the same page, Shankaran said, 'The opposite of that is Indira Gandhi murdabad.'

Upon hearing that explanation, a three-member procession with the sisters leading and Jithen, who was to join school after two months, bringing up the rear, got ready to go around Geethalayam.

'Inkulaa zindaava, inniraanthi moordaava,' they repeated as if it was an incantation.

That night, Chinnamma heard Shankaran's snore vibrate 'Moraaaarjeee', as she lay listening, and remembering reading in the daily about a person called Morarji, who had chances of becoming the next Prime Minister of India.

Jithen liked Thankamani's younger sister Radha, more than his own sisters, his aunt's eldest daughter Thankamani herself, her two younger brothers, and the three sons of Pankaachammavan.

Radha, left leg paralysed due to polio, would be present without fail every afternoon at the time when film songs would emerge out of the new Philips radio in Jithen's house. She wrote down the lyrics of many songs in a beautiful hand, in the empty pages of an old notebook. Jithen understood that the digit two inside a circle at the right end of the second line was a sign that it was to be sung twice. Jithen was surprised at Radha's eyes getting wet when she reached certain lines of some of the songs. He peered into the oblong-shaped sieve of aluminium colour on the radio. He saw nothing there which prompted tears. One day, Radha sang the most beautiful of the songs they heard that day, in the turgid silence that always followed the switching off of the radio.

The darling fisherwoman of the fisherman of Poonthura,
Painted a bindi on her forehead with a smile...

As Radha sang, Jithen sat staring into the blazing sunshine, trying to imagine the scene of the song. Taking the spit from the smiling mouth of Radha, he applied it on her forehead. With the spit bindi and breaking laughter, Radha sang the next two lines,

Before receiving wedding garland,
She received the flaming kiss of man!

It was when Jithen was struggling to mimic those lines in action that he saw the wetness on her eyelashes. From morning, Radha had been consigned to Geethalayam in anticipation of a prospective groom for Thankamani coming from Thattaambadi.

'What's this?' Chinnamma said when she saw Radha, 'Why are you here on a special day like this? Go and try to help your mother, dee.'

'Mother said,' Radha said glumly, 'don't appear before the guests with your lame leg.'

'Oh! I didn't think of it!' Chinnamma said, ratifying the decision.

Having expected a different response, Radha's face fell further. Seeing that, Geetha said, 'Come chechi, the whole day we'll spend singing.'

'No, no,' Rema said, 'let's play with bangle bits.'

'No singing or games with bangle bits.' Radha went inside and opened a window direct in line with her house. 'Today we will sit here. For a long time. Till someone comes and leaves from my home!'

'Who's coming to your home?' Geetha asked.

Radha put Jithen on her lap and sat on the cot next to the window. 'Isn't there a paragon of beauty in my home? A princess?' said Radha. 'A prince is coming to see her!'

While shifting Jithen to her polio-free right thigh, she espied her two brothers going towards her house bearing a package each. Vijayan and Vidyadharan were returning from Kochu Parashu's shop.

'Shu shu!' Radha caught her brothers' attention. 'What all did you get?' she asked.

'Won't say.' Vijayan waded through her inquisitiveness.

'Why da, Vidyadharan, tell me please,' Radha pleaded with her younger brother.

Vidyadharan's heart melted. 'Miccher, laddu, and plantain,' he shouted back and ran to join his brother.

Radha, Geetha, and Rema looked at one another. Incomprehensible to the others, singer Radha let out an imprecation, frowning, 'Oh, it can't be but her last!'

As the new moon approached, the cow in Pankajaakshan's cowshed began to moo as if it were a celestial Kamadhenu, looking at the heavens. None of the children of Ayyaattumpilli, except Pankajaakshan's second son, Shashi, saw the cow in heat, tied to the tripod and mated by Chokli's bull.

The children had school that day. Chokli, who was strongly built like a cast-iron statue, came in the morning with his stud bull to Ayyaattumpilli. Tying the black bull to a coconut tree on the way to the cowshed, he stood stroking the hump on its back. Kalyanikuttyamma went to her husband's bed, woke him up, and informed him of the arrival of Chokli and his bull.

When Pankajaakshan reached, Chokli was already in the cowshed. Fourteen-year-old Shashi stuck around massaging his teeth and gums with burnt husk, watching Chokli lift the cow's tail and examine it.

'Don't children have school today?' Chokli asked, sighting Pankajaakshan. Deferring to the insinuation in that question, Shashi made himself scarce.

Gathering the strong wooden pieces from the compound, and tying them to the poles of the cowshed, Chokli created a tripod. He lighted up the Kajah beedi he took from his lap and sucking in the first mouthful of smoke with a hiss, he told Pankajaakshan, 'Now get the cow and tie it here.'

Double the quantity of smoke that went in came out through his nostrils.

'Let it be after sometime, Chokli,' Kalyanikuttyamma, who had come there by then, said. 'Let the kids go to school. By that time Chokli can have three or four idlis.'

Pankajaakshan, while searching for the container of the dentrifice of burnt husk, asked Chokli, who was sitting on the steps of the backdoor having idlis, 'Do you take this one for ploughing?'

'Nah,' Chokli said, 'for that I have another two. With these useless tiller-shiller coming, they, poor ones, don't have work now. It's now what this guy goes around and earns that feeds even them.'

'I am contemplating whether I should deploy a tiller or tractor in Kainikkulam this year,' Pankajaakshan said, throwing a handful of burnt husk into his left hand.

'Nah, no,' said Chokli. 'It's only if you have many fields that it will be viable, Master. If you let that damned thing into small fields, you'll have to sell all your paddy to pay its rent. Bloody bollocks, tiller! All said and done, can a mechanical bull be like a live bull?'

After the children had left for school, Pankajaakshan moved the cow and tied it to the tripod set up by Chokli. The bull had started snorting and stomping the ground. As Chokli started to untie the bull, Kalyanikuttyamma withdrew to the kitchen. Even while tied to the tripod, Pankajaakshan's cow was standing head down, coyly. Without even looking at the lover approaching from behind, she spread her hind legs. Chokli's face had the grave aspect of a sacristan. Pankajaakshan said, 'Ow.'

Holding his breath and lurking alongside Naraapilla's New House, Pankajaakshan's son Shashi kept watching the mating of the cattle. After a while, he presented himself at the kitchen door, drenched in sweat, and told Kalyanikuttyamma, 'I came back, Ammae. Terrible tummyache!'

Despite Kalyanikuttyamma giving him ground dried ginger and mace of the nutmeg, the boy's tummyache did not go away. As days went by, the pain increased. The source of the pain went lower.

'Listen, we did not call him for the engagement, we should call Vallyettan for the wedding at all costs,' Thankamma told Kumaran the day the wedding of Thankamani was fixed—with ten sovereigns gold jewellery and ten thousand rupees as dowry—after the eighteen-member group from Thattaambadi had left after lunch.

Kumaran was setting aside the vessels hired from the temple. 'When he invited us all for his daughter's wedding, only Pankajaakshan went from here, no?' Kumaran wondered. 'That being so, would he come here?'

Stepping into the stone-paved sunken area near the well for drawing water, Thankamma said, 'Did brother come here and invite us for the wedding? Because we went there when sister-in-law had died, we came to know of the wedding. That was all to it! If he sends a letter informing of the change in date, what? Are we all going to go in a parade there? Pankajaakshan chettan did go. And for that, he got it nicely from the boy!'

Kumaran was using coir fibres to remove the rice stuck to the vessels. When sand and coir fibres worked together, the scabs started to come off.

'Why is the kid like that?' Kumaran asked.

'That now,' Thankamma said, 'he is a mixed breed, no? Then such things can happen!'

Kumaran stopped his scrubbing and gave his wife a hard stare. Since she had been given that look in the past as well, she fell silent and continued drawing water from the well.

Thankamma was unaware of the strange ways of the evolution of Time. It was beyond her to imagine that the same epileptic boy, who currently did not impress anyone, would marry her daughter Radha five years hence and move into Ayyaattumpilli, after hundreds of marriage proposals had come to nought for Radha.

On the afternoon of Thankamani's wedding, Paanamparampath Nanu posited a new theory in Vengooran Thankappan's teashop. 'Shivo,' rubbing his distended stomach, after having gorged himself at the wedding, he addressed barber Shivan, 'Do you know how Kumaran chettan's second child got a game leg?'

'She got polio, no?' Shivan said, smelling the lime he got at the wedding.

'Nah, what polio?' He was silent for a moment, getting ready to launch the most important observation in his gossipy life. Limbering up and stretching his back, he said, 'That girl was born in nineteen sixty or sixty-one. There was a big procession on foot by communists that day, till Thiruvananthapuram. In that, our Kumaran chettan and Shankaran chettan and all joined the march, shouting slogans. Shankaran chettan came away after some time; Kumaran chettan did not give up and continued walking.'

'Till Thiruvananthapuram?' Shivan asked.

'You won't believe!' Nanu said, 'But the guy walked. Not one or two days, thirty days continuously! When he returned, what is left to say? Both legs were practically paralyzed. But he was away from home for a long time, yes? So problems with his legs notwithstanding, he didn't give up on his other activities. Which? That was how this second girl was born. So wouldn't it have been surprising only if she didn't get a lame leg?'

'But Kumaran chettan's legs have no problem now!' Shivan raised his doubt.

'Have these communists ever had any problem that has been prolonged?' Nanu said, 'His weakness got over in a week. It was only the kid who got into trouble!'

Merely imagining the walk from Thachanakkara till Thiruvananthapuram, Shivan felt weak. He felt there was actually a march like this seventeen years ago. However, the barber could still not accept Paanamparampath Nanu's theory that temporary weaknesses in communists could create everlasting handicaps in their progeny.

SEVEN

Caterpillar

27 September 1999

...A curiosity from my old diary: a note of regret about a girl who studied with me up to the fourth class, written in retrospect. I do not know if it's advisable to talk about previous girlfriends to the one I am going to marry. However, I leave the right to decide whether this note about her should be included in the novel or not, to you. If possible, you must also suggest a name when she becomes a character.

I will end this letter with something interesting. Do you know that like authors, real history also desires that the nature of characters and their names should match? What else, then, is the secret behind an old-style bell ringing in the name of Alexander Graham Bell, the inventor of the telephone?

After reading the enclosed note, don't get cross with me; and, without wasting time, do reply quickly.

Is that a tiny channel of sandal that is seen when hair is parted in the middle? Is sandal-coloured skirt and green blouse the uniform of angels?

You did not recognize how shamelessly I aped your habit of biting your lower lip in concentration while sharpening the pencil. You did not pay attention to how I had my revenge for you getting higher marks in the Onam examination, by scoring the same in the Christmas examination.

I sang in light music competitions only for your ears. To win your approbation, I participated in elocution competitions. Drew pictures. Studied hard. Rang the school bell in the evenings. Donned the role of Ravanan in the annual play.

You knew nothing of all these.

Even when we changed schools, and did not meet, I continued to be myself. I saw you in a silk skirt for the festival at the Thachanakkara temple. You laughed at the naughtiness of handsome boys. On the day of the finale of the festival, I was scared that you would be frightened by the one thousand and one mortars that would burst. I alone.

You were not seeing me.

I was crying. I was growing up.

My love, even though there is a proscription against turning and looking back, I will look. I too want write a paean to beauty about what was espied only once.

To deworm children, a more bitter medicine than aloe vera reached Geethalayam—Antipar.

That was the year when the floodwaters had covered Thachanakkara up to its knees. When Chinnamma saw the children happily scratching their anuses during the three days of unexpected holidays, she lost her head. She was already engaged in a struggle against athlete's foot, applying gentian violet with cotton swabs on her feet and the webbings between toes. That was when the children started their finger-battle against the enemy in their anuses.

'What the hell is this now?' she said, rubbing the soles of her feet on the torn gunny bag, used for wiping feet on the floor near the kitchen door, to assuage the scratching in her feet, which the potassium permanganate in the solution could not snuff out. 'When one itching is about to stop, another starts or what!'

There was a reason why Chinnamma had contracted athlete's foot. Hearing of the men getting into the churning river at Punneli kadavu to snare the timber logs hurtling down the mountains in the floodwaters of the Periyar river, Chinnamma too had ventured there the previous week. Looking at the swirling, surging waters of the river smashing against its banks at Thachanakkara and Uliyanoor on the other side, overflowing into the fields to become dark like tea with not enough milk, and forming whirlpools and eddies, Chinnamma was reminded of Muringaattil Leela after many, many years. Thousands of angling lines of the rain, baited with memories, kept falling into the river. A young man, tethered to a coconut palm on the shore by a coir rope wound around his waist, was still grabbing timbers in the maelstrom of the river. Chinnamma, who was standing under the umbrella, fancied that she could land more timber than that man, if she could get a rope long enough. She considered returning home, untying the rope used to draw water from the well, and coming back with it. She saw a big uprooted dead tree on the river from afar. The sight of the fast-approaching tree with the black roots, which looked like mating black serpents as the tree kept twisting in the water, was too enticing for Chinnamma. She felt envy for the man, who at the other end of the taut rope was waiting for the huge tree with anticipation. When he subdued it like taming a bull which was snorting and bucking in the midst of the river, and finally got on top of it and, sitting astride, started propelling himself and the tree towards the bank by pulling at the rope, Chinnamma could not contain herself and said, 'To hell with him! That's enough for his old woman to burn as firewood for a whole year.'

She spent five days, on different occasions, at Punneli kadavu standing with her legs steeped in the slush, gazing at the trees floating past, like unidentified corpses. By the time the floodwaters eased and the river narrowed, she had a bad case of athlete's foot.

She pinched between her toes, grimacing; scratched inserting coir fibre and combs; pulled down embers from the stove and stepped on them. The itching did not subside. Finally, after applying the potassium permanganate solution, which Shankaran had fetched from the Aluva Government Hospital, the fungal infection stopped its boisterous laughter and started smiling.

Since subscribing to the daily newspaper, she had started reading not only the news, but also some of the advertisements with serious intent. When a small advertisement, at a corner of the page in which the news of the miraculous birth of what was called a test-tube baby in England caught Chinnamma's attention, a solution was found for another problem in Geethalayam. The advertisement ran like this, 'Eradicate tapeworms and hookworms completely. Use super Antipar immediately!'

Shankaran got the vermicide that very evening from a new medical shop in Aluva. The insufferable bitterness of the teaspoonful of the medicine that each child had to take before going to bed at night, left a screwed-up expression on their faces that remained even after they woke up in the morning. To make Jithen open his mouth, which he would clamp shut, every night Chinnamma had to slap him. The nights, which awaited the administration of the bitter medicines, swamped the new lessons Jithen had started to absorb in the daytime during his first year in school.

The bitterness of Antipar convulsed through the inner space extending from human life up to that of a hookworm.

The purpose of One-Eyed Kochaappu's incarnation was the total modernization of Thachanakkara kitchens. The weapon of Kochaappu was more potent than the plough of Lord Balaraman and bow of Lord Rama. A compound word, which Jithen in his first year of school could never pronounce properly—the sawdust stove.

Kochaappu and his son from his second marriage visited every house in Thachanakkara, carrying iron stoves, which looked like measuring *paras* with holes. Using the tale of his left eye—which his first wife had blinded using the rib of an umbrella as a precautionary measure to keep him from seeing her affairs with her paramours—as the preface, he slowly introduced his business proposal. His publicity slogan was that one or two coconut husks were enough to cook an entire meal for afternoon or night. The women's minds were set aflame by its enticement. The popularity of the sawdust stove moved from kitchen to kitchen like an epidemic in Thachanakkara. Except in the New House, in which Naraapilla resided, in every house in Thachanakkara, at least one sawdust stove established itself as a squatter.

The fourth of every month, Kochaappu came with a truck filled with sawdust bags. After emptying the sawdust in a mound in one corner of each kitchen, he went away with the empty bags and money. After hacking two forearm-sized branches from the evil-smelling Indian Elm tree, and cutting them to size, Shankaran got ready to begin filling sawdust into the stove. Keeping one of them upright in the centre of the stove and then inserting the other horizontally through the hole in the bottom side of the stove till both met, he began filling sawdust around the right angle formed by the two pieces of wood and when it was filled to a heap, he summoned Jithen and told him, 'Son, now use your leg to compact this sawdust for your mother!'

Jithen used his six-year-old legs to press down on the sawdust in the stove, which was a caricature of the auspicious paddy-filled para topped with the coconut flower. When he got down from the stove, Shankaran pulled out the two pieces of wood carefully. Jithen remained open-mouthed, seeing the narrow tunnels his father had created in the stove. Chinnamma inaugurated the stove using it for warming the rice left over from lunch, for dinner.

One-Eyed Kochaappu was right—before two pieces of husk were burnt, the water in the earthen pot was boiling!

The sawdust heaped on the floor served other purposes too. The children plucked and buried pomegranates in the warmth of the sawdust to ripen them. One of the hens being raised in a new coop built in Thankamma's house—a dotted hen which Jithen thought resembled the fisherwoman Bhaimi—when it was time to hatch, would come and sit on the sawdust heap. Chinnamma drove it away every time shouting, 'Get lost! When it is time to lay eggs, you sluts never choose the wrong house! And now you come here only to hatch! Pho you foul fowl, pho!'

After returning from school, Jithen used to go to his elder aunt's house and stand and stare at the hen coop, without batting his eyelids. The yellow-wood rafters had new tiles on top. There were two sliding doors and a small wooden ladder at the opening for the birds to climb up and into the coop. To save the birds during nights from the foxes which lived in the thickets along the Periyar river, the coop was kept on four laterite stone pillars, as tall as Jithen. The only factor that thwarted Jithen's ardent wish to stay with the hens in that beautiful house, was the unbearable smell of chicken poop. The rooster strutted about with his gorgeous shawl and cockscomb and wattles that Jithen felt were cut out of human tongues. Sometimes, without any provocation, it chased down one of its three female companions and mounted it. Vijayan, the younger brother of Radha, unbeatable in giving nicknames to people, did not spare the hens in his house. Amba, Ambika, Ambalika—these were the names he chose for the hens. When dusk fell, refusing to follow the hens into the coop, the rooster used to fly up into the nutmeg trees of Thankamma or the pomelo or the champaka trees of Chinnamma, and perch there. 'Babbabbabbaba!' a new incantation started to be heard in Ayyaattumpilli in the gloaming. Thankamma said, looking at the rooster sitting at a height, 'It's a relief that roosters don't lay eggs! If he sits like this and lays eggs, will we get even a fragment of it?'

Thankamma distributed the first eggs laid by the dotted hen, and the other two, within Ayyaattumpilli itself. After ensuring that the children had at least one egg each, she started sending eggs to Pooshaappi Stores at the rate of thirty paise per egg, through her youngest son, Vidyadharan. Holding Vidyadharan's hand, Jithen accompanied him on his egg-sale trips. Only on the days when Shivaraaman, Thankamani's husband and a Kerala State Road Transportation Corporation bus conductor, used to come to Ayyaattumpilli, no eggs reached Pooshappi Stores. Shivaraaman, with a wispy moustache and always smelling of talcum powder, had the face of foxes which sucked on stolen eggs. Despite his investigations, Jithen could never discover the source of the new fragrance, which had started emanating strongly from Thankamani after her marriage. By the time she got up in the morning after her first night, she was transformed wholly into a butterfly from a caterpillar. She used to praise, whether warranted or not, the wretched Shivaraaman, who used to slurp his tea reprehensibly, retch and strain his abdominal muscles every time he used the split spine of coconut leaflet to clean his tongue, and at twenty-five had no moustache worth mentioning. On an occasion when she fantasized that her good fortune in getting married had attracted even the special attention of the whole universe, with a puerile intention of engendering envy in her younger sister, arching her eyebrows, Thankamani even said, 'When good times come to someone, even if it's a sibling, some jealousy is sure to be there.'

Gradually, Time started diluting such fantasies of Thankamani. Recognizing that her husband too was as pedestrian as they came, she had nausea. Kumaran and Thankamma were thrilled that they were going to become grandparents.

After he had gone to Kallu aunt's house to borrow a glass of sugar as instructed by his mother, Jithen also got a piece of sea battered by the waves with it.

It was evening. After duly completing her household chores, Kalyanikuttyamma, who had seated herself in the portico to read the newspaper, stumbled over a piece of news, hurt herself, and said loudly, 'Ayyo, hadn't our Lord Mountbatten kicked the bucket yet?'

Though he had read the entire paper in the morning, Pankajaakshan had missed that bit of news. Pankajaakshan, who had been gathering the coffee beans spread in the yard for drying into an old rimless bucket, stopped his work and came to the house. Jithen also reached at the same time, holding a steel glass.

'Amma has asked to tell you to give a glass of sugar,' the child repeated the sentence he had learnt by heart by repeating it over and over again on his way there. Getting up from the floor and taking the empty glass from Jithen's hand, Kalyanikuttyamma said, 'I had thought all those people we studied about in history, must be dead!'

Pankajaakshan took the paper and read the obituary, which was not given prominence. When he read the news of India's last Viceroy being killed off the Irish coast by a bomb explosion on a boat, Pankajaakshan had a strange feeling of being a part of history.

'Oh yeah,' Pankajaakshan also said, 'was this chap still alive?'

Keeping the newspaper down, Pankajaakshan went to Jithen. 'How's your asthma, son?' he asked. Touching his collar bone which was jutting out, stretching the skin like a bow facing up, he told his wife who had returned with the sugar, 'Look at this, Kallu, like a clothes hanger.'

Disliking her husband's sense of humour, Kalyanikuttyamma held Jithen close. After handing over the glass with sugar to Jithen she told her husband, 'You people from Ayyaattumpilli have this belief that you can tell the children anything. Don't forget that the children will keep these in their minds!'

Remembering something suddenly, Kalyanikuttyamma went inside, came out with a small package, and handed it over to Jithen and told him, 'Here, give these to your sisters and you also eat! These are some unniappams.'

As she gazed at him walking away holding the glass and the package close to his naked chest, she said, 'Poor thing!'

On his way home, though close to his chest were two sweet things, within him a thought bitter than Antipar was rising up. Though he was not aware who had died in the explosion in the boat, the death on the sea was felt overwhelmingly. Death by suffocation! He remembered his sister pointing out an old couple, in a house on the way to Aalungal School, who were waiting for their son who had died of asphyxiation. He looked at them every day, as he passed by. They were not weeping. There was a mention about them in the newspaper. His father talked at length about them. It was a bigger death than the one heard of today, because it was not a death in a boat accident, it was in a ship accident. The ship was carrying iron ore to Germany from Marmagoa. The only son of the old couple was working on that ship. The ship disappeared on the high seas. Father said the ship could have sunk lock, stock, and barrel. With water rushing in through the nose and the mouth, with their eyes and ears bursting with immense pressure as they were going deeper, people were sinking to the bottom. Jithen, who had not seen the sea or a ship, could imagine the scene. Without realizing that children who had asthma could vividly imagine death by asphyxiation in all its horrors, Jithen's father kept up his description.

Till Jithen was in the fourth standard, those parents used to live in the rented house in Thachanakkara. Their picture with their eyes fixed on the distance, awaiting their son, came in the newspaper twice. Then they also disappeared from that house. They too fell into the great ocean of Time, were asphyxiated and disappeared.

'The name of the ship which sank was Kairali.' The day before the social studies test in his fourth class, his father reminded him again about the death by asphyxiation. 'Keep it in mind. The meaning of the word Kairali is "Malayalam"!'

EIGHT

Maelstrom

15 December 1999

...It was around this time, twenty years ago, that the World Health Organization announced that smallpox had been eradicated from the world for all time to come. I still remember my father reading that out to my sisters while they were preparing for the half-yearly examinations during Christmas. Father also said 'vasoori' or smallpox marks can be seen on the face of the sanyaasi who was living in the lodge in front of the Thachanakkara temple. My grandfather had to wait for many years to meet vasooriswami face to face, though even the children of Thachanakkara had seen him so many times. Till the day of my death, I will remember that it was in June, when I had passed from fourth standard to fifth, that my grandfather met him for the first and last time.

Darling Ann Marie, if I tell you that doing penance as a sanyaasi is my favourite subject, would you be shocked? The other day I was reading about a Bhutanese satyr somewhere. A sanyaasi who the Bhutanese, to this day, call holy! After having sex with all the women in his land, he set his eyes on his own mother. He confided his wish to her. The chaste woman wept, cried loudly, and cursed her son. But he would not be dissuaded. Finally, helpless in the face of her son's intransigence, with the proviso that no one else should come to know of it, and with great revulsion, she acquiesced. But he did not even touch his mother. Instead, he shouted in joy. Leaving his flabbergasted mother, he jumped out into the street. With the public listening, all of Bhutan listening, he announced, 'Listen dear ones, a woman's mind has been revealed for all time. Understand this: once she is sure that no one else would come to know, for the sake of love, any woman would be ready to sleep with even her own son! This is the truth. Upon my mother, this is the truth!'

At that moment of revelation, the Lothario was turned into a yogi.

Are you frowning? Did you tell yourself that it is another story that the Bhutanese invented to demean women? But take this only as a story. Some stories help us understand life; till we grow up only to realize that life also is a fable.

Naraapilla had tried thirty-four times to meet the sanyaasi—who used to come and stay in the charitable lodge in front of the Thachanakkara temple off and on—but each time in vain. The fact is that the sanyaasi used to stay in the lodge only for a few days a year. But even on the days he was there, for unknown reasons, he never opened the door for Naraapilla.

That lodge stood like a quaint boathouse waiting at the beach of Time for the final journey of some stranger, with its foundation stones displaced by the roots of the banyan tree, its walls covered with creepers, and its ancient roof tiles, stuck to the disintegrating rafters, covered with fallen banyan tree leaves in myriad colours—blackened by dampness, dried and ripened, beat down by the wind or fallen by themselves. From the time Naraapilla heard from Paanamparampath Nanu that a sanyaasi was sojourning in the lodge, he fell under the spell of an unearthly attraction. Thachanakkara folk saw the old man from the New House of Ayyaattumpilli wearing a single mundu and leaning on a green ebony persimmon walking stick, going up to the lodge, knocking in vain and returning, cursing the door that remained shut each time. He used to go there and return in the killing heat of Kumbham afternoons and during Edavam evenings when the dark clouds were in heat. Appu Nair, who was almost blinded by cataract by then, and Paanamparampath Nanu used to accompany him many a time. Even when the sanyaasi was not there, Naraapilla felt that someone was watching him intently through the cracks made by termites on the windowpanes on the right side of the lodge, which always remained shut. Though his eight-decades-old body still retained enough strength to push open the old termite-eaten door of the lodge, Naraapilla never ventured to do that. Not only that, a feeling that an invisible message from the soul of the person inside was breaking through the walls and entering him, reminding him that his time had not come yet, always made Naraapilla trip up. Whenever he felt that he was being assailed by this knowledge, he also felt relieved by the thought that, each time, he was returning from the portals of death. Then, on his eighty-second birthday, the day he decided to recommence his early morning bath in the temple pond and worship Thachanakkara thevar, that inevitable meeting happened.

As dawn was breaking in the east, he was climbing down the steps of the pond, holding the tumbler for pouring water on himself, and the walking stick, which for many years had become his constant companion. The month of Mithunam was on the cusp of its full-moon day. Naraapilla felt that the rain, which had been falling incessantly till the previous day, had taken a vacation on that auspicious day.

'Moolam day of the month of Mithunam,' he said to himself, straining to avoid slipping as he climbed down the steps made slippery by the monsoon. 'In these eighty-two years, this is the first time a Moolam day is without rain.'

Splitting the image of the pale full moon in a thousand shards, at that time someone was dunking himself repeatedly in the temple pond and surfacing. The sounds of the wavelets created by the ripples in that pond, tired from its centuries' old incarceration, began to hit the sodden cracks in the laterite stones and the failing ears of the old man coming down the steps. Naraapilla was terrified by the sight of a form with shoulder-length hair, with its back to him, coming up from under the water. The next moment when he recognized it as male, his fear abated.

The bearded man, who came up from the water, took off his chuttikkara thorth, wrung it dry, flicked it open like cracking a whip, and towelled his head and face. Then, after wearing the loincloth, when he was tying and tucking in his ochre-coloured mundu, Naraapilla recognized him as the one he had been trying to meet for so many years. Seeing the silhouette of the descending old man, the resident of the lodge froze for a moment; then he began to climb up the steps in a hurry. As it was unavoidable that two persons who were climbing and descending the same steps at the same time in opposite directions would meet at one step, Naraapilla stopped the sanyaasi with his stick as they came abreast.

'Listen,' Naraapilla said, 'I've been to see you. I have been trying for many years. I have a few things I need to tell you, Swami!'

At that moment, the spittoon-shaped speaker on the eastern portal of Thachanakkara thevar cleared its throat, from the first tickle of electric current. Then, accompanied by an ethereal tune, P. Leela's voice started to sing the hyms from *Jnaanappaana*. With a regal gesture, which was perceptible even in the dark, the sanyaasi brushed aside Naraapilla's walking stick and climbed up the rest of the steps, without uttering a word. When he reached the top, he turned and looked back. The sight of an old man holding a long stick and a wavy tumbler, which reflected the greying sky in the background of the moon straining to rejoin its original form in the still-rippling waters, held the sanyaasi immobile for some time.

'Come before it's daylight,' saying thus in a solemn voice resounding with solitude, he disappeared.

In that moment of bliss at having received the invitation, muttering something into the darkness of the early dawn, Naraapilla climbed down the steps for his last birthday bath.

After praying and circumambulating Thachanakkara thevar, and generously applying the sandalwood paste that the new, young priest had pinched and dropped into his palm, on his forehead, chest, and upper arms in wide strokes, Naraapilla got out of the temple through the portal on the east side and walked directly to the lodge. It was not yet daylight. P. Leela had completed *Jnaanappaana* and had moved onto *Harinaamakeerthanam*. As Naraapilla felt the coolness of a Mithunam morning touch the grey hairs on his chest, after a long time he felt he was still one among the aristocrats of Thachanakkara. But that feeling did not last long. Even as he carefully went up the mouldy and slippery steps of the lodge with splayed toes, he lost his footing and nearly fell. Leaning the walking stick against the wall, to let his presence known over the sound of Leela's singing, he purposely banged the tumbler on the floor, while keeping it down.

The door opened instantly.

'Come in,' the man inside invited Naraapilla. Holding firmly onto the termite-weakened doorframe on both sides, Naraapilla entered the lodge.

The so-called lodge had space just enough to spread two mats. Two ochre-colour mundus, and a threadbare thorth were spread on a dry, broken bamboo stick, which had been fixed across the width of the room at a man's height. The muddy-brown streaks left on the walls by the water from the rains of Mithunam, seeping through the worn edges of the beams, could be seen even in the dim light. On a wooden plank on the floor at the corner of the room, were four or five termite-eaten spiritual books, a very small oil lamp, and a lotus-shaped incense stick holder made from coconut shell, all spread out. Though the incense sticks had died down, the flame on a wick in the lamp, which was lit in the morning, was in its last throes of getting asphyxiated. Directly above it, in the Sivakasi calendar—hung on the wall, also for hiding its cracks—the devi on her lotus-seat remained unmoved even when Naraapilla entered the room.

The only door and windows the building had were the ones in the front. A bottle of oil on the windowsill, a cloth bag stuffed with many things and tied to a bar of the window—the list of movable objects in the room was complete. Opening the window and the door and taking the grass mat rolled up and stored in the corner of the room, shaking it free of dust, and sitting on it, the sanyaasi gestured to Naraapilla to sit across from him. The old man sat down on the mat with much effort.

Naraapilla saw the sanyaasi's face getting delineated in the gathering light, as he was sitting facing the open door. Naraapilla sat absorbing all the aspects—the beard with a grey streak only in the middle; the matted hair, the abundant smallpox scars on the skin which resembled a freshly chipped grinding stone base; the ochre-coloured cloth, which hid the form from the neck down, sitting in lotus position. He observed that the sanyaasi was probably only half his age, and his face did not reflect the kind of divinity that Paanamparampath Nanu had been foisting on him all those years. Naraapilla cleared his throat, unaware if the sanyaasi was looking down or meditating. After cracking the joints of his two big toes, the sanyaasi continued to remain silent. At that point, Naraapilla started to hear clearly the cawing of the now-awake crows on the banyan tree, above the noise of the gramophone record of Leela.

'The reason for my coming ... There is no particular reason,

Swami,' Naraapilla said. 'There used to be a senior astrologer in Kaniyankunnu. For everything and anything I only used to go to him. After he died, that too stopped! Well, what is your name? Which's your place?'

When he realized that the sanyaasi had no intention of replying, Naraapilla made as if he was getting up and said, 'Well, since I was on my way after my bath, I am not carrying any money. I forgot that you would only talk after getting the hansel.'

'Today's your birthday, no?' the sanyaasi asked suddenly.

'Eh?' Not catching the question, Naraapilla used his right hand to cup his ear. The second time, when the sanyaasi repeated the question, raising his voice, Naraapilla was shocked. With that he sat down more firmly. Like a child whose artifice has been exposed, his smile bordered on tears.

'Tell me all that you have to say,' the sanyaasi said, 'I don't accept any hansel!'

Naraapilla had forgotten his own reference to hansel just a while ago. He felt anxious that the man of divinity sitting across him could read his mind. He took the damp thorth off his shoulder and wiped his brow. Dried sandalwood flecks floated in the air. Words gushed out of him like from a breached dam.

'Swami, I, this me, have lived long. Have reaped much, threshed and measured much, ate much, saw many as children and grandchildren. Saw many births and many deaths. I lived thus, a long time. On the birthday the exact age shouldn't be mentioned, but I will tell you approximately. Not one or two, at least about eighty years! But these days, what should I say, a kind of ... You understood?'

'Keep talking! It's not polite to ask if one has understood every now and then,' said the sanyaasi, keeping his head bowed.

Naraapilla corrected his posture, sitting straight. He didn't hear distinctly what the sanyaasi had said. For a long time Naraapilla had been having a feeling that his ears were sharper in the night and as the day progressed, his sense of hearing weakened.

'Ah, let it be, whatever it is,' saying this sentence, which was a good enough answer for whatever the sanyaasi was telling him, Naraapilla pointed to the corner of the room and continued, 'That flame is going to die. Just extinguish it. There, like that, that's all there's to it. So, what was I saying, Swami, eh?'

Stretching his hand and pressing the index finger on the lamp to douse the flame, the sanyaasi said, 'This. After living all this while, you have reached an age when the wick can be extinguished any day, no? Umm, let me hear the rest!'

It did not appear as if Naraapilla enjoyed it a bit. Frowning, he said with displeasure, 'I told you, I don't know how to say that. Or else, I will put it bluntly.' Looking around, and after making sure that no one was lurking near the lodge, he continued, 'The belief is that after we die we will go to heaven, hell, etc., no? Leave the thing that those who do good will go to heaven; even if some of those don't go to heaven, we couldn't be bothered. But those who have sinned, shouldn't they get an assurance of sorts from somewhere? Do you understand what am I getting at? That is, imagine I commit a sin without the world knowing of it. Then imagine that I carry it with me for the rest of my life without even a fly getting wind of it. If I have a guarantee that I will get a punishment when I reach hell, I can die in peace, no? If not, what will happen? What if I don't get punished in this world or the other world, terrible, isn't it?'

'Terrible for whom? For you or...' the sanyaasi asked with his eyes closed, looking inward.

This time, Naraapilla clearly heard what the sanyaasi had asked. 'For me!' he said. 'For who else? Swami must be aware that the wrongdoer gets a kind of relief when he gets the punishment, whether from God or the court?'

Hearing this strange concept for the first time in their dialogue, the sanyaasi looked at Naraapilla's face. He perceived the old man's heart had kept its dim yellow light in his indifferent eyes, wide open under the grey eyebrows.

'In this old age, what punishment are you expecting?' the sanyaasi asked a little loudly.

'Why should I receive punishment?' A little shaken, Naraapilla looked behind him at the door and said, 'That's right. It's only the one who has sinned need worry about punishment? What I was getting at is not that, Swami. Imagine now that the police nabbed one who's committed a lot of crimes. Did you imagine? Think that he was beaten up in the station or they take him to court and he gets dumped in the jail for a long period. Did you think? When the criminal comes out after all that punishment, his heart will be clean. Clean how? Clean enough to commit another fresh crime! Hee! And not clean in the sense he would lead a straight life thereafter. Understood?'

The sanyaasi smiled with the right side of his mouth. 'I am getting it gradually,' he said, 'but this is not a new problem. When the sinner gets punished, the others get a feeling that the world is going in the right direction. A tiny feeling only. But as far as man is concerned, such a feeling is paramount. Is that not so?'

'Dey, Swami's losing track again!' Naraapilla said, 'Because of that spittoon's noise, I can't hear what you are saying properly. I am a little hard of hearing. I'm hearing only in halves and fractions.'

As if heeding that, the music from the spittoon stopped in the middle. There was a cut in the electricity supply to Thachanakkara. Naraapilla gave the sanyaasi a disbelieving look. With a smile of gratitude for that miracle he continued, 'Swami is talking of humans. I am talking about me. That is the difference. Isn't that a terrific difference, Swami? That is, we know all the canons of this world. We wish that all the people in the world would live and die according to those laws. But don't we believe we alone are not bound by those canons?'

'None of these is applicable to us, right? Is that the way you really intended it?' the sanyaasi asked, concentrating on tearing off the nail on the big toe of his right foot. 'That means even when we live unmindful of others, gifting pain and sorrow to the world, we can remain unaffected by all that—that is what you believe, yes?'

'That's where Swami has gone wrong.' Naraapilla thrust forward enthusiastically. 'Does anyone create pain and sorrow in this world on purpose? No! Such extremely wicked people are not there in this world! We do things for our pleasure or maybe for a little happiness; those appear to be wickedness in the eyes of others. That's all, no?'

The sanyaasi, who had been somewhat indolent till then, became wholly focused on him. The cool breeze slammed the window shut. Naraapilla's face became more sombre.

'Swami asked earlier what sin I had committed?' When Naraapilla started again, the sanyaasi raised his hand in denial and said, 'No, no. That is not how I asked. What punishment are you expecting in this old age, is what I asked.'

'Ha, all right!' Naraapilla laughed sarcastically. 'Aren't both the same, Swami? Let that go, let that go. After all who's Swami to apportion punishment to me, no?' The old man suddenly became silent and sat still, gazing at the floor. After some time, swaying his body to the sides, with a low voice he said, 'Yes, I have committed a sin. Now that I have said so much, I might as well tell you that too. If you ask me if it was intentional, no! Not at all. But if you ask me if it was done without any forethought, that is also not so.'

Through the open door, a ripe banyan leaf floated in and fell on the floor of the lodge. The sanyaasi saw with his inner eye, the grey hairs on the back of the old man feeling discomfited by the cool breeze.

'That means you were the cause of a small, a very small, violation, no? That is all?' the sanyaasi asked.

Naraapilla opened his eyes and looked at the sanyaasi. At that moment, he felt a spasm in his abdomen. A pain that began as a pecking and gradually tore him apart with increasing intensity.

'Pho,' he said slowly, screwing up his face and keeping his hand on the pain. 'When you say small … when you consider it, it isn't such a small infraction. Well, no, you can also say it is small. How many people die from so many causes! Drowning in the river, poisoned, run over by vehicles … no? When you add it all up, one death is nothing, isn't it so, Swami?'

The sanyaasi gave Naraapilla a sharp look. Even though he was looking at the sanyaasi's face, he did not see that at all.

'Can we say that?' the sanyaasi asked, stroking his beard to hide his agitation. 'Isn't each death like the end of the world, in a sense? At least as far as the dying person is concerned? If that be so, every death would be sorrowful in equal measure. That is a usage of us sanyaasis— in equal measure. Whether it is a human being or a monkey, even a lowly chicken, death can create a very heartbreaking emptiness—in the minds of those who love.'

'Eh?' Looking back and ensuring that his tumbler and walking stick were still near the door, Naraapilla asked, 'Did Swami say, chicken? Why are you bringing chicken into matters that concern human beings? I was not talking of the sorrow caused by death. There's this unbearable sadness in murdering someone, even if unintentionally—I have been straining all these three-four years to meet you to speak about that! Tell me this, Swami, we kill the mosquito which sucks our blood, we kill the louse on our head, we beat to death the snake and the mad dog coming to bite us, right? That is no crime and there is no guilt, not a wee bit! Like that, on the other hand, what if someone kills another for some reason? All hell breaks loose, there's noise, there's incarceration, no?'

'Is it right to say so? Are human beings like mosquitoes, lice or snakes?' the sanyaasi asked, with a smile marking the mind of the old fogey sitting across him.

'Eh? Isn't it so? You were the one who mentioned chicken earlier. At least you sanyaasis should say it is correct? Let me say, there are murders which ordinary men commit, this side of the portals of the courts. Hapless common men! Do you know, sometimes, even the murderer may be as innocent as the one murdered. The dead are celebrated by all at all times. Sometimes, the killer may be a better person than the one killed. Do you understand? But people will say he is a villain. Police, lawyers and the magistrates together will toy with him for a period, and then hang him to death. So what about the murder done by the executioner, with the consent of the court? Truly, isn't this like beating to death a mad dog coming to bite you? Even if the one who writhes and dies is a man? Then, there is sin and there is no remorse!' Showing the stubs of his remaining two incisors Naraapilla laughed. Suddenly his face showed a mysterious emotion, fleetingly. Rubbing his tummy in a circular motion, with unfocused eyes Naraapilla said, 'I too may have been killed that way! Then my children would have been happy. Not mere happiness, real beatitude!'

'You shouldn't say so!' the sanyaasi said, with a bitter smile donned to mask his bitter emotions. 'Your children must be happy to have such a wit for their father! But if it's something you can confide in me, tell me, whose death is making your mind so uneasy? In whose murder do you needlessly believe you have played a part? Tell me! Any expiation which gives more comfort than repentance is yet to be discovered!'

The day had broken outside the lodge. An old woman headed for the temple, reciting hymns, peeped into the lodge through the open door. Seeing the back of Naraapilla, seated facing the sanyaasi, she raised the volume of her hymns and hurried away.

'Or give me a chance to divine and tell you!' After meditating for some time, opening his eyes and staring at Naraapilla, the sanyaasi said, 'The death of a child, no? A male child who died while still young from not getting medical attention in time?'

At that moment, Naraapilla felt a devotion towards the sanyaasi. Joining his palms he said, 'Not that one, Swami. How many children like that die from diseases, how many are saved! Even my Pappanaavan's case is like that. This ... This is not that.' Playing host to a feeling that there was nothing further to hide from the sanyaasi, Naraapilla's mind underwent an upheaval.

'One kick!' Suddenly, Naraapilla said in that frightening voice of Ayyaattumpilli stock, 'One kick alone! When that was done, I was sure it was over! What was over? My life! Now can't you see? Who's there to boil and give me a drop of tea on my birthday? If I become bedridden, that would be it, no? Will any son of a bitch even look at me? Oh, I didn't think it would come to this. Or else I wouldn't have kicked that kick. But that kick happened! Didn't everything end with that one kick? See, it was with this leg.' Naraapilla pulled his right leg from underneath the lotus position. The sanyaasi struggled to control himself and stared at the dark leg full of grey hairs. The look on the old man's face seemed to be aiming at tearfulness and losing its way into stubbornness. The atmosphere in that dilapidated lodge became funereal and seeped in silence. He sucked his lower lip into his mouth, as if making faces, and managed to get his equilibrium back.

'But it did not stop with that.' Pulling back his leg, Naraapilla continued, 'She continued for many days with that head broken on those steps. The mother of four sons, with no one by her side was spitting, shitting, smashing her head against the walls—all in that one room. After spending many days like that, the story ended. Here, like this, I returned home after my bath and prayers, and people and excitement at home! Ah, dead!'

Naraapilla did notice the sanyaasi seizing as if struck by electricity and his tongue getting cut, caught between clamped teeth. The sanyaasi lowered his face, unable to look at the face of the old man who was sitting like the dried, shrivelled, corpse of a vulture in front of him. Outside, along the main road of Thachanakkara, the calls of a fish vendor rose and fell with many intervals between them and moved farther. Realizing that he had been sitting for a long time with lowered unblinking eyes, sighing deeply the sanyaasi got up and said, 'What was...' Unable to complete the question, a sob rose in his throat. He rubbed both his open palms on his face roughly, and pulled his beard, and with difficulty completed the question, 'What was the crime she had committed to deserve such a punishment?'

Naraapilla looked up at the sanyaasi. When he felt that some people on the way to the temple had stopped in front of the lodge, the sanyaasi went and shut the door. Looking at the old man with his back full of grey hairs, the sanyaasi stood by the door, breathing heavily.

Naraapilla heard that question clearly. He was sitting and moving his body to and fro, wearing the mask of a long-suffering person labouring under all the tribulations of the world, but relaxed from achieving the purpose of his visit and expecting only some words of solace. He stopped his body movements the moment he heard the question from the sanyaasi. With the expression of a thief, hearing approaching footsteps while hiding in a dark room, Naraapilla turned around and asked, 'Eh?'

The doors, opened by a strong breeze, hit the sanyaasi's body. He opened the doors and looked up. When he heard the sound of the unusually loud rain, unleashed by the burning sky, on the tiles of the lodge, he closed the doors suddenly, moved the latch, and asked, 'What was her crime?'

Naraapilla tried to get up. The sanyaasi came and kneeled

down in front of him and maintained the interrogating posture. Naraapilla trembled at his look. The old man thought that in that closed single room, he was caught in a rigorous test, where he had to prove his eligibility to live even if it was for the next few minutes. Unable to look at truth in the eye with dignity, Naraapilla lowered his eyes. But that did not last long. He then realized a masculine fiend of prevarication, of subterfuge, of treachery for the sake of survival, of false witness for self-preservation, was shaking and rising up in him, surprising even himself. He saw himself as the most gifted actor in the world then. 'Betrayal, what else? A rank perfidy which no husband can condone,' Naraapilla stated in as high a voice that his eighty-two year-old body was capable of, 'she was one who didn't have the basic necessities—to eat, wear, or live. The daughter of Paramu Nair of Peechamkurichi, a man of no means, Thachanakkara thevar will vouchsafe. And to look at … Aeyy! A miserable scarecrow with hardly any redeeming features! She was starving, absolutely starving. To add to it, the disease of eating stones and soil! I married her without much thought, thinking at least I could give her a life. Do you understand? Does Swami know what the folk of Thachanakkara used to say those days about this Naraapilla? The man who used to measure money with a para! It's with such a Naraapilla that she messed with. When we made a new house, a tenant, an outsider, came for the old house. An educated, knowledgeable teacher. One look at him and you could see he's the kind who goes after other people's wives. Hey, pulling wool over my eyes … Poetry recitation, taking her to the beach festival then … How can I say it? Swami can imagine the rest, whatever shouldn't have happened there.'

Since the rain was lashing the place, Naraapilla's voice had reached a high pitch to compensate. He did not notice that the sanyaasi had got up and was furiously pacing the room like a wounded animal. Seeing the sanyaasi lunging at him with the oil lamp he had grabbed from the corner of the room, whirling like a temple oracle, and with a roar like thunder, Naraapilla shut his eyes tight. The next moment he heard the sound of the oil lamp hitting the floor. Naraapilla opened his eyes. The sanyaasi, standing with his head tilted up and with his convulsing arms raised in a clasp, spoke in words broken up with intense pain: 'And how did the poor thing hit her head against the walls at the time of her death? How? I didn't know, I didn't know!' Crying loudly, he dashed his head against the wall of the lodge. The lodge shook all over, as if in an earthquake.

'Tell me, you vile sinner, you ancient creature! Tell me if it was like this!' He smashed his head against the wall again and again. The blisters of lime plaster fell off the walls of the lodge. The sanyaasi's voice rose above the pelting rain outside. 'Tell!'

The trembling of the sanyaasi now spread to Naraapilla like a flame. In his frantic efforts to scramble and get up, he fell twice on the floor. In his panic to escape death, in his third attempt, he managed to stand up erect. As he saw the sanyaasi sitting in a corner, hiding his blood-streaked face between his knees and clutching his long hair, Naraapilla started to convulse and writhe, realizing the epilepsy of his childhood was making a return in his ripe old age. He felt as if the walls of the lodge were closing in on him rapidly and crushing him, as if the entire lodge had become a torture chamber and was being hoisted up on the banyan tree. Froth and bubbles flowed out of his mouth. When he failed to catch the drops of rain falling through the cracks in the tiles with his tongue, he had a glance of his son sitting in the corner of the room, for the last time. 'Pho!' Snapping at his son with vigour, he toppled over, even as he urinated and defecated involuntarily.

Sitting in Vengooran Thankappan's teashop, Paanamparampath Nanu started to dream up, among the legends of Thachanakkara, one no one had heard so far. Some of the passers-by who had ventured out without umbrellas were standing in a row on the veranda of the shop. Nanu, who was aware that along with the strength of the audience, the gravitas of the story should also go up, managed to hook a biggie on the angling rod of his memory.

'Do you know why Kathakali performances are not held in our temple?' he asked Kochu Parashu and Karunakaran Karthaavu. He did not even glance at Vengooran Thankappan or barber Shivan, who had no sense of history. Some of the passers-by interested in the unfolding story, moved closer.

'In that case, I'll tell you, you all listen,' Nanu started. 'Long, long ago, we had a Kathakali programme in our temple. You have this incident of Narasimham appearing and killing Hiranyakashipu or Hiranyaakshan or someone? That was the story.'

'Hiranya Kashipu,' Karthaavu helped him get a fix on the character.

'Ngaa, if you say Kashipu, okay, Kashipu!' Nanu continued. 'The aattakatha drama was going on unfurling. At last, when the time came for the Narasimham to appear, breaking the pillar, it was beyond what the other guy could suffer!'

'Which other guy?' barber Shivan interrupted.

'Haa, the guy inside our temple!' Nanu continued after bringing on the impatience of Thachanakkara thevar on his own face. 'Would the worthy like it if guys come to Parashuraman's temple and enact Narasimham's story?'

'But aren't they both the same?' Kochu Parashu asked.

'How can they be the same?' twirling the index finger of his fisted right hand inside his mouth, Nanu asked. 'In that case couldn't all the ten incarnations have been in the same form? You listen to this without asking qostens! There's this scene where Hiranyakashipu is on his back and Narasimham is pulling out his entrails, no? By the time that scene came, the real Thachanakkara thevar entered and possessed Narasimham! Ah, you won't believe if I tell you, Narasimham split the abdomen and pulled out the orijinal entrails of the actor who was playing Hiranyakashipu!' When he reached that point, he made a pretence of making a deferential laugh by covering his mouth with this hand.

Barber Shivan felt a spasm in his tummy.

'Did he die, then?' Vengooran Thankappan asked.

'Is there any need to ask?' Nanu said. 'With that came the decision that Kathakali will never be held in our temple.'

At that point, Pankajaakshan of Ayyaattumpilli reached in a hurry, carrying an umbrella.

'Did father come this side, Kochu Parashu chettaa?' Pankajaakshan asked.

'No, he didn't,' Kochu Parashu said. 'But these days, does he come out at all?'

'Imagine how much of a pity it is,' Pankajaakshan said. 'Today's his birthday. In the morning, when my missus went with tea, he was not to be seen. That Nampoothiri boy said he had come to the temple in the morning. He has been to the pond and has had his bath there in the morning. Now where has he gone?' As Pankajaakshan was about to close his umbrella, Paanamparampath Nanu came to the veranda and said, 'Did you look in the lodge?'

As Pankajaakshan stood, having no answer, Nanu got under his umbrella boldly. 'Then come, after a long time the sanyaasi has come here. Naraapilla chettan should be there!'

Forgetting their long-standing tiff, Pankajaakshan and Nanu went under one umbrella to the lodge.

Before long, the congregation, which was still standing on the veranda of the shop saw Pankajaakshan and a few others carrying Naraapilla to the New House in the rain. Pankajaakshan, who was walking in the front, was shielding Naraapilla's face from the rain with the umbrella. Carrying a tall stick and a dented tumbler, Nanu rushed into Kochu Parashu's shop and said, 'He was lying inside the lodge. Covered in shit and unconscious, alone. Here, this stick and tumbler on the steps, a lot of blood and shit inside! Ho!'

Dashing behind Nanu, Kochu Parashu, Karunakaran Karthaavu, and Vengooran Thankappan, headed for Ayyaattumpilli.

'Oh my father,' before the throng entered the gate, Chinnamma's scream jolted the rain.

That was a little premature. On that day, Naraapilla still had twenty-seven days left.

NINE

Harbinger of Death

28 June 1999

...The day before Grampa's death too, a mottled wood owl, a 'thachankozhi', had cried in Thachanakkara, announcing an oncoming death. To cry out at midnight to portend death, he had flown across the river from Uliyanoor, the land of Perumthachchan, to perch on the tall trees of Thachanakkara. He had been living in hiding in the innards of Uliyanoor, incarnated as a bird to outlive his pitiable death by a falling wood chisel. The elders of Thachanakkara used to say that thachankozhi used to fly to the house where the son was wishing for the father's death. He sat on the branch of darkness with a head, which could be rotated three hundred and sixty degrees, on the neck which had been sliced through by the broadest of the wood chisels. The heartbeat of one aching for the death of his father accompanied the startling cries of the legendary carpenter's son.

The night before Grampa's death, the bird came and roosted in one of the big trees in Ayyaattumpilli. I was woken up with a start at midnight by his alarming call, which I heard in the darkness outside, and lay with a palpitating heart. My asthma curdled in my chest like a cooing dove.

'Damn,' mother turned to the side in her sleep and muttered, 'wonder who he's come to carry away!'

Jithen had the fortune of seeing Pankajaakshan shouting into the newly-installed telephone in Pooshaappi Stores, loud enough to be heard over at Cherai, about forty kilometres away. Since Jithen had not gone to school due to his wheezing, his mother had sent him to the shop with an umbrella to get pappadam. As he turned, after buying pappadam worth one rupee and getting the purchase entered in the ledger to their debit, he saw Pankaachammavan lifting the handset of the phone. In the pocket diary in his left hand was written the telephone number of his sister-in-law's house. Though it had been written down and given by Govindan Master when Pankajaakshan had gone to attend Chandrika's wedding, it had stayed with him unused for many years. Later, when he used to look at it, he only thought of it as a forgotten sum that either he owed someone or someone owed him. However, on the third day after his father had been carried in from the lodge, when the realization struck him like a bolt of white lightning that, for the rest of his life, his father would become his burden alone, he suddenly recalled the number in his pocket diary. 'My God,' Pankajaakshan said to himself, smacking himself on his forehead, 'isn't this the number that elder brother had given to notify him if father was ailing!'

Using his index finger to turn the dial of Kochu Parashu's telephone a number of times, Pankajaakshan stood listening intently into the receiver with a serious look. After someone picked up the phone at the other end after many rings, he shouted into the phone, 'Hallo … Who's that? Hallo, hallo…'

At that time, apart from Jithen, there were two old men on the store's veranda. Hearing for the first time someone other than Alamboori talking into the phone, the old men and Jithen stood looking with the same sense of wonder at the spiral cable of the phone elongating as needed and Pankajaakshan talking with gestures in reply to the silence from the other end of the phone.

It had been three days since Naraapilla had been stretched out like a cast-iron statue of old age, covered with his faeces, on the rope-bound cot in his unventilated and ill-lit room. On the second day, on his way to the hospital in Aluva, Madhavan Doctor had come and done a thorough check-up of Naraapilla. From a quick physical examination, Achuttan Vaidyan inferred that the bones and internal organs of the old man—who lay delirious and screwing up his face—were unaffected. When he saw that his prescription, with only vitamin B complex for tiredness and cyproheptadine for appetite, which he had extended towards the people standing around, was not being accepted by anyone, he was forced to leave it on Naraapilla's bed. To Kalyanikuttyamma, who ran after him with a crumpled ten-rupee note in her hand after a minute of uncertainty, with the all-understanding smile of a doctor of the old school, he said, 'Aren't you the daughter-in-law of Naraapilla chettan? Keep it with you. You will need it again.'

That evening, before darkness fell, Kalyanikuttyamma pulled down the electric wire running to her toilet and extended it to the New House and lit up a bulb there. The communist husbands of Thankamma and Chinnamma, Kumaran and Shankaran, respectively, had discussed with their spouses the need for providing light in the New House where the old man was laid up. But, though they had not heard each other, both the daughters of Naraapilla differed with their husbands in similar fashion. Though residing in separate homes, their ideas and the words they used were eerily similar. 'What's wrong with you?' said Chinnamma to Shankaran and Thankamma to Kumaran using different pitches, 'At the end of the month, when the electricity bill has to be paid, will father count out and give the money?'

Ignoring the smattering rain, as she stood on a wooden chair and was trying to loosen the wire going to the toilet, when Pankajaakshan, realizing her intent, echoed his sisters' objection,

Kalyanikuttyamma, as the only unfortunate daughter-in-law of the house who had to live in Ayyaattumpilli, said with as much steadfastness as she could muster, 'If I don't do this, there will be no one else here to do this. Aren't you all that kind of pitiless creatures?'

Thus, on the fourth night of his being bed-ridden, electricity reached Naraapilla's bedroom. The first three nights in that room, where a tired, unsleeping lantern kept watch at all times, the three sons of Pankajaakshan had started taking turns sleeping, keeping Naraapilla company. It was when, unable to suffer any more the stench of his excreta and the foul words which Naraapilla kept uttering in his delirium, the three children had baulked at their night-duty that Pankajaakshan recalled the mysterious number lying in his pocket and made that long call to Cherai.

It was getting dark. As he stepped on the soil of Ayyaattumpilli after twenty-five years, Govindan Master's soul shivered. He stood with a cloth bag and a closed umbrella in front of his siblings' houses, now separated by bamboo fences, like a man who had come from another planet. As he gazed at the silhouette of a girl with a limp moving along the yard of the old house through his spectacles misted with the rain, Govindan Master felt disoriented. He heard the soulfully melancholic rendering of hymns by P. Leela, something which was not there in his childhood, coming out of the loudspeakers of Thachanakkara temple suffusing the twilight. He saw in his mind his younger siblings and himself standing in the torrential rains of the past in the places which now had the house with the blue gate and the cowshed with the lowing cows beyond that. Seeing the guest with greying hair, the eldest among the children asked, 'Who are you?'

Kunjuamma came from inside and, gathering her curly hair and tying them up, sensing that some stranger had stepped into the yard at dusk, said, 'My son! My Govinda!' before she vanished into the darkening air. His siblings came out one after the other and smiling sadly at their elder brother dissolved into the darkness like their mother had. Only one of them, an eleven-year-old with his cheekbones sticking out and eyes rheumy, came closer and asked, 'Chettaa, don't you remember taking me from Mother and carrying me when we were returning from Achuttan Vaidyan's clinic, and continuing to carry me even when your legs were aching, without letting on? But, chettaa, what a pity! Amongst us six, only I died early!' With his lower lips trembling between sobs, he too disappeared.

'Achyutha!' a call came from the old house. Govindan Master saw his childhood friend, the wide-eyed Achyuthan come running towards him to show off his biscuit-coloured plastic footwear, ignoring the summons of his father, Menon Master. When the call was repeated, realizing that some of the syllables were different, Govindan Master returned to the drizzle of the present.

'Jithaa!' the call and the child both came from the opposite direction. From the new house with the blue gate. Govindan Master knew the name which was called out. The child with big ears and wide eyes who had stood alone in front of the bookshelf at Cherai, seeking refuge! Time had added a few inches to his height.

Unable to recognize the man who was stepping on the soil of Ayyaattumpilli after twenty-five years, the ten-year-old child turned around and shouted back to his mother, 'Here, Mother, someone's here.'

In that dusk, getting wet in the drizzle, Govindan Master walked towards the New House with a bitter smile.

That late evening, three generations were arrayed near the cot of Naraapilla, to see the middle-aged man standing with his hands folded and head bowed: Pankajaakshan, Thankamma and

Chinnamma, their progeny—three, four and three, respectively—from child to adolescent to youth; the wailing infant who was being carried by Thankamani, the daughter of Thankamma…

'Shush, don't cry baby,' said Thankamma to her grandson, 'here, see who has come, your great-uncle!'

Unable to understand the relationship, the newborn raised the volume of his wails and peed on Thankamma's yellow saree. Govindan Master held close to him the only one he could recognize from the next generation and asked him, 'Which class are you in now?'

'Fifth,' Jithen said, snorting the phlegm from his nose which was lengthening onto his upper lip like tiny tusks.

Then, imitating her sister who introduced her grandson, Chinnamma told Naraapilla loudly, 'Here, Father, take a look at who's here! Your eldest son!'

It did not appear as if Naraapilla had heard her. He had shut his eyes to the sight of a centuries-old fear looking at his life with burning eyes and waiting with its wings closed. 'Pho,' Naraapilla snapped from his bed, 'Go away without killing! Go away without pecking! Pho.'

Govindan Master hung his cloth bag on a peg behind the door and asked Pankajaakshan, 'Who's sleeping here with father?'

Pankajaakshan said with some hesitation, 'Well … that … I and my sons are there. We take turns…'

Raising his right hand and putting an end to the stutter of his younger brother, Govindan Master said, 'From this day onwards, I will sleep here. I have more than enough time!'

Govindan Master stayed for three weeks in the New House, without a break. Kalyanikuttyamma, who used to come thrice a day to the New House to bring food for the old man, bowed in her heart to the man who was so far away from the ruthless behaviour of Ayyaattumpilli stock. During the first week itself, she had offered Govindan Master two new lungis which she had bought for her sons, and three shirts of Pankajaakshan's which were washed and pressed and kept in the cupboard. Lifting and showing the cloth bag which showed signs of mildew, Govindan Master told his brother's wife, 'No, my child, here, I have brought all that I need!'

Noticing how well Govindan Master was taking care of his father day and night—even as Naraapilla tried to dodge him like a naughty child and snorted like a wild animal—Kalyanikuttyamma vowed to herself that she too would lavish the same kind of conscientious care on her own father in Kochi when he would become old, while Chinnamma and Thankamma, who had gone there to borrow some mustard seeds, stood near the grinding stone of Geethalayam, wrapped up in a discussion of some other sort.

'Did you understand, chechi,' Chinnamma said in a voice which, despite her efforts, did not sound like a conspiratorial whisper, 'why someone has dashed from Cherai to here, when it's apparent he's going to die?'

Glancing back, climbing on to the steps under the eaves to escape the drizzle, Thankamma asked her sister, arching her eyebrows, 'Why?'

'Can't you see from the way he's shovelling the shit and pee and licking father clean?' Chinnamma asked, unable to control the seething in her blood. 'If he gets the New House bequeathed to him, would he find it unpalatable?'

Thankamma's eyebrows arched more like a drawn bow. Snapping its bowstring, Chinnamma said the next sentence, 'When I saw the deed-maker Karthaavu going there yesterday, I got the hint. Isn't it enough to take the inked thumb of the dying man and stamp it on the paper?'

At that time, from the lips of the normally righteous Thankamma, a vicious hiss escaped. That was the sound of Ayyaattumpilli boiling in her soul. But when the image of her brother—who could be seen removing, with apologetic care, their father's excreta from the mat and sheets, washing them, and drying them, defeating the wet Mithunam and Karkkadakam months—the very next moment she corrected herself and said, 'Heyy, you are imagining things, girl! Even the land he has been given, he has no time to take up. What to say of this!'

Chinnamma who was holding back the mustard seeds in her hand, ended the brief discussion by handing them over. 'Ummm, you watch now. You'll see someone carrying away everything that has been written and not written, when father's dead!'

As Chinnamma had guessed in her devious mind, Govindan Master was trying to win back something from the fallen man all through the day and night. But the only difference was that it was not money or property. He was only trying to inform Naraapilla, who used to stare at him without any recognition while he was using lukewarm water laced with Dettol to wash his father clean morning and evening, applying the ointment to prevent bed sores, and massaging his back, of one thing: 'It's me, Father,' Govindan Master used to say at least thrice a day, 'an old Govindan!'

Govindan used to blow on each spoon of gruel—which Kothappulakkalli used to make with broken rice, using coconut tree spathes to light the fire—to cool it before feeding his father. The chilli in the chutney often used to make the old man sputter and cough, spraying the gruel into his son's eyes. Wiping off the rice from the glasses, the son continued his efforts. Apart from the medicines prescribed by Madhavan doctor, he applied ayurvedic emulsions and liniments of his own accord. He put ayurvedic *ilaneerkuzhambu* eye drops in his father's rheumy eyes. He pared the black, thickened nails of the toes with a penknife.

Vengooran Thankappan asked Govindan Master, who had gone to Kochu Parashu's shop to buy 501 brand washing soap, with overweening respect, 'Why are you washing all these soiled clothes of your father, Master? Doesn't he have daughters and a daughter-in-law? Otherwise, if you pay four annas, won't that washerwoman do it for you?'

The answer that Govindan Master gave him vexed him to no end. 'For twenty-five years,' Govindan Master said with an inner acceptance full of magnanimity, 'Father has been saving up those soiled clothes for me.'

By the middle of Karkkadakam, Naraapilla could sit up with the help of others. When Govindan Master was dozing one afternoon to get over the tiredness of many sleepless nights, he woke up with a start on seeing a dream, which appeared to be more truthful than reality. In that dream, Naraapilla was shouting at his son, pointing at his own back which had spots of blood as if lashed with a whip, 'You have come to atone for the sins of beating by caressing, haven't you?'

Startled awake, Govindan Master looked at his father who was sleeping peacefully, and let out a long sigh. Though the old man's body had returned to the sleep and wakefulness cycles, with his fall in the lodge, he had lost his sentience. Because of that, no one could find out from him as to what caused him to fall. When Naraapilla could sit up and could drink the gruel from the plate by himself, Govindan Master took his umbrella and cloth bag, promising to return in two days after going to Cherai. Every moment he spent taking care of his father, he was loving his own epileptic son, whom he had left in the care of Sulochana's parents, more deeply. All those days, he had this feeling that he was on a strange pilgrimage wearing his father's slipper on one leg and his son's slipper on the other. Both ill-fitting, biting footwear;

but they protect his lower extremities on life's thorny path. Thus on the twenty-fifth day of Naraapilla's fall, after having lunch at Thankamma's house, Govindan Master returned to Cherai.

'I will come back in two days,' ruffling Jithen's head lovingly, Govindan Master told Kalyanikuttyamma. 'I feel bad not seeing my son all this while.'

TEN

Swayamvaram

23 July 1999

...You know the capacious trough for bathing that you see in movies is called bathtub in English. Do you realize how many evocative words such as bath trough disappear from our lives the way some geriatrics die and vacate the space without giving any grief to anyone?

Forget the love for the language. There is a specific reason for me to remember the trough now. Yesterday, I slept at a friend's place. It was late when I finished work. I had told you that I am ending my stay in a lodge and moving on to a house. I have been searching for a house with low rent where we can stay after our marriage. When I heard that the upper floor in a colleague's house is being let out, I went there to check it out. Both of us had a few drinks and food to our fill from a bar in the city. Since by the time we reached his house it was very late, I decided to sleep there. I was alone on the upper floor that was to be let out. After hearing the rent expected, I had let go of any idea of staying there. Let me tell you something if you won't tell anyone: before I left in the morning, yielding to temptation, I used the bathtub there for my bath. Immersed in its lukewarm water, like a child trying to recall its previous life lying inside its mother's womb, I tried to reminisce about Aluva river. But lying inside that bathtub which didn't belong to me, more than about Periyar river, I was reminded of the temple pond of Thachanakkara and of the centuries-old algae bloom-ridden water in it!

The sight of me lying naked in that bathtub of the fashionable people was amusing. How did the grandchild of Naraapilla of Ayyaattumpilli, who drowned in the temple pond, end up in a bathtub like this? After laughing for some time, lying all alone, I started feeling a little afraid.

•

It was the twenty-seventh day since Naraapilla had been carried home from the lodge.

On that morning, when the Karkkadakam monsoon was performing its dance of destruction, Ayyaattumpilli gaped, finding Naraapilla missing from his bed. In the downpour, which was doing its torrential work seemingly in one breath, Pankajaakshan and the next generation of males of Ayyaattumpilli scoured the yard, the compound, the well, and the streams for Naraapilla. Pankajaakshan did not forget to look for him in the lodge, to which he despatched his youngest son, Soman. Shankaran and Kumaran took leave to join the search for Naraapilla, and went into the rain. Jithen alone could not be a member of the search party. After he had started sneezing following the exposure to rain, Chinnamma had dried his hair and chest and confined him to the house. Chinnamma was heard asking Vidyadharan, who was rushing through the yard with a thorth wound around his head, 'Did you find him?'

The rain swallowed his reply. Taking out a shirt from the almirah, which smelt musty, and offering it to Jithen, Chinnamma said, 'Where the hell has this guy, who's been shitting and spitting in his bed, gone to? Let the goners be gone, you wear this, lad!'

The children and grandchildren had been having misgivings that Naraapilla was casting around for more trouble, even as he was giving the impression of coming out of his bedridden state. Even the seniors of Thachanakkara, including Raambillapolice and Appu Nair, felt that Naraapilla was coming back to life. But after Govindan Master went back to Cherai, things went topsy-turvy. In the absence of a nursing attendant, in those two days, Naraapilla revealed his worst self. Causing the stench that carried even to the neighbourhood, he dipped his hands in his own excreta on his bed, and with the ritualistic artistry of one applying handprints of rice flour on the walls on the eve of Karkkadaka Sankraanthi, he started to press yellow prints on the walls. Sometimes he cried openly with the pathos of being able to leave the imprints of his eighty-two years in this world only in that manner; at other times, pleased with the expression of his artistic talents in yellow, he laughed out loud. The last time Kalyanikuttyamma saw her father-in-law by the side of the rope-bound cot, he was jumping up and down, covered in shit from tip to toe.

'Pho,' Naraapilla snapped, seeing the female form near the door bearing his food. 'If you come to peck at me, I'll kill you! I'll kill you, and I'll die too! Pho! Pho!' His voice boomed for the last time in Ayyaattumpilli.

The person who noticed the dented tumbler on the topmost step of the pond of Thachanakkara thevar was the priest of the minor temple. When he saw the tumbler, which was overflowing with rainwater, he remembered a mendicant he had seen near the pond the previous evening. Realizing that the beggar, who had come stealthily from the thickets beyond the temple, was planning to do his ablutions in the pond, the priest had shouted at him and had driven him off; he even stood guard at the pond for an hour, holding up his umbrella. However, now early in the morning, when he looked at the tumbler—which, sitting on the stone steps and overflowing in the rain, looked like a sculptural rendering of loneliness in metal—the young Nampoothiri could recall its real owner. With a palpitating heart, he looked at the pond, which, gorging on the torrential rainwater and having covered all the steps, seemed vain about its depth and expanse. Then in one bound he reached the main temple and said within earshot of the priest and the deity, 'One of Naraapilla's possessions is near the pond. Also, his children are searching for him!'

That news blazed, disregarding the monsoon, through those who never stopped their ritual baths and temple visits even in the torrential rains. Daylight had not broken through, though it was past ten o'clock. Within no time, the whole village was assembled around the banks of the overflowing pond. A joyous thrill, which only spectators are capable of, went around the pond, the rains notwithstanding: using spades to clear the climbing nettles, siam weeds, and touch-me-nots, the public made their standing space around the square of the pond, as if around an ancient drama theatre, where a tragedy was to be staged. Holding the old dented tumbler his father had used for bathing for years, Pankajaakshan was in the front row of the audience. The boys of Ayyaattumpilli, including Jithen, also got their places in the front row without anyone protesting, on the strength of their grandfather being the one in the pond. Though the public expected some action, when the four khaki-clad firemen entered the precincts of the temple and reached the pond, having reached from Aluva in their firetruck, the scene did not change. Someone's two-year-old stubborn child began to cry loudly, feeling hurt about being denied the right to catch the rain drops by extending his hand beyond the circumference of the umbrella. After a brief consultation with his colleagues, the leader of the men from the fire force called out to the spectators, 'Who here knows how to dive?'

There was a buzz in the crowd. The child crying for the rainwater increased the volume of his wails in the second round.

'We can give it a try!' a young man wearing an ochre mundu, with a sandal-paste mark on his forehead, and carrying an umbrella with broken ribs, came forward and said. Everyone there knew him by face, as the muscled, khaki-knickered trainer who used to lead the branch of a religious organization in the west side of the Thachanakkara thevar temple. The young man took off his shirt and mundu, folded them, shoved them between the stretchers of the umbrella, and gave the umbrella to another man to use. By that time, three more men of approximately the same age, with sandal-paste marks on their foreheads bleeding in the rain and clad only in their underwear, appeared next to him. The audience watched with interest as they descended part after part into the water, in congruence with their descent down the submerged steps. The public whispered among themselves that the corpse would be on the sixth or seventh step, invisible in the muddied waters. The sight of four heads, caught in the net of rain, surfacing here and there spitting out water, and diving again amused the children in the audience. That was when that sight caught Jithen's attention—the girl standing in the front of the crowd across him! His heart did a somersault. Many months ago, she had sowed the seed for the shock that Jithen underwent just then, having completed her fourth standard in Aalungal School and moved to St Francis School in Aluva. From the moment she was seen standing close to her father under his umbrella, and looking steadfastly into the pond, the seed sprouted, and even as one was watching it, it grew into a huge tree of uneasiness.

'Damn,' he said to himself, 'what a time for her to put in an appearance!'

He could easily recognize the small form in a green skirt, amidst the reflected upside-down images of the people on the other side of the bank. Her image was swaying in the wavelets created by the divers. It was impossible to reach where she was standing, by wriggling through the throng. He was certain that even if he could make it through the crowd, he would still not be able to do what he could not, in the four years they had studied together. He was dying to catch her attention by shouting that the man in the pond was his grandfather. However, suddenly with a terrific sneeze a bubble burst in his nose. With a feeling of inferiority, he sniffed in the two tusks of phlegm emerging from his nose and hid himself behind the crowd.

One of the four divers searching inside the pond came to the surface right in the middle of the pond after a long dive, and told the uniformed guys on the banks, 'Saw the thing. Can't hold enough breath to lift it and bring it up.'

The other three young men in competition dived under in the same spot and corroborated that statement. When all of them reported sighting the old man lying steeped in the mud with his limbs sticking up, from the audience women, children, and the weak-hearted men started to leave the area of their own accord, sighing deeply. Still, there were quite a number of people left behind on the banks of the pond. Jithen looked with anticipation at the remaining crowd on the opposite bank. His first love had disappeared, choosing not to witness a poignant sight, which could have stayed throughout in memory.

The young men dived singly and in groups, another two or three rounds. Deciding that retrieving the corpse stuck in the mud from such depths was impossible, they came up on land and sat with their legs spread. Their eyes were bloodshot and protruding, having seen an undesirable sight. Tying a grapnel, brought by one of the spectators, the firemen flung it into the middle of the pond. However, Naraapilla refused to be baited by the flukes of the grapnel. That was when someone suddenly remembered the brick-kiln owner Devassy, who had rescued a drowning lad many years ago at Punneli kadavu, with what seemed to be an interminable dive then. Paanamparampath Nanu, who was lurking behind till then, shouted out that suggestion, 'Shall we call our Achaayan? Wasn't he the one who lifted up from the river alive, the boy from Chammaram?'

Though it was clearly understood who Nanu was referring to, expecting the public's approval, Pankajaakshan asked, 'Who? Our Devassy from the brick kiln?'

With that, a debate began on the banks of Thachanakkara thevar's pond. Listening to an old man holding forth on the remedial rituals required if a Christian entered the temple pond, one of the firemen withdrew to the background and looked once at the temple pond as if tempted. Fearing the possible repercussions if it was revealed that he was a Christian, he turned the side of his wedding ring bearing the name of his wife to align with the palm and looked nervously at the divers who had found Naraapilla's body. At that time, Karunakaran Karthaavu, who was standing to the left of Pankajaakshan, said in a heavy voice that sounded peremptory, 'If he can bring the thing up, call him! If a corpse can lie inside the temple pond, a non-Hindu can bring it up too!'

Thus, Devassy reached Thachanakkara in half an hour on a green Luna moped from Angamaly. Since his brick kiln was not working due to the monsoon, he had dropped anchor at his pig farm in Angamaly. That morning, when he had entered the pig sty, for no reason he had remembered Pankajaakshan's father. Three weeks before, when he had gone to pay the rent for the land leased for the brick kiln to Pankajaakshan, he had also gone to the New House to visit Naraapilla. The moment he stepped into Naraapilla's room along with Pankajaakshan, for some reason, he thought of his pigs. And when Pankajaakshan introduced the middle-aged man sitting at Naraapilla's bedside as his brother, Devassy also thought of his only ram, which he used to lock up every night in the sty along with the pigs. Devassy had a foreboding then that during the last days of the old man on the bed, he would have to render some significant service. He gave his new phone number to Pankajaakshan that day before leaving. When, after writing it under his brother's telephone number in his small diary, Pankajaakshan looked up questioningly, Devassy told him, 'Write it down. You will need it before long, sir!'

The words of the brickmaker, who used to become a butcher during monsoons, turned out to be prophetic.

Before getting into the pond, wearing only red shorts, Devassy took off his thick wristwatch and gave it to Jithen, saying, 'Son, you hold this! Give it back when I return!' There was only a light rain then. The wristwatch resembled a circular pond for Jithen. It was getting to be twelve noon. He saw the big needle diving down to catch the stationary small needle in the glass pond on his hand. Devassy swam up to the mid-point of the pond, dived down, came up empty-handed, and shouted, 'This is difficult. Our small boat is lying in the brick kiln. Two of you go and bring it here. And talk to the boatmen and bring a bamboo for punting. Do you understand what that is? You know the bargepole, that's it!'

Though at first sight they looked made for one another, three things which would never go with one another, came together in front of the people of Thachanakkara: a centuries-old temple pond, a small canoe, and a big bargepole.

Devassy stationed the canoe, manned by a young man, in the middle of the pond. Then the barge pole was lowered into the water. The entire bamboo pole, as tall as six full grown adults, disappeared under the water. Asking the young man to hold the tip of the pole firmly, Devassy took a deep breath. And dived down alongside the pole, swift like a harpoon.

The light rain seemed to be casting seeds at the wavelets in the water. Jithen counted till eighty-two. By that time, catching hold of the right calf of the corpse with his right hand, Devassy had started his ascent to the top using his left hand to pull himself rapidly up along the barge pole. The naked corpse, hanging upside-down from the leg with splayed toes, spiralled in the water, creating a small whirlpool. On the banks of the pond, rose a sound similar to wailing. With the long immersion in water, the heel had turned white and sodden. The leg itself had become darker. Till they reached the banks, Jithen could only see over the water surface the right leg of Naraapilla, held by Devassy. When he saw the pale area like the cutting edge on the dark leg, he felt he was seeing a stone-cutting axe, which had been lost, being brought up from the water. When he realized the person being hauled up along the ascent of the stone steps by the one who swam ashore was his grandfather, Jithen sat down with a breathlessness of such severity as he had never experienced before in the ten years of his life.

The corpse of Naraapilla, so sodden that no hellfire would be able to burn it, lay on the banks of the pond like a depraved icon of the bygone times.

Increasing its tempo, the light rain of Karkkadakam turned into a torrent.

As Naraapilla's body started smoking on the pyre made on the southern plot of the New House, protected from the rain by a make-shift tarpaulin tent, not a single tear came to Govindan Master, who lit the pyre. Govindan Master had reached Ayyaattumpilli on hearing of the death, just before the body reached from Aluva Hospital after autopsy. His epileptic son, Narayanan, had accompanied him. Contrary to misgivings, Narayanan attended the funeral, in its entirety, in silence. When the corpse was moved to the pyre, he even wept.

Unable to disperse quickly because of the rain, the folk of Thachanakkara, who were distributed among the four houses of Ayyaattumpilli, got an opportunity to discuss life. There were opinions that when Naraapilla's body was retrieved from the pond, his right hand had a clutch of dark, wavy hair in it and that it belonged to Kunjuamma, who had met with a premature death. Barber Shivan contended, with his long-standing experience, that more than female hair, it resembled the hair of a man's beard, grown long. There were arguments that Naraapilla was eighty years old and eighty-four years old. There were surmises about the young man who came with Govindan Master from Cherai and who bore amazing resemblance to Naraapilla. Appu Nair, who had fallen faint at Peechamkurichi on hearing of Naraapilla's death, and yet had scrambled up to attend the funeral, only to go 'hari hara' on seeing Chinnamma's sister-in-law Kunthi bawling along with Chammarath Amminiyamma, became subject of discussion. There were various annotations that the sanyaasi, who seemed to have disappeared forever from the lodge twenty-seven days ago was in reality Kesavan, who had left Thachanakkara ages ago; that he was Achyuthan who stayed in the old house of Ayyaattumpilli as a tenant; and yet again, that it was Naraapilla's own son Chandran who had run away from home. There were hyperbolic statements about the time Devassy spent underwater holding his breath while retrieving the corpse of Naraapilla. There were explanations that Christians are able to hold their breath for a longer time; that the Resurrection of Jesus Christ could be accounted for by his power to lie down holding his breath for seventy-two hours; and the technique that enabled singer Yesudas to sing long passages without exhaling was the same one that Devassy used under water. Thus, standing on the burning body of that dead man, people produced baloney, as they always do.

Once the month of Karkkadakam was over, the water in the Thachanakkara thevar's pond, confined for centuries, was pumped out and remedial rituals performed for the purification of the pond after the inauspicious death in its depths. The contaminated water pumped out from the temple pond flowed in streams in front of all the houses of Thachanakkara. Initially, clear as tears and later thick as excrement, the flow continued. A task which looked as daunting as emptying the ocean was successfully completed before Thiruvonam. On Jithen's birthday, the day after Thiruvonam, and the first day after the conclusion of the fifteen-day pollution period following her father's death, Chinnamma, who was at the temple, went up to the pond.

The new day's light falling on the new waters without the algae bloom of yesteryears, like a newborn child, smiled at Jithen without Chinnamma noticing it.

Part 4

Moksha

'Man is the only creature that perishes before attaining full growth!'

—Anonymous

ONE

Portal

15 August 1999

…I got up very late today. Last night, I sat up late, scribbling this and that. Things without any structure or scheme. Considering the existing ways of writing a novel, I do not think that I would be able to write about the life of our times. To invent a new method of narration is more difficult than discovering a continent. Yet, while others are sound asleep, a few are trying to do just that the world over, burning midnight oil. Why do they sit down and spend so much of their time writing, moving between the heart and the mind, into which emotions and thoughts are sieved, like in the two chambers of a repeatedly turned hourglass? In this island of solitude, where neither money nor fame is of use, why does one want to sacrifice oneself? I want to ask these questions to the world once again, standing on top of its head—in the full-throated manner of Ayyaattumpilli stock.

Today is a holiday. I had wanted to go and meet Amma and Acchan at our place. But I am running a high temperature. Maybe Independence-fever. I don't know what I will do the whole day. Like solitude, fever too does help writing. But what's the use of writing? Will anyone want to publish a novel written by someone like me? Or, even if they publish it, these days, will anyone read a novel with involvement? We, who respect the Taj Mahal and the Pyramids for their size, would denigrate a novel for the same reason. Do you know that it is because death is inhered in them that these creations have become so magnificent?

Largeness, we have started believing, is a liability even if it is of the heart. Would there be ten people below fifty years of age in our state who would have read Kunjikuttan Thampuran's translation of *Mahabharatham* in its entirety? If I tell you that, for Malayalis—whose state, Kerala, has a seashore running along its entire length—except for the fishermen, the sea merely represents the time spent on the beach, would you believe it? How much of an expanse! Do we need as much, we may say to each other.

You needn't get alarmed. Even I am not certain that I will write a book about Thachanakkara. In order to use this holiday granted by our Independence, I will set aside the writing and go for a porn movie. In the secure darkness, where moustachioed lives gather and get tired from their collective coming together for a little pleasure.

This cursed loneliness be damned!

During the study holidays before his annual examination in ninth standard, an unknown muse from somewhere made Jithen write his first poem on the empty pages of his mathematics notebook. He was sitting imprisoned in the square pool of light on which the shadows of the window bars fell, with the book on the table blackened with age. With his eyes frozen on the hibiscus plant seen through the window, he turned to a new page of the notebook. The sour smell of the ink of the new pen, which his father had brought from Aluva for use in the examinations, intoxicated him like never before. Like a yellow fledgling in the throes of death, bleeding blue from its beak, the pen shivered in his hand as he started writing thus on the unruled page, surprising himself:

Why does the heart resemble a well, O Guru?
How it had hoped to be like a burning ocean
Thou art an ocean of wisdom, expansive; Acolyte, I
Falter as a soul of the well.
As days pass, will the breadth of the mind
Shrink, and ailments abound?
Majesty unbounded, thou art Ocean,
Becalmed mind, my only companion!
Angry waves swirl like the essence
Of tempests! O Guru, even the well is parched!
Foolish worthies, lowering buckets,
Deem ripples to be the well's waves!
When even tingles bloom, in the confines
Of stone, only a deepening stillness!
I espy only circular sky, will not birds
Be seen, was education misplaced?
One fear remains: would thou say
The well too is the offspring of the Ocean?

Despite a rather unsuccessful attempt to incorporate rhyme and metre migrated from his textbooks, despite the inelegant gawkiness of a novice, Jithen thought that the poem of eighteen lines had something that was intrinsically of his own blended in it—something which, till that moment, was unfamiliar to him. At the same time, it was the verbal body of many unnameable sorrows accumulated lately in his mere thirteen-year-old soul. Acknowledging that it was beyond the powers of appreciation of his classmates and not amenable to parsing by his Malayalam teacher, he signed his name in full, Jithendran, under his debut poem—which was not fortunate enough to find a reader—and shut the book. Then, certain that it was not going to help him ever in his entire life, he opened the book to study geometry, arithmetic, and trigonometry.

Human letters; animal numerals. For Jithen, that was how he perceived his math textbook. He created night and day by closing and opening his eyes over them. His young heart, cooing in his phlegm-filled chest like doves, would start to dream of a child flying over the green fields. The child who discovered the technique of flying high by inhaling, and descending by exhaling. As he would remain immersed in the dream, many household sounds would pierce his ears.

His mother ran from the kitchen to the well and back, her invectives let loose. The bucket hung from the rope, falling into the depths, hitting head first. The pulley, which brought up water with a squeaking noise that did not find a mention in the section about levers in the physics textbook. The clanging of the stainless steel vessels that his father had got as awards for maintaining safety at the factory. The frightening tick-tock sound in the portico, dripping from the clock, swinging its ladle-like pendulum. The Philips radio switched on for the film songs and switched off with a curse by either of the sisters as soon as the news in English started. The cawing of crows roasted by the burning sun. Underneath all these, the incessant rubbing of the cymbals by the cicadas of Thachanakkara...

His ears were large enough to catch all the sounds easily. Made of cartilage, they stood on either side of his big head facing each other like two big interrogation marks. Eons ago, in an incarnation without asthma, one of those ears was used to safeguard a grain of cooked rice kept for Mother upon returning from the celestial world after a feast. Then, the siblings were not sisters with lice-ridden heads; it was a magnificent brother. When starting the return journey after partaking of the splendid feast, a sobering thought arose: there was nothing to give Mother, who would be waiting anxiously, watching his path of return! That was when it was seen: a grain of cooked rice on the tip of the hand that had already been washed. Picking it up, it was kept wedged in the ear. On their arrival home, Mother asked the brother: 'What did you bring for me?' With an embarrassed smile on his face that confessed to his forgetfulness, Brother showed his empty open hands. With a sigh, Mother repeated the question to the younger one. Offering her the rice grain from the ear, the younger sibling said hesitatingly, 'I could bring only this.'

Mother was gratified by the offering. Touching the head of the younger one, Mother said, 'Let the heart of those who see you feel as fulfilled as my heart is now. Let them rejoice seeing your pleasing moonlight!' The mother turned angrily to the son who had forgotten her in his time of abundance, and said, 'Let those who look at you melt. And curse you for the heat!'

That mother was none other than Earth; the Sun and Moon, the siblings. In this story, of the two, which Aunt Kunthi used to narrate repeatedly to Jithen, he was the younger sibling, who would return from the heavens with the grain of rice. Jithen knew that God had given him such large ears to accommodate the big grain of rice from heaven.

Apart from such stories told by Aunt Kunthi with elephantiasis, the illustrated storybooks borrowed from classmates, drawn in yellow and black, detective stories drawn and illustrated by someone called Kannadi Vishwanathan, and the made-up stories narrated by Granpa Raambilla in his neighbourhood, gave Jithen's childhood a power bestowed only upon dreamers. Grandpa Raambilla, with his dark face and broken, deformed teeth, who was continuing as the Raambillapolice of Thachanakkara despite his superannuation, used to narrate stories to Jithen in the afternoons when he had no school, with the innate creativity and imagination of a policeman for inventing stories. He had overcome the black devil of Kaniyankunnu, the cheetah of Chenkottukonam, and the great wrestler of Mammallapuram wearing trousers pressed at right angles to keep them from touching the thighs, body-hugging khaki shirt, cap with a sharply conical top, calves that were strapped with pattis and booted legs. Nowhere did he have to fight. Even before one twirl of the bamboo lathi—which Jithen fancied to be a flute—was completed, everyone would come, prostrate themselves, and surrender.

'I made your uncle a policeman. Who? Your Pankaachammavan! He threw it away and is back home now, no?' Granpa Raambilla repeated often. 'Now you have to grow up for Thachanakkara to have a super policeman! A policeman who will beat all and sundry into a pulp, right?'

Jithen knew that the child, who in his previous incarnation had carried in his ear a grain of rice for his mother, could never be the policeman who would beat up people and extract their juices. Therefore, he maintained silence and did not even acknowledge Granpa Raambilla's desire with a murmured assent. He would look up at the sky on those occasions; at the blazing sunlight gobbling up the tiny arecanuts perched atop the unruly heads of the areca palms, tired from their swaying. Beyond that, the afternoon breeze was playing, blowing cottony clouds into the blue sky. The songs from Akashvani radio station were seeping into the radio without wilting in the sun or blowing about in the wind or getting caught in the areca palms…

Time came flying down from the heavens and touched him. 'When I grow up,' Jithen asked one day, 'will Granpa Raambilla be there?'

The moment he asked that question, Granpa Raambilla knew Jithen had grown up. Children do not ask questions about the future. Apprehensions about surviving and death also do not go with their innocence. From that day on, Granpa Raambilla avoided stories about overcoming cheetahs and demons. One day, when Granpa Raambilla mentioned that behind Naraapilla's death in the temple pond, there was a third party's hand, partly as soliloquy and partly to him, Jithen too understood that he was now grown up.

The days when there was no school, they used to go for walks. In between, Jithen had transplanted to his own grandfather, his childhood affection that he had nurtured for Granpa Raambilla. After the interval, by the time he returned, Granpa Raambilla had prepared many lessons for him. To catch the bandicoots in the compound, they rigged up big bamboo traps with drawn strings. In the evenings, after keeping the traps reminiscent of the bow of Lord Kama, Granpa Raambilla would put a ladder against the corky coral tree and cut down leaves for his pet rabbits. For Jithen, who was waiting below, blood-coloured flowers would rain down. Fetching broken bricks from Devassy's kiln and using clay as mortar, they built small houses for the rabbits. At the same time, every morning, they would rejoice at the sight of the dead bandicoot caught in one of the many traps, with their necks strangulated in the noose and ants crawling over the carcasses. Thorny questions about how building a hutch to raise one animal, when killing another one with nooses and slipknots could become equally pleasurable for human beings, had not started budding in Jithen's mind yet. Jithen also had not recognized the contradiction that it was the same Granpa Raambilla, not fated to father his own children, who loved him like his own grandchild and yet created the lunatic Alamboori from a fine young man called Vasudevan, for the folk of Thachanakkara. Jithen enjoyed the act of Granpa Raambilla's Narasimham, sticking the nail-shaped petals of the coral tree to his own nails with spittle. When the Narasimham killed the father to save the son and roared, pulling out his entrails, Jithen laughed.

Those were happy days. A childhood of plenitude, when rains beamed like sunshine and sunshine drizzled like rain. They were like the easy-to-read illustrated tales, simple and limpid. They passed without complaint or sorrow. Jithen could recall every detail till the day of his death: the upside-down image of the world seen on the drops of water, during rainy days, on the rusting blue-painted gate. In each drop, it was different. Even the tingling that the raindrops caused on the skin as one touched and took them in one's dry palm was different with each drop.

Till his mother had called stridently three or four times, he would stay in Granpa Raambilla's house. He loved that house with a small veranda, two termite-eaten pillars, and a pleasingly cool parapet, more than his own. It was from behind one of those pillars that Narasimham with coral tree petal nails used to jump out. Even when he knew they were not related, he continued to call Thachanakkara's Raambillapolice Granpa Raambilla. He considered that house his own.

Jithen had not reached the age when the world is divided into one's and the other's. The awareness that, like the sky, the air, and the river, everything belonged to everybody, gave each day a remarkable lambency. Time for Jithen was a celebration of today, which had no yesterday or tomorrow. When hungry, noon; when the school bell rang, evening; when sleepy, night; when waking up, morning again…

But there were many people around him who were not like that: His father, who started early in the morning for the aluminium factory, on foot, wearing a white shirt and mundu, after dusting his neck with Cuticura powder to mask the smell of sweat on the shirt he had worn the previous day too; his mother, who would wake up much before Jithen did, and wake up the stove and the vessels and get busy amongst them, doing chores, neither the beginning or end of which she could recall nor knew; his cousins, who would talk of many jobs, do none, and spend hours in front of the mirror, cursing the hair and moustache for not growing or not becoming wavy in the way they wanted it to be; the girls of Ayyaattumpilli who would wash the bloodied rags of their monthly periods each month, with the same abhorrence with which they read their schoolbooks, and chanted the Harinaamakeerthanam hymns in the late evenings... Thus, each of them gave the impression of doing something or running behind some task, which they could not master, and getting flustered. While daydreaming, thanks to the sedation of his asthma medicines, Jithen used to think that if the men of the house did not go to the factories, or the women did not do the household chores, or the boys and girls did not waste time meditating on their bodily emissions, nothing would change in the world. The world would still hang upside-down like a bat on the drops of water on the rusted gate. When he brushed it with the palm, it would just dissolve and spread.

In his thirteenth year, the inauspicious thirteenth, when one is a human child in the perspective of others, yet is starting life as a man, Jithen's mind was muddled more than that of the other Ayyaattumpilli children. Sitting in the toilet, he would ponder for hours over God, a God beyond the temples and tales of His incarnations. He was certain that this place was better than the temple for such ruminations. And when he would stand in front of the steps of the sanctum sanctorum for the evening deeparadhana pooja at Thachanakkara temple along with his sisters, brushing against mature women in the crowd who smelt like elephant dung, his animal instincts would wake up and trumpet. He had started feeling the annoyance of being unable to hide from himself, even when unseen by others, as was the case with God.

As the age of Paramahamsans was past, he could never become a Narendran and thus, become a Swami Vivekananda. Even if he were able to find a Paramahamsan any time in his life, it was likely that Jithen may reject him, considering the inferiority in becoming someone's disciple. However, reinforcing certain precepts of the greatness of man that he received as a child, he had created within himself a guru. It had to be believed that he had foreseen his fate of failing in every test put forth by that guru.

What he had attempted to put down on the unruled pages of his mathematics notebook, during the study holidays for his ninth class terminal examination was this truth. Those eighteen lines were destined to get submerged, one rainy season, by the stinking water that swept in from the gutter outside into his tiny rented house, where he was staying with his wife, away from Thachanakkara, many years after the poem was found serendipitously among the wave-less sea of old books. However, as a poem written by a child in homage to everyone caught in their circumstances as much as in their bodies, and cursed to exist through the drudgery of their lives, those lines had originality and relevance.

Jithen was a child; at the same time, a man. It was more strenuous than living life as half-human, half-animal or half-man, half-woman. Nevertheless, the thirteen-year-old was yet to realize that the fate of every human being is to die before reaching his or her full potential; and that adolescence, which is only a prelude to torments, is the portal to the forbidding fort of turmoil.

TWO

Darkness

30 November 1999

...It's raining outside now. Beyond the window of the rented house, the unbroken greenery of plantain leaves is iridescent. There is rain and shine. Somewhere in the forest, mangy foxes were getting wedded. Rain queries: Demon of masturbation, when are you getting married?

I remember: an adolescence which paid homage to libido. The guilt of it was more enjoyable. The white juice of the forbidden fruit.

The goddess painted by some unknown artist on the calendar printed in Sivakasi. Underneath the see-through blouse of the veena-toting goddess was the strap of the undergarment with a silvery, shining square to adjust the length of the strap. The passion of the artist to make it more realistic. I meditated in front of the goddess; '*Dheeyo yona prachodayaath*'. Instead of the accepted meaning of 'we pray to propel our intellect on the Divine-righteous path to unfold spiritual potentiality and enlightenment', the pervert-poet inside gave it a variant translation—'intellects are propelled by vaginas'.

Then, on the fungus-affected walls of the toilet, images of goddesses started appearing. The time and imagination for creating a thousand Mona Lisas were being dedicated to the pleasure of indulging in a crime committed in solitude. Studies became distracted. Melancholy became a permanent resident in my eyes. In my school uniform, and with a palpitating heart, I went to a theatre with slippery seats. To compound the fear that those below eighteen years would be handed over to the police, the guy at the ticket counter grinned at him, displaying his decayed teeth. The first time he saw the nakedness of a woman he felt as if the screen was steaming; and then, catching fire.

The seats, connected to each other, began to shake in the dark.

A man's libido: a black deed which sacrifices and sends as castaways tens of millions of lives for a momentary pleasure. A heinous act without guilt. A masculine act of zero benevolence. The only throne any man can mount.

On the night of his fourteenth birthday, four years after completing his tenth birthday in the month of Chingam, which followed the unnatural death of Naraapilla in Karkkadakam, for the first time in his life, Jithen heard surreptitiously, in the company of his friends, the moans of a woman in the throes of making love. Binding all the four years together, the Vypin Hooch Tragedy left its black mark on his life story.

The death of Naraapilla had shocked Thachanakkara more than any news, which the newspapers and radio were disseminating. There was a rumour circulating that Skylab, a manmade satellite, which was orbiting out of control in space, could crash anywhere on the earth. Jithen dreamed that, freed from the reins of America, it was shooting through the skies of Thachanakkara as a glowing ember and crashing, aflame, onto the roof of Geethalayam, setting fire to the rafters. When the news appeared in the newspapers that America would handsomely reward those who find the remnants of the Skylab, the treasure-finding dreams of Paanamparampath Nanu got diverted in that direction for some time. His enthusiasm progressed up to lugging the misshapen debris of an abandoned water pump set, which he found in some plot along the river, upto where Kochu Parashu stood, mistaking it to be some vital organ of the Skylab. By that time, the news had come in the newspapers that the debris of the Skylab had been discovered in the western coast of Australia. With that, fears about an errant Skylab ceased. The iron pump, which Nanu had dragged in, lay in a corner of the plot of Pooshaappi Stores, rusting further.

In February that year, the bangle sellers in the Aluva beach helped Jithen's sisters wear 'Skylab bangles' that came with gold glitter and tiny notches. With his hand held by his mother, Jithen walked between the shops with their eye-catching wares, sneezing all the time from the dust. His twelve- and fourteen-year-old sisters followed on either side of his father, hanging on to his hands. He heard his mother say proudly, to all the acquaintances she ran into there, pointing at Geetha who was appearing for that year's S.S.L.C. board exam: 'This year, it is *essessellcya* for our Geetha!'

Jithen saw the Well of Death and magic show for the first time. In a well boarded up with planks, two fearless young men were driving what looked like skeletons of motorcycles, circling the well continuously. The smoke and sound, which arose from the well, gave their rashness an aura of imminent heroic death. After the young men, who wore yellow helmets, finished their ride and reached the floor of the well and waved at the spectators, there was no applause. However, in the next tent, when the magician pulled a starved-looking brown rabbit out of the hat, the spectators, in spite of their knowing that he would have hidden it inside earlier, continued to clap and cheer. On their return, holding on to the parapet of the Marthaanda Varma Bridge, along with his parents and sisters, Jithen gazed upon the picture of the temple painted by the lights, and its reflection on the wavy waters of the river.

No one in Thachanakkara talked about V.T. Bhattathirippad

dying that February in Thrissur, or Akkaamma Cherian becoming one with God in Thiruvananthapuram, two months later, in May. Though the demise of S.K. Pottekkat at Kozhikode had saddened Kalyanikuttyamma in Ayyaattumpilli, that sorrow had been drowned in the stench of Naraapilla's shit-wallowing days and thus been invalidated. Those days of persistent hunger; it was at the time, when even the last grains of the oblation rice for Naraapilla's obsequies were being picked off, that the poisoned hooch frothed in Vypin. The day after Jithen's birthday, on the *Chathayam* day, the Vypin liquor tragedy happened, killing many and sending thousands to the hospital in critical condition. In one stroke, the waves of that news wiped off the horrific death of Naraapilla from the consciousness of the Thachanakkara folk. The names of Malayalis who celebrated the birthday of a venerable soul—Narayana Guru, who had pronounced liquor as poison—by drinking and dying were arrayed on the newspapers. Paanamparampath Nanu, whose tongue used to confuse Hiranyaakshan with Hiranyakashipu, was now able to use the same one to talk of ethyl alcohol and methyl alcohol without mixing them up, sitting in Pooshaappi Stores. The newspapers had explained the various compounds of alcohol in such detail to their readers. With unusual interest, cross-eyed Vengooran Thankappan read the list of people who had lost their eyesight in the tragedy. He could not have imagined then that the list had on it the name of the boy who would later come to marry his beautiful daughter—who, though past marriageable age, could not be married off as he did not have enough money for the dowry at the prevailing levels.

Shantha, sister of Muringaattil Leela who committed suicide by drowning herself, was the life partner of Vengooran Thankappan. Their only daughter, Vasantha, was ogled at by all the young men of Thachanakkara because of her shapely body. Barber Shivan could still recollect the little girl with red ribbons tied to her curly hair, who had come to see her father's new teashop, holding her mother's hand, while the Eagles Club, headed by Vasudevan Nampoothiri, was still occupying one of the rooms in Kochu Parashu's building. Whenever he marvelled that the same girl was thirty years old now, he would sigh deeply realizing that he had been wasting his life cutting hair all the while. 'Ssho,' thinking about the distance he and his scissors had travelled, Shivan would say, 'how time flies in a trice!'

The folk of Thachanakkara, especially the young men, tried many ruses to ignore the onrush of time. One of them was the lewd meditations at the riverbank. The young men used to compete among themselves to pass time by watching their icon, Vasantha, bathe in Punneli kadavu, and indulge in lusting after her in secret. The soul of Leela, who committed suicide, unloved and unwanted, was taking its revenge on Thachanakkara through her niece. With their own sighs and moans drowned by the hissing sounds of the wind passing through the reeds behind which they sat, the young men shot their libidinous arrows at Vasantha's bathing scene. Unconsciously imitating Kama, who used sugarcane as his bow, the left hand of these young men gripped the reeds tightly. In memory of the bulging promise of spring seen through the wet sarong tied around her chest, they rolled around in their sleep. However, none of them had the temerity to stand in front of Vengooran Thankappan and ask for his daughter's hand in marriage. The times of Naraapillas who married Kunjuammas after seeing them bathe were over. For the noon shows in the cinema theatres in Aluva—Casino, Zeenath, Pankajam—movies with larger-than-life women were being shown. The old mores of a man-woman relationship, which started with a formal sighting of the girl by the prospective groom, had lost all its anxieties in the eyes of men who had access to a surfeit of exposed flesh and female forms. They kept lamenting about the inconveniences of ogling and lurking around real women, when their sizes were nothing compared to what were seen on the screens.

It was during this period that Bhaimi, who used to come from Vypinkara with sea fish to Thachanakkara, told Muringaattil Shantha something special. When other women used to buy fish, when the beautiful maiden from Muringaattil only looked into her basket and walked away showing aversion, the broker in the fisherwoman woke up. One afternoon, after assuring her of her receptive mood, the old fisherwoman asked Vasantha's mother, 'Shall I give you a boy to marry your girl who's overdue for marriage? He's from our Vypinkara. They are an aristocratic Nair family. They are moneyed. Lands and fields on top of that. A lad strong of limbs. But then ...?'

Vengooran and his wife weighed the explanation given by Bhaimi of that 'but then' against their own perilous finances. They considered it their good fortune that the blind boy's only condition was that the girl should be beautiful. Vasantha also liked the young man who came to see her in her tiny house, in the company of a grey-haired man. When she has handing over tea and biscuits, he turned his head towards the direction of her sound and she thought his eyes were lovely: there was not an iota of lust in those unseeing eyes.

In the newly-built wedding platform in front of the Thachanakkara thevar, in the month of Meenam of next year, two weddings took place. Everyone in Thachanakkara participated in the weddings, which took place with an interval of seven days between them. In both weddings, more than blessings, sympathy was showered. The naïve women of Thachanakkara wept for the tragedies of a rich man, blinded in the hooch tragedy, marrying a penurious girl in the first case; in the second wedding, for a dark, epileptic young man marrying his lame cousin. Their husbands wiped clean the plantain leaves on which the feast was served, burped, and nit-picked on both the function and the feasts, laughing with derision.

The twenty-one days that Govindan Master came and stayed in the New House to nurse Naraapilla, greatly influenced the future of Jithen, son of Chinnamma, and Radha, daughter of Thankamma. During the days when the young generation of Ayyaattumpilli were getting used to calling Govindan Master with the unfamiliar 'Elder Uncle', these two were the ones who got closest to him. Govindan Master was the first person who asked Radha to sing a song, and praised her for her talent. He gave the translations of some Russian novels he was carrying in his cloth shoulder bag to her for reading. During the breaks in the rain, they strolled through the empty compounds of Ayyaattumpilli. Govindan Master's heart bled for Radha as he looked at the singer dragging her game leg on the damp grass, as she followed him.

Govindan Master walked through the plots of land where the hundreds of saplings once planted by his brother Chandran had become big trees. At the western end of the plot, Govindan Master showed Jithen a coconut palm, which stood like a hapless peacock that had lost its feathers. 'This was our areca-coco palm!'

Jithen looked at that, remembering his grandfather's betelnut cracker. He justifiably assumed that it was a hybrid of the coconut and areca palms, inasmuch as the knife for cutting the arecanuts was known as betelnut cracker. When he started imagining things about the nuts of that magical palm, Govindan Master explained to him that a coconut palm, which had the largest coconuts set apart only for seeding purposes, was called areca-coco palm. The coconut palm, on which coconuts for seeding matured. When Jithen told him how he misunderstood it as a mixed breed of the two palms and laughed, all of a sudden, Govindan Master went silent, reminded of another kind of mixed breed.

Govindan Master, who stayed in the New House—this time, along with his son—for the fortnight till the sixteenth day obsequies of Naraapilla, called his sister one day and asked her, 'Thankammae, did any one of you tell father about Narayanan earlier?', a look of discovery flashing across his face.

Thankamma shrugged, indicating negation.

'Today it was that deed writer of yours who told me,' Govindan Master said with a disbelieving perplexity, 'that father had already granted this house to Narayanan in his will!'

'That is excellent!' Suppressing a start, which arose in her and making sure Chinnamma was nowhere close, Thankamma said, 'Now he has to only get married! Shall we consider my poor handicapped girl, etta? How many times can she be decked up and displayed before men?'

'It's not that I haven't thought about it,' Govindan Master said after a long silence. 'Isn't he the spoken-for cousin of hers as per tradition? Didn't you also marry your spoken-for cousin?'

A low-level grumbling continued till the month of Meenam. As against the news of the beauty of Muringaattil getting married to a blind man, the shock of the handicapped girl of Ayyaattumpilli marrying her spoken-for cousin got attenuated. The month of Meenam arrived. When Narayanan and Radha started their cohabitation in the cleaned and lime-washed New House, their remarkable compatibility and love surprised the folk of Thachanakkara.

It was the union of two loners who had waited apart, pining for love.

After Geetha and Rema both stopped their studies within a gap of two years between them, having failed in English language in their undergraduate examinations, the studies of Jithen, now in his tenth standard, assumed an avoidable seriousness. Shankaran used to secretly feel proud about his son topping his class, despite his frequent asthma attacks. Under the mistaken impression that his son wanted to be a scientist, he used to bring bauxite powder in empty matchboxes from his factory, at least twice a year. In his misguided attempts to create glittering ink, Jithen mixed it with the blue ink of the Bril brand, and spoiled at least four pens irredeemably, filling them with that concoction. By the time he was fourteen, under the expert advice of his two older friends, he got immersed in experimentations for producing a shiny ink from his own body, without the need to add bauxite powder. However, in the moment of his first successful attempt, wild with joy, he lost his balance and, unable to see the results of his experiments, he went under, and ended up swallowing the water of the Aluva river through his nose and mouth. He was just learning to swim; keeping himself afloat with one hand, he was treading water and keeping himself busy looking at a woman bathing on the far bank of the river. The experiment succeeded the moment the woman, who was soaping herself, turned around and looked at him. He lost control, sank, and gulped water into his lungs.

However, the wick continued to burn in him, refusing to be doused by any amount of dunking. On his fourteenth birthday, with the permission of his mother, he went to see the late-night movie in Pankajam theatre along with his friends. Unnikrishnan and Babu, who were close to twenty years in age, were the birthday boy's companions. But that night they did not reach the movie theatre. When Babu started saying in whispers about something more tempting, Jithen's heart started beating loud enough to wake all of Thachanakkara. Babu had seen Vasantha and her blind husband get down from the bus at Thachanakkara in the afternoon of Thiruvonam day. If his guess was correct, they would be staying the night in the Muringaattil House with its disintegrating window panes. Unnikrishnan concurred in Babu's opinion—who was speaking from experience—that the views through the cracks in the window panes were far superior to those on the screen.

'If my sisters ask me to narrate the story of the movie what do I tell them?' Jithen asked, in his eagerness to seek a way out of the plan.

'Isn't this for that?' Handing Jithen a lyrics book, folded in four and stuck inside his pocket, which also contained the synopsis of the movie, Babu closed that loophole too.

Thus, the three of them stood flat against the wall of Muringaattil, holding their breath and listening to the coughs of some unknown person from inside.

They peeped into the house, which had no electricity, and were thrilled to hear a slow, yet mounting feminine moan from inside. A cot started to creak inside the house. Imagining the feminine grunts, which were now coming from inside, were Vasantha's, the trinity outside stiffened in the darkness. As if on the point of climaxing with pleasure, invocations of God arose inside. The plea to be killed came. Then it went high-pitched, hit the floor, and stopped. Realizing that someone had got up and was lighting the lamp, Babu and Unnikrishnan jumped into the alley and disappeared into the night. Jithen tarried for a moment. He needed to sight the owner of the sounds. The light from the lantern inside showed the sight to him though the crack in the pane.

An old woman, swathed in a blanket, came towards the window, holding the lantern. She was still invoking God in the plaintive voice heard earlier. When he recognized that they were the moans of a dying woman laid low by age and sickness that he and his friends were eavesdropping on till then, Jithen was staggered. Coughing and spitting far through the ajar window, unknowingly, the old woman snapped at the spectator outside.

When Jithen reached home at midnight dissembling happiness at having seen the movie, the unintentional question his mother asked him, drove a dagger into his heart, 'Now that you have seen it, aren't you satisfied?'

The next day his mother told him that the aged mother of Muringaattil Shantha had caught a disease called chicken pox and Vasantha and her husband, who had come in the evening of Thiruvonam, had returned the same time, fearing infection.

Jithen never told the truth to his friends, who had swooned that night listening to the sounds through the crack in the window. Instead, he took mendacious pride in being elevated as one of the daredevils who was an eyewitness of the sex act of the beauty.

Without his own knowledge, he was adding his own name to the list of those afflicted by the blindnesses of the new era.

THREE

Fragmentation

28 October 1999

...Like a cobbler who ignores people without footwear, I am sitting with my needle and thread by the side of a highway overflowing with love and friendship. Any wonder that I find flower sandals repulsive?

Dearest girl, it's after I fell in love with you that my feeling that I am a cruel man became a confirmed belief. Before that, I used to have this vain belief that I was someone great; had arrogantly believed that I could love the whole world, all by myself. However, that belief has abated somewhat now. When you start loving individuals, you start hating humanity; and vice versa.

Haven't you felt that every man, to fight with himself, has to blow up trivial incidents? Similarly, isn't there something enjoyable in treachery—though we pronounce the word treachery with a trembling heart? I don't expect an answer. Without fearing one's denigration of the status as a human being, no one would dare reply to these two questions in all honesty. Yes, if you think about it, you shall have to laugh through tears. The hapless man who can be injured by a mustard seed, lights mortars for enjoyment!

Do you know that every man is a child deep inside? A small child who cries standing in the festival grounds of life, lost in the sounds of the crowds and unnoticed by anyone. No one knows where the child in him has come from. But he is there. He is the elephant, the percussion ensemble, and the crowd of the festival. But he doesn't know that.

My freshly-hatched feminist, 'he' refers to a human being; and in that, all 'shes' including you, have been subsumed.

In the land earmarked for him by his father, Govindan Master made a building, close to the alley, with three shops on the ground floor and a hall on the first floor. Thus, a new shopkeeper appeared four plots away from Kochu Parashu's shop. Narayanan, the son of Govindan Master. The husband of Thankamma's daughter Radha. The spitting image of the deceased Naraapilla.

Dividing the hall on the first floor into two, Govindan Master started a library and reading room, with the help of the Cooperative Bank of Thachanakkara. Before the inauguration, many hazarded guesses that it would be named Sulochana Memorial Reading Room or Naraapilla Memorial Reading Room. On this matter, in Pooshaappi Stores, people split up into two groups and held a debate under the leadership of Paanamparampath Nanu and Karunakaran Karthaavu. However, unknown to the others, Govindan Master had another old debt to pay. A memory that remained fresh about a man who visited Ayyaattumpilli in his childhood. A tribute to a guest whom his father had insulted by spitting ceremoniously into the crepe jasmine flowers in their yard, in front of his teary-eyed mother. When the two young painters, standing on the scaffolding in front of the parapet of the top floor with paint and brush, started writing the name of the reading room, it was one which was not in the memory of those gathered below. Nor did they have the courage to ask Govindan Master, who used to come from Cherai to Thachanakkara only on Sundays. The painters standing on the scaffolding, wearing clothes which were dotted with paints of many hues, first pressed a long thread dipped in indigo on the wall. Then stretching the thread, they drew broken double lines on the parapet. The children of the new generation read open-mouthed, the letters one of the painters had outlined with a pencil touching the borders on top and bottom: Kuttippuzha Krishna Pillai Smaraka Vijnanaposhini Reading Room.

Fleshing out the skeletal outline made with the pencil, three lines—'Kuttippuzha Krishna Pillai', the first line in middling blue, the next line 'Vijnanaposhini' in red with yellow border, and the third line, 'Reading Room' in brick colour—appeared in the sky. The new generation that lazily read the lines painted in blue did not understand that time was repaying, through a library, a debt to a great soul for committing his whole life, without family or progeny, to the cause of knowledge.

Aaminumma, who used to come to Ayyaattumpilli bearing tales from Elookkara and Kayintikkara and carry rice water back, had burped for the last time and become one with God. Many of the Muslim children, who used to trade in pomelos from Geethalayam, buying them at thirty paise, had flown to the blazing heat of Arab countries as soon as they became strong of limbs. Words such as passport and visa were uttered at least once a day in their relatives' houses. The sweat those hardworking men spilt in foreign countries, turned to vapour and rose up, mixed with the monsoon winds, and rained in Elookkara and Kayintikkara as green currency. Shankaran, on his daily walk to the factory through that route, noticed new concrete houses springing up at the rate of one every morning on either side of the red-soil path leading up to the Eloor ferry point. Wearing ostentatious yellow and green lungis, these men on vacation used to buy fish from the vendors on bicycles without haggling. Jealousy and intolerance became rampant, running their roots into the mouldy degree certificates of the Nair youth of Thachanakkara, who eschewed all physical work. They translated that into ridicule. They spread tasteless jokes, making fun of religion, caste, and women, whom they considered inferior to them. Manikandan, the son of Paanamparampath Nanu, with a narrative skill which excelled his father's, described to the young men, who had started thronging Narayanan's grocery store, a letter which one of the mothers of Elookkara had purportedly dictated to a scribe, for her son in Dubai.

'Right in the front,' the mother, rubbing her feet sitting on the parapet and arranging in her mind matters according to their importance, is reported to have said to the young scribe, who had got ready with a pen and paper to transcribe the letter, 'write then, I'm clothless.'

'Umm, writed!' the young scribe said after completing the opening lines.

'Th'r isself,' rubbing the scar on her leg, the mother narrated her next problem, 'write, bit by dog.'

'Aah, writed!' adding the continuation, the young scribe said.

The rest of the story Paanamparampath Manikandan completed in a paroxysm of laughter. 'The kid wrote it without leaving a word! What did the son sitting in Dubai read? His mother's letter is full of ribaldry.' With help of gestures, Manikandan repeated the lines of the letter, 'Right in the front I'm clothless th'r isself bit by dog.'

The unemployed Nair youth who had congregated on the shop veranda roared with laughter. As if echoing each laughter set off by the invented story, the dog which had earlier bitten the mother's ankle barked at Pankajaakshan's gate.

Jokesters who found nirvana in creating such stories masquerading as humour, sprouted like mushrooms which needed no fertile humus, in Thachanakkara and Aluva, which enveloped Thachanakkara, and further south in Kalamassery, Ernakulam, and Kochi. The psyche of youth, which could create miracles in any line of creativity, confined itself to an art form called mimicry—which needed neither knowledge nor contemplation. That year, four smart young men, who came from Kochi for performing in the temple festivities, dumped a new performing art called Mimics Parade in Thachanakkara. Their incredible mimicked voices were amplified a thousand times by the huge box speakers rented out from Aluva. A minority in the Devaswom Festival Committee, which had been struggling to bring back the long-ignored Kathakali to the temple grounds, laughed uncontrollably at the mimicry performance, and gave the nervous young men in their sandal-coloured uniforms, an advance for the next year's booking.

One Sunday in April, Jithen was performing, for the benefit of his sisters, some of the mimicry acts he had seen the previous day at the temple. The voice of an Ottanthullal performer, made tremulous perhaps by the lack of audience, could be heard faintly from the temple, where the temple flag had been raised signalling the start of the annual temple festival. Behind Jithen, who was facing his sisters seated in the small veranda behind Geethalayam, Govindan Master appeared. After the unrepressed laughter of his sisters was over, hearing his elder uncle behind him, Jithen turned around. Thankamma, doubled up with laughter, and Govindan Master, unsmiling, stood watching him closely. He was ashamed that his elder uncle would have heard him mimicking the voices, and yet reasonably, expected some compliments.

Touching Jithen's cheeks with fingers calloused from using chalks, Govindan Master said, 'Child, did you like that programme so much?'

Jithen realized for the first time that addressing an adolescent with an incipient moustache as a child had such powers for belittling. He felt the fingers that touched his cheek were both trembling and burning.

'Definitely, mimicking is an admirable skill. But the problem lies in what is being imitated and why it is being imitated,' Govindan Master said in a voice which had in equal measure piety and trace of phlegm. 'Do you know who is the first mimicry artiste in the world?' he asked looking at Jithen and his sisters. As they blinked without an answer, Govindan Master narrated that story:

Once a group of Buddhist monks were accompanying Buddha, asking for alms along a city street. Flourishing commerce had made the place crowded like a festival ground. The original Bodhisattva was moving along, listening to his companion Anandan's doubts and answering them with only smiles. Suddenly, breaking out of its enclosure, a rutting elephant emerged onto the street. Near the stalls of the vendors, danger loomed.

Seeing Buddha leaving the street and moving into a clump of trees by the side of the city, ignoring the plaintive cries of the crowd and the monks including Anandan, his disciples cried out, 'Lord, are you forsaking us as danger approaches?'

There was no answer. Instead, from behind the trees, the trumpeting of a cow elephant was heard—an invitation to the rutting one standing on the street. With the tranquillity of one who has received a calming medication, the tusker walked across to the clump of trees, which was at a distance. The Lord who had trumpeted like a cow elephant behind the trees, reappeared now in front of the crowd, who were saved from being impaled on the elephant's tusks.

After completing the story, Govindan Master said, 'Every art has an invocation to save. It's only souls who contemplate who can be its true sources. What you heard yesterday in the temple was the rowdy laughter of derision and defamation. It may get the crowd to laugh, but will weaken the soul of the individual. Remember one thing—art and the artiste should be the sanctuary of life. In that sense, every art is an enlightenment. And every artiste, a

Buddha. I know, my son, you will be able to remember what I am telling you now!'

Geetha and Rema did not understand anything. Since Thankamma had got into Chinnamma's kitchen as soon as Govindan Master had started his story, she did not have to hear it. However, Jithen could see a blazing old light hiding in the words of his uncle: sagacity was its name.

That coin, unimpressive to most due to obsolescence, fell with a happy, clinking sound into the money bank that was Jithen's heart, which still being immature, was not yet in use.

When he was eighty, the second owner of Pooshaappi Stores, Kochu Parashu, after bequeathing the shops to his forty-five-year-old bachelor son, fell and died on the road. At the time of his death, Kochu Parashu was rich enough to give every inhabitant of Thachanakkara a feast on the sixteenth day of his death, as per the sapindi ritual of oblation to the manes. This was celebrated in a tent, which was put up though it was not the season for rain, with his portrait kept at the entrance, with incense sticks burning in front of it —which gave the wrong impression of a handsomeness which he did not possess when alive—and by sowing satisfied burps, which were created by the hearty feast. With that, a chapter, which, it was feared, would go on interminably, came to an end and a new one started.

With the coming of Narayanan's store on the other side, sales had come down in Pooshaappi Stores. Kochu Parashu's son Vishwanathan, who had become a riddle which Thachanakkara folk could not solve, sat silently in the store that was now into the third generation, unmindful of the tapering business returns. On the veranda in front of him, the lunatic Alamboori became a regular. Alamboori used to sit with his back to Vishwanathan. As he sat staring at the back of Alamboori with his torn shirt and the yellow nylon poonool, the past would create bubbles in Vishwanathan's silence. They had both started the Eagles Club in one of the rooms of that building. It was from this oil-smudged till-box that Vishwanathan, dodged his father's vigil and managed to smuggle out ten rupee notes, to fornicate with Lalitha of Chammaram. Vasudevan from Nedumpilli Mana, who was the president of Eagles Club and then of Arunodaya Club near the irrigation bund, now sat in front of him like a stinking scarecrow. An Alamboori, shunned by all and created by the silence of Vishwanathan, who was filled with self-loathing for having used that silence once as a shield for self-preservation when the police came to Arunodaya Club.

One afternoon, when no one was around, in an attempt to prevent a nervous breakdown, Vishwanathan called out to Alamboori seated with his back to him, 'Daa, Vasudevaa…!'

He did not look back. On the verge of tears, Vishwanathan called again, 'Alamboori!'

This time he answered. Displaying his stained teeth and rolling his eyes smouldering with insanity, Alamboori asked, 'Who's calling me from behind? Who? If it's that reprobate Vasudevan from the Mana, tell him I am not here.'

The mad man lay on his back on the floor and laughed. 'What's the use of calling now? I am sick of smoking beedi butts. If you can, give me a full beedi and help! Enjoy my sizzling to death like this.'

That year, Jithen received the first punishment for considering love to be the first obstacle in life—at the end of an excursion during his undergraduate class. But then, he did not imagine that the incident would insinuate itself two years later into a story he was going to write in two hours. He also did not realize those days that creativity had the divinity to convert tears into laughter and vice versa.

The vehicle they were travelling in was going downhill slowly. All the singing and dancing and whooping had subsided. The return leg of every excursion is boring: lethargic like a siesta and heavy like death.

Sliding the glass with tinted film stuck on it, Jithen looked at the valleys on his right side. Why doesn't looking at mountains and the sea never tire one?

Beyond the wire fences by the side of the road, oranges which could be reached and plucked. Depths which bore silvery clouds in their womb, seemed to invite the onlooker silently to dissolve into the emptiness.

She was in the seat right behind. Possibly dozing. When he turned his head as if without pre-meditation, she was smiling, half asleep. Some of her forelocks were caught in her eyelashes. In the breeze, a drizzle of single strands of her hair could be seen on her face.

'Shall I come to your seat?' she asked.

'Um?' He raised his eyebrows, with its meaning falling between come and do not come.

'Just like that,' she said, 'to look at the mountains!'

'You can see from there also.'

'I can't move this glass.'

Braving the bumpy ride, she moved to Jithen's seat. When the starchiness of the cotton skirt touched his arm, Jithen was irritated. You wouldn't have come to sit and watch the hills, Jithen said in his heart. After this year-end trip, there are no more opportunities to sit by the side and confess. Cry, without anyone seeing and hearing, cry, begging for forgiveness!

'Hic,' she hiccupped. Before she could lean out of the window, the vomit fell on Jithen's shirt. And, blown by the wind, on his face as well.

She had come only to vomit. Her puke stank like shit.

Smell of a cremated love.

FOUR

The Embodied

13 October 1999

...I got yet another reason this afternoon to hate navels.

I was summoned to the boss' cabin, as he wanted to meet me. Acting as if he didn't know I was standing in front of him, he kept on reading a thick book and simpered. Possibly that was the only book he has ever read. Guinness Book of Records. His lime-stained fingers were drumming on the glossy pages. The corners of his mouth were stained by the blood of betel leaves.

Offering the book to me with the page he was reading open, boss said, 'An interesting record. For collecting the dirt from one's navel in a bottle!'

I accepted the book without any interest. It is true. A guy has made that sickening record his own. The smiling navel-scavenger was shown in the picture. I remembered grandfather, who had made imprints of his own palms dipping his hands in his own shit. He was in his dotage. But this guy?

'I told you, to make one's mark in this world, anything is acceptable,' Boss continued, pushing another arecanut piece into his mouth. 'Purity of God ... Isn't that what you said that day? Your contention that leaving such marks would alone be creativity is utter idiocy!'

Looking at him with a bitter smile, I said to myself: working under you in this factory is also idiocy. Drummer monkey ... That is an interesting toy for a kid for some years. But what about the one who manufactures it all his lifetime?

Ann Marie, when we experience some things, when we see a place for the first time, don't we feel it's not the first time? My meeting with him today gave me the same sense of déjà vu. But today it was fatally prophetic. In my twentieth year, in a story I had written believing erroneously that I was a writer, I had encapsulated my life long ago! Alas, I didn't preserve that tale!

Vijayan, the second son of Poovamparampath Kochu Parashu, was the first one to buy a TV in Thachanakkara.

He had gone to great lengths in the path of domesticity on which his elder brother Vishwanathan had failed to embark. By giving birth to two sons with a gap of two years between them, Vijayan's wife had emulated her mother-in-law and ensured that Kochu Parashu's lineage would continue. To strengthen the lineage, she educated her children in the English-medium school in Aluva. To ferry the children to and from school, a school bus came for the first time to Thachanakkara.

One afternoon, crowding round an autorickshaw found halted in front of Vijayan's house with two long steel tubes secured on its top, the children of Thachanakkara connected those tubes with the word Doordarshan. Vijayan disembarked from the vehicle with a big carton and after him came out a young man holding a small plastic bag. There was a debate among the children on whether the transparent plastic-topped thing in his pocket was a pen or a tester, which tickled electricity with its tail and grinned. In the long walkway to the new house built by Vijayan in the Poovamparampath land, the steel pipes were carried with a proprietary air by Vijayan's children in an atmosphere with as much reverence as when the areca palm, meant to be installed as the flagpole in the Thachanakkara temple, was reverentially borne to the temple grounds. When some of the children milled around, trying to lend their shoulder to the pipes, Vijayan snapped at them with as much ferocity as he would at stray dogs.

'Get lost, kids!' The weight of the carton he was carrying reflected in his voice too. After pulling back a little, the children moved in again.

After a short while, the steel tube appeared upright on Vijayan's terrace like a thin flagpole of the new era. The thin aluminium tubes, with increasing lengths, fixed on another tube kept horizontal to the upright pole, piqued the interest of the audience consisting of Thachanakkara children. The crows of Thachanakkara, which were irreverent enough to perch even on electricity lines, were frightened by that antenna that rose into the sky and thenceforth kept a respectable distance from it.

'Umm, enough, enough! Go home now!' Vijayan gave the ultimate decree to the new generation of Thachanakkara peeping in from the window, gnawing at their nails. His ten- and twelve-year-olds stood sweating with pride. The eldest told the bunch of curious children who still remained at the gate, 'We bought it to see the matches! Oh, what fun we are going to have!'

On the way back from the school, one of his friends pointed out to Jithen the wonder called antenna, which was sticking into the sky, with its digits spread out. The silvery comb to bring under control the unruly mops of the hair of the coconut and arecanut palms. Jithen could never forget the first day he saw that antenna during his schooldays, even though, in the following years, antennae on upright poles on the crowns of the houses proliferated in Thachanakkara, standing like ships' masts. He had to forge a friendship with the English-medium students of Poovamparampath, only for the sake of watching television. He handed over his long-time collection of matchbox labels to the younger child of Poovamparampath. It was one of those collections he had decided to get rid of, since he had decided that he was a grown-up. Thus, in return for those moribund labels, he won the right to watch television with its moving images.

He saw: hundreds of thousands of black and white termite wings were quivering in the glass case. Jithen's new-found friend was untying his blue school tie. With a grown-up's expression, he touched one of the knobs of the TV set and the termite wings turned to the white lines of a court. In the middle of the court was a net which touched the floor, on either side of which were men holding racquets and were dressed in white and dashing about, panting. They were wearing white shorts too. The 'tock' sound which arose when the racquet met the ball caused an unfamiliar joy in Jithen's heart. 'Aw, advantage!' Stepping back a little from the TV, the friend said, 'If you like, we can have a wager; Ramesh Krishnan will win this match as well.'

Jithen was watching tennis and Ramesh Krishnan, who had a big posterior not normally seen in tennis players, for the first time. He was hearing the word advantage for the first time. Still, without any hesitation, he said, 'Definitely, he will win this!'

Ramesh Krishnan ran from corner to corner bearing his burden, sweating. There was silence in the house. Only the sound of the ball hitting the racquet resounded at irregular intervals, like the gong of a clock in disrepair. Thighs grew cold from sitting in the lotus position on the mosaic floor. When the friend went inside, calling out—'Mummy, tea…' Jithen pressed his fingers on the sofa-cum-bed by his side. The table cloth on the TV stand, the violet plastic flower on top of the TV, the wedding photo hanging on the wall, all appeared larger-than-life. They all appeared connected to this wonderful thing called television. They complemented one another. He saw a black, plastic umbilical cord going up from behind that wonder box and making the figure of a zero above the window, and then moving up changing the zero to six and moving out along the right angle of the ceiling. The silence was resounding. The ball kept meeting the racquet. He looked agape at the bag lazily thrown on the sofa and the black shoes kicked off by his friend. The shoes had been silenced by the smelly socks shoved into their mouths. Asthma possessed him with a sneeze. He got up and walked out slowly. He heard his friend plead with his mother over the hum of the fridge, 'Mummy, some more time. Till brother comes back from his tuition.'

'Um,' the woman spoke. 'Let it not be every day, do you understand?'

The door handle too felt cold from the silence. God, the fourteen-year-old said, they do not know who they are shoving away!

Once he was in the yard, he looked up again at the silvery comb of the antenna. When he saw the blue sky above it, his asthma eased.

In the next few years, television reached more houses in Thachanakkara. Resembling the soft stem of the plantain on which an incense stick had been stuck, the high-rise antennae stood atop houses, emitting smoke-like clouds. Rendering Poovamparampath Vijayan's black and white TV irrelevant, many installed colour TVs in the drawing rooms, financed by generous loans from the Thachanakkara Cooperative Bank. Under the impression that the height of the antenna was the measuring rod for the nobility of the TV set inside, many of them bought steel pipes longer than required and installed them atop their houses. Through these steel pipes, initially news, then a Hindi film songs programme called Chitrahaar, cricket, and later, *Ramayana*, leaked into the houses. Fed up with listening to the women narrating the story of *Ramayana*, when bathing at the irrigation bund, Chinnamma also bought a black and white TV. She had goose pimples looking at Rama and Ravana simultaneously shooting ten arrows at each other, the arrow heads standing still in the atmosphere for a long time facing each other, and then, to the accompaniment of instrumental music, dissolving. The next day she declared at the bathing ghat, 'What if the TV was procured at a high price and with loan, the war scenes are so real!'

The generation of Jithen passed through the serialized *Ramayana* featuring a simpleton actor called Arun Govil with his powdered face, then through *Mahabharata* which gave more importance to the swish of the costumes than to the precepts of Bhagawad Gita, and then through thousands of cricket matches played with mock competitiveness that hid the bribes and match fixings.

Play predominated at this testing time when children evolved into adults. Television helped an invocation to spread throughout India, with perhaps more zeal than the phrase 'Quit India'. From the open grounds of Thachanakkara, even Chinnamma of Ayyaattumpilli heard it: Howzzat? The new generation screamed the phrase without realizing its significance. In the close-ups in the TV, umpires resembling Wellesley and Mountbatten kept negating the appeals, shaking their heads from left to right.

Sometime during those years, reading the strange term 'athletic genius' in the newspaper, Govindan Master smiled sadly, sitting in his house in Cherai. After two decades, he would smile the same smile when he would hear the word 'book market'. New-age words are born from conjoining those once considered opposites. It occurred to Govindan Master that words such as insight, which were uttered with extreme reverence, had disappeared from the language. 'Body,' he laughed alone, saying a line broken off from a sloka, 'Body comes first, verily!'

Jithen had fallen prey to the peculiar disease of falling in love with every beautiful woman that he came across. He was also in love with homely women. With them having no chance of enjoying ardent masculinity, he could, even in darkness, see the shadow of animal-like helplessness in their eyes. However, his feelings towards beautiful women were different. At twenty, his libido was uncontrolled enough to make him want to rape a beautiful woman in a public place and invite arrest.

Jithen was not handsome. However, he had in him an innate aesthetic sense to create Earth out of Mars in a flash. The brightest example for his aesthetics was the short story he wrote within a mere two hours, which was world class due to its unique theme. In style, it resembled a Colombian author's books, which he had read in the library started by Govindan Master in Thachanakkara. Spending one-sixth of his retirement benefits, Govindan Master had donated some more excellent books to the library. Most of them were by renowned foreign authors. In that one story Jithen had written during his lifetime, their influences were certainly present. The story, which overflowed from a two-hundred-page note with a red lotus on its cover, had as its protagonist an old troglodyte called Bharathan, who had divine powers.

The story ran like this:

Based on hearsay, a woman journalist goes to the mountains alone in search of a sanyaasi who resides there and is supposed to have the extraordinary power of recognizing the smells of colours. Though he had not received any creature after turning into a cave dweller, Bharathan welcomes this girl, young enough to be his daughter, with wild honey and tells her his quaint story without any trace of lewdness. The moment of his discovery that each colour had its own different smell was quite unexpected and magical: its origin was a wager he had laid with his friends as a student.

To win the bet he had to reveal the colour of the underwear of a luscious girl whose ankles were good enough to hurt the Adam's apple of the boys from too much swallowing. With the self-confidence born of the marijuana smoke provided by a friend in the hostel, who hailed from Wayanad, the seventeen-year-old pulled up the skirt of the beautiful girl from behind and produced a twin melon shape of light blue colour before his friends. That night, after leaving a note asking the college authorities to spare the young man who had destroyed her life, the girl consumed the red-tinted blue paint and turpentine, which her father had bought for painting their house, and after lying comatose for three days, died uttering her famous last words, 'A real lover will never approach from the rear.'

What about Bharathan who was responsible for her death? Using the wager money of two thousand rupees, he got a big painting made of her and hung it in the library; survived the legal tangles for abetting suicide; kissed the feet of her father and atoned for his sins; and then roamed all over north India like a sanyaasi. However, he was not able to become a sanyaasi. The reason was a special odour which had entered his brain through his nostrils from the momentary nakedness of the girl that was revealed under the mango tree in the college. Bharathan had known from his later experience that it was neither the smell of new or old fabric nor of the sweat formed between a woman's legs. While dozing in the afternoon breeze, on the veranda of a shop in the North Indian metropolis known as the Pink City, he had an epiphany about that odour.

'That was the smell of the colour blue!' Waking up startled, Bharathan ran through the streets shouting like Archimedes.

Thereafter, Bharathan honed his olfactory powers. He could smell a deeper smell with dark blue, than that of the light blue of that day. The wilted smell of yellow, the iron smell of red, the natural smell of the life-like green, all became distinct with hard practice. He understood that black smelt of death and white had the clean, transparent smell of sunlight. Coming to know of his special powers, a famous magician made Bharathan a member of a troupe of magicians touring worldwide, with a remuneration of two thousand rupees a day. His item was to predict the colour of the underwear of the women who came to see the show. The magician would knock Bharathan's head with his magic wand and declare that he was bestowing on Bharathan the power to predict colours. After that, Bharathan, taking deep breaths, would strut in front of the rich and beautiful women seated in front of the audience, and would announce correctly the colour of the underwear each of them wore, including their hues, through the wireless microphone.

However, as could be imagined, Bharathan could not continue in that job for long. Before long, Bharathan realized that he was deceiving himself by letting his extraordinary powers be prostituted by going along with the rigmarole of getting knocked on the head by the dry wand of his master to pretend that he had acquired the temporary power for smelling colours. Also, in his attempts to smell colours, he also had to suffer the stultifying smell of the venereal diseases of some of the rich ladies in the audience. Even that was bearable—till one day the master declared that Bharathan's item was going to be expanded to include identifying the colours of men's underwear too. When matters reached that level, Bharathan decided that solitary life incognito was better and returned to Kerala and found a mountain which was not listed by the Tourism Department. There he liberated his powers from underwear. He sharpened his powers to recognize the smells of not merely rivers, forests and hills, but also the smell of the subterranean springs bubbling deep inside the earth, of the clouds seeking to escape into outer space, of stars boiling with a sad sound.

Jithen's story continues: as she is about to climb down the mountain after taking photos of Bharathan to include in the article in the weekend edition of the prominent newspaper, the young journalist asks Bharathan teasingly, 'Just for fun, can you guess my ... colour?'

He correctly answers the girl, who thought she was cleverer than him, and had tried to test the man with divine powers: 'I can't, because you are not wearing any!'

The story ends with the embarassed journalist, being given a peroration, as in a classical drama.

'That was not a guess just because I could not get the smell,' Bharathan said with a smile. 'Beautiful women who come to conduct interviews wearing miniskirts, even if they do not make any preparations, should at least take care to keep their legs together. Why should we resort to guessing about things which can be seen directly?'

After reading the story and returning it to Jithen, Govindan Master said, 'Now you should try for a bigger one. There should be Thachanakkara in it. You, me, and your grandfather should be in it!'

Jithen looked once again at the picture of the lotus on the cover of the book. This story was about this flower. Now, one should write about the roots which sucked up the nutrients. That is what Uncle Govindan said: a book about the mud into which our roots run.

Be the Brahma seated on the lotus, which blooms and rises from the mire which fills the navel of the present.

One must create.

FIVE

Omnivorous

2 September 1999

...Yesterday I paid the first rent for our house. For the last few days of last month, I had to pay almost half a month's rent. The house owner seems to have forgotten the ingress of water from the gutter. Or would he have thought that I deserved this wholly? The promise is that by the time you reach after our wedding, everything will be repaired. It is not going to be easy to find another place for one thousand rupees. I can see the displeasure on your face. And now, trying to be cheerful, saying, 'No, no, there is nothing like that'.

Dear Ann Marie, to entice you with a description of heaven, I am not inviting you to death. I think it is unfair to invite someone to my life without giving advance notice about such hells. An injustice like how God brought us into this world without our permission.

I can see the sea, sitting in the office. To forget the bilge water of daily life, this sight is more than enough. If I keep looking at the largest of the water bodies created by God, I can forget myself. I do not know if I can call the gutter a water body. However, gutters have a pride of place among the civilized man's greatest inventions. I can see these mini-streams, which bear the impure blood of the city, emptying themselves at various points into the sea, like tributaries of a river. In a way, this is a water colour painting of human life merging in God. (Or in the Void?)

Oh, what am I getting at? Haven't you heard that old Zen story? The caged tiger keeps going around in the cage, impatiently. A bird flying outside the cage asks, 'What are you doing?' The tiger says, 'I am writing.' The bird asks, 'Writing? What?' The tiger says, 'Cipher.' The bird becomes curious. 'Why are you writing only the cipher?' 'You will not understand now,' the harried tiger said, 'If you lose your liberty, everything is just a cipher!'

The Kuttippuzha Krishnapillai Memorial Vijnanaposhini Reading Room, established in Thachanakkara by Govindan Master, created a Sofia Begum. The best and the brightest among the women he had met in his entire life, Jithen summarized her thus in one of the pages of his diary, a habit which he had taken up for a short time:

Sofia Begum: the only woman with both brain and breasts.

Having recognized that he was a failure in maintaining a daily diary, it was also a revelation that his days were empty and uninteresting. As a child, he used to curse himself for not being born one of the heroes extolled in the heroic ballads of north Kerala, the Vadakkan Paattukal. During adolescence, he used to feel disappointed at the Indian Independence having taken place a quarter century ago. Now, at the start of his youth, he felt if he had been born at least two decades earlier, he could, at a minimum, have become a Naxalite. He could have filled the torn sack of his life with some action promoting common good. Recognizing himself as one jostling for space among a throng of youngsters caught in a life with nothing to look forward to beyond studies, job-seeking, marriage, and building a house, and dreaming of many ways of pleasuring themselves, his soul gagged. Without a person, philosophy, or movement to seek refuge in, time was getting crushed. In old places of moral rectitude everywhere, new greeds had been installed. Life was becoming empty without being able to find a decent soul as a friend or a mate or a guru.

Jithen decided to record, in his diary, some old memories in the order of their unforced appearance, as a method to get over this unbearable emptiness. But that too failed. Many of the memories had got buried irretrievably in the swamp of the past. That was how he embarked on this homework of defining his acquaintances in one sentence. But that also came to an inevitable end. It was not from his Christian male friends, but from his lover, Ann Marie, that he heard the Biblical proscription, which warned against passing judgment on others.

In the afternoon breeze, her long hair was flying and brushing against his eyelids and nose. 'You said you own a Bible?' Ann Marie asked. 'Then tell me, which is the shortest sentence in the Bible?'

'Are you on a path to convert me to Christianity?' Jithen asked. 'You tell me, I am keen to know anything about the Bible. Especially since my girl is a Christian!'

'Then listen.' Leaning to see if her bus was coming, Ann Marie said, 'Jesus wept!'

When he heard that the shortest sentence in the Holy Book was the sob of Christ, after a moment's silence, Jithen said, 'It's also the longest!'

The vehicle that came off the turn was a truck. On its forehead was written with flourish, 'Christ the King'. They both stood disbelieving at the amazing coincidence.

'Now do you want to hear another sentence in the Bible which, according to me, is the most lambent?'Ann Marie asked borrowing the look of a padre. Jithen paid attention.

The sound that was heard this time was that of her bus itself. Folding the umbrella and shoving it into her bag, she said hurriedly, 'Keep this sentence in mind: Thou shalt not judge!'

As he heard the unpainted, genuinely feminine lips of Ann Marie say those words that afternoon, Jithen understood that his diary writing was coming to an abrupt end. But it was only the night before that Jithen had described Sofia Begum in his diary. That was his last judgement. Two days later, he wrote this in the next page:

'Yesterday with the Bible as the witness, Ann Marie told me the truth that we have no right to mark others. Therefore, all the notes herein till now have no validity.'

Ann Marie knew about Sofia Begum, who had become Jithen's friend at the reading room in Thachanakkara. Sofia Begum was a student of MA Philosophy in Maharaja's College in Ernakulam. The most intelligent and beautiful girl of Elookkara, she had wide knowledge and empathy beyond her years. With abiding interest, the youth of Thachanakkara watched her climbing down the stairs by the side of Narayanan's shop every other day, bearing two bound books with the name of the reading room stuck on them. Four or five youths from the new generation, who could not find jobs despite their education, used to meet up on the veranda of Narayanan's shop in the evenings. Other than desire her by looking at the ankles of the beautiful maiden, none of them polluted her either by words or looks; the reason being, Sofia Begum was the daughter of Hamid Master, the mathematics teacher of Aalungal School. His nails had engraved indelibly the fundamentals of mathematics on the brains of the students from Thachanakkara.

Those were the days when Jithen, who was enrolled in UC College for his post graduation in history, used to go to the reading room, which smelt of newly-plastered cement, to help the librarian. In the library, taken over from Govindan Master, and made bigger by the management of Thachanakkara Cooperative Bank, the librarian was the one-eyed Sadashivan, appointed by the governing council of the bank. Hanging behind Sadashivan's seat was a statement of Napoleon that if he were not to be an emperor he would have been a librarian, written in red ink by Jithen on a flattened carton he got when he bought a pair of flip-flops. Turning back repeatedly and reading those words in English with his one eye, Sadashivan became increasingly uneasy. To get rid of his uneasiness, he used to disappear every day without fail into the newly-opened arrack shop near the irrigation bund, installing Jithen in his chair.

A melancholic young man, who used to come regularly to the reading room those days, was a contemporary of Sofia Begum in Maharaja's College, where he was enrolled for his post graduation in Malayalam. Looking at him, sitting at one end of the reading room immersed in some magazine and pulling at his moustache, and noting the uncanny resemblance he had to Jithen, Sofia Begum asked Jithen, 'Is he some relative of yours?'

Taking the book from Sofia Begum, Jithen answered after looking at him, 'No.'

When Sofia Begum told Jithen in a low voice that he was a student of Malayalam in Maharaja's College and had written a story in the College magazine, Jithen felt a desire to meet him. As he went past him after closing the magazine, Jithen got up and attempted to ask him something, but looking at his unfriendly mien, Jithen sat back in his chair.

As their friendship grew, Jithen felt that she was carrying a lot of information in her unveiled head, which could be deemed unnecessary. But in everything she said, there was something that blazed: desires of femininity which neither place nor time can contain. She connected Farinelli, an opera singer who was born in Italy in the eighteenth century and had moved to London, and the new singer Michael Jackson, who used female hormones to retain his talent for singing at high pitch: she had read somewhere about

Farinelli undergoing castration, in those olden times when female hormones were not available. She also told Jithen about another Italian who had conceptualized a bizarre tower in which the first floor was to be a brothel and the tenth floor an astronomical observatory. When she said that in idol worship there was a subconscious sexual craving for inanimate objects, as if to test whether he would be provoked as a Hindu, instead of debating it, Jithen repeated the word fetishism twice and learnt it by heart. After narrating the story of a Greek weaver called Arachne, who in a competition with Athena, wove a tapestry with male penises depicted from many angles, and, fearing defeat, tried to hang herself, Sofia asked Jithen, 'Do you know what that weaver who depicted male penises became in her next life? A female spider who gobbles up the male after mating! From this story, can't you make out that repressed sexuality and art have a connection?'

Jithen laughed hearing her posh language, unfamiliar to Elookkara. 'Why do you collect such information which no one else needs?' he asked her one day in the reading room when no one else was present.

'I want to write a novel!' she said with determination. 'Haven't you read foreign novels? In each, how much information do they cram! I will also write one like that!'

'If filling with information is what makes novels, can there be better novels than encyclopaedias?' Jithen laughed, pointing at the thick tomes in the shelf closest to him. 'There is a novel in my dreams too. But if I ever write it one day, there will be only the story of people, of flesh and blood from Ayyaattumpilli!'

Sofia Begum took out her charming smile, which any critic could have interpreted whichever way they wanted. 'The twentieth century has got only a few years left,' she said. 'In the years to come, if we write tales of families, discerning readers will laugh at us!'

'Then you shall see!' Jithen spoke with a self-confidence which possessed him for the first time in his life, 'I will write a story of families, which Malayalis are always going to read!'

That vow was a little loud. That had used the open throat of Ayyaattumpilli stock. And because of that, it was hollow. Even after living for fifty-four years, he could never bring it to reality. Sofia Begum also did not write her novel. A man of faith became her bridegroom before she completed her MA, and rescued her from Elookkara and writing.

'You have in you what cannot be found in men these days,' Sofia Begum told Jithen the day she came for the last time to the reading room, 'masculinity!'

'If that be so,' Jithen said, 'very soon we shall have to clash! Because the masculinity I have in my blood is the kind that kicks women. Of the basest kind!'

'I like that,' Sofia said. 'I like men who smoke. I like intelligent men who drink, open their hearts, and talk amusingly. If I am certain he is capable of loving, I like the man who kicks women who should be kicked.'

'That is because you do not know of the Ayyaattumpilli blood,' Jithen tried to explain. 'There was once a woman called Kunjuamma who deserved only to be loved. The blood I have in me is that of Naraapilla, who made her eat laterite stones and kicked her to death.'

'There have been no children born with only male blood in them. Won't the blood of the woman you talked about also be flowing through your heart?' Sofia asked.

'I am not sure about that,' Jithen said, 'more than Kunjuamma's, the blood that is flowing through me now is Ann Marie's!'

'Ann Marie?' Sofia arched her unibrow. 'Who's that? Did your mother change her name?'

'Ann Marie is the girl I love. The one I may marry. The Mary who considers me to be Christ! So, how can her blood be not in me?' Jithen receipted the books returned by Sofia Begum.

Sofia rose and said, 'Dey, if you are going to write your novel in such style, it will be very good. When they cannot make out anything, the critics also will praise it.'

'What's with your novel?' Jithen asked.

'Oh, I doubt if it will happen,' Sofia Begum became despondent. 'What you have said is true. If one has to write, one has to write about one's life, one's times, and one's locale. If a woman like me writes one like that honestly, all the above said together would kick her out!'

At the time of leaving, Sofia Begum asked him, 'Have you touched Ann Marie we discussed about earlier? I meant…'

'Only her hands and hair,' Jithen said, 'but not in the manner you meant … No!' Lowering his voice still, he said, 'I have not done it! That's what you meant, no?'

'Till now? No one?' her voice went lower than Jithen's.

'No!' Jithen lied.

From the swamp of his memory, suddenly Laila Majnu bloomed.

They were three. Two women and a boy.

They were to be taken to the newly-built house. Since it was past midnight, there was no light in any of the homes. Jithen's heart was pumping furiously. The key to the house into which people were to move in from the coming week, had been left with Unnikrishnan, the plumber of the house and his friend. There was some piping work left to be done the next day. The opportunities were put together and she was fetched for Jithen by Unnikrishnan. The middle-aged woman accompanying her was not a companion. She was for his friend.

'For a plumber, someone a little aged will be more suitable!'

Unnikrishnan justified his choice. The boy with them was ten years old. Jithen was disquieted by the boy calling the middle-aged woman mother in an insistent manner, often in the darkness.

The gate was locked. Waiting for the light from a passing autorickshaw to subside, Unnikrishnan helped them jump over the compound wall to the other side. To Jithen, who stood to the side, afraid that the women might shout at him if their buttocks were touched, Unnikrishnan said through grinding teeth, 'Just don't stand there staring. Come, push!'

The boy had to be literally pushed over. When he fell in the darkness on the other side, he whined again calling his mother. As the fourth and the fifth, with scraped and burning thighs, Jithen and Unnikrishnan jumped over to the other side.

As Jithen was being let in through the backdoor, Unnikrishnan told him, 'Laila is for you. The other rusted one is for me, but I need to wait till the kid is asleep!'

Laila! Jithen laughed with a palpitating heart. He is then Majnu. The eternal lover who was buying love with the hundred-rupee note stolen from his mother's cupboard.

Someone else's house. The main switch was off. As a matter of abundant caution by his friend. Striking a match, Jithen went forward. Like the arrow that shot towards the sound of water filling the pot, as in the Purana tale, to the pool of urine falling on the mosaic floor.

Laila was squatting and piddling on the drawing room floor.

She told Jithen's face, which was visible by the light of the match stick, that she chose the drawing room because she could not find the toilet even after searching. He took her to another room. When he struck the match, he saw a showcase full of dolls. Unnikrishnan had instructed that they should not use the bed.

'Lailae!' he called with a surfeit of love.

'Do it fast and go!' she said, as if snapping at him.

The body of the streetwalker on which the anaphrodisiac of torpor had been applied.

The first act of sex is like getting power. The preparations start very early. It is decided that many things will be brought into practice. Then when the moment is at hand, doing things in hurry and haphazardly, one comes away like a poltroon.

Jithen waited with fealty for his friend's turn. The squeak of the rusted pipes. The back of Jithen's head kept pulsating from the fear that the kid asleep in the other room would wake up suddenly and would hit Jithen on the back of his head with whatever came to hand …

Sending off the women and the child along with Unnikrishnan before daybreak, Jithen started to wash with water and broom, the floor of the drawing room, which had started smelling of ammonia.

The last scene of the love story of Laila-Majnu that Jithen had to write.

SIX

Odds

23 August 1999

…I laughed when I read your request that I should send at least a couple of lines of verse to you. Baby, what did I send you these six months, then?

Ann Marie, I swear upon my unfortunate lungs, tired from standing on either side of my heart and fanning like the attendants holding the regal, decorative circular fans: the kinds of poem you expect now, I finished writing long ago. Much before I met you!

Instead, I will write some of the thoughts about death, which I had written down yesterday. Please forgive this good-for-nothing fellow who sends thoughts on death to his lover when asked for poetry.

The only couple with total compatibility: Life and Death. Every man ends with a death which suits his life. Therefore, unnatural deaths may happen to penguins and kangaroos, not to humans. However macabre a death it is, we can dig up something from the dead man's life which justifies it. We may be appalled reading about a woman who diced her paramour and put him in twenty polyethylene bags. But if we search his soul, we may find the life of that woman, which had been chopped up into twenty pieces by him much earlier. Isn't stealing a person's life worse than taking a person's life? But to punish that act there are no courts and laws for man.

Our poor minds can only comprehend a system in which punishment is decided after a crime is committed. However this linearity of time is not applicable to Nature. It can punish and redeem a soul at ten, which was going to commit a crime when fifty.

Ann Marie, don't feel nervous thinking this is philosophy. Here is a simple truth: like each life shackled inside its body, every existence is shackled inside its own special circumstances. In both cases, the outcome is death; though in the second case, some may reach heaven.

When two old men, who were living across each other, died in consecutive months, Thachanakkara flung back a book which it had completed reading. The last pages of the book were Appu Nair of Peechamkurichi, confined by blinding cataract, and Raambillapolice, who was called Granpa Raambilla by the children of Geethalayam.

At least twelve years had passed after the darkness of cataract had driven out the whole of the outside world from Appu Nair's vision. Even the house, which his son Gopalakrishnan, the younger brother of Kumaran, who had married Thankamma of Ayyaattumpilli, had built anew after razing most of the old Peechamkurichi House, had become old. The old man Appu Nair had, like a letter which could not be rubbed out, taken refuge on an old cot, in an old anteroom which had not been demolished when the new house was built. He clung on to that cot, which gave the appearance of a disintegrating raft moving through time, pushing out, as ripples, the weak waves of helplessness. The past still burned inside him like firewood, providing fuel for the journey which was close to its destination. Warming himself at that fire, he spent his time talking to the dead. He often mixed up the living and the dead. The age of the dead varied wildly. He was perplexed seeing that his darling sister's hair had gone completely white, when Kunjuamma appeared, her head swathed in bloodied bandages, along with Naraapilla, whose face had been scalded.

'Hau!' he said with bitterness. 'Why are you still walking hand in hand with this guy, Kunjo? Haven't you had enough?'

Appu Nair saw their eight siblings often in front of his eyes. Only because they were dead, they were spared all pain. As they stood before him with the joy of having left this world and smiling without a care, as their elder brother, he joined them in their happiness and laughed out loud.

'Now no one will blame my father Paramu Nair!' Holding his hands up with palms open and level with his face, he said to himself, 'See, except me, all the nine are in good positions.'

Later, repeating that same sentence in another tone, he wept too.

In between the unbroken rendition of his past, one afternoon, an old lady, whom he had not seen before, came and called out to Appu Nair, 'Lord Appu, oy!'

Appu Nair stared uncomprehendingly into the blankness of his cataract. Two shadows blocked the square of light from the window. 'It's me,' one of the shadows said, in a voice from the past, heard and forgotten, 'Kaali Pulakkalli!'

'Hah! Is that Kaali Pulakkalli?' He smiled showing his gums, vain about his sense of hearing, which had become acute, as his sight went down. 'When did you die?'

Kaali who had a ravishing, bright smile during the days when she and Naraapilla used to conduct their sexual acrobatics in the anteroom of Ayyaattumpilli, now stood before Appu Nair as an old woman past eighty and laughed heartily. 'Both of us aren't dead yet, Lord,' the old woman said. 'Your niece in Ayyaattumpilli told me that you have lost your sight. Then itself I had thought that

I must pay you a visit. Can you see who this is? You know my son Velayudhan, the dark kid who used to be with me in Naraapilla Lord's anteroom? This is the third son of Velayudhan. We've come to invite you for his wedding!'

The scene of the harvesting in the fields in Nedumaali appeared before Appu Nair. The cloth cradle hung from the young mango tree convulsed. In that, when the midday sun burned his tender thigh, the little Velayudhan cried, kicking and screaming.

'Where?' After sometime he withdrew his hands, which he had stretched expecting to touch and feel. 'The third son of the kid who lay in that lungi cradle? Ayyo, haven't I died still?'

'Hah, great!' The shadow, which was folding its fingers, counting, told Appu Nair, 'Velayudhan's eldest daughter—in pisheries; the second one—in phorest; the third—in police. Dey, he is that one, who's come with me.'

'Why is there a smell of cow dung?' the shadow and sound in front of Appu Nair disappeared and instead odour predominated. He became anxious and pointed to the yard. 'Who is that, Chokli who's come with the stud bull? Or the buffalo of that heinous guy?' The old man flared his nostrils. He felt that someone was showering semi-dried cow dung patties in the yard. Upsetting the spittoon under his cot, he tried to get up. He staggered up to the portico. Seeing the buffalo, which was standing in the yard swishing its tail after dropping fresh dung, for the last time in his life he went hari hara. The golden bell around the buffalo's neck kept clinging. Appu Nair recognized whose vehicle it was.

The three donation seekers for the Thachanakkara temple festival, who had come with the receipt book and notices, saw Appu Nair collapsing on the portico, just as they were entering through the gate of Peechamkurichi. There was no one else in the house at that time. Cursing the old man for hampering their donation drive, the men who came with the festival notice, started gathering people.

Appu Nair was no more.

The day Shashidharan, son of Pankajaakshan, was elected as the president of Thachanakkara Panchayat, Kalyanikuttyamma distributed rice and milk paayasam to all the Ayyaattumpilli houses.

As she had become bowlegged from sitting down to milk cows, it had given the fifty-six-year old Kalyanikuttyamma a gait that made her sway from side to side. Coming to Ayyaattumpilli thirty-five years ago as a fashionable woman from Kochi, holding on to Pankajaakshan's hand, gradually she too acquired the features of the Ayyaattumpilli stock. While during the initial years, her voice was hardly raised above a whisper, now she bellowed even at the cows like the Ayyaattumpilli stock. By the time her youngest son had started sending money from Pathankot every month, having joined the army, her earlier reservations against walking through the alleys carrying bundles of cut grass for the cows, had completely disappeared.

Prompted by the desire to get rich quickly, when he had cut down all the fruit-bearing trees in their compound and planted rows of cocoa saplings received from the Village Block Office, it backfired on Pankajaakshan. Having learnt to climb trees in the extraordinary circumstances of having been forced to compete with squirrels, the bandicoots made clean holes in the cocoa fruits and devoured the white-covered seeds inside and exhibited their gratification. All over the compound, the cocoa plants stood ashamed with their noses and teats slashed, like Shoorppanakas. With the non-cooperation by the coffee plants, which he had imported from Munnar after being dismissed from service, and

Devassy's absconding after suffering losses at the brick kiln that he eventually abandoned, all avenues of Pankajaakshan's income came to an end and he was left with the occupation of playing cards. Though he was always a loser in poker—which, for some obscure reason, was known as *pannimalarthu*, or flipping the pig, in the vernacular—he kept on playing, with the irrepressible optimism that he would win in the next hand. So, Kalyanikuttyamma had to slog all the while for not only putting food on the table for her three sons, but also for anteing up her husband's wager money for the cards. Though he was of pensionable age, his health was still robust and one day, looking at his wife going to the cowshed with her swaying gait, carrying the milk pails on both hands, he sighed.

'Poor woman, she ain't good enough anymore!' Sipping the rum that had been brought wrapped in his socks by his son during his first home leave, Pankajaakshan passed judgment on his wife, twirling his moustache.

Pankajaakshan could not believe that the beauty who was with him in their honeymoon enveloped by the glass-panes of Munnar, was the old hag of now, staggering around, exhausted by backbreaking overwork. When he was struggling to bear inside him the image of his once-beautiful wife like that of a paramour, Kalyanikuttyamma of Kochi was finding varied reflections of her life in her cows' milk, urine and dung in the cowshed, which now stood where Kunjuamma had been cremated.

Her youngest son, joining the army, had mitigated the anguish of Kalyanikuttyamma, who feared that her three sons were growing up to be worse lazybones than their father. She would smile reading the letters sent by Soman, blowing up his tribulations during the training period in Pathankot. 'My poor son!' Kalyanikuttyamma would talk to the words carelessly flung on the inland letter by her son. 'He was getting to enjoy the taste of living off my sweat here!'

Her eldest son, Venu, was not able to find a job though he was thirty-five years old. His main occupation was standing close to the window and enjoying his reflection in a small handheld mirror. Venu was an ardent fan of singer Yesudas. He had transcribed at least five hundred songs of Yesudas in five notebooks and had learnt by heart at least half of them by singing them repeatedly. Around four o'clock in the evening, wearing only a lungi, and holding a glass of steaming tea in his hand, he would stand at the gate of his house. Looking at the nubile schoolgirls returning to their houses in Elookkara and Kayintikkara, he would slurp his tea with a hiss, and hum some of the songs. At those times, he would feel smug considering himself Yesudas, and also humbled by his readiness to practise at four in the evening standing on the concrete slab covering the gutter in which the sewage water was flowing to the Periyar river. However, the response of the girls to the singer was ever disappointing. They had given a nickname among themselves to the man who appeared with a glass of tea and hummed tunes, when they themselves were hurrying home from school, famished: Tea Demon. When the girls went by, muttering the nickname and suppressing giggles, misconstruing that as their coyness at the sight of his masculinity, Venu ripened his youth standing on that slab for many months.

Venu's younger brother Shashi had chosen politics as his playground, as a carry-over of his smelling the clothes of the women working in the brick kiln, hiding behind the coffee bushes, and watching, again surreptitiously, the stud bull of Chokli humping their jersey cow. Starting off as a leader of a band of men who used to mine sand from the river at Punneli kadavu in the dead of the night, shouting instructions to them from the riverbank, soon he spread his influence to daytime activities too. Shashi had divined that, by becoming the leader of the political party—the one which the sons-in-law of Ayyaattumpilli, Kumaran and Shankaran, had served so selflessly hoping for the prosperity of people of all the world—at least his own personal prosperity could be ensured. The old communists, including Kumaran and Shankaran, were stupefied by the sight of Shashi holding forth on the workers' rights at the various public places in Thachanakkara, an exhibitionism much like the one undertaken by his brother Venu during the evenings with his glass of tea, standing on the slab. Once, when his credentials for becoming the leader of a party known to be one of the working class, he declaimed his irrefutable allegiance in front of thousands of the party followers in the temple grounds in Thachanakkara, with such vehemence that even Nature's cardinal points took notice:

'No one dare teach me about the workers and their sweat.' Remembering the sweaty clothes of Rebecca that he used to savour, hidden in the coffee plants, Shashidharan said, 'I have reached here only by having known all that, be sure!'

Shashi had fed power into those words by tying in the soul of some comrade, who had fought with mere bamboo spears. Without realizing that he was enjoying even then the results of the sweat of someone else, the Thachanakkara folk used to whistle and cheer him on. Thus, in his thirty-third year, Shashidharan, the second son of Pankajaakshan of Ayyaattumpilli, took charge as the youngest ever president of the Thachanakkara panchayat.

That day, Kalyanikuttyamma felt her cows were lactating more. She made milk paayasam using raw, semi-polished rice and sent it instead of milk to the eight houses in the neighbourhood. Geethalayam, which was next door earlier, was now two houses away. In the forty cents of land, which Chinnamma had sold at different times for meeting the wedding expenses of her daughters, outsiders had built two houses that stood like excrescences. The compound walls all around had made the topography of Ayyaattumpilli a maze resembling Ravanan's fort. After handing over the vessel with the paayasam in her left hand to the wife of the youngest son of Thankamma, standing at the gate of the old house, Kalyanikuttyamma walked past the many compound walls, and Narayanan's shop towards Geethalayam, with another vessel of paayasam in her right hand.

'Chinnammae!' Kalyanikuttyamma hailed, going round the house up to the kitchen door.

Chinnamma appeared at the door, holding sheaves of coconut spathe, which she was going to insert into the sawdust stove.

'Here, some paayasam,' Kalyanikuttyamma said pleasantly, holding out the vessel, 'for celebrating the kid winning the election.'

'Oh!' Flinging the spathe away, Chinnamma said with a scowl, 'I thought Kalluchechi had come to give me a naazhi of milk free.'

As Kalyanikuttyamma turned around, tired of such jibes, she also heard this: 'Here also there's a party worker! Dey, sitting and smoking his beedis, doing nothing, after quitting the job! Not having the money even to buy a gas stove! Hohoho!'

Kalyanikuttyamma made haste. She had to deliver paayasam to six more houses.

In the month of Medam, when the standard for the temple festival at Thachanakkara temple had already been raised, another death in the neighbourhood shook Jithen badly: the life of the childless Granpa Raambilla, who had become a solitary soul, following the death of his wife, and had ended up in the Aluva Government Hospital for sixty-four days, untended by anyone. That day, a phone message came to the UC College from the Government Hospital, for Jithen. As he was getting out of the Principal's room after reading the scribbled news of the death left on the table, Jithen was asked, 'How is the dead man related to you?'

Sitting in the bus for Aluva, along with the three members of the students' association, Jithen also thought about it: who's the dead man to me? Last month he had described another deceased as the father of his mother's sister's husband. Otherwise, his grandmother's brother. But how can this death be defined?

'One who became all alone, an ordinary man!' Jithen told his friends. 'And because of that, our close relative!'

That evening, accompanying the emaciated corpse in the ambulance from Aluva, Jithen had a nightmare with his eyes wide open: on the fifth day after the cremation, when everyone was gathered for immersing the bones and ashes of the cremated body in the water on the day of sanchayanam, Alamboori appears suddenly, grabs the earthen pot in which the bones have been kept, runs towards the irrigation bund, and laughs and claps his hands, after sending the pot floating in the waters of the bund.

But that nightmare did not come true, despite no sane person coming forward to do the ritualistic submersion of the bones in the river.

Despite the irrigation bund being the most suitable water body for Raambillapolice to dissolve in.

Despite Raambillapolice becoming Alamboori's father, morally responsible as he was for having created a new man called Alamboori, burying Vasudevan of Nedumpilli Mana.

SEVEN

Religious Rivalry

5 November 1999

...Yesterday too my boss started a fight with me. 'There is no great place for humanism in professionalism!' he tried to justify himself somewhere in our argument. 'Possible,' I countered, 'but we are yet to start calling all inhuman behaviour professionalism!' Probably because I went to bed with the thoughts of that showdown in mind, I had two nightmares in the night. Strange nightmares which translated emotional turmoil into a different state. I will end this letter by writing about those.

First dream: Both of us were sitting, listening to ghazals. The singer sang with a pained heart:

It feels good to cry by the walls,
Looks like I too will end up mad ...

Suddenly, you leaned on my chest and started weeping. Our relatives and friends came and stood around and leaned over to look at me. That is when I understood: I was dead! I could see it all. Hear everything. But I couldn't move. The old model tape recorder, swathed in black leather with only the record button in red, started to play another Hindi song:

If there are no tears to shed,
What is the fun in crying?

You translated that into Malayalam in the old style, crying.

From the other side of death, I was getting ready to say that, in translation, it had lost its soul. But by then the people were jumping in joy and congratulating the translated version.

The second dream was this: A dance performance in the Town Hall by Yamini Machayya, a Telugu. The unparalleled sensuality of Bharathanatyam. Bewitching gesticulations which reached out to even the last row. Seductive face. Majestic beauty oozing from the movements of limbs. As I was leaving, I buy her from the organizers. Stuffing and mounting in an expansive posture and hand gesture, I install her on the veranda of the rented house.

For the crime of insulting India's performing arts, a gang of moral police encircle the house, armed and screaming obscenities.

Jithen wrote his first poem in his thirteenth year. Even though it was written in the inauspicious thirteenth year, it was not a love poem. The theme of the eighteen-line poem, which was titled 'The Well and the Sea', was the angst of a small child who wished to attain greatness and yet doubted whether he deserved to be great. In a short story he wrote when he was twenty, other than undergarments, there was nothing on love. But in between these, when he was fifteen years old and seventeen years old, to be exact, Jithen wrote two love poems. The first one blindly imitated the style of a poet Malayalis had mostly forgotten about. A poem out of its time. Once, later in his life, when he got to read it again, mercilessly forgetting the anguish of the time he had written it, he laughed heartily. Looking at time making a farce of something which was genuinely admired once, he laughed again, shocked. The poem of his fifteenth year ran as follows:

> In the solitude of beautiful dreams, you
> I saw many a time, my beloved

Why did you forbear, from speaking to me?
Why did you not even caress me?

Then, lines which were more laughable:

If I am not desired at all, darling,
In my dreams, could you not murmur?
With your golden dreams
May you bless this mortified soul!

If rhyme more than love defined this poem, the poem written in the seventeenth year, showed a lover trying to be in with the times:

The hibiscus plant beyond the window,
A forlorn girl this
Though draped in green plenitude,
And wearing the heart outside
How can love be felt, as my mind
wanders searching for something …
Is sighting another fragrant flower
Afar, the reason why?

Nevertheless, in none of the many letters he had sent during the six-years of tumultous courtship of a girl called Ann Marie, and in the ten months after getting a job in the land of the Zamorin, was there a single line of verse. Life had presented him with such bitter experiences that he gave up not just versification, but poesy as a whole. He was taught the unforgettable lesson of unrequited love by a classmate of his, whom he had loved with melting heart and tremulous mind, by anointing him with vomit which smelt of faeces, during the return leg of a college excursion. And in the attempt to forget that, in his first tryst with a prostitute along with his friend, misfortune surfaced in the form of a pool of ammonia-smelling urine in the drawing room of some unknown man.

His desire to enjoy the female form unseen, was stymied when God punished him by making him hear the whine of a sickly aged woman through a termite-eaten window pane. His poesy ended there. He found Ann Marie there. The turn in the life of that girl who was to join a convent and become a nun as soon as her graduation was over—caused by his love, his care, and his masculine protection, gave him the jitters. It happened more or less like the romance of Govindan Master of Ayyaattumpilli. Govindan Master had told him of a poetry contest that a magazine conducted forty years ago, as if only to bring them together. It was a sentence, more venerable than a poem, which someone had scribbled on a blackboard in UC College that brought Jithen and Ann Marie close. Jithen did not find anything in that petite girl, a graduate student of Malayalam, which made her desirable. It more or less ran contrary to the first encounter Naraapilla had in the temple pond of Thachanakkara with this grandmother. If it was the nakedness revealed through the wet clothes that tormented his grandfather, it was the spirituality which shone in the girl who was to become his wife that beckoned Jithen. That goodness, which Jithen had deemed women to be incapable of, called to him more than any nudity. That even upended his concept of women. She delayed her entry into the convent, a wish of her father, by following up her graduation with a post graduation and a degree in education. With the support of her brother, two years younger to her, she continued to wait for Jithen for six years. To avoid detection by her parents, she used to, after reading them, burn Jithen's letters, sent in the name of her brother, Joshi, to the seminary where he was training to be a priest. However, from the day Jithen came to her home in Angamaly and asked for her hand in marriage, granted grudgingly by her father Varghese through a grunt, since her brother too supported her, she started preserving the letters of her future husband. But they were only one tenth of the letters he had sent her; the last forty letters, to be exact—the forty extraordinary missives, which she had salvaged, many years later in another place from the sewage water that invaded their rented house, and safeguarded for the rest of her life.

He finally revealed his secret romance that he had cleverly hidden during the long years spent in applying for jobs, to his mother during the Vishu after he had landed the job. 'Amma, you needn't shout needlessly now!' Jithen told his mother who was stirring the curry on the stove. 'I am going to marry a non-Hindu girl.'

A firecracker bomb went off in Thachanakkara temple, where the flag had been hoisted signalling the annual festival. The nerveless hand of Chinnamma dropped the ladle into the pot. Her hand got scalded in her attempt to take it out. He had come home for his first vacation after getting the job. Licking her scalded finger and tasting the curry using the ladle, and without looking at Jithen's face, Chinnamma said, 'Many have told me about you sitting and chatting with the Muslim girl from Elookkara in the reading room. If your fancy is to marry girls like her, I won't have the likes of her in these premises!'

'This is not a Muslim girl!' Jithen said, 'The girl you are talking of has got married and gone away. This is a Christian girl. Ann Marie, who has been waiting for me for six years, forsaking even Christ!'

'Pthtoo!' snapped Chinnamma fearsomely. The same snapping Naraapilla did when he heard of Govindan deciding to marry the out-of-caste girl from Cherai. But this one was more fearsome. It was not for out of caste, but out of religion!

'See the fate of the guy here who married disobeying his father? With an epileptic son and a dead wife, now he has come back with books and a library, shamelessly! I will not permit it while I am alive!' Chinnamma called out stridently to her husband, 'Dey, did you hear this?'

'I have told father,' Jithen said, stepping out of the kitchen.

'And...?' Chinnamma asked.

'He said let it be as per my wish.'

'Pthtoo!'

Ann Marie was the child Kalappuraykkal Varghese had promised for the Father in Heaven. But in her eighteenth year, the Lord Almighty made her sit alone one afternoon in an empty class in UC college, and changed the course of her life. She, who was to join a convent after her graduation, ended up obeying the call of life, which was more powerful than the call of God, and became the beloved companion of Jithendran of Ayyaattumpilli.

Since she was born after the premature death of her two elder siblings, who were delivered before term, her father did not think twice before committing her to the convent. He had already decided that there would not be a suitable husband in the whole world for his daughter who was as beautiful as, and more energetic than, his wife. While taking Ann Marie—who had irises like white stone, inherited from her father, who was known throughout Angamaly as Cat-eyed Varghese—home from the hospital, he stopped at the church on the way, and without any provocation, made a brutal offering. 'As my bride, this one's mother destroyed her own life.' Taking the child in his arms and shaking off his flip-flops, Varghese continued, addressing the church, 'But I shall not allow her child to suffer the same fate! Here, from the Kalappuraykkal family, one more blessed bride for you!'

Hearing that unexpected avowal, Varghese's wife, Susanna from Kongorppilli, and her mother who was with them, were stunned.

'If thy wish be that, thy will be done,' Susanna said smiling at the church, the very next moment, more to Christ than to her husband.

From the time they had converted to Christianity, the Kalappuraykkal family maintained their allegiance to Jesus Christ by offering a girl to the Church, in every generation. Varghese used to boast that when the Portuguese—who introduced pigs and boars to Angamaly, which were called pork locally—chose women as nuns for the Church in Angamaly, among them was the sister of his great-great-grandmother. In that claim, which had less historical accuracy and more of old wives' tale, he always used to include the part about the pigs.

'Why did the Portuguese bring pigs to our land?' Ann Marie, as a child, asked her father.

'That is their way in Portugal!' Varghese said sitting on the parapet and drinking arrack. 'All the garbage in their cities is cleaned by these pigs, no? No salaries to be paid, and when they are fattened with the garbage, they can be slaughtered in the kitchen and eaten too!'

Varghese had made a habit of drinking at home, to get over the premature deaths of Ann Marie's elder brothers, who perished before they could toddle. When the third child turned out to be a girl, he continued to drink on that score as well. By the time the fourth child, a boy, was born, arrack had diluted his blood. Intoxication sieved out the past from his soul and dumped it outside. The calluses formed in Ann Marie's ears from hearing her father recite, as if from memory, the tales beginning with the advent of Thomas the Apostle landing at Kodungallur, were hard enough to resist even the call of God. Yet, since her verity was more divine than the vow made by her father, Christ was a friend to her from her childhood. The usage, the Bride of Christ, stirred an infatuation in her soul. The day her father told her about the Angaadi kadavu in Angamaly, which Thomas the Apostle reached via Mala from Kodungallur, she experienced Christ mingling in her blood. However, she could not suffer a string of people—

starting with Thomas the Apostle to the young men who were shot to death in Angamaly during the *Vimochanasamaram* in the late-fifties against the communist rule in Kerala—turning out to be her father's relatives in the alcohol-fuelled tall stories that he used to narrate.

'Wasn't Arnos Paathiri taught Malayalam by Kunjan Nampoothiri?' Quaffing a mouthful of arrack, and winking his light-coloured eyes, Varghese would try to tie up history with the hem of his mundu. 'One of the relatives of that Kunjan Nampoothiri is the first Christian in our family. Now, don't you get the secret behind our complexion?'

Varghese's younger sister, Justina, who was fortunate to go to Italy, was the model woman for Ann Marie for all times. She used to await for the uplifting sight of her aunt, pure as Mother Mary and merciful as Jesus Christ, coming towards her house after alighting from the autorickshaw at the beginning of the path hidden by the rubber trees, once every three months. With the advent of Doordarshan, as a child of the new generation whose sight reached the poles, she could establish the resemblance between her habit-wearing aunt and bashful penguins. The line of Kalappuraykkal women enticed to wear the habit had come to an end with Justina, Varghese's only sister. Though delivered by Susanna of Kongorppilli, Varghese had reckoned on Ann Marie, being his daughter, continuing with the tradition of donning the habit. That reckoning had come to nought on that day, in the empty classroom in UC College. The bearded young man standing at the door of the classroom asked Ann Marie, who had been sitting and copying out the notes from a friend's, oblivious of his presence, 'Who wrote this on the blackboard, is it you?'

Ann Marie read the sentence, which had not caught her attention so far, off the board.

'Man is the only creature that perishes before attaining full growth!'

That was the Chemistry classroom. The students had gone for the practical classes. Even in the previous class session, there seemed no reason for such a sentence to be written on the board. Like another misplaced sentence, Ann Marie who was a student of Malayalam, was sitting in the Chemistry classroom and transcribing notes.

She showed her open palms indicating ignorance. The melancholy eyes of the bearded young man smiled. 'Then we should find out,' he told her, 'not who wrote this on the board, but who said this the first time!'

They introduced each other giving names and course details. 'I am Ann Marie, Malayalam BA, first year. I came looking for an empty room to transcribe notes,' she said.

'I am Jithendran,' he said. 'MA History, second year. Some unknown power brought me here. Perhaps to read this line; or else to meet you; if not, then for both!'

Ann Marie thought she heard the bell toll in the church. And that the sunlight had dimmed outside.

'Search and you shall find,' he told her. 'And if you come to know of it, tell me also. Among the things I have read so far, this is the most authentic sentence!'

He turned and walked back. She wrote down the sentence in her notebook. Underneath that she wrote a biggish J. Making it the common initial letter, she wrote Jesus Christ and Jithendran in two rows, and in different styles.

'Search,' she said to herself, smiling, 'you'll find!'

Though both of them searched for two years in their own ways, they could not find the author of what was written on the board that day. But that sentence, which they had assumed to have forgotten forever, had to enter their lives once more. But by that time, they had got married and had become the parents of two grown-up girls. They had even become grandfather and grandmother. He was fifty-four years old and she was fifty years old. The words of that sentence, which had entered them from the blackboard of life, and whose authorship remained anonymous, were the last words of the middle-aged Jithendran.

EIGHT

Creation Song

31 July 1999

...Like lava into the weak throats of monomaniacal volcanoes, something rises and boils over, with a roar from my innermost soul. A non-somatic retching is troubling me. Can you imagine the anomaly of someone, after majoring in History and doing a post-graduation, becoming a supervisor in a toy factory? Beyond doubt, I am a true representative of the modern-day youth. An imbecile who's making rubber monkey dolls, after forgetting all history. A counterfeit Brahma!

Have you thought of toys other than from the perspective of a child? Definitely, the top-selling toy in the world must be the balloon. A child starts touching human life through a balloon. Isn't every balloon a distended form of emptiness? A rubber edition of what Ezhuthachchan, the father of Malayalam poetry, called water bubble. If it is their fragile nature that makes balloons more childish than balls, the same reason lends them a philosophical quality. Have you noticed the sense of wonderment which reflects in the eyes of a child as it sees a balloon, which it has been knocking about, burst? At the time of death, once more that thought about life has to flash in every man's soul: where did that thing of entertainment vanish as vapour?

Even after going past his childhood, a man's fascination with toys doesn't end. Do you know how Gandhiji described the Eiffel Tower, which the world celebrated as a wonder? As Paris's toy! Leo Tolstoy had declared earlier that the iron tower didn't have an iota of art. In the vanguard of those who protested against the Eiffel Tower was the world-class storyteller Guy de Maupassant. However, it was our Gandhiji who found the mot juste for criticizing that folly in steel: 'So long as we are children we are attracted by toys, and the Tower was a good demonstration of the fact that we are all children attracted by trinkets. That may be claimed to be the purpose served by the Eiffel Tower.'

Girl, when the world is filling up with mere toys of objects and facts, I feel like throwing away my life!

On his first visit, before getting into the old building, which stood facing the sea, with strange-looking maps on it's walls drawn by the salt-laden sea breeze, Jithen tarried a while on the seashore. The waves, which were calmed by the tears of millions of years dropping on them, came, prostrated at the feet of humans whose longevity was only a few decades, and kept retreating.

That was March 1999. As if on a clock, Jithen could track time looking at the sun on the eastern wall of the sky. Thousands of repetitions of this day—which rolls the sun up the invisible hill in the sky, and in the evening pushes it down this side into the sea and laughs and claps like how Naranathu Branthan, that beloved lunatic, did as his daily routine—await him. Jithen remembered: thousands of monkey dolls of the same size and colour, not yet manufactured, await him. The rest of his monotonous and dry life, untouched by creativity, awaits him like the pedlar on the seashore. Thinking about that, the twenty-seven-year old Jithen smiled with pain.

The magician sea that amuses the spectators by spreading and pulling back his frothy handkerchief each time to reveal a clutch of yellow-legged crabs. The same sunshine that fell on

Vasco da Gama five hundred years ago shone on the wet armour of the crabs and their tong-like pincers. One of the mother crabs, coming out of the children's tales written by the sea, told a parable to its young one:

'Why are you stepping sideways? Walk ahead and prove your straightforwardness to the world.'

The young crab smiled. 'Teach me how to walk straight,' it said. 'Mother, show me by walking yourself!'

The mother crab started to flail, trying to walk ahead straight. Acknowledging that the habit of epochs was pulling it to the side, she stopped moralizing and withdrew into the waves.

Jithen turned around and looked once again across the road at the institution where he was going to work. The sanctum sanctorum of drummer-monkey toys. Half an hour later, he found himself sitting in a chair in front of his boss, on its second floor. He was going to listen to his boss describe the toys, with the realization that the same exam-fever that used to afflict him from the age of five in the month of March, was being rekindled within him. He sat there nodding his head like a doll-man, looking at the betel-juice stained mouth of his boss.

Assistant Creative Officer—that was his designation. Not merely his academics, even his creativity, which was noticed in the university, was a criterion for his selection. However, he knew that his designation notwithstanding, there was little scope for creativity in his job. The company only expected Jithen to play a supervisory role between ten in the morning and six in the evening. In between, he should test the tautness of the drumhead and whether the fully-keyed toy plays as long as claimed in the advertisement.

'America, Hong Kong, and Japan are the best in the manufacture of such toys,' his boss said. 'There is a big difference in that the monkeys they make use cymbals. To tell the truth, this cymbal is only a variation of our own *ilathaalam*. Their monkeys are dressed in trousers with red and white stripes and yellow-coloured vests with red buttons. The eyes have big red circles drawn around them.'

His boss continued the description. For Jithen, words of another world and another time, dropping off from another life, seemed to fill their glass-walled room. Words of deceit, like clods of earth of faux mass and like dry leaves devoid of any life. They started to rise up to his knees, his chest and his neck, and began to suffocate him.

Taking the toy monkey left on the table by the attendant and caressing it like his own son, the boss said, 'Taking away the cymbal from the foreign toys, I fixed a miniature chenda. A little bit of creativity!' He displayed his betel-stained teeth. 'With that, the sales of this guy doubled. Within India and outside, equally.'

'Creativity?' Jithen pricked his ballooning pride with a needle-like question, 'How long will it take for him to evolve into a human?'

The boss frowned. He jumped up, making the chair scrape the floor and said, 'Come with me. Now I shall tell you about production.'

The word 'production' sprayed red-coloured arecanut grits on Jithen's forearm.

After walking along the passage, Jithen climbed down the stairs behind his boss. His boss explained to him how the toy monkey, called Musical Jolly Chimp, made by a Japanese company fifty years ago, was resurrected in a company in Kerala as a toy playing a drum.

'The machinery inside is the same, then and now,' quoting a sloka, the boss shone his torch of erudition on to Jithen's face. '*Vasamsi jeernaani yathhaavihaaya, navaani gruhnaathi naroparaani* ... Like a man leaving out old worn-out clothes, and wearing new clothes when necessary ... Haven't you read the Bhagawad Gita?'

Taking off from the last two syllables of the sloka, which sounded like nail in the vernacular, a joke which could be pegged to it flashed in Jithen's mind, 'Is this nail or screw, sir?' pointing at a metal spot hidden in the fur on the back of a toy monkey he could lay hands on, Jithen asked.

'Screw,' the boss said, missing the joke. Knocking against the spiralling word, arecanut grits sprayed farther.

As he lay in the room in the lodge that night, with the realization that the basic pitch of the cicadas in Thachanakkara and the land of the Zamorin was the same, Jithen had an epiphany. The snippet of the sloka from the Bhagawad Gita, which was crawling like a worm in the daytime, was now growing wings and soaring. A flash of thought, which could neither be transcribed into the letters meant for Ann Marie or his mother, nor expatiated on intrinsically, as, for thousands of years, it was lying unsaid. Even in the last few centuries, when reading and writing had become popular, no one had verbalized it. There were debates and discourses on what was written and spoken, all the time and at all places. There was constructive criticism and destructive criticism on creativity. Studies and tributes on books containing original thought happened at least a thousand-fold. However, only one thing remained. And it was that which was blooming in all its fragrance within Jithen that night.

It was an idea fundamentally against the Bhagawad Gita. Jithen imagined that the heart of the book he would write would be this. To coin a single phrase to connote the concept, which needed more time and energy to ponder over its ramifications, Jithen chose 'Creation-Song', or 'Creation-Geetha', to avoid over-complexity.

In that hot and humid March night, after crawling into the newly put up mosquito net and sitting in the lotus position under the creaking ceiling fan, with the unbridled enthusiasm of his twenty-seven years, Jithen started to write down in his old, hardcover diary the concept that had only started toddling, along with directions for amending and developing it further later. What would have been recreated in his own inimitable flowing, poetic style in the novel, which he never got to write, would remain in its skeletal form in the diary, like this:

> We have discussed Arjuna's dilemma over a thousand times. Sitting in our pooja rooms, we read about Lord Krishna advising a perplexed man, in the battlefield of a war that both sides considered righteous, that it is not a sin for the warrior to extinguish the lives of those arrayed against him, without having to ponder over their souls, which man can neither create nor destroy. Thus, we conveniently overlooked that in its narrowest sense at least, the Bhagawad Gita is a Song of Annihilation too. The quintessence of the Bhagawad Gita was the contrivance of converting one who turned away from violence, into a killer. Through thousands of years, riding on hundreds of interpretations, it became the fundamental testimony of a country, of a civilization. Both the guilty and the innocent equally lay his or her hand upon this Song of Annihilation, to take an oath in the courts that whatever he or she was going to say was only the truth. The case was not different with followers of other religions. Solely due to the reason that they were God-given, all the holy books were full of pronouncements and deeds against humanity. Thus, the insistence that man was the son of God remained, for thousands of years, contradictory. Considering that it was a strange power of creativity than intelligence, which was the factor behind elevating man as the only legitimate son of God from among the other creatures, which should be the moment of dilemma that should sadden man the most? The angst of the man who is unable to create should be more than the regret of the lone man about killing, as he stands between

> two groups facing each other, ready to battle, within the rule of nature of killing to eat. That would present a deeper and more intense authentic dilemma—than Arjuna's. When an individual or a language or a culture stands lost, unable to give rise to any great creation; when a new generation passes through a period of mindless celebration and empty cores; when the modern-day Arjunans sit helpless, unable to undertake any original work in lines, colour, words, or music; we need a new song which will lay a hand on the shoulder to energize and exhort, to wake and create, rather than kill and win. A human song promoting creativity instead of all the belligerent and violent Bhagawad Gitas. A Creation Geetha, which can distil and preserve all the creative essences of the evanescent human life.

Jithen spent his first Sunday after joining duty in the lodge itself. After writing a letter each to his mother and Ann Marie, he went out and breakfasted on dosas and tea. From the kiosk nearby, he bought a *Mathrubhumi* weekly and a movie magazine with a voluptuous south Indian actress on its cover. In the weekly, which lay unopened during the whole day, Jithen discovered accidentally in the night, a short story written by someone from Thachanakkara. He remembered Sofia Begum after a long time. He remembered her pointing out, while sitting in the Thachanakkara library, the young man from her college who used to write short stories. Jithen had no news about that young man's life thereafter, even hearsay. Hoping to discover something about it, he read the story with interest. Unfortunately, the story gave no indication about the provenance or life of the author. It was a story about a famous painting of a renowned foreign painter. Jithen remembered reading a story by the young man in this same weekly, around the same time he was pointed out by Sofia Begum—it was about an earthquake somewhere in north India. Jithen felt an uncontrolled contempt for the newbie writer who could not dig up raw material for a story in Thachanakkara or even in Kerala. He lay with his eyes shut for some time, after closing the weekly. Then, rising, he made an entry in the diary using the word 'mean', and then having a rethink, he tore off the page. When he got up the next morning, he tore open the envelope containing the letter for Ann Marie, and added a few sentences. That was a note of confession. For many years, informing Ann Marie of such atonements was a habit. However, in the added lines he had made a change on purpose—he wrote that he had described one of his colleagues as a meanie, and not that he had done that with the short-story writer.

After amending the date from seventeenth March to eighteenth March, he put the letter in a new envelope. It was the first letter he wrote to Ann Marie after getting the job. The first among the forty letters she had saved for her lifetime.

NINE

Abandonment

12 November 1999

...I am abandoning my attempts to write the book for two or three reasons. The first reason is the realization that a dreamer like me is incapable of narrating the story of the Ayyaattumpilli family and at the same time recording the sentimental history of Malayalis of over a century. If I am not able to bring in this one book, as per my dream, all the dualities existing on this earth—between man and woman; upper caste and lower caste; capitalist and worker; haves and have-nots; man and God; common man and creative mind; child and adult—and their connected emotions, it would be better if I don't attempt it.

Now even if I accomplish such a strenuous task, the trepidation whether it would be appreciated as much as it deserves, is one of the other main reasons standing in the way of the book being written. Like mosquitoes in a latrine, I see around me a lot of people who have constricted thoughts. They may be seeing man as one who can produce only excreta. The mosquitoes in latrines can define man as only one who wanders around everywhere, eats whatever is available, produces faeces and collects it in concrete receptacles. They merely need his blood. But they still consider it their bounden duty to evaluate him, though they meet him just once a day. The naïve mosquitoes cannot comprehend that, when he gets out every day, pushing open the door, his day of incredibly varied experiences is just beginning. I am aware that butterflies are also present in this world, not just mosquitoes. But tell me, have you ever seen a butterfly among Malayalis, recently?

This letter is rather lengthy. I find it surprising that it was only after filling nine pages with my desultory daily activities that I thought of my novel. However, I shall close after writing the third reason for not writing the novel. I fear that the person, who ventures out on an arduous and intensively long creative effort as writing a novel after entering a life of domesticity, will only be a bad head of the family, a bad husband, and a bad father. An artist should be free of all such shackles—if he dreams of superior art. Do not reject it as the immature thoughts of a twenty-seven-year-old. If you try to prove me wrong, the loss is only going to be yours. Therefore, my girl, I am ready to sacrifice a great book only for loving you!

Dear one, please forgive me for the arrogance of sending this letter without striking out these words. Though rather sombre, please understand that this is nothing but a reflection of human dignity.

For the fish transported from the river to the glass bowl in the living room, its memories of the life spent in the river become a fable: a flowing story, written on water by someone for someone else. Now, with the feeling that it was not part of that story, it starts to enjoy the artificial security created in the still waters within the transparent bowl. It considers the rubber doll that sits nearby and spits out aerating bubbles, its relative. It feels proud without reflecting about the world view, which it never had but which it can now have by pressing against the glass of the bowl. It even develops a respect for the hand that throws down the feed at the appointed time. Thus, it slowly forgets its river.

A fish can do that; but a human being cannot.

As he sat in the glass case of his transplanted life and reminisced about Thachanakkara, he would get caught in the net of feeling that he was at both places simultaneously. He would start feeling that Thachanakkara was a book yet to be completed, or perhaps would never be completed, and that he was only one among the thousands of sub-characters in that book. Some had torn out the page on which he appeared and had kept it elsewhere. One letter of the page ponders over that big book with torn pages.

Jithen did not go to office that day because of asthma set off by such thoughts.

When he went to Thachanakkara for the first vacation after getting the job, during Vishu, he presented a walking stick to Govindan Master. His mother had indicated in her letter that it was his seventieth birthday. Jithen remembered the green ebony persimmon walking stick his grandfather had hacked out for himself to support the stoop brought on by age. He realized with a shock that, nowadays, there were no people in Thachanakkara who stooped as they aged. It was not just in Thachanakkara; old age had wiped off its stoop the world over. Jithen had thought that stooping with age was the body bowing before mighty Time, when the body leaves its posturing after all the joyous dancing with life's passions were over, recognizing the decay setting in. As time went on, the wisdom of that realization got attenuated. However, Govindan Master, who had completed seventy years, was missing among the old men of the new generation who dyed their hair and who, even with broken spines, leaned their body backwards without stooping.

Happily accepting the walking stick presented by Jithen, Govindan Master said, 'The proverbial third leg, no?'

Narayanan's daughter came and inspected the walking stick of her grandfather. She called out to her mother inside the house.

Radha, who had greyed at forty, came with a knife and took the stick in her hand; as if he was still the child who used to hang on to her hand, she asked Jithen, 'You have brought this for the lame me, haven't you?'

Uncle Govindan walked without the walking stick by the side of Jithen for some distance along the plot where the debris of the burst crackers of Vishu were scattered. 'Have you decided?' Uncle Govindan asked.

'Yes,' he said. 'It's been six years since it has been decided.'

'Did you tell Chinnamma and Shankaran?'

'Mother said she won't be let into these premises.'

'The same sentence which my father said! What about Shankaran?'

'Fortunately, father is still a communist.'

'Umm,' Govindan Master said after sighing deeply. 'Find a house for rent near your place of work. Then take her there. What is the name of the girl?'

'Ann Marie.'

'Convey to her the love of an old revolutionary. Love her till you die. There is no better walking stick than a heart full of love.' he bowed down and picked up a fired flowerpot cracker which was lying steeped in the soil. He blew the soil off the flowerpot cracker, which had illuminated the darkness of the previous night, and handed it to Jithen, saying, 'Remember always, life is only this much!'

Carrying the corpse of that half-burnt cracker, Jithen stood alone for a while there.

After the first rainy season, in which the sewage water had come into the house, Jithendran married and brought Ann Marie to the rented house in the land of the Zamorin. Four months had passed after shifting from the musty lodge room to the rented house.

Jithen had got on rent, the half portion of a tiled house owned by a disease-ridden, moaning old man and his second wife, who had been abandoned by their children. The younger sister of his dead first wife was the second wife of the old man. It was her second marriage too. The old man, isolated by the death of his wife and the disowning by his five children, had taken her up, who had been alone for forty years after being prematurely widowed. His was a special case of misfortune. In the first few days of their cohabitation itself, the old man realized the fact that she was closer to the ever-open doors of death than he himself. The honeymoon had turned to embers even before it had started. He spent the rest of his life pottering around taking care of the moaning, bedridden wife. When his meagre pension was not enough for the household expenses and medicines, the rent paid by Jithen came to his aid. On either side of the separating wall under the age-blackened tiles covered by ripe-yellow and dried mango leaves, two types of honeymoon from the opposing poles of life were being staged.

After midnight, when Ann Marie would stifle her sexual cooing, which she thought was excessive, by covering her mouth with her hands, Jithen would forcibly remove them.

'Don't worry,' he would say panting, 'she's moaning louder than you!'

That was true. As taught to him by a crack in the window at Thachanakkara when he was fourteen, the moans of sex and death were surprisingly similar. Jithendran also saw them competing often with each other under the same roof.

The new bride of Jithendran was one with the mien and heart of God. That made his life complicated and liveable at the same time. Ann Marie came with a simplicity which allowed her to survive with one dress and with the magical powers of feeding hunger and quenching thirst with only water. That was the greatest dowry someone like Jithendran could receive. The meagre stipend during his training period, created a tinny, ringing sound like that of coins given in alms in the emaciated piggybank of their honeymoon. However, she melted those boulder-heavy feelings of inferiority in his heart with mere smiles. After sleeping with Jithendran, who could not afford an alarm clock, she would get up at exactly five o'clock in the morning. When arising from the bed, she had neither rheum in her eyes nor signs of dried drool, which could be seen even in the faces of angels. She would kiss the trumpet-like ears of the sleeping Jithen—who lay like an aborigine run over by a truck after the previous night's wild lovemaking—and then begin her daily chores, which would stretch till eleven in the night. Deaf to Jithen's pointed remarks, dumb to the extent of making no complaints, and suffering him with the patience of God, she managed the household work. Till she signed on the wedding register, she thought that she was waiting for six years under the sentence written by someone unknown on the blackboard of the Chemistry classroom at the UC College. She was offering herself to a man who was more tortured than Christ, after she had been offered by her father to the Church. She had survived undeterred for six years, within walls at Angamaly made of conservatism, amidst clenched teeth and tears, for a life with Jithen. More than her love for Jithendran, there was something that was pulling her towards him: the anxiety that he would be orphaned without her. The belief she could transform his life from something insipid like water, to one spirited like wine, bubbled within her all those years. Till the mature intervention of her brother, Joshi, who had been anointed as a priest by then, won a grudging permission from her father for plighting her troth with Jithendran, she carried that relationship like a crown of thorns upon her soul. The three hundred and fifty-six letters sent in Joshi's name to the seminary, were brought by him eight to ten at a time when coming home, and Marie Ann used to read them in secret and burn them. However, the forty letters sent to her home address in the ten months after Jithendran's meeting with her father, she kept securely with her degree certificates. When all her certificates got wet and were destroyed in the sewage water, which invaded their rented house, she managed to salvage completely the forty letters and summarized notes of Jithendran's novel. Along with Jithendran, who had given up completely on the novel, suspecting his capability for writing, she had to spend her life bearing those letters like seeds, which could be sowed sometime—first, through the first few months of marriage in straitened circumstances and then through the two-and-a-half decades with material wealth.

During the initial months, Jithendran often wished that she would quarrel with him on some pretext. Like all husbands who surrendered to guilt, he too tried his best to find some fault in his wife during the honeymoon period. Naraapilla's blood coursing through his veins made him suspect every iota of goodness in her. Quite needlessly, he compared her to his mother. Chinnamma of Ayyaattumpilli was one capable of raising hell singlehandedly, and put the Pandemonium to shame. Though his desire for peace was the reason for him to accept a job so far away and offered an uncertain training period and a paltry stipend amount, he found the peace that he now had quite unbearable. His tendency to shout in a manner surpassing his own mother surprised him. He used despicable words when the tea went cold because of his forgetfulness, after he had sipped the first mouthful hot and had left it: 'Oblation to the manes,' after spitting out words foreign to her, he trembled. 'Were you carried here on your bier to give me this cold tea?'

He slipped into greater self-loathing seeing his own desperate attempts to give the impression to his mate that he was undergoing sufficient mental torture and abuse to commit suicide.

However, his attitude was not a complete put-on. The crux of his problems was in his inability to countenance that life would end with death. He was a soul capable of manifesting creativity above average. His aptitude for singing, which filled his bathrooms once in a while, was enough for him to win plaudits as well as the respect of a town. If the plots and concepts that he had imagined could be turned into a short story or a poem, he would be treated on par with any renowned litterateur. There were times when he indulged in self-congratulation, feeling that Michelangelo himself would have shaken hands with him if the sculptures he had dreamed up could be realized. He was sure that at least on some occasions, he did think that contemporary artists were worthless, not only because he was a cynical Malayali. He always made it a point to look down upon speakers, with a disdain they deserved, for having made a name for themselves as great orators merely by repeating the same thing over and over again. In short, he was getting despondent bearing collectively, all by himself, the many doubts which many young men, in many places, were undergoing in myriad ways. Jithendran used to pine for creating something by which he would be remembered in this world after his death and not for the reason of producing offspring alone; but smothered by a dark lethargy, which covered his times like the dark clouds of Karkkadakam and unable to follow his heart's desire, he grew flustered. Though dejected by the people reproducing like mosquitoes in the new age, which was a pool of sewage water, and consequently deciding that he would remain childless, he still indulged in sex without remission. The number of used condoms he used to throw into the dilapidated toilet of his old house bore witness to this. Those exertions were born of a tragedy of not being able to recognize his extraordinary powers to create something new. His sexuality was merely the physical reinterpretation of his intense creativity. He was surprised by his unbecoming behaviour that he passed off as dictated by the circumstances, after he had reached the earth as a guest, invited to partake of celebrations of the body. He wished strongly to flee from the desire to create something during his lifetime which would survive his death. He tried to take refuge in the belief that time for all creativity had ended and such attempts were futile. He started feeling that, in the book that he was trying to create in the form of a novel, every line written about the new era was like something which had been translated inelegantly from another language and given to him. He feared thinking of the preparations that he had to do for writing about Naraapilla of Ayyaattumpilli, his life and times, and about Thachanakkara. The names of the huge trees in the lands of Ayyaattumpilli, the birds which sat and sang on them, the flowers which bloomed at its fences, all had disappeared from his mind. The couplet which his great-grandfather had created and his grandfather had recited to him as a mnemonic for names of the seven mountains, which had created Periyar river from their sweat, had also been forgotten by Jithendran for times to come.

Thachanakkara was not just a place, it was an era too. When one looks back into the past, the magic of place and time fusing together happens. When they both get blended and solidify, pictures that become like conservative memories, get painted. They can be renovated repeatedly by adding colour; but they cannot be repainted. Naraapilla cannot be found in them as an old man sitting in front of the TV, holding the remote. Kunjuamma cannot be painted in it as an old angel, floating down the escalator in a shopping mall, along with children and grandchildren, holding plastic shopping bags. None of the moveable or immovable items of the new era, can be seen even as a shadow on the wall where they have been drawn. Can it be said, because of that, their lives were pointless? Jithen asked himself: can it be said that they were undeserving of becoming characters in the great book of human life? Can a child who receives a rubber monkey doll, which plays the drums, be said to be superior to the one who creates his own toy using immature coconuts and spines of the coconut leaf?

Jithendran felt the memories assailing him, much like the peacock being struck by lightning from the dark clouds, seeing which it had been dancing in ecstasy. He, who had many years ago given up writing definitions of the people in his acquaintance circle, wrote now in his diary:

I am a peacock dancing with burning feathers, struck by lightning from dense clouds. But in the forest without an audience, this fire dance is futile.

TEN

Zenith

1 January 2000

...This may perhaps be the last letter I will be sending you. Do not fear. Next week, as soon as our wedding is over, I shall be bringing you to this rented house of ours. Then, till one of us dies, like one of the compounded consonants of Malayalam, our souls are going to be in a knot which cannot be untied. The two separate 'me, me' feelings are going to be one. Shall I tell you which is that compounded consonant?

'Mma'!

To throw light upon two lives coming together, God, who has planted this compounded consonant, whether in amma which is the vernacular for mother, or in umma which is the vernacular for kiss?

Girl, my new year greetings to you! Greetings for the new century! Greetings for the new millennium! Standing on the corpse of the times past; conveying my aadaraanjalikal—respectful condolences.

Oh, let me also write about this interesting thing, lest I forget it later: aadaraanjali literally means joining of hands respectfully in front of someone. The joke is that you can do that to any living person. But for Malayalis, that word connotes death—we always see a corpse beyond the word aadaraanjali. It has come to this that the Malayali will join his hands respectfully only in front of a dead man! Ann Marie, if I am the one to go first, you should tell the world without fail: Do not come with your aadaraanjali now and wound this soul!

My darling, my condolences to you for sincerely loving a man of straw! My aadaraanjali once again for those who died living, lived dying, and are yet to be born and die, in this wondrously strange world!

I am locking up all these scattered papers of mine, so that they do not hamper our honeymoon. I also feel, perhaps I may never open them again. Last night, when the whole world was celebrating, I was penning the last lines in them, hurting both my body and heart. Thinking perhaps they may hurt you, contrary to the usual practice, I am not sending these to you. Later, if you are able to dig it out of my papers, you can read that. No, you need not keep these in your memory. Please delete from your memory all this information about the book, which I will never be able to write.

The day Jithen's boss came to know that a group of representatives from an American company was coming to take over the toy factory of the drumming monkeys, he declared he was resigning. Three days later, in the farewell party organized by the staff of the office and the workers of the factory, he seemed to be very emotional. He chewed the betel leaves adding more tobacco that day; he applied more lime on the betel leaves. As he sat on the stage listening to phoney encomiums, he stuffed more and more tender betel leaves into his mouth. In his return speech, which sprayed betel juice on to the microphone, he was on the verge of tears. He took all of thirty minutes to describe how he indigenized a foreign toy and the changes he made to it. He informed the audience with a sad smile and stutter, caused by emotion, that he foresaw that the toy would undergo changes, though the American party had assured him that when the factory was taken over, the workers would be retained. He said, 'Times are changing.' And then lowering his voice dramatically added, 'For people like me, this would be unbearable!'

The expensive silk-saree clad, middle-aged lady sitting in the front row of the audience, dabbed her eyes, making sure that her makeup was not smudged. The sparkle of her diamond necklace was reflected on the glasses of her husband speaking on the stage. She looked with pride at her husband, who was relinquishing his post at the age of fifty-six, even when four years of service remained. When the boss declared that a life of ease would be alien to him, and he would start writing a book on the ordeals by fire he faced in his job and his achievements, the entire audience, except Jithen, clapped. When he declared that it was his unshakeable faith in God that brought him to where he was and the primary lesson he learnt from life was that good people would always receive God's help, his wife looked up at the ceiling of the hall and lifted her two hands holding the tasselled vanity bag as a mark of devotion. In the opinion of the boss, the hardest test he had to face was six months ago, the day the year two thousand started, in the form of the Y2K imbroglio that was feared to affect their computer systems. Fearing that if the computer systems were to shut down, the company's productivity and quality would go for a toss, he could only take refuge in God. There God came to his rescue and saved him and the company from the Y2K problem, about which the whole world was quaking in fear.

The boss went on with his speech. The heat in the hall was unbearable. The workers sat listening to the speech of the outgoing boss, fanning themselves with the thick notice distributed specially for the farewell meeting, and sighing deeply. To suppress asthma, which was threatening to break out, Jithen took out an Asthalin tablet and swallowed it with the aid of his saliva. That assuaged his lungs and anaesthetized his brain. Though he started to slip off into sleep twice, he hung on for some more time, feeling the eyes of the speaker on him all the while. But the third time, he lost control. He fell asleep, with his mouth open and head resting on his left collarbone. The insincere bombast assailing his ears gradually faded away. In its place arose, a parade of venerated Malayalis, their heads held high and eyes gleaming with self-respect, about whom he had read in the hundreds of books borrowed from the Thachanakkara library. Some of their faces were not familiar to Jithen; and where faces were familiar, he could not recollect their names in the other world of dreams.

The sage, who came holding Shree Narayana Guru with one hand and Dr Palpu with the other, asked, 'Do you know me? This is my guru and my father.'

Smiling kindly at Jithen, who stood ashamed at not being able to recall his name, he said, 'Do not worry. Consider it a matter of pride, your inability to recall.'

A tall man came with his body, which had turned blue from poison and asked, 'Don't you know me? Don't you have any recollection of this man from Thiruvananthapuram, who died from Adolf Hitler's poison?'

'One Mr Pillai?' Jithendran hazarded a guess.

As he moved on, the man said laughing, 'You got only the caste right, didn't you?'

They were coming, one after the other. Unable to make out the mother, as tall as a tree, who was walking away with Captain Lakshmi and Mrinalini Sarabhai on either hip as if they were babies, Jithen scratched his head raw. After that, a radiant person came, whom he had not seen before and asked, with the intonation of a quiz master, 'I astonished Karthika Thirunal Maharaja with a sloka I composed when I was fourteen years old. Who am I?'

Seeing that there was no answer forthcoming, he hummed a famous lullaby as if it were a clue and smiled.

'Irayimman...?' Jithendran hit the wall.

'...Thampi!' he completed his name, and walking forward, patted Jithendran's back. 'Any child can remember lullabies.'

They went past like a procession. When the last man had disappeared, the applause started and continued for a long time.

After sometime the applause stopped. Jithendran woke up from his sleep, alone inside the hall.

Before the first thunder of the monsoon season, as if in preparation, Ann Marie started to arrange the limited items in the rented house, according to category. She had been warned about the sewage water, which would come in from the gutter during heavy rains. From the books lying scattered underneath the cot and in the corners of the room, she selected the better ones and stacked them on the table, close to the wall. The rest of them were bundled into a bed sheet and put on a termite-eaten teapoy, which had been lying from the beginning in a corner of the room. In the only almirah, she kept all their clothes and in the space which remained, she kept two or three glass bowls and music cassettes, which were deemed to have served their purpose. Then she kept an album on top of it, from which people, who had been imprisoned in the stillness of a square, were dissolving themselves into emptiness.

Jithendran had taken away his degree certificates and testimonials of his extra-curricular activities in the morning to show to the people who were taking over the company. He was very disturbed after he had returned from Thachanakkara the previous day, where he had gone alone. After informing her of his mother's decision to sell Geethalayam and the land adjacent to that, he told her, 'As per current valuation, I will get at least two million rupees as my share. Damn, what will we do with all that money?'

Jithendran had heard of the possibility of him being appointed as the new boss of the factory. If that would happen, he could leave this foxhole and take Ann Marie to an apartment with full amenities in the city; he would be able to buy all the appliances he needed and drive his own car; he would be able to buy a mobile phone and an internet-enabled computer. If so, he would be able to easily forget the far-away Thachanakkara and the Ayyaattumpilli blood.

'If so,' he said in the morning, 'in the eyes of others we will be able to lead a decent life! To damnation!' The bitterness that showed up in his face as he said this, was something which would stay with Ann Marie all her life, to be regurgitated from time to time.

After stacking up everything, when she saw some space in the bottom shelf of the almirah, she suddenly remembered her suitcase kept under the cot. She had kept the forty letters in the hide-coloured suitcase which her brother, Joshi, had given her. During the first few days of her life in that rented house, she had moved Jithendran's incomplete notes on the novel and his diary into the suitcase. But now she had to give them a safer place. She had vowed to herself that if the water from the gutter came in, whatever else may be affected, she would save these letters and notes at any cost. She was ruled more by the guilt of having had to burn, fearing her father, the three hundred and fifty-six letters which she received from him before the forty, than by the loathing Jithen felt towards his creations.

She dragged the suitcase out and took out the letters, the diary with its torn cover, and the bundled-up notes. Even the oldest letter would be less than two years old. Suddenly, from amidst the notes, she saw a sheet of folded paper, written in red ink. She was seeing it for the first time. It was a small note, written with letters as broad as fingertips. Ann Marie was shocked when she realized that the writing, which was turning brown from red, was in dried blood. She read from the paper, which sat trembling in her shaking hands:

I always shuddered at the thought of the moment when God would send me that question. 'Show me proof,' he would ask ruthlessly, 'proof of a light you have lit for the coming generations, in the hundreds of thousands of hours you have spent in the world for the pleasures of your mind and body.'

I will stand with my head bowed. A feeling of inferiority at least sixteen times more than I had when I was alive would start to consume me. Then I would not have the strength to go again through those few moments when my heart also throbbed like a full moon while still on this earth.

I ate, drank, fornicated, lived, died. Like the louse in the hair and the lion in the jungle. Like a thousand creatures in between them. But as a man, what did I do to outlive death? No, I won't have an answer. My backpack will be empty; my heart too.

'Nothing, my lord,' I will say. Then I will add a sentence which apparently has no pertinence to the question: 'There is nothing heavier on earth or in hell than an empty heart!'

Ann Marie heard the rain coming down in torrents, smashing its head against the roof tiles. She put all the papers in a yellow plastic cover and then into a bigger white plastic bag. After some thought, she swathed it in her wedding saree, which she took out of her suitcase. When she was keeping the bundle in the almirah, she shut her eyes and pursed her lips, as if she were dropping money into the donation box in churches and temples.

The wooden almirah stood in front of her like a wooden ship preparing to ride the flood of sewage water.

He came in the night to give audience to Jithen from the unknown—the large, unused plot of land lying across the alley in front of their house. A fox whose face had become elongated from howling.

During the initial months of their honeymoon, because Ann Marie's judgment of the quantity of food to be made for the two of them slipped up and they had no refrigerator to store excess food, Jithen had to throw the leftover food into the thickets in the empty plot: leftover rice and curries, which would be spoilt by the next day, as a travel snack for the unknown movers of the night. When Jithen would throw the packet into the thicket of colocasia plants—standing with their wide water-repellent leaves as if seeking alms, in the front of the swampy portion of the plot, which Ann Marie had christened as Colocasia Field—he would hear sounds of biting and snapping, sending the leaves into shivers. Those territorial cries of creatures with animal bodies were a declaration of their presence, which would not reveal if it was a battle to satiate their hunger or the exertions of sharing. During a break at ten o'clock in the night in the first rain of June, when Jithen went with the leftovers, one of them stepped out fearlessly from the colocasia-covered swamp. He mistook it for a dog first, looking at the silhouette, but when it came within the oblong area of light from the open door of the house, it was clear it was a fox—the vocalist who provided the background music of howls during their condom-clad, late-night copulations.

In the first meeting, they stood still on either side of the alleyway. Then Jithen turned back holding the packet of leftovers, and brought Ann Marie there. She was enthusiastic to see a live fox, as foxes had become practically non-existent in Thachanakkara and Angamaly. Abandoning the dishes she was washing, Ann Marie went silently with her husband up to the alleyway. In the square of light, which came through the door of the house, four foxes could be seen waiting for them on the other side, as if under a spotlight on stage. With their tails tucked between their legs, pointed ears held up, heads lowered till the ground and eyes looking up, a family of foxes.

Standing on either side of the alley, the meeting of two different types of families was staged. In the cool breeze, the colocasia field was making waves in the night. A thousand cicadas, unable to determine whether it was from within or without, were making the night noisy. After standing still for some time looking at the human couple, the male fox started his howl, which the vixen and their children took up faithfully. Hearing that, standing in the darkness, Ann Marie smiled widely like the Dutchman's Pipe flower.

Reaching up to her husband's ear, she whispered, 'Do you know what he was telling his wife and kids, pointing at you? There, behold a strange animal with a moustache. A mighty one who sleeps wearing a cover, to prevent procreation!'

When the fox family cut their concert and walked back into the thickets, Jithendran returned with Ann Marie to the house, after throwing the leftovers packet in the direction of the retreating foxes.

Jithendran lay without sleeping, his mind caught in something other than the poltergeist-like rain. Fearing the water from the gutter, every now and then, he kept feeling the floor with his hand in the dark. Ann Marie was sleeping with her head resting against his armpit.

The foxes forgot to howl that sexless night.

Twenty-seven nights went by in that fashion, repeating themselves. In the days between those nights, Jithendran's future had been set.

To get into a consensus with the new life, Jithendran had to make only very little effort. When suggestions were sought for new ideas to take the company beyond the drummer monkeys, suppressing some of the spontaneous, irreverent thoughts, which sprang up in his mind, he shifted to English to don a mask of seriousness, and shook them out one by one—he began with the introductory statement that evolution from the monkeys is essential in the case of toys too; and since transactional power in money is in the hands of adults, the company should develop toys which would attract this segment as well. The company should concentrate on the miniature figurines of the geniuses, who were dead and gone. The company should take upon itself the onus of providing each head of the family with such life-like miniature dolls that would cater to his interest. For instance, if a person is interested in sopaanasangeetham, the company should be able to provide miniatures of one of its practitioners, standing and singing with an idakka. A scale model of idakka, hung with sixty-four woolly testicles, will hang from his shoulder. The song will flow out of the open mouth of the plastic miniature, which should be drumming on the idakka. Not just accomplished singers, but Kathakali artistes, danseuses, film actors, even litterateurs can be made as the new-age toys for adults. Jithendran made his point by thumping on the desk that he was sure that these dolls, which could be priced high, would take their place in the living rooms of modern homes if they were marketed as invaluable offerings to those householders who have not had the opportunity to meet such geniuses face-to-face or appreciate their art and craft adequately. If the list of venerable Malayalis were to be exhausted, then the company could do a national and international selection to create miniatures of dead geniuses.

When Jithen's sham enthusiasm had scaled those heights, one of the white men sitting across from him got up, shook his hand and offered him a salary that was double of what he had expected, and invited him to take up the responsibility of leading the company from the next day itself.

After he had assumed the new post, twenty-seven days were being completed on that day. After making all the arrangements to move to the new apartment next morning, they were preparing to spend their last night in the rented house. The rain had been coming down heavily from the late evening onwards, with enough ferocity to drown the moans of the old, sickly lady on the other side of the house.

Around midnight, Jithendran woke up from a nightmare with a start. He saw the solar system shrunken into a small basket with the planets stacked crushingly in it like tomatoes. One of them, blue as if poisoned, was crawling with human worms. Suddenly a sinewy hand with white nails appeared and took it out and threw it into a gutter called the Milky Way. Realizing that one of the worms, which went flying out of it, was he himself, he opened his eyes, with a hollow feeling inside him. Hearing his heavy breathing over the sound of rain, Ann Marie also woke up.

Jithendran felt the floor with his right leg. His guess was correct. For the first time after their honeymoon had started, the water from the gutter was making its presence felt. He heard its wavelets even above the racket the rain was making on the tiles. Ann Marie had told him the day before how the hundreds of used condoms he had ejected into the toilet during his many months of stay in the rented house had blocked the toilet. He could guess that if the water from the gutter would continue to enter the house, the filthy pool it would create would contain his own excreta, flowing back from the toilet.

Before his foot could get more wet, he pulled up his leg. The couplet which his grandfather had taught him about the Periyar river, which flowed irrigating the faraway Thachanakkara, came to his mind. But he could not recall entirely the seven mountains which nurtured Periyar, mentioned in the couplet. He failed to recollect the name of the washerwoman with the beetle on her cheek, who used to wash clothes in Punneli kadavu for many decades. The names of the engineers mentioned on the plaque on the Marthaanda Varma Bridge, beneath the etching of the silver-edged conch, would not manifest themselves, however hard he tried. Neither could he recollect any of the stories, which he had heard so many times, about a teacher and his family who were tenants in the Ayyaattumpilli house. Imagining thousands of such details fleeing from the book he wished to write, he sat on the bed, panting and holding the hair on his chest. A primal lust to implant on the earth some sign of his existence, to extend his legitimacy beyond death, filled him. He undressed himself in a hurry and subjected his wife, who woke up from her sleep, to his will. It was their first act of copulation after marriage without prophylactics. Ann Marie's eyes shining in wonderment of the experience could be seen even in the darkness by Jithen. A drop of water making its presence felt on his head made Jithen look up. Seeing a stream of water falling towards his head through a crack in the tile caused by its trembling in the thunder, he caught the water in his mouth, by stretching his neck back. It was the beginning of a mediocrity which would extend interminably till his death. He felt that his body was a torture chamber of clay with his soul enclosed in it, and suspended high over a thoroughfare. He felt an acute thirst amidst the torrential rain. Even in middle of his sexual thrusts, he stuck his tongue out and drank the water falling off his head. The thirst-driven Jithendran drank through his eyes, nose and mouth. Mixed in his centuries-old blood, a survival instinct was manifesting itself, uncapped. His excitement heightened. At the point of climaxing, more than at the seeds of life gushing from inside him, he snapped open-throated in the Ayyaattumpilli manner at death, which had been squatting inside him for twenty-eight years, staring at his soul, 'Ppho!'

That sound, which emanated as if from a soul being torn asunder, was the mid-point of a life which went on for fifty-four years. That snap which was against a measly existence, was the mid-point of two centuries and two millennia.

Epilogue

Dawn was breaking.

Ann Marie had spent the night reading and rereading the words written twenty-six years ago, without bothering about their chronological order. She felt all the tiredness of travelling the distance of about a quarter century within a single night. Sitting amidst a bunch of old papers and a diary, she yawned, relaxed her back, and stretched her legs on the dark green bedsheet. She heard the joints of her fifty-year-old toes crack. As she saw the light of dawn seeping in without permission through the windows she had forgotten to close the previous night, she turned to the side, stretched out her hand, and switched off the light. The sight of the light at the top edge of the toilet door, like a straight line, made by a chalk, created the feeling that her husband was, as usual in the morning, standing inside and peeing, sleepy-headed.

Saddened, she switched off that light too.

Ann Marie started to arrange the letters lying on the bed. In each of them, comprising five to six pages, closely written on both sides, she had underlined certain portions with black ink. The lines she had left unmarked were those she could not understand fully or appreciate as a young woman: in some, five or six lines; in some, two or three consecutive paragraphs. Suddenly, an illusion of the book, which her husband had wanted to write flashed within her eyelids, intoxicated by the heady feeling the letters had stirred in her. She had hallucinations of the sentences which she had underlined, along with the dates and in the chronological order, being printed as the opening lines of each of the chapters of the book. She saw, as if in a flash, in the last chapter of that mythical novel a passage which had been written with blood from his right index finger and now was seen as a note in a brownish, almost black colour in one of the letters. Her head was reeling from the sensation of all the descriptions of the happenings in his village and the histories of his forbearers—which he had written in the hundreds of letters she had read and burnt fearing her father, during her six-year-long wait—crowding into the book. Though they were in the vernacular, she could not read the thoughts and emotions replete in them. In the white pages, being flipped as if by a breeze, she could clearly see words like Kerala, Thachanakkara, Perumthachchan, Periyar and such standing out. And religion, Narayana Guru, caste, Gandhiji, Christian, communist, house, temple, pond, sea, siblings, shit ... And in between all those words, singular thoughts and a wonderful amalgam of memories, which were simple and complex at the same time, like cave paintings.

Ann Marie stretched her hand to touch the book. When the palm her face was resting on between the two pillows on her lap slipped off her chin, she was startled awake. Segregating the letters and the loose papers, she secured them with rubber bands and left them on the bed. Keeping the diary, which showed signs of the wear-and-tear of twenty-five years, by the side of the heap of papers, she headed for the bathroom. Wearing a sandal-coloured nightgown, with the confusion of a moth still circling a flower despite dawn breaking, she walked barefoot over the new cool and slippery floor tiles. Her movements were affected more by the previous night's sleeplessness than by incipient old age. Since she still felt that she was travelling trapped inside a yet-to-be written book, she used a finger, wetted with her spittle, to open the door of the bathroom, as if it was a sticky page which refused to turn. She recognized her silliness, and with a self-deprecating laugh entered the bathroom.

The void created in the world by the death of fifty-four-year-old Jithendran last September was, at the most, only as big as the air trapped inside this flat, which was lying unused. Beyond that, the void had nothing special to do with the twenty-seven other apartments in the building, or in the many apartment buildings which had filled Thachanakkara, or in between them the bungalows that stood proudly, rubbing their midriffs with their neighbours. The heads of the houses of each of them were trying to get ahead, competing with one another, leading lives that could not be very different from the life which Jithendran had set off on in his twenty-eighth year, a quarter century ago. The same life that Jithen had lived peacefully in another part of the world for the last twenty-five years: gossip, bragging; being judgmental; cursing society without reflecting on oneself; denigrating one's own mother while singing praises of mother goddesses; an unjustifiable estimation of one's own children and abhorrence of others' children; friendship with neighbours with the smiling incisors hiding the grinding molars behind; the schadenfreude of seeing respected people in society being maligned in the press; the inability to compliment another person to his face; declamations that all societal values had been undermined, in order to hide the guilt of one's own goodness drying up inside; with aging, despite the lack of faith, stumbling in devotion confined solely to the gods of one's own religion; the insistence that only another man's sexuality is pornography; the despondency from the feeling that one is deserving of greater things than what has come by; and above all this, a scorn nurtured inside for every soul outside the ambit of one's own four-member family...

In his fifty-fourth year, impelled by an unexplained urge to be in the land of his birth, after leaving his job, when Jithendran moved to an apartment in Thachanakkara, he did not encounter any dissonance anywhere. When he saw the people around him live in the same manner that he did, with the same false prestige, marking time to an invisible drum with the same rhythm and duration, he did not find it unnatural. The new generation of Thachanakkara did not recognize him. The scattered few of the Ayyaattumpilli lineage who remained, need not have felt for Jithen anything more than a sympathy in the guise of a weak affection for one of them who had migrated to somewhere far away after marrying a Christian girl, many years ago. Standing on the balcony on the eighth floor of the apartment building, which now stood on the ground on which he used to play cricket and which now towered higher than any of the sixers hit then, Jithendran could see, beyond three or four more tall buildings that bore the banners of clothes put out for drying, the land on which the clutch of houses called Ayyaattumpilli once existed. Looking at the skyscraper coming up amidst dust and smoke raised by the groaning machinery on that arena where Naraapilla and his wife and their successors played out their grand drama of life and death with a flourish, he would sit on the balcony, sipping tea. The scene of a lame girl with a songbook in her hand, and a snotty-nosed, shorts-wearing boy hanging onto her skirt, walking through the grounds, would flash before his eyes on the screen put up by the dust. He would hear the sounds of many throats calling out his name with many intonations from the past, over the growl of the concrete mixer: Jithaa! Jithen! Daa Jitho! Their pitch would change depending on whether it was summer or the rainy season. On the dilapidated steps of Time with missing stones, Jithen would see the wails following each death in Ayyaattumpilli amalgamated in the atmosphere like the photos of a conflagration taken from many angles—still photos of the bellowing. The sadness would pile up within Jithen, like the one felt for the floodwaters that, once in a while, would start from the river, reach the floor of the house, exchange pleasantries with the children of Ayyaattumpilli, and then recede, which conversely made only the grown-ups happy. At that point, he would roll up his sails of memories and turn back. He would start imagining that the burqa-clad, middle-aged woman sitting in the back of the luxury limousine zipping along the widened roads to Elookkara and Kayintikkara was perhaps the girl who did not wear a veil and, once upon a time, went around collecting strange world facts for writing her novel. Unable to recollect her name, he would become flustered. Pity, he would tell himself. When she did not write that book, this is what she did: obliterate her memory from Time. When he saved himself from a book, this is also what he did.

At those times, he would feel nauseated by the thought that he was dangling, hung eight storeys high at a crossroad, and his grandchild's diaper, shoved inside his underwear, would become damper.

On such a Saturday when he decided to have alcohol instead of tea, afraid to sit in the balcony, he went in, towards Ann Marie.

'I have this strange feeling, Ann Marie,' he told his wife as he arrived in the kitchen to fetch the drink, not knowing that it was the last day of his life. 'Your Bible says that God made Man in his image.'

'My Bible?' she asked. 'When did it become my Bible alone? All right, tell me what you feel!'

'Oh, sorry!' he said. 'The matter is this: if God were to read it, he would be the one to laugh the hardest. Because, more than anyone else, God knows that man is not at all his son!'

'The man searching for the alcohol bottle in the kitchen certainly may not be the son of God,' Ann Marie said. 'But do you want to make such a judgment against all men? Is this the same man who went to war with his boss over the usage of "As creative as God himself!"?'

Jithendran seemed not to have heard that. He chose a bottle from the top of the shelf, with his eyes closed.

Even before he opened the bottle he was intoxicated as he was reminded of his youth and said, 'Ann Marie, man is the bastard child of the Devil! The mischief done by the Devil the day God was resting! When he hears that man has the features of God, the Devil must be laughing. Now the only thing for God to do is keep quiet: to avoid a household devastation that would be as destructive as a battle of planets!'

As he left bearing the glass, the bottle, and the cashew nuts, Ann Marie was overcome by the desire to write down that concept somewhere. The synopsis of the twenty-six years enveloped in darkness. She also heard her husband's curse from the living room, angrily shutting down the TV after checking the various channels.

She realized that her husband had started viewing every facet of human life darkly. He was a wick smouldering without oil. He was about to be extinguished.

It was ineluctable for people like that.

Hearing the calling bell, Ann Marie hurried to the living room. Since she had left her spectacles in the bathroom, she bumped her knee twice on the way. She ignored the calendar of the year two thousand and twenty-six scraping noisily against the wall and hastened to open the door. Suddenly, the calendar fell off its nail right in front of her. Without waiting to put it back, she looked through the peephole. She was shocked for a moment to see a middle-aged man resembling the person who had died last month, standing on the other side of the door. She rubbed her eyes and looked again.

When she realized that it was not her husband, she opened the door.

'May I come in?' asked the visitor, who was holding a book in his hand, in a voice that was not familiar. Ann Marie invited him in silently. Though he had come up to the seats, without sitting down, he offered the book in his hand to Ann Marie. 'I came to give you this,' he said, 'a novel in which you are also a character!'

For a moment her breathing stopped. Accepting the book with a trembling hand, she read its title:

A PREFACE TO MAN

When she opened the cover page, after flipping through four or five pages, she was stunned to see printed, within quotes, a passage she had underlined the night before in one of her husband's letters:

> If a human child, who is born fearless, independent, and above all, creative, ends up craven and bonded in sixty or seventy years, spending his creativity solely for procreation, and finally dies as a grown-up child in the guise of an old man, and if this is called human life, my beloved girl, I have nothing to be proud of in being born as a man.

She raised her head and looked at him in disbelief. Picking up the calendar from the floor and rolling it up, he said, 'I am from this place. Perhaps your deceased husband may have known me. For a long time, I have been writing this book for him. A long tale about your husband and his family history!'

'But…' she tried to say something. 'But…'

'I know.' He turned and looked back, located the nail from which the calendar had fallen off, and said, 'For the last twenty-five years you were away. But that doesn't matter.' He continued after hanging the calendar back on the nail. 'Those years are not in this book. I have left the space empty here for the readers to add their own lives and fill in the blanks.'

'But,' with difficulty she completed what she was attempting to say earlier, 'I don't know you. I haven't even seen you. I also do not understand how you could do something which my husband desired very much to do but never could!'

The book handed over by him sat trembling in her hands. With a smile tinted with a time-transcending sadness he said, 'I know you. We have also met once.'

She gave him a disbelieving look. As she stood as if in a trance, riffling the four hundred and eighty pages of the book with her thumb, he told her, 'It was at least thirty years ago. I had come to meet a friend who was doing Chemistry in UC College. Seeing no one in the classroom, I asked around and was told that everyone was in the laboratory for practical classes. I waited for him there for a long while. Because of the boredom and loneliness, I took a piece of chalk lying on the floor and wrote on the blackboard a sentence which had occurred to me at that time. That was when an eighteen-year-old walked in with some books in her hand. In order to not disturb her, as she seemed to be in search of a place to sit and copy down notes, I left hurriedly. I do not know if you remember; that girl was you!'

Ann Marie's mouth went dry. Her legs were sweating copiously. 'I never saw you,' she said, 'possibly because I wasn't looking. But I still remember the words you wrote on that board. That was the beginning and end of my marriage!'

'Oh, that is interesting,' he said. 'Some silliness! Let it go, don't worry about that. Please read this book. Effectively, there is no difference between your husband not being able to write this and I being able to do so. Beneath every mountain it is the same lava which is boiling. It may be spat out by weak mountains. We call those mountains volcanoes. And some people with fiery heads like that, we call writers. In effect all are the same—nothing but heaps of soil! None of us owns the fire inside and the light it spreads!'

After saying that, he stepped out and disappeared into the light.

Ann Marie woke up from her strange dream. She was dozing, sitting on the same seat used by her husband during his last moments, leaning against the yellow cushions. She had no recollection of reaching there from the bathroom. Feeling the strong breeze starting to blow through the window, she got up. The calendar near the door started to swing in both directions and make the scraping sound. She stood for a moment, trying to recollect the name of the book she had seen in the dream. Suddenly, the calling bell sounded thrice and the calendar flew off the nail on the wall and on to the floor. Stepping on the calendar unintentionally, she moved to the door.

A great hope filled Ann Marie from somewhere. It was a faith that it is possible for a light, which smouldered like an oil-less wick inside a tortured empty soul for a quarter century and then was extinguished, to be resurrected in three days, or in three years, or if not, at least in three centuries. A corporeal resurrection possible in the son of God may seek other avenues in mere mortals: in another body, in another place, in another time.

She felt her empty life was like a book that had been closed by someone after reading it. The door to the flat stood like its hardcover. Someone will open it. She, a recent widow, will be discovered as its first chapter.

Feeling trapped between dreams and reality and getting endlessly repeated in them as if in two mirrors kept facing each other on either side of her, she got ready to look through the fisheye lens of the peephole on the door.

Glossary

Prologue

Anupallavi is a recapitulation of lyrics sung in *Pallavi*, the first section of the *Varnam* (short metrical composition in Carnatic music). Charanam follows *anupallavi* and can occur towards the end of the varnam. Multiple *charanam* stanzas, can be sandwiched between pallavi and anupallavi.

Onam is the harvest festival of Kerala. During the ten-day-long celebrations, the front courtyard is decorated with flower carpets showcasing freshly plucked, seasonal spring flowers and colours endemic to Kerala.

Lungi is an informal, coloured variation of the more formal *mundu* (usually white or ecru with/without border), worn wrapped around the waist and allowed to hang down. It is worn by men, and sometimes also by women.

Kaattuchembakam: Invocation to *Chembakam* or Flower of Wild Champak tree known for its enticing smell. The invocatory phrase to the beloved, 'Oh, my *kattu chembakam*' is from a popular Malayalam film song, sung by A.M. Raja.

Prana in Indian philosophy indicates 'life force' of the soul.

Nair is a socially prominent Hindu caste, many of whom had martial lineages and were feudal overlords. During and after British rule, Nairs enjoyed prominent positions in Government Service, Medicine, Education, and Law.

Part One
DHARMA

1. The Address

Manvantara: In Hindu mythology, Manu is the progenitor of all manavas or human beings. According to the Bhagavad Gita the lifespan of one Manu, one manvantara, is seventy-one mahayugas, and each mahayuga is 4,320,000 years.

Kindi: A traditional hand held pitcher with a spout, usually of Bell metal, used to carry water for *puja* or cleaning.

Thorth: A loosely woven, thin body towel used for drying the hair and body, used ubiquitously by Malayalis. Women wrap it like a sarong while bathing, and men don it around the waist while bathing or working in the fields. When worn on one shoulder, instead of a shirt and, with a mundu, it can indicate respect and formality.

Kadavu: River ghat for bathing, washing, and boats to dock.

Thiruvithamkoor: Erstwhile kingdom with Ananthapuram as its capital. Included present day Thiruvananthapuram, the capital city of Kerala.

Marotti oil: Hydnocarpus oil, used as fuel and medicine in India and China.

Palaka: Wooden plank used as a stool for seating, especially for eating. An uruli is a wide-bottomed, traditional vessel for cooking.

Vidhooshakan: A jester in classical Sanskrit theatre.

Koothambalam: The temple-theatre for Koothu and Koodiyaattam performances.

Kuduma: Tuft of hair knotted at the back of the head, especially by Brahmins.

Aattu: Blistering, blasting snap, usually to express derision and contempt.

Chettan: It is a common suffix added to refer respectfully to an older, male sibling. Chechi is the corresponding feminine form.

2. The Ancestors

Para: A traditional measuring vessel for paddy, shaped out of the base of the jackfruit tree. The largest among paddy measures, a para can hold around 8 kg of rice. Even today the nirapara (para filled with paddy) is the auspicious sign of prosperity and an inevitable part of festivals and celebrations.

Advaithasharamam: Sree Narayana Guru's ashram at Shivagiri, Aluva, with the motto 'All men are equal in the eyes of God'. Gandhiji had a historic meeting with him there in 1925.

Naanu Guru: A derogatory reference to Sree Narayana Guru (1854–1928), saint, sadhu and egalitarian social reformer from the Ezhava/Thiyya community (an avarna or lower caste), who defied Brahminical tradition that allowed only a Brahmin to install idols/deities, and installed Shiva's idol. He rejected casteism and promoted new values of spiritual freedom and social equality, based on universal education to all castes.

Nanu: A colloquial nickname for Sree Narayana Guru.

Pulayan: A member of the Pulaya caste, was denigrated as the lowest caste, deemed polluting untouchables. They led wretched lives, in the casteist madhouse that was Kerala.

Shivarathri festival: At the extensive sandbanks of Periyar river in Aluva. The devotees of Shiva offer prayers and honour their ancestors, and fast through the night of the grand festival.

Hari-Hara: Authors' coinage to indicate incredulous amazement. Hari and Hara are Vishnu and Shiva, respectively. The reference is to the son supposed have been born of the relationship between these two males.

Thevar: A corruption of deva (devan), which may contextually mean God or demi-god.

Vaikom Satyagraha (1924–25): Was an agitation against untouchability in Hindu society, centred around Sri Mahadevar Temple at Vaikom. Supported by Gandhiji and Sree Narayanaguru, it secured for the lower castes (the avarnas) the right to break prohibitions and enter the temple and use the public roads around the temple, prohibited to the avarnas till then.

Swadeshabhimani K. Ramakrishna Pillai: A writer, editor-journalist, and political activist, famed for his brave stance against the atrocities of the *Diwan* and the King of the erstwhile princely state of Travancore. He was known by the name of the newspaper *Swadeshabhimani* he edited. He was arrested, exiled and his newspaper and press confiscated jointly by the officers of the British Raj and the King.

Tharavad: Ancestral homes of Nairs (and later, for also, Ezhavas, Muslims and Christians) jointly held as the common property of the members of the joint family. It also, signifies a moneyed and weighty heritage.

Sambandhams: A form of marital system, or cohabitation, practised by the Nairs, which was contractual and dissoluble at will by both parties. A woman could have Sambandhams with a male of her same caste or of superior caste.

Marumakkathaayam: Matrilineal System, common among Nairs, which placed the Karanavar, or the oldest maternal uncle as the head of the ancestral house, or tharavad, and his nephews and nieces as beneficiaries to jointly held, indivisible family property. It was one of the few traditional systems that gave women some liberty, and the right to property.

The Second Nair Act of 1925: Took away the right of nephews to be direct heirs of their uncle's property, leading to the dismantling of marumakkathaayam and the eventual breakup of the joint family system.

Pudava: A wedding mundu set or sari that a groom formally offers to his bride, as part of the Sambandam or marriage ritual.

Gurudevan: Literally, Lord-Guru, the popular name for Sree Narayana Guru, especially among his disciples.

3. Thachanakkara

E.K. Nayanar: A leader of Communist Party of India (Marxist), was the longest-serving chief minister of Kerala, and held the post three times. He was very popular for his rustic dialect and earthy humour.

Advaitha Vedanta philosophy: Propagated by Adi Shankara or Shankaracharya. Young Shankara's timely, on-the-spot decision to become a sanyaasi or ascetic is supposed to have saved him from the clutches of crocodiles that caught him while he was having a bath in the Periyar river, now known as the Crocodile Ghat at Kalady.

Sree Padmanabhan: The Kings of Thiruvithaamkoor (Travancore) serve the kingdom as Padmanabha dasas or the vassals of the principal deity Padmanabhan of Shree Padmanabha Swami Temple. In Thiruvithaamkoor, the State currency was Chakram coins and the Travancore rupee.

Chakyar Koothu: A classical performance art of Kerala, a solo narrative performance dealing with stories from Hindu epics, interspersed with mime and comic interludes. A traditional equivalent of the modern stand-up comedy act, in Koothu, the Chakyar satirises the manners and customs of the time and spares none. His wit ranges from innocent mockery to veiled innuendoes, barbed pun and pungent invectives.

Aattakatha: Literally, a 'story for dancing and acting', it is the lyrical libretto used in the classical dance drama of *Kathakali*.

An Anna (ānā): Was a currency unit formerly used in India, equal to 1/16 of a rupee. It was subdivided into 4 Paise or 12 Pies (thus, there were 64 paise in a rupee and 192 pies).

Vaidyans: Traditional apothecaries, practitioners of Ayurvedic medical treatment.

Lord Parashuraman: As an adolescent, he obeyed his father, Jamadagni, and beheaded his mother whose chastity his father doubted. However, using the boon his pleased father offered him, he brought his mother back to life.

4. Glorious Mother

Naazhi: The smallest of paddy measuring pans, capable of holding around 200 grams of paddy.

5. Two Kinds of Rivers

Sayyip: A corruption of the Hindi word sahib, which means 'sir', 'master' etc.

Pattar: A corruption of the Sanskrit 'Bhattar' for Iyers and Iyengars, who were Tamil Brahmin migrants in Kerala.

'Veena Poovu' ('Fallen Flower'): Kumaran Asan's highly philosophical poem is an allegory of the transience of the mortal world, told through the brief life of a flower.

Gurudevan at Shanthiniketan: Rabindranath Tagore.

Edappally Raghavan Pillai and Changampuzha Krishna Pilla: The popular romantic poets of twentieth century.

'Changampazha': Naraapilla's deliberate mispronunciation of Changampuzha's name, the celebrated and influential Malayalam poet known for his romantic pastoral elegy, *Ramanan* (1936), which sold for an unprecedented 100,000 copies, shows the ignorance and arrogance of Naraapilla.

Kuttipuzha Krishna Pillai (1900–1971): Noted Malayalam literary critic, who was initially an admirer of Narayana Guru. He is known for being an atheist.

6. Casteism

Guru Nithya Chaithanya Yathi (1923–1999): Philosopher, psychologist, professor, writer-poet, succeeded as the head of Narayaṇa Gurukulam, following Natarajaguru, who was in turn the successor to Narayana Guru.

Swami Chinmayananda (1916–1993): A Hindu spiritual teacher who founded the Chinmaya Mission to spread the knowledge of Advaita Vedanta. He was a *savarna* (Menon caste) by birth, and the first President of the Vishwa Hindu Parishad, an ultra nationalist Hindu organization for the revival of Hindu religion and culture.

Illams: Traditional Nampoothiri houses.

Yogakshemasabha: Progressive organization that worked for upliftment of the Namboothiri community.

V.T. Bhattathirippad: The author of the revolutionary play *Adukkalayilninnum Arangathekku* (*From the Kitchen to the Stage*) was a social critic, well-known dramatist and a prominent freedom fighter who was a key figure in removing casteism and conservatism that plagued the Namboothiri community of Kerala.

Antharjanam: Literally, 'people inside the house', and referred to Nampoothiri women, who led restricted lives bound by rituals, traditions and rules.

Temple Entry Proclamation of 1936: Issued by Chithira Thirunal Balarama Varma, the last Maharaja of Travancore, abolishing the ban on low-caste people entering Hindu temples in the state of Travancore.

Sir C.P. Ramswamy Iyer: The Diwan of Travancore from 1936 to 1947.

Chattambiswamikal: A great scholar saint of Kerala (1853–1924), and a contemporary of Narayanaguru, he tried to reform the caste-ridden Hindu society. His father was a Nampoothiri and mother a Nair, yet, he gave voice to the distressed castes and women.

Ayyankali (1863–1941): A Pulaya by birth, was a social reformer who fought against discriminations against lower caste Dalits, for their right to education, fair wages and use of public roads and amenities.

8. Outsider

S.K. Pottekkad, Malayalam novelist, short story writer and travel writer, who won the *Jnanpith* Award in 1980 for his novel *Oru Desathinte Katha* (*The Story of a Locale*).

Zamorins or Saamoothiris: The titular name for kings who ruled the erstwhile kingdom of Kozhikode (Calicut).

9. Crepe Jasmine

Yakshis: As per folklore of southern India, are reputed to waylay men with their beauty and drink their blood

Kosavan: The potter caste; used only for alliteration here.

10. The Circle

Melmundu: A piece of cloth to cover the upper body of woman.

Vishukaineettam: The hansel given by elders to children and those younger to him on the day of Vishu.

Part Two
ARTHA

1. Transformation

Temple Entry Edict: Proclamation by Maharaja Shri Chithira Thirunal Balarama Varma and his Dewan Sir C.P. Ramaswami Iyer in 1936, which abolished the ban on low-caste people from entering Hindu Temples in the state of Travancore.

Kavu: The scared grove, presided over and protected by a deity. It can also include richly bio-diverse natural sacred spaces seen near traditional homes and temple premises. Muthappan is the colloquial usage for deity.

Avarnar: A blanket term for people of lower castes, as *Savarnas* is for upper castes.

2. Seed

Mappilas: Malayali Muslims.

Chechi: Suffix added to women's names as a mark of respect and to indicate seniority. Literally, elder sister.

Therandukalyanam: Celebration that marks the onset of menarche in a girl and day of her first menstruation.

Velathis of Veluthedan community: Women of washermen/washerwomen community.

Paayasam: Dessert served on auspicious occasions, usually at the end of the traditional feast, the sadya.

Thiruvaathirakkali: Dance is performed by (traditionally by Nairs and other upper castes) women on the day of thiruvathira in the month of Dhanu, as a prayer to Lord Shiva for conjugal harmony and marital bliss.

Nilavilakku: The traditional lamp integral to all rituals and ceremonies in Malayali Hindu families, is lighted in homes at sundown by young girls as a daily ritual. Art forms are also performed after the nilavilakku is lighted auspiciously.

3. The Decade

The Vimochana Samaram (liberation struggle) of 1958–1959: Was a combined socio-political and communal agitation launched by the Catholic Church, the Nair Service Society, and the Indian Union Muslim League, which led to the premature dismissal of the world's first elected communist government led by Chief Minister E.M.S. Namboodiripad. The unprecedented reforms in education, land, and labour reforms initiated by the government invited opposition and outrage.

Mannathu Padmanabhan: Nair community leader of significant stature, who unified the Nairs under the community organization of N.S.S (Nair Service Society).

Kantambechcha Coat (the patchwork coat): The first colour film in Malayalam.

EMS: The popular short form for Elamkulam Manakkal Sankaran Namboodiripad (1909–1998), the Indian communist politician and theorist, and the first Chief Minister of Kerala state in 1957–59 and then again in 1967–69. A member of the Communist Party of India (CPI), he was the first non-Indian National Congress chief minister in the Indian republic, and headed the world's first democratically elected Communist Party government. The communist government under EMS initiated radical reforms that alarmed its critics, forcing the Congress Ministry in Delhi to make an anti-democratic dismissal of the ministry.

4. Siam Weed

Appa, Appan, Achan, etc.: Are common ways of addressing and referring to the father.

Vada: Popular fried snacks made of ground pulses.

Poonool: The 'sacred thread', a thin consecrated cord of cotton, worn by Brahmins, as a reminder to observe purity of thought and deed, and pay respects to parents and God. During *Upanayana* or the initiation ritual, the sacred thread is tied diagonally across the chest, to symbolize the transference of spiritual knowledge.

Poromboke: Unassessed lands, or wasteland which are the property of Government, and reserved for public purposes or common use of the people.

5. Meanie

Chetta: A mean, base, scoundrel. Chetta is also an abbreviation for 'chettakkudil' or thatched hut, usually belonging to the lower caste and the poor.

Kamanthan: A desi corruption of Kabhandham, or headless corpse. Kabandhan was the headless demon in the Puranic legends.

Panickan or Panikkar/Panicker: Usually is a professional astrologer.

Thrikkakarappan: Clay idols of the deity Thrikkakarappan, shaped like geometric cones, installed in front yards of Hindu houses during Onam festival, often along with flower carpets.

Pulayi: The feminine form of Pulayan, a lower caste, usually labourers and menial workers.

Your Nair: Contextually, Nair can also mean a woman's husband.

6. Crescent

Chenda: A cylindrical percussion instrument used widely in the state of Kerala, made from wood and leather, with a length of two feet and a diameter of one foot.

Sanchayanam: The ceremony, usually on the third day of cremation, for collecting the bones from the funeral pyre in an earthen port, for eventual submersion in a river or the sea.

Kochettan: Second eldest brother, or chettan.

7. The Birth

Chathayam: Sree Narayana Guru passed away on chathayam day.

Thulaabharam: An offering given to the deities of temples – usually of fruits, grains, coconuts etc. – equalling the weight of the devotee.

Vamanan: The fifth incarnation of Lord Vishnu, depicted as a dwarf.

Putthaleebai: A corruption of the name of Gandhiji's mother, Putlibai Gandhi.

9. Iconoclasm

Udukku: A membranophone instrument used in folk music and prayers in South India. Its shape is similar to other Indian hourglass drums, with a small snare stretched over one side.

Poothana: Was a she-demon, sent by her brother Kamsa to breast-feed and kill baby Krishna. She entered his house, *Ambadi,* in the form of a beautiful woman (Lalitha).

Lakshaarchana and Udayaasthamana vazhipad: Poojas in a temple when the deity is offered hundred thousand flowers ritual (*lakshaarchana pooja*), and periodical ritual worship done from dawn to dusk (*udayaasthamana pooja*).

10. Treasure Chest

Ammayi: A suffix added to female names to indicate the relationship as an aunt.

Edathiamma: A suffix indicating sister in law, especially the maternal status accorded to the wife of an elder brother. From 'edathi' (chechi/sister), and amma (mother).

Pappae: Colloquial usage for brother.

Kaaleeyamardhanam: A dance commemorating Krishna's subduing of the arrogance of the feared Kaaleeya serpant, by dancing on his hundred and ten hoods.

Kunjalam: A decorative hair accessory worn at the end of the braid, especially as part of dance attire.

Thechi: Jungle Geranium flower

Devatha (feminine of 'Deva'/Devan): Female goddess, or demi-godess, or even an exceptionally beautiful or good woman.

PART THREE
KAAMA

1. Sequel

Jnaanappaana: Considered as the Bhagavad Gita of Malayalee, *Jnaanappaana* is an intensely devotional poem of the sixteenth century, written by poet Poonthanam Namboothiri as a paean to his favourite deity, Lord Guruvayoorappan.

Harinaamakeerthanam: The sixteenth century devotional song written entirely in Malayalam by Thunjathu Ezhuthachan, the father of Malayalam poetry.

P. Leela: Popular Indian playback singer, recognized for her mellifluous rendition of devotional songs.

Achaayan: A term used to address elder males belonging to Travancore Christian communities.

3. Mixed Breed

'The name of your Guru': Narayana Guru, here, is mentioned derogatorily as the Guru of the Thiyyas (lower caste), in a momentary surge of casteist pride on the part of Govindan Master.

Chattambi Swamikal: A sage and a social reformer of the Kerala Renaissance and a contemporary of Narayanaguru. Though born a Nair, he challenged caste inequalities and Hindu orthodoxies.

Chettathiamma: Elder sister-in-law

5. The Old Man

Anusooya and Priyamvadha: The inseparable and beautiful companions of Shakunthala, the heroine of Kalidas's renowned classical play, *Abhijñānaśākuntala*.

Shashtipoorthi: A Hindu ceremony celebrating the sixtieth birthday of a male, whose children offer prayers for the well being of their parents, who in turn renew their marital vows. Usually, it is celebrated only by the rich or families of high social standing.

6. Oxen

Miccher: A local corruption of mixture, a fried mix of peanuts, beaten rice, and vermicelli made from powdered Bengal gram.

Kamadhenu: The divine bovine-goddess described in Hindu Religion as the mother of all cows, Kamadenu is the miraculous 'cow of plenty', who showers devotees with whatever they seek.

Valyettan: Literally 'big brother', for eldest brother.

7. Caterpillar

Amba, Ambika, Ambalika: The three princesses of Kasi that King Bhishma had carried away from their wedding venue, for his brother, Vichithravirya, the King of Hastinapur – as recounted in the Mahabharatha.

Unniappams: Fried dumplings made from powdered rice, jaggery, coconut.

8. Maelstrom

Hiranyakashipu: An Asura from the Puranic scriptures of Hinduism, who was killed by Narasimha avatar of Lord Vishnu, who appeared with a lion's face.

9. Harbinger of Death

Perumthacchan: The 'master craftsman' is an honorific title that is used to refer to Perumthacchan, an ancient and legendary carpenter, architect, woodcarver and sculptor from Kerala.

Pappadam (poppadum): A thin, disc-shaped Indian food typically based on a seasoned dough made from black gram, and crisply fried or roasted, to be served along with rice.

Ilaneerkuzhambu: A cooling medicine of eye-drops made from tender coconut.

10. Swayamvaram

Swayamvaram: The ancient custom of kings that allowed their daughters to choose their life partners, from an array of kings and noble suitors invited for the function.

Part Four
MOKSHA

1. Portal

Lathi: A typical baton, about 5 ft long and made from bamboo, still carried by policemen in India.

3. Fragmentation

Mimics Parade: A very popular mimicry show, which was a launchpad for a quite a few talented actors and comedians in Malayalam movies.

6. Odds

Yama or Kaalan: The God of Death, who comes when a death is imminent. He rides a water buffalo and wields a loop of rope in his left hand to pull the soul from the corpse.

8. Creation Song

Ilatthaalam: Made from bronze, is a musical instrument which resembles a miniature pair of cymbals.

Maddhalam: A cylindrical percussion instrument used widely in Kerala, made from wood and leather, with a length of two feet and a diameter of one foot.

10. Zenith

Nataraja Guru: Son of Dr Palpu, who took reins at Adhvaithaashram, after SreeNaryana Guru's Samadhi.

Dr Padmanabhan Palpu: Social reformer and bacteriologist, who founded the Sree Narayana Dharma Paripalana Society (the Propagation of the credo of Sree Narayana, or SNDP) for the socio-economic advancement of the Ezhavas and Thiyyas. Narayana Guru was SNDP's first President.

Chempakaraman Pillai (1891–1926): An Indian independence activist, and ally of Netaji Subash Chandra Bose, based in Germany and reportedly killed by the Nazis, on Hitler's instruction, by food poisoning on 26 May 1934.

Captain Lakshmi: A revolutionary Indian independence activist and officer of the Indian National Army of Subash Chandra Bose, and the Minister of Women's Affairs in the Azad Hind government.

Irayimman Thampi: Renowned Carnatic musician as well as a music composer and vocalist in the court of Swathi Thirunal. His compositions include the well-loved lullaby '*Omanathinkal Kidavo*'.

Sopaana Sangeetham: A form of singing, primarily based on Jayadeva's *Geethagovindam*, rendered by the side of the steps (sopaanam) leading to the sanctum sanctorum of a temple.

Idakka: An hourglass-shaped, handy percussion instrument, similar to the pan-Indian damaru. While the damaru is played by rattling knotted cords against the resonators, the idakka is played with a drumstick.

All the Short Stories That I Wrote Were Preparations to Arrive at This Novel

An Interview with Subhash Chandran (the Author)

Fathima E.V.

P.S.

Insights
Interviews
& More...

All the Short Stories That I Wrote Were Preparations to Arrive at This Novel

Fathima E.V.

You have often said that everything that you wrote before* A Preface to Man *was a powerful commentary on the making of* A Preface? *Do tell us about your transition from a short story writer to a novelist.

It can safely be said that *A Preface to Man* is a novel that looks at the contemporary world, simultaneously, from both philosophical and experiential perspectives. Through the tale of the fictitious village of Thachankkara on the bank of Periyar river, I have tried to depict the story of Indian life of the past hundred years, tracing it through its emotional history. In fact, the synopsis of the novel was published sixteen years ago in the weekly *Mathrubhumi* as a short story titled *Novelsangraham.* The thirty-first chapter of this novel was also published eleven years ago as a short story. The long and short of it is that it was a long meditation. During this period, the form of the novel itself was overhauled many times. The first version had 72 chapters. From the beginning, I had imagined the novel to be divided into four parts corresponding to the fourfold division of the *Purushartha* in Indian philosophy: *Dharma, Artha, Kama* and *Moksha.* Eventually, I was able to condense the history of hundred years and its hundred plus characters into 42 chapters. From this perspective, all the short stories that I wrote were preparations to arrive at this novel. The moments that I desired an Indian novel should encompass are what I tried to recount in my short stories. I had always hoped that this novel would be included in the history of great novels created by Indians. I have been writing stories from the age of seventeen. Now I am forty-three years old. Within this span, I have published five short story collections, besides three collections of memoirs. However, it was only after the publication of my novel that I realized how dear the reader holds a writer, how cherished a writer is. Only a novel has the ability to present life in its complex totality. Perhaps that is the reason why readers often feel characters resemble them. I was shocked out of my wits when I received two pairs of gold earrings once, with a note saying 'To be worn by Jithendran's daughters'. That golden prize that some unknown reader sent was a recognition for the sum total of my life.

'We have art in order not to die of the truth', said Nietzsche. Is writing not an escape from death, to exist beyond death, to not forget? What are your hopes for Man?

I do not believe that human life is something that is destined to just flare up, only to be snuffed out. The magnificent brilliance of creativity is never a decorative lamp in human existence. It is the essential sunlight required by our souls. There is no need to fear that it will ever be extinguished. Creative artists will remain beyond hundred or thousand years, till human race itself continues to exist. They will succeed in creating works in different fields, illumining the eras to come. Maybe on a purely individual level, man may end up losing this optimism. The protagonist of this novel, Jithendran, is one such soul, a creative soul who has lost his optimism. Life is not a story that will conclude, underlined solely by either cheer or gloom, as we all think. It is a continuity. Every word that I write is never mine alone. The life that I live is not unique. Even if I were to die, the emotions and thoughts that I harbour in secrecy will blossom and come to fruition in the earth through many others. This continuity of creative light can be seen in the fiery hope that suffuses Ann Marie, in whom the entirety of Jithen's words remained stored, even after Jithen's death.

In a novel marked by diligent descriptions, did you, at any point in your writing, have to undertake any particular research?

Didn't I say that I was trying to write the emotional history of a century? Along with that, a meditation on creativity also happened to become an integral part of it. I studiously edited and pared down many things that had already been written down, reworking obsessively on the draft for greater accuracy. Though I had grown up on the shores of Aluva river and had seen dead bodies floating in the river, I had never seen how a body lost in the water was revived by divers. For a long while, I had struggled to lend authenticity to the details in the scene in the novel when the corpse of Naraappilla, who is a main character, had to be pulled up from the depths of the temple pond in which he had drowned. While the scene that I had struggled to realize through ten years of creative effort continued to nag me, in an astonishing coincidence, I happened to come across an actual case of death by drowning. After years, I was standing near the riverbank with my friends. When we realized that one of the young men who was bathing in the river ghat had drowned, we jumped into the river. Though we searched for a long time, we failed to find him. Finally, an expert diver from the village of Uliyanur on the opposite bank, retrieved the body from the depth, with great effort. Thus, I chanced to witness a scene in which a corpse was retrieved, and in the final edit rewrote the scene. The details for the episode where Devassy dived to haul up Naraappilla's corpse were chanced upon at the last moment.

***A Preface** is a novel about the cultural evolution of Kerala, as much as it is about Jithendran, a Malayali. Given that the construction of the plot itself is, in its many turns, fashioned around varied responses to the philosophical and political ideas of Kerala Renaissance, to what extent does it explore the changes entailed, which subject male authority to critical interrogation? How does the ideational history of the narrative examine the male centric authority inherent in Malayali public discourse?*

On many counts, Kerala is at the forefront among Indian states. A state where education and literacy tops, where the proportion of women dominate the man-woman ratio. The place where Vasco-da Gama's ship landed, in his search for a sea route to India. The birthplace of Sree Narayana Guru, esteemed even by Mahatma Gandhi. The state of forty-four rivers, bordered by the beautiful Western Ghats on one side and the long ocean stretch on the other, and the birthplace of the globally respected art forms like Kathakali. The state that proudly says that the last Cheraman Perumal, a Hindu, went to Mecca and became a Muslim. The land in which the world's first elected communist government came to power through people's choice. We are, at present, living in a period when all these proud achievements have taken a beating. Unfurling their hoods, religion and caste have started meddling in public life. We seem to be closing our eyes against the radiance gifted by the Renaissance era. Woman has morphed into a mere sex apparatus. One of the chapters in the novel examines the transformation of the umbilicus—from a mark on the body that is constant reminder of your rupture from the Mother—that has now become symbolic of an enticement to sex. One needs to only look at how copiously Indian cinema uses the belly button, solely as an erogenous image for sexual titillation. There is a chapter titled 'Darkness' in this novel. It introduces the young men of our times who, under the cover of darkness, eavesdrop on the moans of a woman on her deathbed, laid low by age and sickness. Mistaking the grunts of old age to be the lusty moans of a beautiful woman in coitus, they masturbate in the darkness. The infamous Hooch tragedy of Vaippin occurred in our state, during the birthday celebrations of the great man who taught us that alcohol is poison! Thus, this novel reveals such areas of darkness that Jithendran passes through in his adolescence and youth.

Given the large canvas, complex time scheme and bewildering crowd of character, how do you explain the novel briefly? How much of a critical engagement does the novel have with the contemporary age, and how far does it reflect the exigencies of the times?

It can perhaps be said that the novel is an elaboration on the profound sentence that appears at the beginning and in the middle of the novel: 'Man is the only creature that perishes before attaining full growth'. However, it is not just that alone. The book is also a reminder of the greatness that the same creature is also capable of! Our contemporary age is becoming increasingly unacquainted with the word 'greatness'. The lack of greatness has even been exalted into a theory. World over, evil seems to be winning in projecting virtue as a weakness or failure. Wounded by the scenario, my heart had wailed, manifesting as this novel.

How do you chart your movement from short stories to full fledged fiction? Are their aesthetics different?

By instinct, stories are closer to poems. They are the word pictures of man's emotional moments. If short story is a photograph, the novel is a videograph. Both have their own aesthetics. If short story writers are God's stenographers, novelists are surely his chosen holy brides. In this sense, novelists are more blessed in being able to touch God at least once in a while. This novel gives its readers the choice to read each of the four parts of the novel as separate, independent narratives. Each chapter has that kind of completeness. Yet, this novel is an illusory book that reveals itself for a moment in one of the early morning dreams of Ann Marie, a character in the novel.

A Preface *has a painstakingly wrought structure, which holds a tight rein on its craft, in terms of its plot, language and time scheme. Was the emphasis on form consciously attempted for innovation?*

The book that Ann Marie's husband yearned so fiercely to write appears in her dream as a bolt of lightning. In her dream, she even knows the exact number of pages that the book has. When you reach the end of the novel, you realize that that book too has the exact same number of pages. Thus, a dimension of magic has also been incorporated into the novel. This is something that we are not too familiar with in Indian novels. In a novel of nearly 400 pages, I have paid more than adequate attention to craft, to steer clear of tedium.

You have written that you have been overwhelmed by the responses of your readers, who often equate your characters with the people

in your life. Could you recollect instances in your life from which the narrative has drawn its energy?

I have not seen my grandfather. However, I painted Naraapilla with some of the residual colours hoarded from the stories I heard from my mother and others. I have only used my grandfather's DNA in Naraapilla. There is no other similarity, either in life or death, that Naraapilla shares with him. Not just the characters, but every image in the novel is created thus. Yet, it is not like how a stone carver makes the grinding stone and its roller, *mano* to grind with. The carver is not a sculpting artist. A sculptor does not continue to replicate his creation. Symbols created artificially will only obstruct the flow of reading. It is true that a sculpture is made from rock. But is it merely rock? Far from it!

Acknowledgements

Both Subhash and I are very grateful to Lakshmy Rajeev, who happened to come into our acquaintance at the right time, connecting us to the delightfully purposeful Kanishka Gupta, who put us to our publisher, HarperCollins India and its ever-patient Minakshi Thakur, and Prerna Gill. Special mentions must be made of Jojy Philip who typeset the draft, while maintaining his cool in incorporating last-minute changes, and of Girija Padmanabhan, my fellow Kannurite at HCI.

I am deeply indebted to my friend Nandakumar, for having strayed into my translation out of curiosity and offering to be a willing accomplice for the sheer pleasure of discovering a potential translator within himself, and painstakingly reading through my careless errors while motivating me when my interest flagged. Adept at using internet resources, Nandan assiduously tracked oversights in chronology and mismatched quotations in the original, which were subsequently changed by Subhash. More than anything else, I am grateful to Nandan, for helping me keep faith and not give up, sometimes out of sheer lack of time and laziness, and sometimes because it was too demanding. There are many, whom I cannot thank enough, from the ever-suffering Riaz,

Hannah, and Aamir, who bore my obsessive translation sprees without complaint, even as they ate up most of my vacations in Sharjah; my friends, M.V. Narayanan, always my rock, and Santhi, who put me to N.P. Sajesh, who in turn introduced me to Subhash.

I thank my friends, Manoj, Nishad, Sunil P. Elayidom, Tommy John, Jurgen Quibbler, Maya Nair and many others who stood through my vexing doubts and uncertainties. Needless to say, Safia, Tasnim, Kouser, Aysha, Abid, Sana, Shahabuddin and Jaleel, who were unwavering in their faith in me, even as they are still unwilling to forgive me for not completing my own novel that has been in the half-born stage for many years now; my word-driven parents, Nafeesa and Mayan who initiated my love for reading; and Harris, Ashraf, and Parveen for their support. Two absences I regret and miss more than ever are, my little mentor, Nazreen and my dear guide, T.K. Ramchandran.

HARPERPERENNIAL

Harper Perennial presents special editions of its finest books in translation

Age of Frenzy
Mahabaleshwar Sail
Translated from the Konkani by Vidya Pai

A Life Incomplete
Nanak Singh
Translated from the Punjabi by Navdeep Suri

Mohanaswamy
Vasudhendra
Translated from the Kannada by Rashmi Terdal

The Music of Solitude
Krishna Sobti
Translated from the Hindi by Vasudha Dalmia

No Presents Please: Mumbai Stories
Jayant Kaikini
Translated from the Kannada by Tejaswini Niranjana

A Preface to Man
Subhash Chandran
Translated from the Malayalam by Fathima E.V.

The Secret Garland
Andal
Translated from the Tamil by Archana Venkatesan

Shala
Milind Bokil
Translated from the Marathi by Vikrant Pande

The Weary Generations
Abdullah Hussein
Translated from the Urdu by the author

Written in Tears
Arupa Patangia Kalita
Translated from the Assamese by Ranjita Biswas

HARPERPERENNIAL

Bhima: Lone Warrior
M.T. Vasudevan Nair
Translated from the Malayalam by Gita Krishnankutty

Chemmeen
Thakazhi Sivasankara Pillai
Translated from the Malayalam by Anita Nair

Ghachar Ghochar
Vivek Shanbhag
Translated from the Kannada by Srinath Perur

Hindutva or Hind Swaraj
U.R. Ananthamurthy
Translated from the Kannada by Keerti Ramachandra & Vivek Shanbhag

The Liberation of Sita
Volga
Translated from the Telugu by T. Vijay Kumar & C. Vijayasree

A Life Misspent
Suryakant Tripathi Nirala
Translated from the Hindi by Satti Khanna

The Sea Lies Ahead
Intizar Husain
Translated from the Urdu by Rakhshanda Jalil

Selected Poems
Joy Goswami
Translated from the Bengali by Sampurna Chattarji

Wild Animals Prohibited: Stories/Anti-stories
Subimal Misra
Translated from the Bengali by V. Ramaswamy

Wild Words: Four Tamil Poets
Malathi Maithri, Salma, Kutti Revathi and Sukirtharani
Translated from the Tamil by Lakshmi Holmström